LONELY HEARTS
(MEMOIRS OF LUST AND LOVE IN CYBERSPACE)

J. Christi

A special acknowledgement goes to my husband, without whom this book would not be possible.

CHAPTER ONE

This is a very personal love story – very much like every love story I've ever known, and yet like no other. It's my love story. The one I keep close to my heart, and pull out when I need to feel that my life meant something to someone once. I was important to him, and he loved me as no other ever has, or ever will again. And, I loved him in exactly the same way. I write down these words from my heart, so I'll never forget even one moment of the beauty Henry brought into my life. I want to relive it over and over again, to experience the joys of these memories that have become so precious to me, and I want to experience all the wonders we shared as I read about them each time I pick up this journal.

How it began is strange, almost mystical. It made me wonder if, just maybe, we all do have some sort of predetermined fate. It started a few weeks after my Dad passed away. I had a special relationship with my father, I was his princess, and he loved me totally and unconditionally. Now, he was gone, and I felt empty and very lonely. I missed him so much.

I was unhappy in a marriage that lasted too long, and I was married to a man who was so much into himself, that he was incapable of feeling love for me on the level I needed from a man. Don was probably the first man I ever let get close to me. I was nineteen, and in many ways still a child, when I married him. Once married, my life started to evolve around him, and I soon felt trapped. For thirty years, I ached for something, not even sure of what it was, but I knew that it was missing in my life. I needed to reach out and try to find the dreams I lost, and to find myself. I struggled for months, knowing that if I were ever to find peace and happiness in my life, I must find what I really want in the deepest part of my heart, and I realized that I was not living *my* life. I was living someone else's view of what my life should be. I was the good daughter, the good wife, great Mom, and the sassy Wall Street executive, but all these roles that I played, weren't me, or what I needed to be. My life was devoted to other people, and my own needs were lost in the scheme of it all. I knew that was not the way it was supposed to be.

When my Dad died, I realized how quickly it can all end, and how we can loose the dreams that go with living. My Dad's dream was to be an artist. Instead, he became an architect building things the way other people wanted them and not from his own creative ideas. He never achieved his goal as an artist. I made a decision that week to do whatever I had to do to take my life back, before I was too old for it to matter, as if it could ever cease to matter.

Being true to oneself is not as easy as it sounds. When the people you love suddenly realize that you are no longer putting their needs before your own, you encounter resistance. As a mother, my children's needs always came first. But, my children had grown up. They are capable of taking care of themselves, and I had to put their needs into proper prospective. I wanted to be loved for "who" I am, not for what I did for the people I care about. I am not by nature a loner. I don't think anyone is a loner by nature. I was fifty-one years old and wanted to share my life with someone, but not just anyone. My husband no longer shared my life. We lived in the same house, but went in two different directions. I wanted to reach out and find someone who could love me the way I needed to be loved, who wanted to experience the adventures of life with me, and have the same drive and passion that was inside of me. I wanted a soul mate, and if I could not find such a person, I would rather live alone than continue in a life that was sucking every drop of blood left inside my body which is what I felt was happening in my marriage. I decided to look for someone who felt as I did about life.

I finally reached into my heart and found the courage to tell my husband that I was unhappy in the marriage and wanted to separate. That was difficult, because rather than believe that I was unhappy, he felt that I might be going through the 'change of life', and that these feelings that stirred inside of me, would somehow go away over time. I never expected him to understand. He never understood anything I felt in all the thirty-two years of marriage we had together. This was his typical attitude to just about everything I said. I was not going to let myself fall into the trap of trying to work out my problems with a counselor, which would have only prolonged my agony. I may not have known what was missing in my life, but I knew what I didn't want. I told him that I needed to be out of the marriage. Of course, he didn't really believe me at first.

Once that was off my chest, I felt free to reach out to find a friend, with a clear conscience. I'm not the type of person who can lie to anyone and feel comfortable about it. With my new computer, I went into the vast world of the internet, and did some research. I found a few "personals" websites and began searching for a kindred spirit. This wasn't about finding someone to replace my husband. I felt lonely. I needed friends. I hoped to find a friend, and let the relationship take on its own meaning and lead to whatever happened. I wanted to be totally open and free to new experiences and new people. When I went on the personals' websites I felt like I was in a supermarket of men. Finding a friend was a lot of work.

Being of Italian upbringing during the 1950's and 60's, it was ingrained in me that I needed a man to protect me. Going out on my own totally alone was frightening.

I responded to a few ads that I felt had some merit. The questions from these men were always the same. They wanted to know my height, weight, marital status, what I did for a living, and a million other nonessential "details". Hardly anyone wanted to know what I dreamt about, or ached for. I combed through so many ads, trying to find someone special who I could relate to, and who could relate to me. Many were married men, bored with their wives, and looking for sex. There were some newly separated and divorced men testing the single waters. I even found a paraplegic who wanted sex, although I couldn't imagine how. One man was into bondage, and many others were lonely men just drifting through life. The list was endless. But, once in a while, I'd find one who seemed to be sincere, and so I would email him back and forth for a while to see if our minds connected. Out of that, after about five or six emails, if I thought he showed promise, we'd set up a meeting. I tried to make these first dates simple. Usually, it wasn't anything more than a cup of coffee at a local diner after work, so as not to tie up too much of my time, if I decided I didn't like him once we met face to face.

The first man I met was Frank. He was four years younger than I, had been recently divorced, and had joint custody with his ex-wife of his thirteen year old daughter. He ran a plastics company and rode a motorcycle. The conversation went well. I wanted to like him, because a ride on his bike sounded exciting, but there was something missing in his eyes. To me, the eyes are very important. I was looking for a certain type of warmth, and a spark. Maybe the spark is a sign of intelligence, or it's all in my imagination, but Frank's eyes were dull. I got the ride on the bike, and we parted friends, but I knew I didn't want to see him again.

The next fellow I met was Perry. Perry was my age, but was living with a woman thirteen years his junior, who had an alcohol abuse problem. He had been living with her for eleven years and wanted out of the relationship, or so he said. His eyes were average, not very inquisitive, and during the whole conversation, I felt he wasn't telling me the whole truth. After that, there were three others, with similar stories, and I was becoming very disillusioned with the whole male population. Then I answered Henry's ad. His ad itself wasn't much different from the others, but his responses to my email were unique, and so it began. This was his ad:

> *Fifty-two year old male looking for someone who wants to have fun and is looking for new beginnings. I enjoy watching the sunset, walking on the beach, and poetry, and I am looking for someone interesting who I can share my thoughts with.*

> *I am married (soon to be separated), but I have been with a cold wife for too many years and now I am looking for warmth as the clock keeps ticking and I need to change my life while I still can. Everyone needs to be happy so if you need someone to fill the gap in your life also, maybe we could connect.*

CHAPTER TWO

I decided to respond.
April 12, 2000
Hello:

You seem intriguing. I'd like to know more about you. I'm starting a new chapter in my life (new beginnings) and am looking for new friends. Things have not gone well in my marriage, which lasted far too long, and I'm trying to make changes in my life. I have been married for 32 years to a man who likes beer more than sex and who spends most of his spare time on the golf course. My three children have flown the nest and I find no more reason to stay married to him. Maybe I'm expecting more in life than is possible, but I know that something is missing in my life. My husband and I have grown apart over the years and we don't have anything in common any more.

I'm Italian and it is in my nature to be naturally "warm".

Regards, Julie

April 13, 2000
Hi Julie:

I'm sorry that your life is not going well. What I do to relieve the boredom has recently been looking for someone who also feels there's something missing in her life too. Julie, for me it's not motorcycles, or skin diving, or sports cars (although I did keep the car), that fills that spot. It's being able to be wrapped in the arms of someone who I care for and excites me... to share not just sex, but intimacy and closeness. In fact, although I must admit that sex is one of my favorite pastimes, intimacy and closeness are in some ways, much more important. Too many marriages loose that feeling. That's the main reason mine is coming to an end. I like to have fun, be happy, enjoy, and sample life. Also, I much prefer sex to beer. I only drink beer when I eat hot wings and they are so bad for you, that I don't do that often. Don't misunderstand me - I am by no means a prude. I drink occasionally. I fall down from drinking about once in every ten years. So, I am not a drunk.

Let me tell you about me. You may as well know the truth up front. I'm fifty-two, 5' 8" tall, and weigh 175 lbs. I'm in good shape for someone over fifty. 44" chest, 33" waist, and in better shape than most guys younger than me, but I fought the battle of the bulge all my life, and I work out regularly. I'm about ten pounds overweight. I take pride in my appearance. Time has taken its toll on my hair, salt and pepper (whole lotta salt), and I have a bald spot in back. The top has thinned out also. Is your heart racing? Oh! Wow! A short bald guy – just what I wanted. I like good music, good booze, good company, and dirty sex. I'm basically pretty average in regard, I guess. Julie, I have never done this before, and am only looking now, because my obligation to my family is over, my nest is empty now, and it's finally my time. I'm not the kind of guy that is out there just looking for vulnerable women to have sex with. I can get sex any time I want it, as anyone can. That's not what I'm after. First, I want an interesting companion. Someone who I can share my thoughts with, and have a decent conversation with, and someone whose company I enjoy. Hopefully that person will also be my friend, and confidant. After that, where it goes, it goes. I'm not made of stone, and I most certainly want a strong physical relationship with someone that I hit it off with - someone who enjoys me as much as I enjoy her company. I know this is a little long winded, but I want you to know that I am not playing a game. I'm real and I would be very interested in continuing to exchange email and learn more about you. You can ask any question of me that you want. I tell the truth. I'll be interested in hearing about you, and look forward to hearing from you. Please tell me what you are looking for.

– Henry

April 14, 2000
Hi Again Julie:

I know that writing you again before you have had a chance to reply most likely isn't the smartest thing to do if I want to get to know you. I am sure it makes me look pushy and desperate. I am neither of those things. I wrote to you again, because I wanted you to know that I reread your letter a couple of times, and between the lines, I really do understand you. I also understand that when you said your husband likes beer more than sex, your comment had very little to do with either beer or sex, but rather refers to what has become a lifestyle. If you just need to unload, it's OK to write me. Sometimes it's better to be able to speak freely and openly to someone you don't know that's going through the same thing. I think you sound like a bright, adventurous, fun person, being wasted. Now, if you think I'm only writing this to you because I'm desperate, you won't reply. But, I suspect you will see your male counterpart in this letter, so I will hear from you again. And, that would be welcome. – Henry

April 17, 2000
Hello Henry:

You seem to have unusual insight into my feelings, as if you too are going through very similar circumstances. I am inclined to get to know you better. I like short slightly overweight men who are going bald and gray. You are comfortable with yourself and that's a very positive attribute. I'd like to take things slowly and see if we have things in common through emails before meeting. Is that OK with you?

I'm fifty-one years old and am also about 10 pounds over-weight. Weight seems to be a lifetime struggle for me as well. My eyes are green and I have dark brown hair. I color my gray, so it doesn't show. I'm not looking for a quick affair. I am looking for a friend. I must admit, with my children gone, I am lonely. Sometimes you just need someone to be there when you need a shoulder to cry on or laugh with you when you are having a good time. Do you understand what I mean? I've been married for thirty-two years and it may seem strange to you that I waited this long to make changes in my life. But, I don't connect with my husband any more. I haven't connected with him for a very long time. There is something missing in the relationship.

Regards, Julie

April 20th, 2000
Hi Julie:

Thank you for responding. I have a feeling that it may be worth the wait. If you read your own letter and changed thirty-two years of marriage to thirty years, then you know all there is to know about me. Our lives may have many parallels. I know what you are after, and it's not an affair. You are looking for a companion that will pay attention to you, and make an effort to understand WHO you are. You want a friend. Someone to talk to with similar circumstances in their lives, so they understand what you are living through every day. Julie, that is me.

I would love to find someone to have a close physical relationship with. After all, I'm not made of stone, and we all need that intimacy, and closeness. Sometimes, even the act of making love has little to do with sex...although that is a nice fringe benefit. But, a physical relationship is easy to come by for someone. Sex is easy to get. I want more. I want closeness, and to be able to connect with someone who brings happiness back into my life. After that, who knows? But, that is off, maybe someplace in the future, so believe me I am not prowling the net looking for vulnerable women to take advantage of. So, there is no pressure in that direction. Just write again, and we will (I hope) find discovering each other to be what we are both looking for. Please respond and tell me more about yourself, and what you need in your life. - Henry

April 23, 2000
Hi Henry:

I'm certainly glad that you are not prowling the net looking for vulnerable women. I guess I am a bit vulnerable. But, for some reason, I feel comfortable with you. I find it amusing that I am talking to a complete stranger about my life. You have a way of prying without intruding. I feel that you are right about sex and the real need for intimacy and closeness.

I want to write stories. It's just a hobby now, but I wish I could do it full time. I've written two novels which are at home in a drawer. I'd like to get published someday. I earn my living on Wall Street, but my heart is in writing. I've written a few erotic stories. I enjoy writing about sex.

My instincts tell me to leave this marriage. The kids are out of the house and it's just me and him. And I no longer feel I want "him" in my life. We have grown too far apart. Enough about me - tell me more about you.

Regards, Julie

April 24, 2000
Hi Again, Julie:

I am so happy that you responded. It seems that we have more in common than life style. I am also an aspiring writer. I write science fiction. I once had a short story published in Omni Magazine. I am a scientist and engineer to earn a living, and lover of the arts. I work very close to the Shopping Mall. You write erotic stories? Well, want to do some field research? Sorry! But, like all other men, I tend to be a part-time human being, and a full-time pig, so any hint that there may be sexual suggestion involved, gets my interest. If you just ignore it, I'll stop eventually. Now back to reality.

The truth of it is, I understand you so well, because I walk in your shoes every day. Thirty years ago, when I was twenty-two, and so much in love and newly married, I was a different person than the man I am today. I have been many different people over the years getting here, and so has my wife. Do phrases like "hang in there for the kids", "he did nothing wrong", and "how can I throw away thirty years", ring a bell?

One day my youngest son (who is 23) was sixteen came to me very upset, because he and the girl he was dating were "having problems", and he told me he loved her, but he was so unhappy. I told him that life is like a scale. All people bring a balance of good and bad into your life. The trick is to have people in your life that tip the scale to joy and happiness. If you have people who make the heartache side of the scale, the heaviest, then you must save yourself from them and move on. You will live only once, and for a very short time. Use it for YOU! Don't try to save an ideal that no longer exists. Guilt always turns into resentment, don't let that happen.

It was that day the light came on for me too, and I realized that I had an obligation to my children, but when that was fulfilled, I could finally begin life for me while I still had the chance. I told my wife how I felt about fifteen months ago. Things are a little "tense", and we even have now reached the point where we have separate bedrooms. For a variety of reasons, we will stay together until late summer, when we will most likely put our house up for sale. I have very mixed emotions, but…

I am not telling you what to do, and my life is not together enough to give any advice beyond this…follow your heart, and do what your instincts tell you to do. They are probably right. - Henry

April 29, 2000
Hi Henry:

I understand completely why you are still living together with your wife, but also trying to live separate as well. It's not easy. I'd rather sleep alone than with "him". We also have separate bedrooms.

I find that whenever I write romance, my characters end up in bed. I guess that's normal. Or, maybe through my writing I am living the life I really want to live.

I don't look for the same things in men as other women. The eyes are very important. I think I can read a person by looking into their eyes. As an example, I find Einstein's eyes intriguing. You can see intelligence in them from his pictures. Because of those eyes, I find him very sexy. Does that sound strange to you?

Regards, Julie

May 1, 2000
Hi Julie:

I have also tried my hand at writing romance, and my characters also ended up in bed. But, that's where romance finally takes you. Sleeping alone increases hormone levels, and makes one more creative in the erotic sense. In other words, lack of sex makes you horny. Believe me, I know as I think in another couple of weeks, I will retain "virgin" status again.

Writing is a great creative outlet, even if you don't get published. Keep trying, but mostly write for yourself. I write, also paint, draw, and I am into antiques, plants, music, good food, sun & surf, dirty sex, good booze, the theater, museums, great friends, my sports car, oriental philosophy, old movies, dogs, and taking a chance.

As a scientist, it is my nature and my career goal to be an unbiased observer. I have watched life (mine, as well as others), and learned some fundamental truths. That is what you are identifying within my letters. That is why you see yourself so clearly in my description of your pain, and disappointments. I am fifty-two, and I remember when I thought that twenty-one was old, so I guess it's all relative. But, my experience has taught me one thing very clearly. Good judgement comes from experience, and experience comes from bad judgement, so don't be too hard on yourself. I'm stuffy, perhaps, and certainly hard to get to know. But, if Einstein's eyes invoked that feeling of warmth and softened your heart, so that you wanted to bed him, as you said in your email, then one look into my eyes, and you will feel that urge overwhelm you, and the rapid beating of your heart, and the increasing thickness of your breath, will only stop when you have me in your bed. There, the "stuffy old man" will reawaken the woman in you. (See, I told you I could write.) – Henry

May 1, 2000
Hi Henry:

You seem to have so much insight about life. You really have an interesting way of saying things. And, I think you can "write" as I see from these emails. Tell me about your sports car. I like older cars. I like to refurbish antiques and make them look like new again. I've restored quite a few pieces of furniture over the years.

What is your favorite sleeping position? I like the "spoon" style position myself. It's close and intimate. I like my lover's arms around me in that position. It makes me feel safe and secure.

So, what type of scientist are you? Are you a "sex" scientist?

Regards, Julie

May 2, 2000
Hi Julie:

So, you like cars. Mine is a 1952 MGTD. She is green, cute and fast, and my second biggest vice. (Are you cute and fast? If so, you could be my first biggest vice?) It's the first car I ever worked on. I practically built it from scratch. Originally, it was a basket case that was on its way to the junk yard. Now, after four and a half years' work, it's the prettiest car I've seen around, and it turns a lot of heads. I am not a car guy, but I am an antique sports car guy, and I just love the hell out of this one. And you are into refurbishing antiques too. We have so much in common, it's becoming scary.

My favorite sleeping position would depend on two things. Who I'm with, and how horny we both are. If it's sleeping you're asking about, then the closer the better. I like that contact, and "spoon" style is the only way to go to get that feeling of intimacy and closeness. It's the best way to cuddle, and it's my favorite too. But, if it's after love making, then I would prefer something more sensual. Like having my partner literally sleep on top of me with my arms wrapped around her, face down, with her head nestled into my shoulder, and her legs draped over my hips, preferably still joined intimately together. Well, you asked... See,

15

you caught me at a horny moment also. But, these days, I seem to be horny all the time.

As to what kind of scientist I am, it's not a "sex" scientist. My field is geophysics and civil engineering. I am a materials designer. If you wanted to build a dam, you would hire an engineering company to draft the design of the dam. Most likely, they would specify that it be made of concrete. I would be the guy they would come to, to design the concrete in such a way as to withstand the pressure of the water behind the dam, or, any such materials application. I am an expert in dams (concrete and soils), airport runways (asphalt). In fact, all the metropolitan airports' runways have been designed and manufactured by me. Highways like Route 80, Route 24, Route 287, etc.) bridges, shopping mall parking lots, etc. I bet you're sorry you asked now.

Sex is just a hobby of mine, and I have been trying to perfect my hobby all of my adult life. If something's worth doing, it's worth doing right. It also helps that I'm a pervert with an overactive imagination. And, you are such a tease...

- Henry

May 2, 2000
(I attached a picture of myself with this letter.)
Hi Henry:

I don't think you are a pervert, just horny. Your job doesn't sound like you. Or, the way I perceive you from your letters. It sounds like it's full of numbers crunching. I hope you enjoy this picture I am attaching. I like the way you look in the picture you sent. But, you look a bit stuffy in that suit.

You do, however, have an overactive imagination. You have an interesting hobby.

Regards, Julie

May 3, 2000

Come to Papa baby! You look like that, and you sleep - alone. What a waste. Here's me, and the car...

(He sent me a picture of himself and his car.)

May 3, 2000
Hi Henry:

I think you look cute in that picture. I don't feel that we are totally strangers any more. I'm really getting to know you. Do you write to other women? There are a few others I write to, but I find that you are the most intriguing. For some strange reason, you make me feel like I'm 25 again. I was born and lived in Brooklyn most of my life. I have a real strong "Brooklyn" accent. Have you ever been to Brooklyn?

I tried to get into Mensa when I was in my twenties. They told me my IQ is in the top 5% and you have to be in the top 2% to get in. I hope you are not afraid of women who know how to think. - Julie

May 3, 2000
Hi Julie:

Well, after the communications I have sent you over the last two days, are you still talking to me? I write to two other women.

One is in Delaware. We correspond about art and cooking, but that's all. There is another lady I met on the web. She lives in South Jersey. We did meet for dinner, and she is a very nice person. I enjoyed dinner with her very much, and would like to repeat the experience. But, it will always stay only dinner. She is not my type in that way, but a real nice person to have a conversation with. As far as you feeling twenty-five, well if you want, I can run my hands over your naked body, and tell you how you feel to me. I lived the first nineteen years of my life in England, so I didn't get to Brooklyn. If we had dated, I'd remember you. And, as it happens, I used to be a member of Mensa, when I was younger and when things like that mattered to me. Talk later. – Henry

(He sent me more pictures of himself.)

May 3, 2000
Hi Henry:

I think you're cute and I love the car. Do you still have a British accent? But, the suit really does looks stuffy.

- Regards, Julie

May 3, 2000
Hi Julie:

I'm cute? Thanks. I'm not as stuffy as I look. The head shot is a corporate portrait. The one in the gray suit was taken at a friend's dinner party, and the other one was at work. Stuffy occasions, not a stuffy person. So, you like the car. I knew you would. And, yes I have a slight British accent left over from all those years in England. How about a naked picture of you? That was a tease and probably is pushing my luck. But, then wait until you read the nasty stuff I wrote to you. Maybe it will be the last time I hear from you. But, if you respond to the letter in a positive way, things could get interesting. – Henry

May 3, 2000
Hi Henry:

You will not get a naked picture of me. I'm sure you were teasing. How "interesting" things get depends on you. I guess you've never been told that you are "cute" before. Are you one of those stuffy corporate execs? I don't like jackets and ties. "Casual" is my cup of tea. Do you even own a pair of jeans?

The car looks great! You must have a lot of fun with it. - Julie

May 4, 2000
Hi Julie:

How are you today? No, I haven't been told I'm cute before. I'm not stuffy, but I must admit that I do have some of that British reserve left over. I am also a casual person, but a bit of a clothes horse. I try to dress correctly for the occasion, and I always look in the mirror before leaving the house. I hope you don't think me vain. I run around in sweats most of the time in the house during the summer. At home, I seldom wear anything other than shorts and a T shirt. And, I do own jeans.

I thought that you would dig the car. Most of the parts are from Volkswagen, the scrap yard, modified Chevy and Ford parts, and some (in fact many) I made myself, or adapted from something that was never meant to be on a car. For example, the chrome wire looms that go from the radiator to the head lights are actually water supply tubes for a toilet. I'm glad you like it. Thanks. Oh! And it doesn't have a back seat. But, my regular car does...hehehehe...I haven't made love in the back seat of a car since . . . well let's just say that drive-in movies were popular at the time. And, yes, things are becoming interesting - if I could just figure out where it is all going. Have a good day. Try and enjoy the weather. Hope you will be in touch. - Henry

May 4, 2000
Hi Henry:

You sound like you might be horny. Am I right? Tell me about yourself sexually? What is your favorite position when making love? I want to know more about you. How did you learn how to fix cars? Who is your favorite author? Favorite singer? Tell me about your fantasy or ideal woman. What would she be like? I need some help with the novel I'm currently writing. Can you come up with an unusual way to hide a body? The novel centers on someone who has discovered an inexpensive way to produce solar electricity. Do you know anything about that? As much as I like to write about romance, I also like to have an interesting storyline to go along with the romance and flush out my characters. - Julie

May 4, 2000
Hi Julie:

In response to your lunchtime letter:

Yes, I am real horny. It's been a while and your letters don't help me one bit. Every time I read them, I get hornier. Thanks! You do realize that if we ever met, and we hit it off, and you're receptive, we may not survive the encounter.

So, did you enjoy the description of the position I prefer after making love? Who knows, if things go right between us, perhaps one day in the future you may get to try it with me. Stranger things have happened... you will enjoy it a lot more than just the description. I'm not pushing you, so don't run away. We can stay pen pals if you want, and for as long as you want. It's just that any encouragement from you sets my hormones going. I've told you before, it's been a while. And, that brings me to your question. "What is my favorite position during sex?" I'll tell you mine if you tell me yours. I will tell you, but I hope that I don't offend or embarrass you. All of them. Have you ever made love on a straight back chair? It's really fun. I love to have sex, and I think I still remember how, although I enjoy some positions more than others. In fact, whatever excites my partner the most, as I have always believed that if a woman is having a great time, then I will get the benefit from that, and have a great time too. You see, if I can get her horny enough, then her reaction to that would be enthusiastic reciprocation, and the end of her inhibitions. Now, don't blush, because I'm going to get explicit here.

I like petite women, or at least women smaller than I am. Remember, I'm 5'8". I would rather not have to stand on tipsy toes to kiss her. Also, a petite woman is easier to position, and they tend to be more 'acrobatic' during sex, and I like to have the woman take her turn on top, her hair brushing my face to the rhythm of our love making. Watching her breasts sway to the same rhythm. I like to take my time, and really enjoy my partner's body to the fullest. I don't think intercourse is the only way to make love. Intercourse is just one item on the menu, perhaps an entree' but not the whole meal.

I like sensuality. For example, I am a voyeur. I like the lights dimmed, but not off. A candle is better, and I like to use my sense of taste as much as touch. To taste her lips and mouth, to nibble her ears, and kiss her neck. To trace that little hollow at the base of her neck with my tongue, to gently caress my lover's nipples with my lips, bringing her to full arousal, before slowly working my way down her body to bury my tongue between her thighs. Do you like getting extended oral sex? I mean for hours. I love to hear those little moans only that produces. Now, I have to take a cold shower. But, just about anything my partner enjoys will be fine with me. I have a real open mind about sex, and view it as a gift that is meant to be enjoyed. As far as I am concerned, in the bedroom it is no holds barred, as long as both partners are willing participants. However, I'm not into pain, sick, or weird. I'm into "feel good" sex. The bedroom should be a place to fulfill fantasies and just let oneself go, allow the animal side to come out, play without inhibitions, and just have a good time. I believe in communication in the bedroom, telling your partner what you want, or don't want, and making sure that both leave satisfied, with smiles on their faces. Nothing turns me on more than knowing I'm turning her on. See, I told you I was horny. Hope I didn't shock or offend you too much.

And, now for something completely different...I knew nothing about taking cars apart and putting them back together. I just bought a book and followed the instructions like I was building a big model kit.

Favorite author – that's tough. It depends on the work. Oscar Wilde (Picture of Dorian Grey) Isaac Asimov (Foundation & Empire), Algenon Blackwood (Any Horror Yarn). Oh, and ME of course. I do like the writing style of the author who wrote Jurassic Park, and I dig spy novels. I like lots of different kinds of literature. My love of literature and music depends greatly on my mood. I enjoy reading.

Favorite female vocalist – Diana Krall, slow sultry jazz. She puts me in the mood to relax, and of course Gracie Slick (Somebody to Love), and Diana Ross, the Supremes – love Motown, and I've always had a thing for Shirley Bassey.

My fantasy woman – that should be a secret, but I may as well use this letter to shoot myself in the foot, so here it goes... ideally, she should be auburn haired, any length, but too long just gets in the way, and I think shorter hair is attractive. About shoulder length, or a little longer would be perfect. I like green or blue eyes from an esthetic point of view, but big brown eyes knock me dead also. She is petite, and pretty, not beautiful, but attractive. I don't care about breast size. I like them all, but breasts in proportion to body size, would be a big plus. I used to like 'big boobs' when I was younger, but lately, I'm leaning more and more towards average to smaller breasts, as a prefer-ence. They tend to hold their firmness longer. I also like dark nipples. Skin that fits would also be good, and exceptionally horny would be great. My fantasy woman is also one that is warm and giving and sensual. She has some brains, and is not a control freak, and she enjoys my company out of bed. She is someone I can talk to.

Now, the same questions to you...

Your novel sounds intriguing. I would like to read it when you have it done. My novel is also underway. I'm about 2/3's of the way through my millionth rewrite. I have helped design sev-eral solar assisted buildings, both passive and active. Why do you need to hide a body? Hope you will still communicate with me after this letter. Talk to you later. – Henry

May 4, 2000
Hi Henry:

I could tell that you have quite a bit of that "British reserve" left in you from the way you handle yourself in your letters. I hope you don't think that I'm a hillbilly. But, I can clean up real well when I must. I like to have <u>fun </u>with the people I know, and as you have already experienced, I <u>love</u> to tease... I'm glad you know what "sweats" are, and that you actually own a pair of jeans. That's very good, and another point in your favor.

Whatever made you decide to come to America? Are your parents in England? I look in the mirror before I leave the house also. It's a habit I developed a long time ago. No, I don't think you're vain, just concerned about your appearance. My thoughts have a tendency to sometimes jump around a bit. I hope that doesn't confuse you.

I can't get over how resourceful you are. The things you did to get that car in shape are pretty remarkable. I like a man who knows how to work with his hands. I'm impressed!

Now to answer your "hotmail". . . It was pretty hot, I must say! You must have been exceptionally horny when you wrote it. ☺ You sound like a very sexually *generous* man. Is your wife crazy or just numb? I'm sorry if my letters get you that way. I don't mean to, really. It's just the way I write. I tend to say exactly what's on my mind. You are very easy to talk to. I consider writing a letter is like talking to a person. You seem to have a very good understanding of my feelings, and perhaps have some of the same problems I have. I also find flirting a bit of a relief from the day to day tension, and enjoy it. So do you! You realize that you were practically making love to me in your letter. . . (Got my panties wet too!)

It's interesting how you describe the type of woman that attracts you. I'm sorry, but I don't think I fall into the "petite" category. I stand 5'6" in stockings, and have a larger than average sized chest. It's my Italian heritage. (I'm not fat, if that's what you are wondering, but not skinny either.) I work out at least 5 times a week to try and stay in shape. I've never really thought about the way a person looks, to be sexually attracted to them. I don't believe in "casual" sex. I would have to become intimate with a man, and grow to admire him, and then the sexual attraction just seems to develop by itself. The things that attract me to a man are not physical. The sexual attraction stems from my being able to respect him and look up to him. It is very difficult for me to find a man who I can "connect" with mentally. I wasn't joking about what I said about Einstein. I also like sensuality. Besides, I look a lot better in candlelight. Everyone does.

Yes, I love oral sex. Who doesn't? I like giving it when I'm getting it. I enjoy just about every position also. I like being adventurous in bed. I enjoy body massages with warm oil, and just playing around with each other's bodies for hours. I prefer the man to take the initiative, and dominate the sexual encounter. I like it when a man makes me feel desirable and wanted. I like to bring out the tiger in the man. I'm into "feel good" too, not pain. I'm not offended at all. How can you offend me when you hardly know me? Do you talk like this to the other women you write to? I bet you don't.

I like country music and my favorite author is Ayn Rand – because of the way she writes, not what she writes. I don't agree with her philosophy, but love her style of writing. I also enjoy John Grisham and Marry Higgins Clark. I am currently reading a book entitled "Nobody's Safe." I am always reading something or other. I also enjoy reading Playboy and Penthouse Magazines. The articles are pretty good. Men's magazine articles are always much more fascinating than the ones you read in women's magazines.   I also love primitive hot romances.

Tell me about your novel. What is it about? Maybe someday I will let you read mine.   I might even let you read one or two of my erotic stories. First, I have to feel I can trust you. My writing is full of me.

I thought you told me that you were the person who mixes the cement. . . no, I'm sorry, just the one who writes the recipe for the people who mix the cement. Now, you say that concrete is not your primary expertise. I had no idea that you were involved in solar energy. I've always wanted to build a solar house. There is a beautiful one in Maine that sends its excess energy right into the power lines, and the owners get credit for it. You can see it on the internet.   I love the idea of being totally self-sufficient.

This letter is getting pretty long, isn't it? I'd better end it now and do some work for my boss.

BE HAPPY! -Julie

May 4, 2000
Hi Julie:

Both my parents have passed away years ago. I came here because I just wanted to visit the states. That was in 1967, and I'm still here, a citizen, of course. I have lots of things to talk with you about that have absolutely nothing to do with sex, but most of it, I will save for another letter. For right now, I want to address your reaction to my 'hotmail' letter. And, I want to use this opportunity to turn you on. I think looks are initially important. Generally they are what attract first. But, over the net, it's the mind that attracts, and your mind attracts me very much.

And, your photo delights me. Yes, my wife is numb. We make love doggie style. That's where I sit up and beg, and she rolls over and plays dead. I haven't made love the way I would like for a very long time. And no, Julie, I don't correspond with anyone the way I correspond with you. I think we have 'something' – I don't quite know what yet.

Your letter both pleased and surprised me. I agree with you. I also have to be connected to someone before the heavy breathing starts. I also am not into casual sex. Sex should be an expression of your feelings; it should not be used to create those feelings. Sex is the most intimate you can be with a person. I want to know that person first.

I did know that I was making love to you in the letter. That was my intent. Did you like it? Did it give you any ideas for your erotic writing? So, it got you a little hot, did it? I'm so glad. I hope it fueled your fantasies and made you even hornier. Just imagine what the real thing would be like. I think you would be a very enjoyable bed partner if your reaction was "wet" pant-ies. Perhaps one day we could ease each other's horniness. This afternoon wouldn't be too soon. I can tell you that your response to my letter made me "rise" to the bait.

Seeing as you enjoyed my letter, here are some more horny thoughts I've been having about you. I hope that they turn you on, and make you realize that I am not that stuffy.

Five foot six is just fine. A little shorter than I am, good kiss-ing height. And, a bigger than average chest...do you really think I would turn that down? I think that they would be just fine swaying over my face as you straddle me rocking back and forward, making love to me, as I take each breast in turn, lick, and gently suck your erect nipples. And, your hair is the perfect

27

length to cascade over my face so that I can breathe in your natural perfumes while you are driving me deeper and deeper inside of you. Finally, we will both explode in a rush of orgasm, and you collapse sweating and exhausted on top of me into that sleeping position I talked about, and with me still inside you, as we fall fast asleep. I like that you enjoy getting and giving oral sex. That particular position is absolutely my personal favorite, as I love getting it as much as giving it. And, I really like giving it. I would love to send you through multiple orgasms with my tongue. I would pay attention to every square inch of you. When we are done, you won't get horny again for quite a long time. The tingling between your thighs will last for days. You will sit at your desk thinking of our time together, squirming in your seat, to recapture the feeling of my tongue on your most sensitive areas, or the feeling of me deep inside you, when I give into the waves of pleasure that had centered in my lions, finally surrender to that irresistible urge, and let go, giving you all I had. You will be warm and moist between your thighs all day. You will think about me running my hands slowly over your naked body using baby oil, as a smooth silky way of gliding my hands over you in a sensual and long lasting full body massage. You will remember how we kissed pressing as close as we could, our tongues exploring each other's lips, face and mouths. You will think about how I nibbled the back of your ears, while I reached around you from behind, to cup a breast in each hand. And, how you held my head with your hands holding me close between your thighs, and how you straddled my face to take full advantage of what I was doing to you. You will think about how you pulled on my hips while I laid on top of you thrusting deep into you. You will think about how we made love in the shower. You will think about how you held your breasts together while I slid stiff and hot between them. You will have to sit there all day because of the wet spot that will form on the seat.

When you go home that night, you will rush to the computer, to see what I have sent you, and after reading what I have to say, you will make an excuse to go to bed early. You will need privacy because you will not be able to keep your hands off of yourself. You will lay there in the dark, touching your erect nipples, and gently massaging your wetness, pretending it is me there with you, touching you. Your orgasm will make you fall asleep satisfied in that bed, for the first time in a long time.

Well, how was that? One day I'll write you a sexy letter.

- Henry

May 5, 2000

Henry, Henry, Henry...what am I going to do with you?

When are you going to give up science fiction, and write for the much more lucrative "romance" market? Did anybody tell you that romance outsells science fiction, three to one? I guarantee that your very first novel will be a blowout best seller! You are definitely wasting your talents thinking up cement mixing recipes...Your true vocation lies in the field of writing sex!

In answer to the question that haunts you – Yes. By the time I finished your letter, my panties were drenched. But, what I did to my body last night when I went to bed is not open for discussion, as much as I know that you are dying to know. It will only encourage more sexy talk, and you will totally forget that this body has a BRAIN as well. And, a pretty smart one at that! Maybe if you cut and pasted that tantalizing letter into a note to your wife, and left it on her pillow tonight, you'll get lucky. Smile.

I hope I don't disappoint you because I am not going to tell you about all the luscious things my mouth and tongue wanted to do to your cock last night. Instead, I am going to ask you a question, and I hope you will be honest with me, and give me a truthful answer. What is it about me that makes men always want to get sexual with me? I thought that when I was a younger woman, it was because I was pretty and had a great looking body. Now, I'm fifty-one, I'm not exactly a Barbie doll any more, and yet for some reason, it doesn't matter. All men want to do with me is get sexual. I mean you haven't even met me, and that picture I sent you was not sexual. I even cropped out my breasts to avoid any thought of sexuality. In fact, that picture is just plain ordinary. There is no way that picture could have provoked sexual thoughts. On the internet, no one has ever seen me, and yet all I get is sexual communications. I gave up going into chat rooms, because every single man in every single chat room that started a conversation with me usually started by asking "What are you wearing?" Or, they would say "I'm not wearing any clothes." Sex is not the only thing about me. I must have asked you a dozen questions in my last letter that you just weren't interested in answering. That's fine. You don't have to be interested in those things. I think you are intelligent and fun. I really do. And, I just don't know what you think of me. In fact, I'm starting to think that you think I'm just another "Internet Bimbo".

- Julie

May 5, 2000
Good Morning Julie:

I hope that you are well rested after last night. So, you want to get down and be serious. OK. Let's be adults and let's be cruelly honest with each other. First, while reading this letter, keep in mind that I want you as a friend. Not a "female" friend, just a friend. And, please recognize what is real, and what is play.

Julie, if you want me as a friend, then we MUST be honest with each other. It's the only true way towards friendship. I apologize in advance because honesty usually hurts in the short term, but it is worth it in the long run. If you reread some of my earlier letters, you will remind yourself that I do have empathy for you and your life. I do understand very well who you are, and what you want. I do have insight into you. My question to you is, do you know who you are, and what you want? I recognize very clearly that you have a good and sharp mind. If you didn't, I would not be wasting my time with you. I know that this will sound arrogant, but I consider the vast majority of people not worthy of my time. You are a notable exception. You are a ray of sunlight in a dark lonely world full of ignorance and stupidity. And, I most certainly do not think you are a brainless bimbo. First, I will answer your letter's last question. "What is it about me that makes men always get sexual with me?"

When you tell a man that you write erotic fiction, when you tell a man you are horny, when you ask a man what his favorite sexual position is, what do you expect as a response? You solicit that kind of response, and have actually initiated the 'sexy talk'. I even asked you if it offended you, and you responded that it didn't, and that it made your panties wet. That's a green light for more. My letter was sent to you for entertainment purposes (your entertainment); because I thought you needed to be diverted and entertained. I thought it would add some "spice" to your life, and make it less boring. No harm or evil intent was meant.

Now, let's talk about if you wanted that. Please allow me to ask you some rhetorical questions and please answer truthfully.

1) If the letter's content was not what you wanted, why did you read it all the way through, instead of stopping as soon as you realized what the content was, and why did you reread it;

2) If it didn't entertain you and titillate you, why did you lay in the dark thinking about what I had said to you, and why did it turn you on? I truly suspect you enjoyed your body last night, and that you used what I said to you, as a fantasy;

3) Why did you tell me your panties were drenched if the letter was in any way unwelcome;

4) Why did you tell me what you wanted to do to me with your mouth if you don't want more of the same?

Julie, the bottom line is, I meant no harm, and just thought that you would enjoy it, especially as you write erotic fiction. You send very mixed signals. I told you in the beginning of my "shot myself" letter that I have many things to talk to you about. Julie, none of those things are sexual in nature. I am interested in answering all of your questions, and I have many for you, and many subjects I would like to discuss with you. I recognize in you someone with whom I can relate intellectually, and psychologically. If you want to save the "sexy talk" for your other internet playmates, I will be very happy to relate to you only on a cerebral level, if that is what you want. It is more important to me that we continue our correspondence so that our minds can relate to each other, and we can help each other through the rough spots in our lives with some emotional support when needed, than it is to have cyber sex. Besides, it would be easy for me to go get sex if that is the only thing I wanted. It's available everywhere. What I want from you is to develop a trust and a friend in you. If I misread you, I am sorry and baffled. I thought we understood each other. If you want this relationship to continue, then please, help me set the ground rules. I don't care if you look like a Barbie doll or Hulk Hogan. I don't care if you are a sex crazed nympho, or a lesbian, and therefore out of my reach. You don't have to use any sexy anything to keep me around, just be you that is enough for me. Your friend under construction.

– Henry

May 5, 2000
Hello Henry:

You are right. It probably was my own fault that you wrote that wonderful erotic letter to me. I don't mean to confuse you, but I want to be valued for more than just sex. I don't want you to lose sight of who I am.

- Julie

May 5, 2000
Hello Julie:

Thank you for an honest response, and know that letter didn't confuse me further. It just put some things into perspective. Julie, the reason I devoted that letter to just sex is because I wanted it to have some real impact on you. I felt that if I mixed it with everyday small talk, it would not have been so – sensual. I did not ignore the other things in your letter. I just didn't get around to writing to you about them yet.

And, no, I did not loose sight of who you are. I have told you that I truly do want you for a friend. Look Julie, I love sex, after having corresponded with you, I know you love sex too. You're not a bad looking broad, and you are very attractive in a strong sensual way. I am attracted to you, not because of the photo, but because I see hiding behind the light conversation and sex talk, there is a real person. I know who she is. The whole point of this letter, I guess, is to tell you I'm a horny guy who would give you a night to remember, and I am very prepared to do it. You just turn me on. But, if it never happens ever, and we never actually meet, I still would like to be your friend, and confidant. Julie, you don't know me, but I assure you that you can trust me. I would not do anything to cause you pain or harm. You can count on that. I enjoy the sex talk also, but I enjoy your mind even more. I love the fact that I am able to reach out and effect you physically with just the written word. But, that is not what our relationship should be based on. I really do respect your mind, and want to know you as a person. If anything else happens, it happens, but it is not the reason I am writing this to you now. The reason is very simple my dear. Male or female, I would like you anyway. I can be a good friend to you, because I will never ask for anything in return.

Best regards, Henry

May 6, 2000
Hi Henry:

I want so much to jump out of this life I made for myself. I am so unhappy in my marriage, but I also feel guilty about upsetting the applecart. I don't want to hurt Don. My children don't want me to leave him. I feel guilty about that. But, there is also a side of me that tells me that I must go. The alternative is throwing away whatever is left of my life. I think that you have the same problem. How do you do it?

-Julie

May 6, 2000
Hello Julie:

I was going to print out all of your mail and answer it point by point, line by line. But, AOL, in its infinite wisdom, deleted much of it. So, I will answer that which I recall. I want this letter to answer your questions regarding my marriage, and yours, as this is the most important of all our subjects. How old are your children?

Julie, you speak of feeling guilty concerning your children. It is a difficult decision to make, and I cannot tell you what you should do. I can only tell you of my experience. I have not been happy in my marriage for the first eighteen to twenty years. I couldn't tell you why I felt that way at that time, so long ago, but I do know that I felt as though something important was missing. I just didn't know what it was, but at one point, I decided that I needed to make a change of some kind. While thinking about what that change would or could be, feelings of guilt overcame me, both for my wife's sake, and that of my children. Although I have been going through the motions with some good days, and some bad, for all these years, I felt that this was most probably the best life I could have. My wife loved me, so how could I have these feelings that did not include her? After all, she had done nothing wrong. And, how could I leave her to raise those children alone? How could I leave my children without a full-time father? If I left, would I risk loosing the love of my children? I didn't know, so I stayed. Did I do the right thing by staying? I cannot say. I look at my children with pride. They turned out to be good and kind men who are making their own way. Did they turn out that way because I stayed? Who knows? But, I do know that whenever a parent leaves a marriage, it hurts the children, even if those children are adults. So, not leaving then, only postponed the hurt that they will feel now. I also know that there are many unhappy children in a two parent marriage without love between their parents. There are many very happy children in a one parent scenario that has love in it. I also felt so guilty about leaving my wife, which also made me stay.

But, you know Julie, guilt and obligation are not things that bring you personal happiness, and are not enough reason to make you stay in a situation that is missing so much. There are only three choices for you. Stay, go, or stay and find what you need elsewhere. If you stay, can you look at your life, say this is what it will be for the rest of my life, and am I content? If not, then go. Can you find peace alone? Heartache will be your companion for a while, and then freedom will begin to shape your life into what you need it to be. Then, the hurt will fade, and the guilt will end, as you start finally to live your life the way it should be. Can you afford to sacrifice your life, the only one you will ever have, to someone else, who doesn't appreciate what you are giving up for him? Or, do you want to take advantage of the time that is left, and use it to finally live life the way you should? Without negativity, instead love, self-expression, away from another's rules, and your growth not stifled anymore?

You married too young, and this is the price you pay to grow up. Over the years you and your husband have grown and changed from the children that you were when you first married. He has become old before his time; the spark is gone from his eyes when he looks at you. There is no fire in your loins for him. If you met him today for the first time, would he move you? Would you want him, and seek him out as the man with whom you want to share so much of yourself? If the answer were no, you would seek another, then you know you need to go, for both your sakes. But, you lack the courage to do it. How can you be so brave, but lack the courage to do this? For this is the hard road.

You wish he would tell you to go, get out of his life. Oh, you would cry and grieve the loss of your marriage, but deep inside, you would feel relieved – finally the end, and he would have to take the guilt for it, as he told you to go. That would make you feel better. So, it's fear that makes you stay, fear of the guilt of being the one to end it. Fear that you will take the blame. Many people stay married long after the marriage should end. The reality is this – a thirty plus year marriage, by anyone's standards, is pretty darn successful. Few marriages last so long. You have nothing to be ashamed of, if it ends. You won the race anyway. Being in a marriage that long makes you scared to venture out into the world alone. After all, you have never been alone. You think that you cannot make it alone. In fact, although you need solitude, you are also afraid, not of being alone, but of being lonely. But, when is it your time? When you lay on that bed on the last day of your life, will you feel sad for the opportunities lost and life sacrificed? You owe it to yourself to be happy. Either reconcile with your husband, and say this is my life, or leave, and find a new way. It isn't that you want to be happy all the time; it's just that you are so tired of being so sad.

I have decided that life is a scale. On that scale, sit the people who drift in and out of your life. Each person brings into your life some happiness and joy, and some sadness and control. As long as the side that weighs the joy is the heavy side, keep that person close to you. When that person makes the side of the scale that brings sorrow too heavy, then you must move on, to save yourself from such a destructive force. For that will suck the soul from you, and kill who you are.

The other choice is stay, and get what you need elsewhere. This is a workable choice, but a dangerous one. If you eventually intend to leave, and you stay, only for convention's sake, for your children, or for financial reasons, but you have left the marriage in spirit, leaving physically will just be a formality one day. The only advantage to this choice is that you can once again experience the affection, desire and joy that you have needed, like food or air, for so long. It would be good to end the long emotional fast. But be warned, if you do this; remember you are vulnerable, because of that deep need. Be careful whom you pick to fill that void, because try as you might, you will fall in love with love, and be swept away in spite of yourself. Make sure it is someone who will not hurt you or take advantage of you at such a vulnerable time.

My need, like you, is to have someone close, to show affection to. My need is to make love and not just have sex. My need is to lie at night, my arms around the one I care for, like two spoons in a draw, holding tight, knowing she cares for me too. My need is to feel happy again, and positive about life. My need is to discover who I am. My need is to be me. My need to live has all finally become so heavy on my spirit, that I can no longer avoid it or ignore it. That is why I am reaching out to find a friend; fore I can wait no longer to save my life. Am I sorry I stayed? Should I have left earlier? I don't know the answers to that. I do know that I do not hate my wife. In fact, I would not turn my back on any friend that I have. Especially one I have known for thirty years. So, how can I turn my back on my wife with whom I shared a life for thirty years? I have told my wife all about the way I feel. She is not happy about it. We sleep in separate bedrooms. That is my choice, not hers. She would welcome me back into her bed tonight, if I would. But at what price? To give up all that I now recognize as the pieces of my soul? I would go to her bed, if things were better. I would not go there to make things better. It is still difficult for me to leave, but I cannot live with her anymore. I wish and hope that she would be my friend. I still love her, but I just cannot continue under her domination. I don't want to spend the rest of my life watching TV, and doing her bidding. There is more to life than letting the time pass by. I now intend to live it. Life, especially now at fifty-two, is short. How much of it is left? Each day that passes, convinces me more that I need to make a fresh start. I am not the same boy she married so long ago, but then she is no longer that nineteen year old girl either. We are adults. It is just too bad we evolved in different ways, and now have so little in common. It seems that all we have shared is hard work, and the kids. I cannot tell you what to do, only reiterate your choices. Stay, go, or stay, and fill the hole with someone else.

Whatever you finally decide (and it may take years for you to make up your mind), I hope I will still be counted as your friend. I know it is the most difficult choice that you will ever make; fore it affects others, and is not just a choice for you. Whatever you do, please don't throw yourself away. If you stay, he must understand what is happening, and change. If he is unwilling or unable to understand and change, then you know what you must do. Like my wife, he will be in denial. Like me, you will be viewed as the one with "the problem", fore he has not changed. Don't believe it. Your problem is those around you, not you. Surround yourself with beauty and friends who bring you joy, love, and care about you. Avoid those that bring you heartache. Welcome the chance for love, and live your life.

Julie, follow your instincts and follow your heart. They will tell you what to do. And, they will be right. If you have enough love in your heart, your children will be much better off with a happy mother who lives without their father, than one who pretends to be happy with him for their sake. They see the truth. Do you want them to grow up having the view that they now have of your marriage? My kids, now grown, admit that they have known for years that something wasn't right between their mother and me. They will not like it, if and when, we finally part, but they will understand, and they have told me that they will not shut me out, because I have bared my soul to them. I talk to my kids about how I feel, and they know that I am a person. I almost have enough courage to do what I know I must do to save my life. Every day I get more adult and braver. I think by the end of this year I can finally hold my head up, be me, and pay the price. In the long run, I will have a happy life. The short run, in the beginning, will be agony, and I will count on my friends to stop me from drowning in the pool of self-pity and guilt I know I must temporarily endure. But, I will make it, and my wife will too. In fact, she is not happy either, so this is a chance for both of us.

Any support you need that I can give, regardless of the direction you take, I will gladly give you. You see, when you asked me how I feel, and what I am going through, all that I have ascribed to you is I. I hope this makes you understand me better, and makes you understand that you are not the only person who feels the way you feel. Always remember you cannot continue your life the way it is, because it is using you up. Something must change before you are all gone. And remember, you are not alone. Your friend – Henry

May 7, 2000
Hi Henry:

Thank you for taking the time to write me that long letter. You have such an uncanny insight into my life and feelings. I believe you are struggling with the same guilt and feelings that I have been struggling through. When you have a thirty plus year relationship – leaving that relationship takes a lot of thinking and considering the people who are affected by your decision. Like you, I know that if I don't make a change in my life, I will regret it. You are right, time is going by and my life gets shorter each day. It does take courage to leave. For some reason, you seem to be the only man who has ever moved me with just the written word. I find I am able to open up to you in these emails.

I left him once before in 1997. My son (my baby) went into the Navy and there were no more children living at home. I just moved out and went to live in the city. It lasted about a year. He begged me to come back to him and even promised to quit drinking. He got the children on his side. They felt sorry for him. Everyone was making me feel guilty. I eventually relented and I did go back to him, but it only lasted for about two months and then he went right back into his old routine. We don't have the same interests any more. I married too young. But, three wonderful children came out of that marriage, so it wasn't all bad.

I would have left him sooner, but my Dad had a stroke in 1998 and I moved my parents in with me because my Mom couldn't handle the stress. My Dad died recently and my Mom moved into her own home as she couldn't deal with living with the memories in that house. I kind of put my life on hold for the past two years. Don did help me with my Dad. I could never thank him enough for that. But, now I just want to be free. Maybe that's selfish, but it's what I have to do to survive. Have you ever dreamt about just taking off and leaving everyone? Do you think what I am looking for is even out there?

Regards, Julie

May 7, 2000
Hello Julie:

I still owe you a long letter to address all of the many questions and subjects you have raised, and I will begin composing it today. The purpose of this quick note is to tell you something you should already have figured out, and probably have, but are afraid to admit to yourself that this sort of thing actually exists. You said that I was the only man who had ever moved you in that way with just the written word. You said that I have an uncanny insight into people's lives. No, I just have an uncanny understanding of you and insight into your life. You say I "know" you – this is true. Why are these conditions, although so rare, so true? You asked me if what you were looking for is even out there.

The reason I seem to know you so well is very clear. You just won't let yourself believe it possible. Don't you remember the wish you made that night you cried all alone? Don't you realize yet that fate has granted your wish and allowed you to stumble on what you have been searching and longing for, and missing, in your life? Don't you know yet? Haven't you figured it out, that I am the one you wished for?

- Henry

May 8, 2000
Good Morning My Dear Julie:

I intend to answer all your questions in depth. Please be patient, just a little longer, as I need time to answer you right. I think once I answer you, then you will feel that the entire situation between us is indeed 'spooky", and I will be able to read what you have written without reading into it what isn't there. I especially want to talk to you about your feelings of guilt where your children are concerned, and you asked me about my feelings. I would like you to understand me too. In reference to fate – do you believe in fate and synchronicity? Do you read Shakespeare? (One of my favorites.)

Should thee, nay, all of us; believe fate might
the hunter be, and we are but
merely the prey, and not at all the captains
complete of our destiny, that we
secure in our arrogance, believe us so to be.

No, that's not the bard's words, but my own...talk to you later...
enjoy the gorgeous weather. Your secret friend

– Henry

May 8, 2000
Good Morning Henry:

So you write poetry too. Is there anything you don't know
how to do? And now you're my "secret" friend. You are right
about that. No one knows about you. I also am a poet and have
had my poems published in several anthologies. - Julie

May 8, 2000
Julie:

Thank you for the quick and kind response. But, as a hard
rule, I never give advice. I just show the truth. The truth here is
your obligation and responsibility to your children ended when
they became able to support themselves, and legally, when they
reached majority. You owe them with your heart. I understand
that. But, these are not little kids in their formative years. You
cannot live your life for your kids. They should not be a factor
in this decision. When your kids are living on their own - you
have bought back your life. That's the deal you make. If you
stay, then stay because you love Don, and can't live without him.

And every day you wake, you wake up thinking of him. If those reasons are not there, then like me, you must try and find the courage and the strength, to save yourself, before your strength is finally sapped by this unhappy life of yours, and then you will be trapped forever. Either way, don't hang the blame for your choice on your children. I am sorry if I have overstepped, but I would rather loose you, by telling you the truth, than keep you, by telling you what you want to hear. I will help you if I can. But, tell yourself this because it is true. You don't need me, or anyone else to save yourself. You can and must do it on your own, to have true freedom. Anything I will do for you has no price tag. Just help me to find the strength to do the same thing in my life. Perhaps this is why we have drifted to the same place in time.

My next communication will be emotion-free, and more light-hearted than this email. I think we both need a break from the subject we have been discussing. So, on to something else. I am sending an attachment. It's a serious letter and answers some of your questions about me…

Take care, my friend.

– Henry

Attachment:

My Dear, Dear Julie:

Where have you been all my life? Apparently, we have insight into each other's lives. My life mirrors yours so closely, and we have very similar, if not the same, feelings. I have lived with constant control and waves of negativity from my wife for many years. It has broken much of my spirit. I have either had to go along with whatever way she wanted our lives to be, or put up with attacks and her control pressures. Everything always has to be my wife's way. I told her just over fourteen months ago, that I was afraid of her. Whenever she approaches me, I tense up, waiting for her sharp tongue to tell me that I had done something wrong, or not correctly, or giving me a guilt trip. She is one of the most negative people I know.

I poured my heart out to her, telling her how I felt through streams of tears; telling her I still loved her, but my heart was breaking; telling her that I was not rejecting her, and that I wanted her as my wife, not as my keeper, and not as my mother. I wanted a wife, a lover, and a friend. She was stifling me. I needed her permission, either direct or implied, to do just about anything I wanted to do. For example, we have few friends; most have been chased away by her overpowering need to run everything. If I spent any time at any activity without her (for instance, trap shooting one Sunday morning per month), first, I would be told I could go. She was giving me her 'permission' to go. And, every time I went, I would return home to a cold shoulder, while she claimed nothing was wrong. This has been a pattern for many years.

I sought out the support of an old friend (Sophia), that I have known for twenty-five years. I am the godfather to her thirteen year old daughter, and she is the godmother to my youngest twenty-three year old son. We were so close, that Sophia's own mother (she is an only child) refers to us as brother and sister. I made the mistake of being honest with my wife when I emptied my soul to her that day. I told her I had other people in my life that I cared about, and in fact, loved. My best guy friend (Mike) is one, and Sophia another. Wilma began a relentless attack, both on me, and on Sophia. She accused us of all kinds of wrongdoing, none of which were true. She told me to get out of the house, and that she despised Sophia, blamed everything on her, and demanded that I cut her out of my life forever. I refused. That fueled the fire of her unreasonable jealousy. We have been to counseling, only to have her storm out after two sessions, slamming the door, and telling the counselor that she didn't need anyone telling her how to feel. I continued on my own for thirty more sessions, just to have someone to whom I could bare my soul.

So far, over the past year or so, she has demanded I leave at least a dozen times, and then reconciled anywhere from a day to a couple of weeks, later. This roller coaster ride is killing me. I finally moved out of the bedroom. I talked very seriously to her a week ago, and explained to her that if there was ever to be any kind of reconciliation between us, she would have to give me some space, and stop trying to impose what she wanted on me, allow me to heal, and give me time. Just because <u>she</u> said that everything is OK now, doesn't mean that <u>I</u> think it is, and to please give me the space I need to think things through. Of course, she did not. Even though we sleep in separate bedrooms, I wake many mornings with her lying in bed next to me. Even though I tell her this is not changing anything, and to please let me alone for the time being, she does not listen, and acts as though nothing is wrong, except when I go into a depression because of her not giving a damn about what I want and need. Then, she suggests I see a doctor and get medication to make me feel better. The point is that she has decided that we will reconcile, and even though I told her what I want, she doesn't care about what I want. She has decided for us both, and that's the problem, and it has been the problem for so long. She manipulates and controls everything I do. I have to escape before it's too late, and I'm so gosh darned lonely.

I turned to Sophia for some moral support. Late last spring, we went out to dinner together, and both complained to the other about our lives (hers sucks too). You know, Julie, sometimes things happen between friends that cannot be explained easily. We made love that night. It wasn't planned. It just happened. It is the one and only time in thirty years that I have been unfaithful to Wilma. It was also one of the best nights of my life. We made love nonstop for five hours, and then fell asleep in each other's arms. When we woke, just two and a half hours later, we immediately began to make love again nonstop for another four hours. There is little we didn't do to each other. I could not believe that it could happen. Also, I didn't think I would be able to "stay interested" for that long. I climaxed five times that night. I didn't think I could do that either. It did us both so much good. For that one night, our troubles didn't exist, and we just lost ourselves in each other. We are still close friends, and we both understand what that was. The exchange of caring and affection felt so good. Just to be close like that is something I haven't felt for twenty years. But, it did remind me of what life should be about, and that's enjoying it, before you die. My life is most likely two thirds over already. When is it going to be my time?

I want out so much, and yet it remains difficult for me to hurt my wife and make a clean break. Guilt keeps me there. Only now, guilt is turning into resentment. My eldest son (twenty-eight) is returning home from Texas this July to be married in the gazebo in our backyard. So, I don't want to "rock the boat" too much until after the wedding. I don't want to screw up his day. Also, my youngest son graduates Rutgers College in a couple of weeks, and will be out of the house as soon as he finds employment. He wants to go real bad, so it won't be long. I think by the end of the year, if possible, I must get away before she kills what I have left of myself. But, I feel guilty. Yes, it will crush her because she still doesn't understand what's wrong. I find it hard to look at her, because she always looks so sad. But the love I have for her is the kind that you would have for a sister, not a wife.

When we sell the house, and after paying off the debts – credit cards and what's left of the mortgage, etc., there will most likely be little left. But, we will be debt-free. I earn an above average income as I am the Vice President of a large corporation, so it will take little time to get on my feet. My wife works (just started a year ago, after being at home for the entire marriage), and makes about $24,000 a year. I will need to supplement that. But, as I said, I make a good living, so life will still be very good for me if I left on my own, and had to support her. I am a very successful guy. I made it to the top of my profession (internationally) from rock bottom, in fourteen years. I am a problem solver and a consultant to the NJ DOT, the Port Authority, the FAA and other government agencies, and "think tank" groups. I have over six hundred people working for me. My IQ is the highest of anyone I have met so far in my life, and yet, she treats me like an idiot and a child. I have given her everything she has ever asked for. We live in the nicest house in our town. I have kissed her butt for years. So why does she treat me so poorly?

I will not enjoy living alone. I am going to hate being lonely. I want to share my life with someone who has a connection to my feelings, and me to theirs. If you are not on the same page as me, you are at least in the same book. You are someone who I can talk to, so that I can have an intelligent conversation to discuss ideas with me without thinking me crazy. God, what I wouldn't give for that. I have never come across my intellectual equal, at least not one that could understand the emotional side of me too. Where is she? Are you her? I would welcome a woman who could beat me at Scrabble or Trivial Pursuit, and yet, still be the kind of female that I would want to take to bed. Brains and sexual attraction, is it possible? The mind is the best sex organ. Make love to the brain, and the body will follow. You asked about finding a soul mate out there. It isn't poppycock. I believe that we have many soul mates, all having different qualities and strengths. They turn up in our lives, not by accident, but by some design. You and I have a connection here that neither of us can deny. I have never felt so close to anyone, so fast, ever. Julie, this letter has by no means been sexual in content, and I am being very serious when I say this. I'm not being cute. I hope you understand why I am saying this, and don't take it as 'hitting' on you, because I'm not. I'm just going to say what I believe to be true. We, my friend, are destined to do three things. Become lifelong friends; help and give support to each other, through this difficult period in our lives; and, at some point, we will become lovers. Perhaps only for one night, perhaps over a period of years, but we will make love to each other. I feel it is inevitable, and unavoidable, because our connection appears so strong...and, it has little to do with physical attraction.

I am a poet, and do write poetry for my own amusement. I am VERY impressed that you have had your work published. I'll show you mine, if you show me yours. I'll be in touch.

Most Sincerely, Henry

May 10, 2000
Good Morning, Henry:

I agree with you. After this response, we will return to lighter subjects, full of fun and laughter. Before I answer your letter, I have to correct your math. But, you never make a mistake in math, do you? You did this time. You see, you said that your life is two third's over. With medical science today, your life is only half over. That means you have at least another fifty-two years left. And, if you take supplements and vitamins, you'll live even longer than that. I think you should try to make the most of those remaining years.

Why did you allow your wife to take control of your life? Is it because it takes less energy to give in, than to argue? Coming from an Italian heritage, I find it hard to understand how any woman can dominate in the way you describe. But, I know it happens. Maybe you should have married an Oriental woman - one born and raised in Asia. You realize that Wilma will never change. I think you've already decided what you have to do to save your life. Like me, you are afraid to live alone. On the other hand, you don't want to jump into something just for the sake of companionship.

I suggest that after your son's wedding in July, you take a vacation by yourself. Don't tell anyone that you are going to do this until after the wedding. Wait until you are ready to pack, and then drop the bomb. Once you are away, you will see how much you enjoy doing things by yourself. I think you might find that you will love it so much, that it will give you the courage to move out. I've vacationed alone before I left Don the first time in 1992. I had a ball. I ate when I felt like it, went to wherever I wanted to go, and did what I wanted to do. I had one problem - I stayed out in the sun too long, and had no one to put ointment on my back to ease the pain of the sunburn. But, it was worth it. And, my husband survived my burst of independence.

It sounds like you had a great thing going with your friend, Sophia. What happened to that relationship? Did you let it die? That certainly was a night to remember, but if it was that good, why not repeat it over and over again? Sometimes, you can find love that way. You may have been giving each other moral support then, but you had the seeds of a very special relationship going there also.

I think your wife might try to hold onto you by refusing to sell the house. It will be her way of trying to control you, once she sees that you are taking your life back. If you are to be successful when you leave, and I think you will leave, you can't let something like that be an important factor. Your dreams of being debt-free will probably have to be put on hold. Treat it as a problem that you will resolve in the future, and don't let it be an issue that could spoil the rest of your life.

Yes, you and I do have a connection. I don't know what it is either. We both love to write, and have similar problems. But, I'm not quite as petite as I imagine you prefer, and you do have a mustache. I don't know if I want to kiss a man with a mustache. I think that mustache adds about ten years to your face. Well, it's the truth. You'd look much better without it. You've probably had it for thirty years. As long as you're making changes in your life, why not do something drastic, like shaving it off?

I could tell that you have a relatively high IQ after reading your first letter. Most likely, yours is higher than mine. You are better educated also. But, for what I lack in education, I make up for in "street" sense. I was born and raised in Brooklyn, and had to scrape for everything I got in life. College wasn't an option my parents offered me. I had to do it on my own, at night, while I raised three kids. When I went back to work, I was determined to be successful. I've passed every test and hold every license in the securities industry. I started out as a secretary twenty years ago, and am today the director of two departments in a mid-sized brokerage firm that is also an investment advisory firm. I make a six figure income, and I earn every penny of it. I'm also very good at what I do. Like you, I am the problem solver in the firm.

So, you think we'll become lovers, do you? Maybe. Who knows what the future has to offer. And you write poetry also. I suspected you did. Take care of yourself, Henry. And, try to be happy. - Julie

PS: I've attached one of my early poems for you.

THE SHELL OF MY DREAMS

Without you…

> *My fingertips don't feel the warmth*
> > *of a child's cheek*

> *My ears don't hear the music*
> > *in city streets*

> *My eyes see only clouds*
> > *hiding the sunshine*

> *My nose can't smell the fragrance*
> > *of Spring roses*

And,

> *My life is covered by the*
> > *shell of my dreams.*

May 11th, 2000
Hi Julie:

I still need to write you a long letter to answer the rest of those questions. Thank you so much for your kind and thought provoking letter, which I will answer in full, at a later time. Please try and be patient with me. It is becoming very busy at work, and home is horrible. We had one of those talks on Wednesday, and I did not enjoy it. Fill you in when I write, but I have to tell you that your letter helped in what I had to say to her.

Your poem is awesome. Thanks for letting me see it. I printed it out and have it framed on my office wall. The story I had in Omni magazine was published, I believe, in 1974, and has been discarded by my wife as unnecessary, along with photos of me, etc. I tried to contact the magazine a couple of years ago, and they told me that it was not available at that time. But, I am sure I will be able to get it from them, as I didn't try real hard then, and I cannot believe that they don't have old copies of their own magazine. I attached a poem of mine for you, to make up for not sending you the Omni story. Julie, what I said to you, I meant. I wrote this last night for you. Talk to you soon my friend.

- Henry

PS: At some time in the not too distant future (your choice, and no pressure to do it), would you like to get together for drinks or munchies? Don't worry; I am not planning on having you for dessert. We've been writing intimately for over a month and we have never met. That in itself is odd.

Taketh now, thou this,
my mistress of mystery,
keep it safe with that part of me
that thee now possess.
A sweet kiss to dream on,
is what unto thee now I offer.
Use it through the long night,
to be not alone.

- For the Lady Julie

May 11th, 2000
Dear Henry:

I enjoyed reading your poem. It is quite good. Yes, I agree that it is time that we meet. You are right. We have been writing to each other almost every day for over a month now and have never met. It's time. I feel I know you well enough, but I should be cautious. We should meet someplace public. I could meet you there. You used the word "munchies". That was a surprise.

- Julie

May 11th, 2000
Dear Julie:

You know, the more I hear from you, the more I am getting to like you. It's too bad we have taken this long to find out the other was out there. I could have used a friend like you for many years.

I think that poems are the language of love, and that they have been used forever as an aid to seduction. For that reason alone, they will sell. What could be better than reading a collection of erotic poems to the object of your heart's desire? It is a great way to selectively get the message across without having to address it directly.

Do you like this?

Jane kissed me in the spring,
Robin in the fall,
But Brenda only looked at me,
And never kissed at all.
Jane's kiss was lost in jest,
Robin's lost in play,
But the kiss in Brenda's eyes,
Haunts me to this day.

You would be wise to check me out before meeting me, and come in your own car, so you can run away, if you feel you need to. Also, it should be a "public" place for your safety. Not that I'm dangerous, but it is just good practice, considering you don't know me. So, I understand, and am glad you are cautious. I am not troubled by your caution at all. And, I am very happy to wait until you are ready – if that's a day or a year, you will still be around. Why did you seem surprised by my use of the word "munchie"? I'm not that stuffy. I do know how to get the munchies. After all, I am a product of the 60's.

Have a good one...day, that is...your perverted and horny friend – Henry

May 11, 2000
Hi Henry:

You are such a good poet; I would love to try an experiment with you. I will start a poem and then you add a line and then I will add a line. So here it goes:

I feel your scent through the soft seductive whisper of the breeze.

I am looking forward to seeing how you continue this. I hope I bring a smile to your face.

- Julie

May 11, 2000
Julie:

You got much more than a smile from me. As you lay like a cat on the hearth, the dying embers of the fire casts a warm soft glow that bathes your nakedness. My hand caresses the shifting patterns of bronze and gold on your skin, and explores the dark, warm, damp, secrets of your womanhood. Your quivering thighs part, to welcome my gentle touch, and poetry washes over you as tangible as any wave the sea has ever made. You float in that erotic soft gentle sea. Borne up by each wave as it passes, drawn down by each wave that recedes. For that moment in time, nothing else exists for you, except the ecstasy of being a woman so touched by a man.

So, can I write or what?

Here's the next line for our joint venture...

I would beat with your heart as it beats,
I will follow your soul where it leads.

Your turn kitten – Henry

May 11, 2000

Purr.......You can definitely write. So, when are you going to give up writing the asphalt cookbook, and science fiction, and begin to write pure romance? I see you like to explore, too. Smile. Were YOU throwing out signals? I hope you're laughing, because I am. I had to do some editing to our poem.

Tell me if you like what I did to it:

I feel your scent through the soft seductive whisper of the breeze.
I beat with your heart as it beats;
I follow your soul where it leads;
I taste passion on your lips, as your mouth consumes mine
in a soft meaningful kiss.

May 11, 2000

Hi Julie, and how are you this evening?

Of course, I was throwing out signals. I was describing a part of one of our future encounters. What do you think? That I'm dead? Because that's the only way I can stop. Sorry.

Now, as to switching from asphalt and science fiction to romance... This is the first time I have ever tried my hand at romantic or erotic writing, including romantic poetry. But, then again, this is also the first time I have had someone to inspire me the way that you do. Yes, I did like what you did to our poem. You are one hell of a writer, Julie, but with all respect, I do have a suggestion. I believe the rhythm and mood would be better served, if you changed the word "meaningful" (it's kind of industrial), and the word "consumes" (too strong) to perhaps "as your mouth meets mine in a deep sweet kiss". Forgive me for being a critic, but let me explain why I think the changes would work. I have always thought that the most powerful sex organ is the brain. If you give your brain unambiguous detail, or graphic, or too much clear data, it stops using much of the imagination. So, I think erotica should stimulate the imagination, not the groin, let the brain do that. If you reread the erotic letters I sent you, cold and critical, and without allowing your natural reaction to take over, you will see that in no case was I really explicit. The most graphic word I used, I think, was "nipple". You supplied the rest, with your imagination. My job was to stimulate it. Please indulge me and allow me to illustrate what I mean. I could say "I want to eat your pussy", which is not such a bad idea, actually. It gets the point across, but lacks romance. I think it's what you imply, and don't say, rather than what you do say. Would you rather be "made love to" or "fucked"? See what I mean. Now back to the "I want to eat your pussy". How's this instead?

Julie lay there, in the moonlight, her skin looked like fine alabaster, and her lips curved into a seductive half smile - the keeper of the secret garden I longed to explore. The gates slowly parted and my nostrils filled with the opening flower's perfume. I longed to press my mouth between those petals. I longed to kiss that swelling pink bud, to taste that musty hidden nectar. I didn't have to tell her. She knew. She lay waiting for the fire of my desire for her to take control.

Anyway, I hope you don't mind the suggestion, and indulge my example. I don't mean any disrespect to your writing skills. They are just a little different than mine. What do you think, anyway? Did my example do anything for you? Are you starting to get that churning 'I've got to do him' feeling? And, incidentally, I make love the same way I write. I hope that's a good thing. I need to sleep on the next line of our poem. And Julie, you have the power. Just the opening of your email "purr" got my heart racing. With one word – that's pretty good.

Be Sweet – Henry

May 12, 2000
Hi Henry:

So purring gets a rise out of you. I'll have to remember that. I'm glad that I inspire you. You write so well. I am looking forward to reading some of your other work. You have a way with words. It's a talent.

- Julie

May 16, 2000
Hi Julie:

I am sorry that I haven't been in touch lately. Everything is OK with me, but the "you know what", has hit the fan. At work, now that the weather has broken, we are pedaling as fast as we can, and I'm working an average fifteen hour day for the next week or two. Please don't forget about me. I hope you are OK. I will write ASAP, most likely by Friday for sure. Keep well, toots, and thanks for thinking of me.

Your secret buddy, Henry

May 17, 2000
Hi Henry:

I watched an interesting movie which made me think of you and your wife. It's called "American Beauty". You should see it.

I did something crazy. I bought a motorcycle. It was a good buy and riding one is something I always wanted to do. But, it's crazy because I don't know how to ride a bike.

Here is a poem I wrote for you.

ALMOST LOVERS

As you dip into my thoughts and feelings,
A relentless hunger to be captured in your arms,
Burns me from the inside out.
My body yearns to feel every inch of you,
as you tease my lips apart,
and I loose myself in the depths of your eyes,
while you kill me with your passion.

Issuing a silent invitation
between the lines of your verbal coaxing,
the gentleness of your teeth
slowly nibble on my toes,
then your tongue slowly slides between them,
sending erotic sensations up my leg
to the point of my arousal.

As you begin on the other foot,
sensations ripple out
making me moist with desire.
Your tongue makes love to my ankles
I am lost in the ecstasy of the moment,
As your lips travel up to the backs of my knees.

May 22, 2000
How are you, Julie?

Finally, I can take five and write you. I took your advice and rented "American Beauty" and watched it with my wife. During the movie when Annette Benning is on the couch with her husband, and they are about to make love, then she stops him, because he might spill some beer on it, I turned and just looked at my wife. The shit hit the fan. We have finally come to the understanding that we are divorcing. We told our kids (I bet you have questions about their reactions), and I have agreed, that I will give her the house, and will pay for it, and provide her living expenses. I will purchase a townhouse for myself. I think two bedrooms, garage and basement, should be fine. Just as long as it is within a twenty-five mile radius of where I work. That takes in a lot of ground. I looked at a couple in Basking Ridge, and up in Sussex, but not quite what I want. Anyway, my wife is actually helping me look for something suitable. We may be able to do this without bloodshed. I hope so, because even if it is unrealistic, I would prefer to remain friends with her. We have shared, and will continue to share so much, including our sons. Besides, there is nothing for her to fight about. She is making out way better than any court would award her, so there is no reason to fight in court and embarrass each other by parading our dirty laundry out in front of our kids. The marriage is over, so there is no reason to fight at home. You know, it is weird. But, once we agreed it was over, the tension just dissolved, and a feeling of relief came over me. I slept better that night than I have for a long time. Although I still have very mixed emotions, this does not make me happy. But, now Julie, I can look to an uncertain future. My future before was very certain – unhappy. Now, I have a shot. You will see it that way too.

I miss our almost daily communications, and perhaps we could resume them. I have really missed you. Where are we at, with our poem? And, that special one, just for me – why did you stop at the knees? I would go about eighteen to twenty-four inches higher, then linger. And, what's wrong with sending signals? Signals and innuendoes are fun, but sometimes you just have to say what the hell, and ask, "do you want to screw, baby?" Oh, it might be whispered seductively, as "I want to make love to you, my darling," or it might be very subtle, like sucking and kissing your earlobes, or kissing your neck, and then running my tongue across your collar bone, or just looking into your eyes, but, we both know what that all translates to. So, if you happen to miss any of my more subtle innuendoes...well, you get the idea. So, are you going to try out your motorcycle this summer? I will take you for a ride in my car, if you're game. But, you know that would entail meeting me. Thank you for your consideration, Julie.

Your dark side – Henry

May 23, 2000
Hi Henry:

"American Beauty" is a spoof on the life of the "baby-boomers" in America today. I could see why it won so many awards. At least you now know that you are not the only one with these kinds of problems. I'm glad it helped you come to a decision. How did the kids take it? Better than you expected, I bet. Kids know when things aren't right between their parents.

I would like to make a few suggestions for you to think about. Why a townhouse? You seem like the type of man who likes to tinker around the house. I don't think you'll be happy in a townhouse. Have you looked at smaller houses? Check out an area called Lake Arrowhead in Essex. It's really beautiful, and you can purchase a house there for as low as $100,000. You are used to a house with a yard, without a board of directors, and all the bickering nonsense that goes on in some of these townhouse communities. But, why are you allowing your wife to help you choose your new residence? I thought you wanted to be free of her dominance. Will she decorate it for you too? Will she choose your colors? You are so used to her doing all these things, that you have grown dependent on it. That's not good, Henry. You've got to buy the house YOU want, not what she wants you to have.

I know what it feels like to move out of the home that belongs to you. I'll be moving from a 5,100 sq. ft. house to something probably in the area of 1,500 sq. ft. But, it's just me, and I'll have it all to myself. I never even used half the space in the house I'm living in now. Also, I've decided to rent for a year. Interest rates have gone up a notch. All the tech stocks are going down. Most of the owners of the tech stocks are people in their 30's and 40's, who over the past two months have watched their net worth in the stock market get cut in half. These are the prime home buyers. This is bad for the real estate market. I think in about six months to a year, the real estate market will decline. Houses are very overpriced now. I'm not worried about a mortgage, because I can get an adjustable rate one when I decide to buy. When rates go down again, and they will, because it's just one big cycle – then I can always refinance at a lower fixed rate. I think that any house you buy now will be ten to twenty percent cheaper in a year. I could be wrong, but I usually go with my gut instincts, and I'm usually right about these things, or at least have been right in the past. I've bought and sold houses over the years, and have made substantial profits on each of them, by just using common sense, and studying basic economic principles.

And, Henry, everything in life is uncertain. The only thing you know with certainty is that someday you'll die. Think of how boring life would be if we knew everything that was going to happen to us before it happened. The uncertainty is what makes life wonderful and challenging.

In answer to your question, we are not anywhere with our poem. If you remember correctly, we had a difference in opinion as whether to go "soft" or "hard" core... I purposely only got as far as the knees in my poem, just for you. I thought you might like to write the next two verses yourself. Maybe we should write them together; over a glass of champagne to celebrate your new found freedom (I don't believe I said that!). That definitely was a signal! My brother's getting married this Saturday, and I made a commitment for the following weekend. However, after that, I would like to go for a ride in that car of yours. But, I don't know too much about you. I don't even know your last name. What if you're not the upstanding citizen you portray yourself to be in your emails?

I haven't learned how to ride the Harley yet. When I was taking motorcycle lessons, I fell off the bike I was learning on. It scared me. Luckily, I didn't break any bones. I haven't given up, but I am finding learning how to ride a motorcycle more difficult than I anticipated. Also, the bike I bought is a little too much bike for me. I bought it from my cousin, and thought

I was getting the deal of the century. It's being repaired, and I haven't even ridden it yet.

Well, Henry, I think this letter is longer than I wanted it to be. So, I'll say so long for now and start my day.

Sincerely, Julie

May 24th, 2000
Hi there Julie:

It was so great to hear from you, and I love those long letters. They are just not long enough. The kids were not happy about their mother and me announcing our intention to divorce, and although they haven't said so, I know that they blame me, and tend to 'take sides' with their mother. I have absolutely no problem with that. I feel that if they were to lend their support to either of us, I prefer, and am glad it is to their mother. I think they will both come around eventually, once they see that I have no intention of giving their mother a hard time. Besides, they have known for years that there were problems. Kids, even grown up kids, are damaged by divorce, no matter what. But, we can't live our lives for our kids once they become adults. Wilma and I are making a real effort to show them both that we are not enemies, and I am sure that will have a positive effect on them. They both understand that their mother and I still have love for each other, and will try to do this with the least amount of pain. The reason I am considering a townhouse is because I have lived in a house with a yard, and grass to cut, roofs to fix, and siding to be painted and maintained, for all of my married life. I am tired of being a slave to my property, and I am not into grass cutting, hedge trimming, etc. anymore. I need a break from all of that. But, I've just started looking, and may very well end up with a small house anyway. I know Lake Arrowhead well. I live about ten minutes away from it. It is nice, and the downside of townhouses is exactly what you painted.

Wilma is helping me look, at my request. Two sets of feet are better than one, and she has the time to contact real estate people and set up appointments for me, etc. She is not dominating me in this, as it is at my request, and she is helping in the spirit of our new found cooperation. And, no, she will not decorate it, or have any input on my final decision to purchase. I am finally free of her dominance. My secretary and a couple of my friends are also helping me find a suitable place. And, the nice part is, I don't have to go until the spring. I'm not being rushed out of the house, and can take my time and get exactly what I want. I also expect the prices of homes, etc. to come down in about six months or so, which is one of the reasons I am stringing this out till the Spring. I know it sounds weird that my wife is helping me find a place, but it really isn't a dominance thing. It is a tradeoff for the deal I offered her. You are right on the money about the stocks. My net worth in the stock market has taken a hell of a hit. When do you think that you will be ready to strike out on your own? I hope you know that regardless of our relationship, I am ready to help you in any way I can.

Julie, not everything is uncertain. If I stay with Wilma, it is very certain that I will not have a chance at being happy. As far as a difference of opinion regarding our poem is concerned... it is not a difference in opinion, just a suggestion. So, send me what you think will work so I can do the next line, and then we will see if it works.

So, toots, you admit to sending signals – cool. I'll buy the champagne, you tell me when and where. You know you are right, I didn't tell you my last name, and I know yours. My last name is "Lancaster", and so now you can track me down if you need to. I work in at a large quarry called Rock Hill. You have most likely heard of it, if you live in the area. I am one of four vice presidents there, and the chief trouble shooter, designer, technical dude, and negotiator. I have about six hundred people that work for me. Hard to believe that someone this nuts could hold down that kind of job, isn't it? You say you don't know much about me. Yes, you do. You have the ability to look inside me. But, if its facts you want, just ask. I have nothing to hide.

Why not sell the bike and get something a little smaller that you feel more confident with? You sound like a natural for a bike. You will ride in my car for sure. How about taking it for a picnic someday? That would be so cool. I know you will dig it. But, now I guess I have to do some work, so I'd better log off for now. I will work on your "Almost Lovers" poem when I can get my mind out of the gutter long enough to concentrate on it. I don't understand why, when I have never met you - why do you have the ability to turn me on?   It isn't fantasy, but it is some-thing. I guess I just feel your empathy. Enjoy your day. – Henry

PS: Almost forgot – Hope you enjoy the wedding. Is it local, or are you traveling? This weekend is supposed to be beautiful after all the rain we've been having. I'm getting kind of moldy. Work on those tan lines, sweetie…

May 24, 2000
Hi Henry:

I've been so busy with my brother's wedding. He's having it at the Waldorf and the rehearsal dinner is at Tavern on the Green. My brother is going all out on this. I can't wait until it's over. My three kids are in the wedding party, had to get hotel rooms, a hairdresser. The lists of things to do goes on and on. I prefer a much smaller type of wedding myself.

It sounds like you are working things out OK with Wilma and your sons. It's not easy. I worry so much about hurting the kids and I don't want to hurt Don either. Everything you told me about Wilma makes me think that Wilma sounds like she would be the perfect woman for Don. He's German and a person who is constantly cleaning the house. It drives me crazy. We should introduce them. Are you going to be able to handle doing your own laundry, cleaning the house, and cooking for yourself? Most men have issues with doing those things.

You and Wilma should draw up some sort of an agreement concerning money. You want to make sure that your kids inherit whatever assets there are between you if anything happens to either one of you.

I've been thinking about meeting you. I'm afraid that my Brooklyn accent will turn you off. I'm sure that I sound like a hillbilly compared to your British accent.

Got to get back to work.

- Julie

May 25, 2000
Hi There Julie, Sweetie:

Hope your day is going well. Wedding at the Waldorf, rehearsal dinner at Tavern on The Green - well, that's top draw. I hope you all have a great time, and I truly wish your brother success in his new marriage. But, I tend to agree with you, I like a little lower key affair myself. My oldest son (who, as you know, is getting married at the end of July) will be married in my back yard gazebo, and we are having a catered bar-b-que at a small hall close by, with a large open field and pavilion.

He will have about 75 to 100 guests, all close friends and family. He and his future wife felt that it would be so much more intimate than a formal sit down type dinner. Seeing it will be outside in July, the guests could come dressed comfortably, and just have a good time.

Thank you for your concerned thoughts in your last email. Your comments are well received, and thought provoking. You are right regarding inheritance. Wilma and I will draw up a document that will cover all of that in a fair (to everyone) and equitable way. I will tell you more about that later.

Of course, I am very discreet regarding anything that may bring hurt into my wife's life. I have no desire to hurt her further. If Don likes to be led around by the ..., then Wilma is his girl for sure. And, it will give Wilma something to do and keep them both busy. Then, perhaps we can go run and play.

I have thought about purchasing a house instead of a town house, and am actually looking at both. I guess the town house search is more to explore my options than cast in granite. I am looking to spend about $120,000, and I am targeting the spring of 2001. I would miss playing in the dirt. I am an avid gardener, from tomato plants to flowering trees, ponds, and of course my collection of bonsai trees. But, in any event, I am certainly not going to move or anything until after the wedding. Apart from feeling like a guest in my own house, it would put a cloud over the day for my kid that he doesn't need on his wedding day. At least for that day, Wilma and I will be together as David's parents.

I have done my own laundry and ironing for years. And, I happen to be a great cook. In the past, I have worked as a carpenter, machine mechanic, plumber, roofer, small engine and appliance repair, etc. So I am quite good with my hands and can maintain a house myself, without many problems. I'm just tired of doing it.

So, you live ten minutes from Lake Arrowhead. I live in Lewisburg, which as you know is right down the road. I guess we are closer to each other than we thought. Most likely, not this weekend, but next, my car (the toy) will go to the mechanic for it's Spring start up, then I would just love, not only to give you a ride, but perhaps we could head out somewhere neat for that picnic. We will have to get together and plan and plot it. Actually, I would also like to give you a ride (in the innuendo sense). Hey, I can't let a whole letter go by without at least one shot, can I?

Now, I'm going to take you to task. You have excused or apologized for your Brooklyn accent several times. Why? One accent is no better than any other (except mine, of course) – it is part of who you are. I'm used to Brooklyn, Hoboken, and Jersey City type accents. Also, you said once that I might think you a hillbilly. No Way! I am not and cannot afford to be a judgmental person, besides; your obvious intellect excludes you from the hillbilly club. Besides, I have never met a hillbilly with a Brooklyn accent.

Now, a loaded question...Let's meet, or if you would prefer, let's talk. I would love to hear that Brooklyn accent. If you have the moxie, call me during the day at work, if you would.   I warn you, my British accent will make you horny. Seeing that the commuter bus lets you off at the mall, and I work so close to the mall, I thought we could meet somewhere real public so you feel safe – like Maggie's in the mall for instance, or Ken's Trackhouse Jazz Club in Dover. Someplace like that.   Or anyplace you care to suggest. Now, Julie, if you would rather not meet, that's OK. We will continue the way we are, and I will not be the least bit offended, disappointed, but certainly not offended.

Do you want to work on our poem? Send me the latest version. I don't mind if it's soft or hard core...whatever works. I also have some ideas for the next couple of verses of your "knees" poem. I still need to take some time and write you a sexy letter for your entertainment purposes. And, you can consider the entire letter a signal, if you wish.

Julie, the more I hear from you, the more I like you. I am so glad we met this way. It has given us a chance to get to know each other. And, I think we do know so very much about each other. Not facts, necessarily, but I do know that we feel for each other. It's nice, and just a reminder, your letters can never be too long.

You have a great day, toots. Best regards, your mystery (for now) friend and ardent admirer – Henry

May 25, 2000
Hi Henry:

Your son's wedding sounds like it will be a very nice and charming affair. (If it rains, it'll be unforgettable.) I did something like that for one of my daughters when she married. She also preferred "informal". We had beautiful weather, and it was a great success. July is a safe month, weather-wise. Imagine if he picked rainy May. . . My brother's new wife wants the <u>best</u> of everything. I think he is doing this grand affair more for her than himself. I'm still trying to get used to having a sister-in-law who is younger than my daughters.

You are looking for a house in about the same price range I am. I might go a little higher if I see something I really like. There are many houses in Lake Arrowhead in just that range. I know, I could never give up my gardening. I use a landscaper to cut the grass, and do the heavy stuff, but I love to plant flowers. I even have a small herb garden. I'm trying to find a house with an old weeping willow tree, because I love them. I think that it's the most beautiful tree there is. In every house I own, I plant one. I never get to see them grow old though. I never seem to stay in any one house for more than six or seven years.

From the way you talk about yourself, I don't think that you would be very happy in a townhouse. They are for people who don't enjoy taking something ordinary and making it into something extraordinary. I don't see you as being that way, certainly not when you do what you have obviously done to that car of yours. There's nothing at all to "fix" in a townhouse. I'm a woman who plans on living alone, and I wouldn't buy one. Not that I'm anywhere near as handy as you are, but I love to paint and fix things up and make them look like new again. That's half the fun of owning a house. My current house was built in 1997. It's new and I hate it, because there isn't much to do with it.

I am overly self-conscious about the Brooklyn accent, because I know it doesn't sound very professional. I think it may have hurt my career a bit. I could have gone to speech classes, as my mother did, and gotten rid of it, but I like it. It's me. As you say, it's <u>who</u> I am. I'm not exactly a hillbilly, but I tend to prefer "casual" over "formal".

So you think the British accent will make me horny, huh? Wait till you see what the Brooklyn one does to <u>you</u>. . .

For somebody who <u>claims</u> his wife controls his life, you are one very <u>aggressive</u> male.   The character somehow doesn't fit the role. I'll ward away the butterflies, and meet you, but it will have to wait two weeks. Don't worry; I don't need to go on a crash diet. I prefer to meet on a weekend, when I'm not so stressed out, and I'm tied up till the 10th. After work, I'm pretty much harried from the long day and the commute. All I want to do is put my feet up, or soak in the tub.

Do you really think we should meet? Are we ready to meet? You call me. I'm shy. I know you can figure out how to get the number of where I work, because I emailed you from my work email address. What will I say to you? I feel like a teenager again…

Our poem:

(Made some revisions – tell me what you think, and add a few lines, if you like.)

I feel your scent
through the soft breeze;
I beat with your heart as it beats;
I follow your soul where it leads;
I taste the passion in your lips,
as your mouth takes mine
in a meaningful kiss;
then, our tongues intertwine
in a slow intimate waltz.

(You take it form here. I'm not sure of the word "waltz", may change it. Any suggestions?) I will answer the rest of your letter tomorrow. Good night, and smile when you dream of me.

- Julie

May 25, 2000
Hi yourself:

Suggestion: change "waltz" to "embrace".

Then...

With one look, you have possessed me;
With one look, you became what I hunger for.

Julie, if we wait until we are ready to meet...we may never meet. And, I will call you. Butterflies?

- Henry

May 26, 2000
Hello Julie:

I think you have a charming voice, and there is nothing wrong with your accent at all. I am very glad I called you. It was fun to hear your voice. The ice isn't broken enough for our meeting quite yet, but there is a good crack in it now. It will make our meeting easier. By your reaction, it sounded as though I gave you a "gotcha".

As far as your accent holding you back in business – I think that is probably true for some of the starting positions in a company, but once you have a track record, it no longer counts. Talent and intellect will always be recognized, so please don't be self conscious about the way you speak. You truly sound as refined and professional as anyone I have ever spoken to.

In your email letter, you say that for someone whose wife controls his life, I am an aggressive male. Well, actually, my wife does not control my life. The problem is she tries to control it very hard every day, and punishes me when she does not get her way. I am afraid that because I have been "worn down" over the years, I have found it easier to just roll over sometimes, and avoid the conflict. I truly am not aggressive in the negative sense, but I am not weak either. A weekend meeting would be fine with me, any day or evening would be OK. Whatever is most convenient for you will work for me, and you get to pick where. You mentioned that after work, you like to put your feet up, or soak in a tub. If you need someone to wash your back or give you a foot massage, just give me a call. I am very good at both. And, I do enjoy the finer things in life (which is why I enjoy you), but actually, I am quite an informal person. I can't think of anyone, for example, that I call "Mr." or "Sir", or any such subservient salutations, even in business. If someone objects to me using their first name, then I don't do business with them. I don't like pretentious people, and I don't ask anyone to call me anything but "Henry" – even lower echelon employees. I feel that is a meaningless affectation, and does not show respect either. Actions show respect, not titles.

And, Julie, I own several pair of blue jeans, lots of tee shirts, and sweats. So, I'm not as "tight-assed" as you may perceive me to be. I much prefer a casual and easy going, low key lifestyle. Most of the time at work, I sit in my fancy office looking like I am on the way to the beach. I also love willows and enjoy flowers very much. In fact, a hobby of mine is flower arranging in the Japanese style (what a manly macho pursuit). I must warn you of some things about me. I don't play the macho game as I am confident in who I am, and couldn't care less if people think that some of my hobbies tend to be feminine in nature. Anyone who knows me would not hold that opinion for very long anyway. But, I do tend to "take charge" in the bedroom. I am not suggesting that you find that out in person, it's just a peek into my personality. Anyway, I'm rambling, so I'd better go before I say something I shouldn't. Have a nice weekend.

Your secret playmate

– Henry

May 26, 2000
Hello my "secret playmate":

Do you really like my Brooklyn accent? I think meeting works best on a weekend morning. Does that work for you?

- Julie

May 26, 2000
Julie:

If you would like to meet on a weekend morning, may I suggest breakfast together on any Saturday or Sunday? And no time is too early. I like to get up early, especially on the weekends. I find those little snatches of death that we call sleep to be a waste of time, and I don't like to miss the day. I also stay awake at night until past midnight most nights. Although I must admit, I do succumb to an afternoon nap once in a while. Mornings are the best, because no one is up and there is little traffic. It's quiet and I can be alone with my thoughts, relax, and talk to the birds. You know those little peckers are smarter than they look. I like to get up around six AM on Saturday and Sunday, and ride my bicycle. There are several diners around our area. How about the Essex Café? But, anywhere would be fine. Mornings, huh? Afraid to meet me in the dark? But, what are you more afraid of, me or yourself?

- Henry

May 26, 2000
Hi Henry:

How about Cranbury State Park? Have you ever been there? It's very nice and quiet. There's a small lake there and it's very pretty. Or, maybe the Essex Café for a cup of coffee. Is 7:30 AM too early for you?

- Julie

May 26, 2000
Hi Julie:

Do you want to meet in Cranberry State Park? I know where it is, but have never been there. If I try to ride my bike that far I will need an iron lung and a week in bed (alone) to recuperate. I have an old clunker bike from the twenties that I restored, and I ride that around town. It is very heavy, but good exercise. If we decide to meet at the Essex Café, that's fine too. The lake does sound like a possibility for our car ride/picnic. However, I'm game for anywhere you name, and 7:30 AM is most definitely not too early. Well it's time to cut the hedges.

You know there was a time I did all the hedges in one day, just bulled into it, and put the cuttings into the shredder, and then I used them as mulch. It took about 13 to 14 hours of hard work, but that way it would only take one day, and it was done. Now, I spread the job out over about three weeks. It's not because I can't do it physically. I'm not going to fill all my free time with work any more. Been there, didn't like it. What I would like is some alone time and a social life. The clock is ticking and time is on my side. It's on your side too. Every day is one day closer to a second chance. Just keep focused on the clock, Julie. And if you were waiting for me, I sure wouldn't be taking a nap. I would be trying my best to wear you out. Enjoy the Waldorf, get some booze into Don. Maybe it will motivate him.

Smile

– Henry

May 29, 2000
Hi Henry:

Well I'm glad that wedding is over. I had a great time. The food and service was wonderful. The Waldorf is everything that it's supposed to be. My brother even had a cigar hour in the hotel's lounge after the wedding party. He thought of everything.

Your hedges sound like quite a project. I thought of you. It's time. Why don't we meet this Saturday? Does that date work for you?

- Julie

May 30, 2000
Hi Julie:

It sounds like you had a real good time at the wedding. I wish your brother and his new wife a successful marriage. They certainly went top draw. Still didn't get the car out yet. The spring startup is slow this year, but I plan on having it on the road within the next two weeks. I hope! Well, finally the hedges are done. They are eight feet high, four feet wide, and circle the entire property. They create a private and very ornamental backyard, and have arches, etc. cut into them. Lots of work, but they look so good.

As far as this Saturday, I would enjoy meeting you for breakfast. And, don't worry about the butterflies. It's not a date, and we don't have to impress each other, just be yourself. Think of it as two friends meeting that haven't seen each other for a long time. We will just eat breakfast, and have a good time BS...ing. Then, I'll give you a hug, and we will both go home. Of course, you know that the first meeting is always the hard one. So, the sooner we get that over with, the better. You have nothing to be shy about. I'll write you more later – got to earn my paycheck.

- Henry

May 30, 2000
Henry:

You must have quite a garden! So you have a little farm. I have a little herb garden. Do you grow herbs also? I also like to garden. This is another thing we have in common. What made you decide to grow vegetables? Are you Italian with a British accent? How about meeting in the Café's parking lot at 7:30 AM on Saturday? Does that time work for you? I'm nervous.

-Julie

May 30, 2000
Hi Julie:

When I die, I want to be buried in my garden. It is very beautiful. I love flowers and plants, and enjoy landscaping, etc. We also have a small ornamental pond that sits next to the gazebo. My outdoor bonsai are displayed next to the pond – very pretty. And, I have a veggie garden that will knock your socks off. It is a high intensity garden that has unbelievable yield (in 20% of the space, I get 300% more yield than the conventional garden). I'm a scientist, and I approach my garden like an outdoor lab. (I'll miss working in it.) The hedges were planted about ten years ago. I ordered them bare root from a Miller Nursery catalog. They were only one or two twigs per plant, and about two feet high when I planted them. They are Amour River Privet Hedges. When you move, perhaps I could be your gardener? I can grow just about anything (including cash crops.

If they ever make it legal, I'll be rich, because I can grow huge mutants). Plants seem to love me. My office is also full of plants. All my friends give me plants that they have given up on, or believe dead or dying, and would most likely be destined for the compost heap. I bring them back to full health, and so far, I haven't had too many failures.

I am looking forward to our breakfast meeting this coming Saturday. The Café's parking lot is fine with me, too. Do you still want to meet at 7:30 AM? That's OK with me. If you can't find me, we can navigate by cell phone to each other. I drive a green new model Lincoln town car with tan colored interior. You can't miss me. I'll be the guy trying to look confident, suave, debonair, sexy and cool. Are you nervous? Stay in touch, have a great day.

- Henry

Hi Henry:

What made you decide to grow vegetables? You have a green thumb. Maybe you'll give me some of your home grown veggies when they are harvested. I like organically grown veggies. I'll find you on Saturday, don't worry. You know I'm nervous. And, you are too, in spite of your debonair attitude.

- Julie

May 30, 2000
Hi Julie:

In answer to your question regarding my veggie patch – when I moved into the house 18 years ago, I knew nothing about growing any plants, so I either purchased books and magazines, took books out of the library, or watched every garden show on TV. I also joined the Rodale Garden Book Club, and studied, studied, studied. I am an obsessive person with any kind of research, so I attacked gardening the same way I research any other subject, and learned all I could. Then, I tried out what I learned in my yard. Each plant is planted in soil especially prepared for the requirements of that particular plant. For example, I got my picture in the newspaper a few years ago for growing the largest zucchini on record in New Jersey. Also, I came in second for the biggest tomato. I compost and do not use artificial fertilizers or bug killers. Each Spring I take samples of the soil and do a variety of tests on it to determine the ph factors, and the various trace elements, etc. in the soil, and match that against the needs of whatever I intend to plant in that area. Then I amend the soil accordingly. You should see it. Local farmers and neighbors have been convinced over the years, and have adopted many of my methods. They come to me often for help. As I said, I dig plants and I think I understand them. I do grow some herbs, but not many. I grow a horse radish that will make you cry from 50 feet away. It makes a great hot sauce for seafood, and my tomatoes, well you only need one slice for a sandwich, and then it hangs out of the bread by an inch or two. My peppers are also huge. Due to perfect soil, I can grow flowers and shrubs that should not survive in the area. My back yard is lush, and you are right, I will really miss messing around in the garden if I get a townhouse, as gardening does relax me. But, I guess I'll just have to find a substitute. I thought that sex might work, but it has been so long, that I may have forgotten how. So, tell me about the stuff you grow. You said you like flowering trees. My favorite is pink dogwood and rhododendrons. Too bad they don't flower all year. It seems that the more we talk, the more we have in common. Scary, isn't it? As I said before, I am nervous, but I think that as soon as we meet, that will vanish. It's the anticipation. Talk to you later, Julie. Have a fun day. - Henry

May 31, 2000
Hi Henry:

I enjoyed the description of your garden. I just use Miracle Grow in my soil. My Dad used to put fish heads, egg shells, and coffee grains in with his soil. He grew tomatoes and other vegetables in the back yard. How do you keep the bugs away from your veggie plants? I have a lemon tree which I grew from a seed. The problem is that the tree never flowers. I wonder if I'll ever get lemons from the tree.

When I was in Italy, I noticed that they have so many fountains. I always wondered how they built them. I would love to put one in my backyard that worked without electricity. Do you know how it is done? I'd better keep this short as long letters are harder to answer.

- Julie

May 31, 2000
Hi Julie:

I'm glad you enjoyed the description of my garden. Miracle Grow is Ok, but compost is lots better. Your father had the right idea. Fish heads or fish emulsion is probably the very best all round fertilizer. The coffee grains do nothing for the soil, but they are the worms' idea of filet mignon, so they attract lots of them. Worms are the best farmers in the world, and just by them being there eating the coffee, they benefit the soil greatly as far as structure and nutrients go. Egg shells contain calcium carbonate and adjust the ph of the soil much in that same way as lime. So, he did the right thing. It is not that I am a genius with plants; it's just that I read quite a bit, and remember what I read, and that's all. I will bring pictures of the yard on Saturday.

And thank you for saying that my writing shows talent. That means a great deal to me as you are no slouch yourself. It isn't that I am a perfectionist (although I am); it has more to do with me being compulsive obsessive. When I am interested in a given subject, I tend to obsess about it, gathering information, etc., until I completely understand the subject. (I even did that with sex.) Luckily, my genes allow me to retain, when I want to, all that I hear and read, so I tend to become an expert on the subject I am researching, and when I know all about it, then I move on to something else. That is what has made me successful in my careers (plural). This is not the first career I have had. But, when I get as far up the ladder as I can go, then it's time to switch to something I know nothing about, and repeat the process over and over. This engineering career that I have now is just one of many. I have been a paralegal, physicist (applied physics, astro, planetary physics, and quantum), engineer (several disciplines, including running a wind tunnel for the Navy), gunsmith and weapons designer, botanist, psychologist, hair dresser, beautician, carpenter, all around contractor (roofing, plumbing, house building, mason, etc.). I have operated a bulldozer, been a welder, electrician, truck driver and pilot. I've designed energy efficient buildings, including solar supplemented. Designed waste-water treatment facilities (environmentally friendly), and other stuff before starting this career. I worked for some time in a government sponsored facility that used to be referred to in those days as a "think tank" (Lawrence Livermore annex in Washington). I am not trying to impress you, truly, because there is nothing here to be impressed about. I only told you this, so you could understand me better. I can design your fountain, if you wish. I do know how the Romans did it. They used water wheels powered by the kinetic energy of the water flow to raise the water, then allowed gravity to increase the pressure, so that it would arrive at the fountain with enough pressure to power the fountain. But, to do this, you must have flowing water. If you do not have flowing water, then use wind power. I know how to do that too. When I see you, I'll draw you a diagram. Speaking of drawing, would you be interested in seeing some of my art work? As to your question about your lemon tree - lemon trees take about eight to twelve years to mature old enough to bear fruit (depending on variety). So hang in, time is on your side. And the last question in your letter (how do I keep the bugs away). I don't. The plants do it themselves. I'll explain when I see you. And, there is no such thing as a letter from you that is too long. Looking forward to meeting you more than I can say.

See you on Saturday. Best - Henry

May 31, 2000
Hi Einstein:

I'm not sure if I'm intimidated, or not. Smile. Being a mother, I guess I am a psychologist and hairdresser, but I don't know how to drive a truck or bulldozer, or fly a plane. I can tell you everything you ever wanted to know about running a brokerage firm or Wall Street, even how to sue your broker and win, but I never designed a waste water treatment plant. I like the fact that it was environmentally friendly. I do my own tax returns, if that counts for anything. My Dad designed underground missile silos for the Army Corp. of Engineers about 30 years ago, so I guess I know a little bit about guns. Maybe not, but it's in the genes. Smile. I think you are probably the smartest man I ever met. But, then I didn't meet you yet. How did you end up working in a rock quarry? And, how did you find the time to do it all, and get married, raise two boys and big terrific beefsteaks to boot?

I like the "compulsive obsessive" part. And an expert on sex too. Was Dr. Ruth your Mom? Since I'm selling the house, I won't be building the fountain this year. But, I might just take you up on your offer to design my waterfall and pond when I buy the next house. I'll look for something that has flowing water on the property. I don't think I want a place that is very windy. I bet you really could design it too. So, now that you've conquered the "rocks", and tried out all the variations of cement and asphalt recipes, what will be your next endeavor? You definitely could be a best-selling author, if you put some time and effort into it.

I have a feeling that you are like me and you don't make friends easily. It's hard to find someone you can actually talk to who understands what you are talking about.

I am looking forward to Saturday more and more.

- Julie

May 31, 2000
Hi Julie:

Thank you for the kind words, but please don't be impressed. I just have a strange mind that works on its own. I can't take credit for it. It is a physiological abnormality. I don't consider myself smarter than anyone else. I just remember stuff that interests me, and then I try like hell to make money out of it. My brain is just a big filing cabinet. I'm just not that smart. I know that this is true, because there is so much I don't understand, and so many mistakes I make.

I did not have many friends when I was very young, and hid myself in food. Oh boy, was I fat. At nine years old, I weighed 125 lbs., but when I hit fourteen or fifteen, I began an active social life, mostly because I slimmed way down after studying about nutrition, discovered women, and had plenty of friends of all ages. When I was seventeen, I dated a woman of twenty-six for a couple of months. Not bad, eh?

I am considering researching sleep as perhaps my next career move. I mean the study of it, or not doing it. But, who knows – this has become an easy racket, so I just might hang in. The money is hard to walk away from. My present obsession is oriental antiques and art.

You are right about one thing though, I still do have difficulty finding people I like. I don't have very many friends (my choice), but I do have a million acquaintances. The friends I have, I have had for many years, and cherish. With me, I either like people, or I don't. I don't think that there are any shades of gray with people that I meet. I know that I like you by your correspondence, so I couldn't care less what you look like. So, please, don't be intimidated. I'm just a regular guy, but I tend to be a little intense sometimes, and can become fixated on a problem almost to the exclusion of everything else - a flaw in my personality. But, I can be a loyal friend, and I never ever set out to harm anyone on purpose. As far as women go, I know what the word "no" means. I promise you, that you will be safe with me, so please don't be concerned about that.

Finding the time to do what I needed, and need to do, was and is easy. I just don't have much "downtime", and read or draw or write, etc., while watching TV, or write (record) while driving. If I do two or three things at once, I find that I can fit almost everything in. It is only people, to whom I give my undivided attention, and dogs. I like dogs more than most people. I am not a stupid person, but my wife treats me like a child. I will give you a thumb nail sketch of how I ended up here at my present position, when I see you on Saturday. Synchronicity did it.

Hey! I hope that none of this scares you away. I just reread this, and I sound like a nut case...sorry, but I really am not. And, don't put yourself down by saying that your accomplishments do not equal mine. Yes, they do, in spades. I'm not smart enough to understand stocks, etc. One look at my portfolio will prove that. I have the highest possible respect for what you have done. You are a self-starter, for sure. I have to give you credit. There is much you could teach me. You also have good insight into life. Ramble, ramble...guess I should say goodbye before I bore the hell out of you.

Take care, Julie

– Henry

June 1, 2000
Hi Henry:

Whenever you write to me, I will always answer, if not immediately, as soon as I can. It's my nature, as is yours, so it seems.

How could you not think that you are smarter than the average individual, with all the accomplishments you detailed to me? Everyone makes mistakes – it's all part of the learning process. I know that I'm smarter than most, or maybe can just think faster, but there are things that other people can do, that I cannot do – such as swim. I do not know how to swim. I envy the people who can. I have tried to learn on numerous occasions, and have failed. There is an innate fear of the water that I have which I cannot seem to overcome. My mother told me that I almost drowned when I was 3 years old. Although I do not remember the incident, I think somehow it is the cause of my fear of going into water over my head.

When you were 17, having a 26 year old woman, seems very much in character for you. Mentally, you were probably on the same level at some point, even if physically, she was a woman, and you were still a boy. I know I dated older men when I was 17. I considered men, or I should say, boys, the same age as me, to be very immature, but then I didn't know you, did I?

Why do you want to research "sleep"? Do you have problems sleeping? I have done some research in herbs, and can give you some advice in that department:

Insomnia could be caused by several things:

1) It could be mental. For example, all the feelings you repress where your wife is concerned (when she treats you like a child, and you don't kick her butt), will haunt you when you are trying to fall asleep. Try a warm bath and an herb called *valerian*. Or you can try letting out your frustrations by screaming.

2) Something so simple – like slow digestion, or basically eating too late. Try drinking *peppermint or chamomile tea* before bed. These herbs will help you to digest your foods.

3) Congestion – try *basil bayberry or eucalyptus.*

4) A low intake of copper. Eat lobster, cooked oysters, seeds or nuts.

5) Iron deficiency – take an iron supplement.

6) Believe it or not – too much aluminum in your system will keep you awake. Stop drinking soda or any other drinks that come in aluminum cans. Drink only beverages that come in glass containers. Also don't cook with aluminum pots and pans, and never use tin foil to wrap your foods.

7) Stop taking antacids, if you take them.

8) Low magnesium – take a supplement.

9) Some people have had luck with Asian herbal remedies. There's a store in New York City – Kam Man located at 200 Canal St. You can get them there. Look for Jie Yu, Xiao Chia Hu, Tang Wan, or Xiao Yao Wan. Don't ask me what they are; I'm not sure which one would work best for you. It all depends on the color of your tongue. Don't laugh – it's true.

As I said before, it's amazing how similar we are. I also cannot just watch TV. I must read a book, write, or be doing something else at the same time. It drives Don crazy. He can't understand how I do it, and I can't understand how he can just sit there and watch TV, and do nothing else. However, I don't have a death wish, and when I drive, I don't do anything else. I've been in enough fender benders over the years, to know my limitations.

I'm always trying to make money out of what I know, too. Maybe with your knowledge of various industries and my knowledge on how the stock market works, and moves, and how to best leverage your funds, we could put our heads together and come up with a few good investment ideas for ourselves.

You'd probably make a great stock analyst. You could specialize in natural resources. You may find me picking your brain from time to time. If it gets annoying, let me know, and I'll stop.

I don't make friends easily, but when I like you, I really like you. And to me, there is no such thing as gray – only black or white. Gray people are confused. I hate confusion.

Henry, I don't care about the way you look either. It's your <u>mind</u> that intrigues me. I find you fascinating.

I've had a dog most of my life. I don't have one now, because the last one I had was hit by a car, I never replaced him because there is no one home all day to take care of a dog. I plan on getting one when I retire. I love them too. All breeds.

You don't scare me, and I don't think that you are a "nut" case. However, you are one of the few people who I am actually going to meet from the internet, face to face. So, I am a little bit queasy.

You could be a serial killer, or rapist, regardless of what you say; I have no way of knowing that for sure. People on the internet are notorious for lying. I've caught a few in a lie now and again. So, I'm taking a chance by meeting you. So are you, but you being the man, and the physically stronger form of our species, having the advantage? I can't let my fears prevent me from doing things all the time. You know what they say, "no guts, no glory".

I probably could go on, and on, and on, but I have to earn my salary, and right now I should be doing some work for my boss.

Sincerely, Julie

June 1, 2000
Hi there Julie:

I think that perhaps we were twins separated at birth. Too bad I didn't know you when you were seventeen. It would have been interesting.

Thanks for the information on sleep. I found it interesting and informative. I have printed your letter and added it to my research files on the subject. You know much more about herbs than I. Although I also have an interest in Chinese medicine, in fact all "folk" medicines interest me. Actually, I don't have trouble sleeping myself, and the form of research I am interested in, is learning about sleep. Let me explain, if I may. What is sleep? No one knows for sure. Is it a physiological need, or physiological need? Does it have to do with light? If it's physiological, then why do many microbes cease activity when light is removed? What about plants? Do they classify as sleeping when photosynthesis ends? What triggers sleep? No one really knows. If we can discover what the trigger is, then perhaps it could be turned on or off at will. This could dramatically change employee productivity. We already know that light has a dramatic effect on mood. Night shift workers are subject to depression, but if the light is increased in intensity, and the bulbs used are true color bulbs that simulate sunlight, the depression due to working the night shift, tends to diminish. Also, it is well understood that sunlight or any light bright enough to alter the pupil size when opening your eyes after sleeping, will trigger certain chemical changes in the serotonin levels of the brain. This has the effect of waking you up. Interesting, isn't it? So what I want to find out is fundamentally, 'what' is sleep?

I would love to collaborate with you on a money maker. We must talk further. Now, as far as me being dangerous - I hardly ever kill people, and I am not a rapist. You do have some things that will protect you, however - my photo for one. Leave it in a safe place. Also, you know where I work, my name, and the town I live in. Check me out. As far as being physically stronger, I think you may have me there.

Although it would be easy to lie to you, I haven't. If you feel in the least bit uncomfortable, then don't meet me. I'll understand, and will not be offended. Or, if you want, bring a chaperone. That's OK too. I also don't tend to meet people from the net. It is a wise practice to be cautious, especially for a woman. There are many predators out there. You and I have been corresponding for a while, and I am sure that you have formed an opinion. Got to go. My boss just walked in. See ya – Henry

June 1, 2000
Hi Henry:

I also stay up later than I should. When I wasn't working I found that if I woke up at 4 AM, before the children woke, I could do my best writing. So, I did that for a while. Now, I sleep alone and get up to go to work way too early to do anything except get ready for work.

For protection purposes, I told a friend about meeting you. Just in case you are a nut case, someone will know who I was with tomorrow morning. Maybe I'm being overly cautious, but you can never be too careful.

When you get to know me you will see that I see people as either "black" or "white" and I can't tolerate people who are "gray" who are always in the middle and are afraid to be on one side or the other. I tend to overanalyze everything, but I always take a stand. If I don't know something, I just look it up. The internet is a wonderful place for research. I don't make up what I don't know. I find out the answers.

- Julie

June 1, 2000

Julie, this just keeps getting weirder and weirder. You exhibit exactly the same sleep/productivity patterns as me. And, what I found most interesting was your comment about looking things up. When I was in kindergarten, my teacher told my parents that there was something wrong with me, because I told her that I was not interested in trying to retain facts, just tell me where I can look it up, if I need the information. I was about five years old. So, you also have some of the same attitudes as I. And seeing people as black or white, and being tired of "gray" people, is an absolute personality trait that matches me completely. I also overanalyze everything and everybody.

It is a very good idea that you have told a friend about meeting me. It will help to give you peace of mind, and shows me that you are not an idiot when it comes to your safety. There are just too many dangerous people out there. I am not nervous any more about meeting you. I like you already. But, what if you attack me? I haven't been with a female in a long time, and you have told me that you also sleep alone. What if you are an exceptionally horny sex crazed nymphomaniac that is just looking to jump my bones? Not being with a woman in so long has made my resistance to feminine wiles very low, so if you pressured me, I would probably cave in, because right now I am so weak when it comes to resisting a woman's advances. So, please, please, be gentle. (Smile.)

I am really looking forward to our meeting. It is rare to meet a kindred spirit, especially one so full of fire, spirit, warmth, and intelligence. This is going to be fun. But, I must warn you, that when we meet, be prepared. Please don't run. Just a hug, and maybe, just maybe, a kiss on the cheek...but come naked just in case.

Fondest regards – Henry

June 2, 2000
Julie:

I'll be there for sure at 7:30 AM, or earlier if you like, at the Cafe Parking lot. See you tomorrow morning. - Henry

CHAPTER THREE

The first few moments I sat across from him at the cafe felt awkward. It seemed I had so much to say, and yet the words stuck in my throat. I wasn't sure exactly how to begin. I think he was feeling some of the same things. He kept staring at me with those inquisitive eyes that seemed like they were smiling at me from behind his glasses. His eyes were soft, emotional, yet very alert, and you could tell that nothing slipped by them. They reminded me of Einstein's eyes in that famous picture of him you see every once in a while in a magazine or ad. I've noted that most people try to avoid eye contact, but not Henry. He used it all the time. The way he looked at me, especially when he thought I wasn't paying attention, was almost erotic, like he was going to gobble me up in one big bite. His eyes made me wonder what he thought about the way I looked. Did he think I was pretty? Was he attracted to me? Was my neck red? My neck and chest always blush when I'm nervous. It's uncontrollable, and I hate it, because it lets people know how nervous I am. I wanted to look calm and sophisticated, not like a teenager on her first date.

I don't know how we started, but once we did, we couldn't stop talking. If I thought his letters were interesting, his conversation was so much more interesting. It was great to be able to question and respond to a statement as it came out, and not in an email that will be answered later. We spoke of the science fiction novel he was working on, my novel, aliens from outer space, the second amendment, his art, my photography, philosophy, gardening, our marriages, our children – the list was endless. I found everything we talked about fascinating. We found that we could converse about anything together. With him, I had no qualms about saying I knew very little about a subject. He seemed to really enjoy telling me about things that were new to me. I already knew from his emails that I met my intellectual match, and it was fun exchanging ideas with him. We could have talked forever, but we kept the timeframe to approximately three hours - within reason. After all, we both had to get back to our "other" lives.

I think he is a little shorter than he originally told me, and he is most likely the same height as I am. Like he said in one of his emails...a good kissing height, I thought. Comfortable - I wouldn't have to bend or stretch my neck. He had broad shoulders that gave him a sense of arrogance, and the way he carried himself, like a man always in full control of the moment, made him seem somehow taller than other men.

When we walked back to our cars, he opened his trunk and showed me some of his drawings. I was impressed with the quality of his work, and his sense of creativity. He showed me several pictures he drew of naked women. They weren't sexual in nature, but rather artistic, yet with a slight sense of erotica. I could see he appreciated beauty, and had a fetish for large breasts, even though he denied it. One picture was of a woman who could have been me, from the neck down. The breasts were lush and full with the nipples at just the right tilt – almost identical to mine. Then, he put his pictures away, closed the trunk of his car, held me briefly, and kissed me gently. It was a quick kiss, lingering just for a few seconds, designed to say "goodbye" – nothing more. But, it was thrilling in that instant; I could feel the pleasure slither through my veins. Our eyes locked, and we each wanted more, but dare not say so to the other. When I left that meeting, I was sure I had met a truly amazing man, definitely one of a kind, and one I wanted to know much better. I was sure we would become lovers.

June 3, 2000
Hi Henry:

I just wanted to let you know that I had a very nice time this morning. Although I know that we have never met before, you seemed so familiar. I felt very comfortable talking to you, and listening to all your ideas and feelings. You are one of the most interesting and talented men I've met in a very long time. Our time together was too short. I hope to see more of you.

- Julie

June 4, 2000
Hello Julie:

I also would have spent considerably more time with you, if we could have. I would have enjoyed all day. The time flew by for me. Perhaps next time. I hope that this was the first of many. Julie, I resolved from the very beginning to be up front and honest with you. So, please understand where this is coming from. This time I'm not being 'cute', and I hope this doesn't scare you away. First (and this is the OK part), you are the first person, male or female, that I have met in several decades that I feel I can talk about anything with. I find you very stimulating on that level. You are the very first and only person, who I have met in thirty-five years, who is comfortable disagreeing with me on a cerebral level, on subjects in which they know I have a certain level of competence, and yet, you make sense, and have logical and well thought out opinions. Most people, I find, navigate through life as reactionaries bathed in blissful ignorance of the truth. Basically, they think about nothing. So, I think you are an interesting person who I would like more contact with for intellectual reasons. Also, and this is the part I am somewhat nervous about saying, but when we parted, we gave each other a hug, a nice hug, and I kissed you on the cheek. That was the only part of our time together that seemed unnatural and awkward. Although it was the very first time we had met, it would have felt so much more relaxed and natural, to have held your body close to mine, and given you a long deep soul kiss, while my hand caressed your body. You see, I feel as though we have always known each other, and it felt like that would be the most normal thing for us to do. Especially, as when we hugged, I felt you relax, soften, very slightly, yield to my touch, and you leaned into me. It felt good. Did I imagine that from you, or did you also feel that you would have liked a longer, closer hug, and perhaps a real kiss? Now, don't worry, I promise, I'm safe, and I won't attack you. I swear that I know what the word "no" means. But, I do find you extremely sensual, and your eyes knock me out. So?

You see, I want to stay in touch with you, and see you again very much for a bunch of reasons, and I expect nothing from you. I would like your friendship, and I will not push you towards a physical relationship with me. I would be perfectly happy to remain just friends, but you do turn me on in so many ways. So, I figured, 'what the heck', if I said I'm going to be honest, then say it now, after that first innocent meeting, so that this doesn't start going somewhere that you don't want it to go.

Also, Julie, I realize that this is way too early, and not the right time to be seriously saying all of this, but meeting you was such a unique and impactful event for me, and I didn't expect it to be that way. I don't plan on trying to manipulate you, so I am not going to wait for the 'right time', and Julie, you don't even have to respond to what I have said, if you don't care to. Be in touch, enjoy the sunshine. – Henry

June 4, 2000
Hi Henry:

Beautiful day, isn't it? I could always tell when you're nervous. You start to misspell words. Smile. I'm going to get right to the meat of your letter. Yes, the kiss 'goodbye' felt awkward. It was "sweet" and it should have been "meaningful". We've been corresponding for over two months. I feel like I know you more than "sweet". Smile again. I am not a forward person, but we are being honest here. I am attracted in that way, too. I didn't think I would be. I didn't think that you would be attracted to me in that way. I'm not exactly petite. But, there's something in your eyes that I find incredibly sexy. In plain English, if your lips would have 'consumed' mine, I don't think we would have parted at ten-thirty. Your back seat looked very comfortable.

I also felt that we could converse about anything and everything. It was so refreshing to be speaking to someone who actually "thinks". Most men are afraid of my intelligence and I have to hide it. But, with you, I could be open and free with my thoughts and you responded with intelligent statements. I am looking forward to more meaningful conversations with you.

I have to go now because someone is looking at the house with my realtor. Right now they're in the living room and working their way through. Let's hope they buy it. – Julie

PS: I hope I'm not being too forward. I am kind of afraid of the way I feel about you.

June 4, 2000
Dear Julie:

I knew I didn't imagine it. I must admit that the body image that I have always been attracted to has been one hundred and one pounds of fun, sixty inches high, preferably green-eyed, small breasted, and with red hair. Well what do you know?

You, I find unbelievably sexy. You are like some exotic flower that gives off an irresistible perfume that draws me closer and intoxicates me. Looking into your eyes made it difficult for me to keep my hands off you, and I longed to reach out, touch you, and pull you to me. If I had only known for sure how you would have reacted, but I wasn't sure if it was only wishful thinking on my part. I guess we must be connected after all. Actually Julie, this is strange, as this has never happened to me like this before. What happened to the slow build up, the learning to trust, the games. Isn't this backwards? Even if we only meet briefly the next time, I will taste your tongue for at least one long deep slow kiss, and it will be very meaningful. I long for the day when I can taste all of you. I told you earlier that this was going to be inevitable... - Henry

June 4, 2000
Dear Henry:

If I weighed one hundred and one pounds, I would look like I came from Ethiopia! That is, assuming I had the strength to stand up. I'm glad to see that you've broadened a bit, your idea of what is sexually attractive. Smile. For someone who prefers "small breasted" women, your artwork says something entirely different. Your so-called 'hooker' drawing, particularly, had breasts very similar to mine. I don't know if you noticed me looking at her a bit longer than the others, but I was stunned at the similarity. It's amazing about the "green" eyes, too. Does your wife have green eyes, also?

All kidding aside, I don't think that people find bodies sexually attractive. The bodies are just the shell. Human bodies aren't so different than other animals. Do you think that dogs or horses care about how the other looks, whether fat or thin, brown or black, when they mate? The sexual act is the same with them. They just mate with whoever's in heat. My theory is that our bodies are similar to animals. However, our minds differentiate who we mate with. My mind wants to meld with yours. Your body and my body will be the conduits. I believe that our environment and society dictates what the average person conceives as attractive, and what is not. If you were wearing a suit and tie, I would have found you just as attractive as I did when you wore jeans. However, I felt more comfortable with you in the jeans. Smile. Remember I said the 'average' person. We are far from average, you and me. - Julie

June 5, 2000
Hi Julie:

You certainly are very, very, far from average. I liked you way before we met. I understood you as soon as I read that first email. I don't know why I could read between the lines of your letter, and how I saw what was hiding in there, or why I felt compelled to respond. It must be a heightened sense of awareness where you are concerned. I agree with you that we are driven by the same impulse and reactions as animals in many areas, and especially, sex. We use our minds to select our mates. How we select our mates is an interesting subject for me. We all have the same parts, and in the dark we feel very similar to each other. The true sex organ, even what we want during sex, what we feel is erotic desire, what brings us to climax, and why we need to taste the other person, starts and ends in the mind. But, it's the body that gets the bonus.

I find you more sexually attractive than I have any woman in many years. I still truly expect nothing from you, but I do hope to make love to you. I don't want to quickly have sex and go, although making out in the back seat of my car sounds terrific. I want to take our time, all day and all night, to the next morning, would be ideal. I want to bring you to climax over and over again. I want to hold those wonderful breasts in my hands as I kiss and lick your nipples, bringing them to stiff arousal. I want you to lie on your back, your legs draped over my shoulders, as my tongue explores you, while I listen to the low moans and heavy breathing that I am creating from you. I want to leave you drained, satisfied, tingling, and thinking about the next time.

Well Julie, at least now there is no doubt in your mind how I feel. I think about you, and my knees go weak, my breathing becomes faster, and my pulse quickens. You are going to drive me crazy. I think I am infatuated. I recognize that obsessive side of me surfacing, and it scares me too. If none of this happens, I still want to thank you for making me feel this way. It's been a long time. I would also like to spend the day with you on the beach, just sitting back watching the surf and taking up the entire day just talking with you. A perfect day would be a sweater day, overcast and breezy. The beach will be almost deserted, with the surf pounding the shore. You, sitting with me on the cool sand, leaning back on me for support, my arms wrapped around you to keep you warm from the chill air, holding you close. Perhaps we will have a blanket and a thermos of coffee. We will loose ourselves in our secret thoughts, revealed to someone who will not ridicule, and will take the time to listen and understand. And, Julie, as much as I want to make love to you, if I must choose only one of the two scenarios that I have talked about, then I would choose that windy day at the beach.

Have a great day, and thank you for having the courage to be honest. - Henry

June 5, 2000
Hi Henry:

Your descriptions of the scenarios of us together are heavenly. You really got my juices flowing. You definitely know how to write about sex because you got my panties wet. But, I must say I am attracted to both scenes. I wish I could just close my eyes and go there with you right now. I definitely enjoy your writing. I have some information about writing you might enjoy reading and would be happy to fax it to you.

Although I love talking to you, I feel you are far more ahead or advanced than I am on most subjects. - Julie

June 5, 2000
Dear Julie:

You say the nicest things. Thank you for saying you "enjoy" my writing. Coming from someone like you, it means a lot to me. I would appreciate the information you have regarding writing. Thank you for thinking of me. Please fax it to me.

As far as being ahead of you, I think we just know about different stuff. I have a feeling that neither of us is too far ahead of the other, only in some subjects and some ways. It will be more fun exploring the differences between us than the similarities. It will help us both to grow. I am so strongly and strangely drawn to you. I really love the idea that my brief email got your juices flowing. I wish I were able to take advantage of your condition right now - to touch and taste that wetness, to kiss you long and deep, our tongues searching each other's mouths, our hands exploring each other's bodies. I hunger for you, Julie. When I write to you and receive a reply like you just sent, I must admit, I get as hard as a rock. I can't wait to see you again, if only for that one long, wet, meaningful kiss. Now, I have to go take a cold shower.

I know that you are vulnerable and lonely right now. So am I. And, I do not intend to take advantage of that. As a friend I won't let you do anything that you shouldn't. You must wait until you know what you want, and until your mind is clear. Don't allow the hunger in your body to cloud your judgment and do some-thing that you will regret later. This is a friendship that I want to last. I don't want you to come to me unless you do it without reservation, and without inhibitions. That won't happen until you have developed trust in me not to hurt you or take advantage of you in any way. And, that will take time. The friendship is more important to me, and the closeness we can achieve is more important to me, than starting a physical relationship with you. If we allow that to happen, it will be wonderful and fulfilling for both of us, but we must both be ready for that, and it should not be hurried if it is to have any quality. And quality is so much more important than quantity. I can wait, and I can also pass it up, and just stay friends. It would sadden me greatly to loose you now that I have found you. You are too rare to risk loosing by being in a rush, or forgetting what has brought us together. So, for now, you are Julie, my friend, and just being that makes me so very happy, it will be up to you if and when you become my lover. I'll be in touch, and I have to work on our poem. Only now, it will have more fire. - Henry

June 5, 2000
Dear Henry:

So you love the idea that you had the ability to get my juices flowing with a few words on paper, huh? Imagine what would have happened if you wrote a whole short story. . . But, didn't you send that email to accomplish just that? Henry, there <u>is</u> a method to your madness, isn't there? I think I will enjoy the adventure of exploring the differences between us with you. In fact, I look forward to it. And, I am certainly glad, that as a "friend" you won't let me do anything I shouldn't. That is quite a relief. But, what <u>exactly</u> is it, you think I should or shouldn't do, Henry?

Actually, you give very good advice. I will do as you say, and wait until I know exactly what I want, and my mind is clear, before doing something I may regret in the future. I have no inhibitions, (that could be good or bad) but it will take time for me to develop <u>trust</u> in you, or anyone else, for that matter, fore even though we write to each other, and have stolen glimpses of each other's souls, you're still a stranger to me in many ways, and I am a bit afraid of strangers. For example, when we were having breakfast, you invited me to go shooting with you at the quarry. I would have loved to go shooting with you, but in the back of my mind, the idea of going to a lonely quarry with a stranger, who had a gun, no less, frightened me. I kept thinking about how easy it would be to bury a body in a quarry. So, as much as I would like to go, I will have to decline. If you ever change the location we could do this at to a crowded gun range, I might take you up on your offer. I think after you mentioned it, you realized what you were asking me to do. Trust can only be developed in time.

Many good things came out of that meeting for me. It made me put some pressure on my realtor to sell my house; I even lowered the price a bit. I just feel once I'm out of there and have separated the assets between Don and myself, I will be free. I feel like I'm in limbo now. I want to begin to live my new life, and I'm stuck in this charade called "a marriage". I know that you know exactly what I feel like. Don keeps holding onto some image he has in his mind about our marriage, and I know it's just a dream. He won't accept reality, and I don't want to hurt him, if I can possibly avoid it. How much should a person sacrifice? When and where do I draw the line? These are my biggest dilemmas. I want to do the right thing for myself, and am not quite sure if I have a right to hurt another person, even if I believe that what I do will be right for him too.

I don't know where or how you and I go from here. Although, I'm sure <u>you</u> know. I will follow your lead on this one. I can't imagine a relationship with you that is not physical. I intend to give you a more meaningful kiss for sure, the next time we meet. You can take that any way you want to. And, if you really can't wait to see me again, as you say, you can always catch me at the Mall's "park and ride". You already know my schedule, and the color of my car. I am very much predictable and easy to find. - Julie

June 6, 2000
Julie, My Dear:

Yes, I want very much to see you again soon, and I will stop and see you one night at the bus stop. I am not sure what day, due to my late afternoon appointment list, so it will be a surprise. At what time do you arrive at the park and ride? Yes, I do love the idea that I can arouse you with the written word. I think the reason I can, is because I am describing what I really would do, and you recognize that.

I said I wouldn't let you do something you shouldn't. You asked me what I think you should or shouldn't do. OK, I'll tell you. I think you should give in to your desires, and make love to me. I also think you shouldn't do that until you are sure that it is what you want, and not do it because it is what I want, because it wouldn't just be sex between us. That would be easy to walk away from. For me, it would be the start of something more important, a closeness that can only be achieved between a man and a woman by being intimate with each other. That kind of sharing is why it is called love making, because that is what we would be doing - creating a feeling and bond for each other. You must be sure and confident that it is the right thing to do.

I have said this before, but the only advice I will ever really give you is follow your heart, and follow your instincts, because they are most likely right. Only you know what is really inside of you, and what you want and need. Let that be your guide. And, never ever do anything just because someone else wants you to do it – including me. You have done that for too long, and that is why you are so unhappy.

When I spoke about inhibitions and that I wanted you without any, I wasn't talking about shyness or holding back in the bedroom. I was talking about being inhibited in our relationship in general. And, I know you have some of those inhibitions. A good example is the uneasiness you feel about shooting at the quarry. When the day comes that you feel that you would not have a problem being in a deserted place with me, where I could 'bury your body', and yet feel comfortable and safe - in fact safe, because I am there with you, when you trust me to protect you, that's when the time will be right for us to take this further.

And yes, I do know exactly the way you feel in the marriage. I also want my new life to start. The clock is ticking every day. I cannot let my life slip away through my fingers anymore. The big problem for me is the same one you have. We care for our spouses very much, and feel guilty and selfish, because we don't want to hurt them. But, we are hurting them every day we stay. They must have the chance to heal too. Both are as unhappy as we are in the marriage. I am afraid to reconcile again, because when I look to the future, I see nothing changing in the long run. I know if I gave in again, I am sure in the short haul, everything would be great, but I know in my heart that the marriage will slowly slip back to where it is now. Then what? It may take ten years to go sour again, and I will be ten years older and ten years more beaten down. Maybe then I won't be able to muster enough courage to save myself. This may be my only chance for escape, and to finally be me for the first time ever.

Where do you and I go from here? One step at a time, and if that step feels right, then we try the next step. I want to meet you at the bus stop when you return from work, but, only if you are comfortable with this, and have no second thoughts. And, Julie, we are becoming closer, so don't be afraid to tell me "no". It would not harm our relationship at all, if you did say "no". I do know what "no" means, and will respect that from you without any problem.

If we meet, then after saying "hello", I will drive out to the edge of the parking lot, away from the other cars. You will follow me there in your car. I will get into the passenger side of your car and take you in my arms. I will kiss you hungrily, lick your lips, kiss your ears, and taste your neck. My tongue will caress your tongue slowly, intimately, meaningfully. I will caress your breast, feel your nipple harden through your clothing, and I will kiss it to arousal. I will hold you close and tight, look deep into your eyes, and then kiss you good night, but not goodbye. And then, we will part. And that will be our second step. - Henry

(At this time, I sent Henry this poem I had written for him after we first met.)

TAKE ME TO THE STARS...

In laughing brown eyes hidden behind shiny glasses,
I could see the parts of you, that you usually hide, and
That small hint of desire that peeked out at me,
Opened my senses to the man in you, and
I didn't expect that to happen.

I wanted to taste the passion,
I know waited so patiently in your lips,
And I wanted your mouth to tenderly take mine,
For one brief second in time, the kind of time,
That is recorded on a clock without hands.

Take me to that place created by your mind;
To that other galaxy you spoke of,
Where I can adventure with you,
Exploring to the fullest, experiencing all the sensations
Of orgasmic ecstasy that exist in the universe;
To that place where fantasies take over so we can fulfill
The hidden longings in each other's soul.

June 6, 2000
Dear Julie:

I don't have to wait until you are famous for your poem to me to be worth something. It is worth a great deal to me now - more than you will ever know. And, I am very eager to receive a reply to my letter. If you address our meeting, the kiss I want to give you, the hug, my caress, it will be a very important reply, and a very interesting read. I am not sure what I am more afraid of, you saying "yes", or you saying "no". - Henry

June 7, 2000
Dear Henry:

Now, I can finally respond to your very thought provoking letter. I was extremely busy yesterday doing what I get paid to do. I will answer each question as honestly, and as best I can. I didn't want to rush through it and give you less than you deserve.

I love surprises. There is something very special about the sudden jolt that can only be experienced by a real true surprise. Whether you surprise me or not at the "park and ride" is your call.   I warn you, you may find me without my lipstick on, but I promise you a warm smile, for I will be very happy to see you, regardless of whether you call, or choose to surprise me.

I'm not sure exactly why you are able to arouse me with the written word <u>and</u> your spoken words. (I happen to find talking with you very stimulating.)   Maybe it's because of the reasons you say, or maybe it's just the fact that I'm a hot-blooded Italian, or that you are a very good writer, and smarter than I in many areas. But, for whatever reason, I think you enjoy putting me on the spot from time to time. I think you enjoy watching how I wiggle my way out of the traps you try to ensnare me into. I've never had casual sex with anyone. I was a virgin when I got married. That's the truth.   In fact, I can count on the fingers of one hand, all the men in my life that I ever had sex with (and I wouldn't even be using all the fingers.) . That doesn't say too much for my fifty years of living. But, then maybe it says a lot about me. It all depends on your viewpoint. You see, I am the type of person who needs the "close bond" in order to make love. Otherwise, without that bond, it feels awkward, and in the end, leaves me empty.

I <u>am</u> following my instincts, and I have yet to discover whether or not those instincts will lead me to do what is right for me, where <u>you</u> are concerned. So far, they haven't let me down. I generally make snap decisions about people based on my instincts. And, my instincts tell me that you are a very rare and special person. I think I realized that after reading your first letter. Something connected in that letter, and I decided that you are someone whose friendship I would not want to risk loosing. But, I will not do something just because you want me to do it. Whatever I do, I will do it, because it is what <u>I</u> want to do, as well. I promise you that, and I know you will accept my decision because you are a very special and rare individual.

My definition of "inhibitions" is different than yours. When I was talking about going to your quarry, I was discussing "trust", <u>not</u> inhibitions. I also was using good common sense and being cautious. Let me put it this way. If you had a daughter, would you allow her to go to a deserted quarry with a man she doesn't know much about, with guns, even if she does find him intriguing? I don't think so.

In the book I am writing, a quarry would make the perfect background in a kidnapping scene I'm developing. I've never been to a quarry. So, maybe after I develop that "trust" I spoke about, I will take you up on your offer. I'd love to see it. That is the truth. Tell me, could you bury a person alive in a quarry? Would they be easily found by workers? How long could one survive in such a situation? What if the person who buried that person, wanted them to stay alive for a certain period of time? Could they entomb that person sourrounding them with rocks with just enough air so that instead of suffocating them in hours, they could starve them to death, which would take, I guess, about a week. Although if the person had water, I think it could take longer. What do you think? (I told you I'd pick your brain.)

I feel that we have some of the same problems concerning our marriages. I think I learned quite a bit from my first separation and subsequent reconciliation. I learned that people don't change, even if they want to change. Certain things are inbred, and will stay that way. Either I can accept them, or I can't. I wrote a poem many years ago about my marriage and living just that way. If I can find it again, I'll send it to you. You'll appreciate it, I'm sure. But, you are right – ten years from now, we might <u>not</u> have the strength to save our own lives.

Henry, I am not afraid to tell you "no". I think your description of a meeting in my car could be innocent and exciting. Maybe I need to see if you can 'physically' make my toes curl the way your written words do. If I find out you do, I may be in big trouble. If not, at least I'll know. What if you make my toes curl, and I don't make yours curl? Will you promise to be honest about that with me? I will be honest with you as I've been from the beginning. Somehow I suspect that we may not be able to stop, once we start. Are you prepared to run that risk? I'm not sure I am ready yet, so I will begin to "trust" you, and ask <u>you</u> to be the "strong" one between us, if that situation occurs. If you feel that you may not be able to do this, please warn me now. Henry, regardless of what happens between us, if your predictions are correct or not, I want you to know something. A woman can go her whole life never hearing the beautiful things you said to me, and I will always treasure and cherish in a little corner of my heart, all the beauty you have given me this past month. I feel alive again. For that, I will always be grateful. - Julie

June 7, 2000
Hi Julie:

Thank you for replying so honestly to my letter. You also made me think. I do want to surprise you, because surprises make life unpredictable and exciting. Our meeting at the park and ride, I think should be planned this time, because this time it is such an important meeting. This meeting will answer a lot of questions for both of us. I would like to meet with you on Thursday. Yes, that's right – tomorrow evening. Would you like to? I warned you, so you can wear something...appropriate... don't go to any extra trouble. A teddy would be fine.

I thought that you might find this poem interesting, as it sums up many of our mutual fears:

She has kissed me on my mouth,
And although I wanted it so,
And although I know she wanted me,
Tonight my heart is sad;
Her kiss was not so wonderful
As all the dreams I had.

But, that is not what is going to happen to us. Because, when I first looked at you, I felt that rush of passion. While we talked, that passion grew. When I see I have email from you, my heart quickens before I even read it. I have thumbtacked that drawing that you said reminds you of yourself to the wall next to my bed. Before I sleep, I try and imagine your face on that drawing. I know for sure that our first embrace, our frist kiss, will be everything that I want it to be. I know that when you feel that passion in my kiss, you will melt into me, and respond with your own hunger. When I hold you for the first time in my arms, you will crush your body against mine as your nervousness and doubt fades. When I nibble at your ears and kiss your neck, your breathing will become thick and sensual, and you will ache for me to touch your body. When I run my hand over your breast, you will quiver with excitement, and wish we were in a more private place, than your car. While I gently roll your erect nipple between my fingertips, your tongue will devour my mouth. When I bend to kiss that aroused nipple, you will hold my head against your breast. You will feel the warm wetness between your thighs. You will long for me to touch you there, but I won't. Because if I do feel the wetness of your passion, and if you feel the firmness of mine, we will not stop until we make love right there in the car. And, that we cannot do, not yet. Not until we have that trust and bonding between us. I do not want casual sex. I also don't need all of my fingers to count the number of women who have shared my bed. I have turned down sex from more women than I have accepted. Empty casual sex will also leave me empty and wanting. I don't want to just have sex with you; I want the sex to be part of our lovemaking, and not all of it. I want it to be an expression of the way we feel and connect to each other.

You said that you think I enjoy watching you wiggle out of the traps I set for you. Julie, you have no idea how much I would love to see you wiggle. Julie, please continue to use your intelligence, common sense, and cautiousness. In fact, I urge you to. I want you to develop a deep abiding trust in me. That will only happen on it's own. I don't want to push it, because pushing is the easiest way to make trust run away. So, take your time. Take it slowly. As slowly as you are comfortable with. Because, this way we will build something that will last. You are right in feeling uncomfortable going to a deserted quarry with a man you barely know. I forget that, because I know what is in my heart. I know that I will do you no harm. I will protect you, but you don't know that yet.

I am very happy that you like the things that I have said to you, and call them beautiful. It's easy to say 'becautiful' things to a woman who has such a beautiful soul and such a gentle spirit. You have touched me in ways that I didn't think possible again. I am very lucky that the woman who has inflamed me, charmed and beguiled me so, is also so attractive and sensual. I think of you as a reward, only I can't decide what it is that I have done to merit a reward such as you. I also feel alive for the first time in a very long time. Thank you.

I truly feel like a teenager about to go on his first date. I have that empty hungry feeling in the pit of my stomach. It is caused by the fear that now I have found you, I might do something, or say something stupid and scare you away. You see, you also own a piece of me. - Fondest regards - Henry

June 7, 2000
Hi Julie:

I bought another pair of jeans – black. I'll wear them to work on Thrusday. The guys here at work will have a heart attack when they see me in jeans, and they would never believe the reason why I am wearing them. I bought the jeans to show you that I care what you think. I will always try to put my best foot forward with you. I value your opinion of me, and although I know you actually could care less how I dress, I also know that jeans are more your style, and you do favor them, will feel more relaxed if I wear them, and I will take any help I can get.

It's about 11 PM, and I am off to bed, but I know that I won't sleep very well tonight, because I will be anticipating tomorrow. In fact, I don't think that tomorrow will be very productive at work, as you will be foremost on my mind. I will go crazy until I get to kiss you and hold you in my arms. I was teasing about you wearing something appropriate. I was suggesting a loose something, so I could slide my hands up under it, and touch your bare back as I embraced you (maybe if I felt around under there, I might find something else interesting to). But, it was just wishful thinking, and a tease – not to be taken too seriously. I am looking forward to this so very much. I really can't wait for the first taste of your mouth. See you then... Have a good night. – Henry

June 8, 2000
Henry:

I am anxious to see you too. In fact, I didn't get much sleep last night just thinking about it. Your letters have made me very excited about our meeting. Is there such a thing as being overdressed for the back seat of a car? - Julie

June 8, 2000
Hi Julie:

Well, thinking of you kept me up most of the night. I'm not just talking about not sleeping. If thinking of you puts me in that condition, can you imagine what being with you, up close, will do to me? I am glad that I have will power, because you will be hard to resist.

So, the anticipation of our meeting disturbed your sleep also. That's great! I had suggested that I get in the passenger side front seat of your car, because I thought that you would feel more secure if you were in the driver's seat of your own car, in case you were nervous that I would drive away and kidnap you, if we were in my car. But, when you asked if you could be overdressed in the back seat of a car, ehmmm... If you are prepared to risk a back seat, may I suggest that the back seat of MY car is bigger, and will give us more room? If I get you in the back of my car, then as far as being overdressed goes, I would like to undress at least part of you. I would like to touch and caress the satin smooth skin of your back beneath my fingers. I want to release your bra to caress all of your back as I hold you close in that deep wonderful kiss. If I could have my wish granted, it would be to kiss you and taste your ears, and then work my way slowly down your neck as I slide your bra up over your breasts. Then I would continue to lick and kiss the base of your neck, across your collar bone, then across your chest, down your breast, and then, take one of your erect nipples in my mouth, and tease it with my tongue. Then, I will work my way slowly back up again to your waiting mouth. Julie, just thinking about that possibility makes me light-headed. So, what is it to be? Your front seat or my back seat? Either way I am looking forward to this more than you can imagine. My heart is pounding like a trip hammer right now. I don't know why I feel this way about you. I have never experienced this intensity of wanting someone before. I have never found anyone who excites me the way you do. You are unique. Am I bewitched? Tonight is only eight hours away, but it will be an eternity for me. – Henry

June 8, 2000
Hi Henry:

My back seat is pretty big also. Your letters are like foreplay. They are getting me more and more excited about our meeting tonight. You make me feel like a teenager again. - Julie

June 8, 2000
Julie:

I love your honest approach to us. Your back seat would be super with me, and I am pleased that you don't need the "security" of that consul between us. This way I can slide up real close to you. And, all I truly hope for is one long deep kiss. I won't try to do anything that may make you feel uncomfortable or uneasy. Don't feel I'm trying to set traps for you. I would be a liar if I told you that I didn't want to touch and taste you tonight. Yes, I want to caress your naked breasts. Yes, I want to feel the sensation of your aroused nipple between my lips, and hear you moan with desire. But, what I would like to happen, and what will most likely happen, may not be the same thing. And, that's OK. Wishful thinking is just that - wishful thinking, a fantasy, a dream, a hope that may or may not, come true. I expect nothing from you at all, and I am greateful and flattered that you have even consented to meet with me again. And, yes, I do think it would be smart for us to take it slowly, step by step. But, I have a feeling that several steps may be taken tonight. Please don't worry. I know how far to go, and I know when to stop. I don't want to throw away our chance, by being impatient for you, no matter how much I desire you. If I touch you at all, it will be because I know for sure you want me to touch you. And, you do know how to say "no", if I should missread you. I can't wait to see you... - Henry

June 8, 2000
Hi Julie:

I can't seem to let you alone today. It's because I am getting more excited and more horny with each minute that passes. The anticipation is killing me. I write to you the same way I would talk to you. My accent is my accent, so whatever I say will be in that British accent, and I am so happy that you think it is sexy. I hope that you will be in big trouble tonight. I mean trouble controlling yourself. I plan on trying to arouse you to that extent. That would be great, and the answer to my prayer, but I still promise I will not let you cross the line into something you will regret. I would like to take you all the way up to that line, but not over it. I wish I could hear you beg me to touch you and make love to you. To have you wrap your legs around me and beg me to slip inside of you, as you grinde your hips against mine, and have you breathlessly whisper that you want me to bury my face between your thighs. That would nice. But, a promise is a promise, and even if you do that naked and sweating (I have imagined that), I will keep that promise no matter how difficult it will be for me. I won't let you cross that line, not yet. I will not take the chance of screwing this up. So, when you see me, relax, and enjoy the encounter. Enjoy the kisses and enjoy my fondling. It will be fun for both of us. More fun and intimacy than either of us has had in too long a time. That is a promise. Only four and a half hours more – tick...tick...tick... - Henry

PS: I have a great parking spot all picked out.

June 8, 2000
Henry:

I am counting on the fact that you will keep your promise, take this thing slowly, and you will only go so far as I let you. Your emails are definitely foreplay. I hope the bus is on time and you don't have to wait very long.

- Julie

June 8, 2000
Hi Julie:

I always keep my promises. My jeans get tight whenever I think of you. It's true I have been fantasizing all day about some of the things that I would like to do to you, and that I would like you to do to me. I am sure that my jeans will be a whole lot tighter later today, say around six-thirty, or so. I don't care if you don't show up until ten o'clock, I will still be waiting breathlessly for you. And Julie, you and I both know that you don't need the phone call. The anticipation alone will make you wet, and me hard, by the time we see each other. You ask, what are you getting into? Something that is very nice, that will feel good, will heat up your blood, make you feel alive, and that you will totally enjoy and want a lot more of. And, that is also a promise that I will keep. Three and a half hours...tick...tick...tick - Henry

CHAPTER FOUR

The commute home that night seemed to take forever. When the bus finally pulled into the 'park and ride', I could see his big Lincoln parked there, waiting patiently. I instinctively knew he would be waiting. The vibes I got from his emails made me believe that Henry was probably the most reliable person I'd ever known. Later on, those instincts proved to be right. He has never been late for a single meeting with me. I'm generally on time also. But, for me, it's more because I can't wait to see him again, than because I'm a reliable person. But I've found over the years that being early for a meeting, usually gave me an edge over the other parties involved, at least for business purposes.

As I stepped off the bus, I could see his eyes smiling from behind his glasses. I was nervous. I wasn't afraid of him, but more afraid of not being everything he seemed to think I was. I didn't think any woman could turn on a man as much as he said I did to him. I knew that much of what he said was purely fiction, designed to entertain me, and fuel the pump, but regardless of whether or not he meant it, it sounded so good, and I enjoyed it so much. His last few emails seemed to have built up this meeting in his imagination to such a height, that I was afraid I would be a big disappointment to him, and no matter how good it was, it couldn't come close to the picture of this encounter he already had in his mind.

After we greeted each other, a bit awkwardly, I drove behind him and followed his car to the spot in the parking lot he chose. It was deserted, like he said it would be. We got into the back seat of my car. The first few minutes were awkward, and we talked about the differences between his Town Car back seat, and my Continental back seat. But, one thing led to another, and before I knew it, he was holding me, and kissing me very tenderly. I remember mostly the warmth of his lips. He took off his glasses, and his eyes captured my eyes. My breath caught in anticipation of what his fingers began telling my body. He brought his mouth down on mine again, and then trailed his lips to the sensitive spot behind my ear. All pretense of resistance I had, melted away. He teased and tormented my ear with his teeth and tongue, and made my whole body come alive. Then, his fingers moved to one of my breasts, and he kneaded the nipple between his thumb and forefinger. My breathing became uneven, and at that moment, I ached for him to take me right there in the back seat. He raised my bra and opened his shirt. His hard chest against my soft breasts felt indescribably wonderful. I loved the feel of the soft hairs on his chest against my skin. The sensation electrified every nerve in my body. He took my nipple in his mouth while gradually moving his fingers down to my knee, then my upper thigh, just below my crotch, and began to tease the skin of my thigh, making me want him to go further, but he didn't. Except that, he very briefly pressed his arm up against my wet crotch. Now, he knew without a doubt, that I was already drenched with the juices of my passion for him.

I could see the bulge in his pants, and I brushed my fingers over it briefly. The hunger in his eyes was real, and I knew he wanted me as much as I wanted him. But, he kept his promise to me, and we did not go over the line. I know that if he hadn't held back, I don't think I would have been able.

That night, just kissing and cuddling, in the back seat of my car, was probably the most erotic experience I have ever had in my life. He made me feel like a sex-starved teenager again, and wish I could erase the past thirty-two years of my life, and start all over. I didn't realize how much I needed someone to want me, the way he did, until that night. The experience inspired a poem that I sent him via email the next day.

HENRY'S MAGIC

Forever frozen in the cold embrace of my thoughts
Are the gray shadows of my broken dreams.

> *You looked through my mind,*
> *And listened to my tears -*
> *Showing me sunshine,*
> *And through the powerful magic*
> *Of your gently whispered guidance,*
> *You nourished my starving soul*
> *With kindness.*

I was amazed at what I felt when I looked deep into your eyes,
Eyes that have no end, and twinkle with a promise.

> *Your kiss that lingered so softly*
> *Was too strong to ignore*
> *You read my body,*
> *And made me tremble with desire.*

I would have stayed with you all night,
Touching, kissing,
Discovering the hidden secrets of your soul,
Hoping to fill the oceans of need
That came in one erotic heartbeat,
When you nuzzled my neck
Then did that thing your tongue did to my ear,
Making my hunger burn from the inside out,
As my needs turn desperately toward demand
And my body becomes unbearably awake,
To your every touch and taste.

Henry, you make me feel that good!

June 9, 2000
Julie, Julie, Julie:

What did you do to me? Thank you for the poem. It is beautiful and sensitive. This one is shorter, but for you:

A wind is blowing over my soul.
I hear it cry the whole night through.
There is no peace on earth for me,
except for the time last night,
I spent with you.

Even though what I have to say today may sound like all I am thinking about is sex, it is not true. As I told you last night, if you want to get together for just coffee and conversation, for however long a time, that it would be OK with me. I just adore being in your company and talking with you. We don't have to get physical to keep me around. The physical part is wonderful, but not necessary to me to keep our growing friendship together. Thank you for the best couple of hours I have spent in a long time. You filled so many of my fantasies last night, and you started me thinking of even more. I love the taste of your lips. I loved your reaction to me nibbling your ears. It answered my prayer when you let me lick your neck and kiss your mouth. I loved the feel of your nipples hardening with desire beneath my fingertips. The feel of your erect nipples in my mouth, and against my tongue excited me in a way that was hard to control. The touch of your naked breasts on my chest gave me a feeling of closeness and comfort that I could no longer remember having, and thought that I would never feel again. Your tongue in my mouth told me things words cannot say. As I ran my hands across your body, your legs, and thighs, I was filled with desire. I wanted you so very much last night. It took every bit of my willpower to resist you. When your hand touched my crotch and felt my excitement there, I wanted you to caress my stiffness and lick, kiss, suck me, and feel my passion swelling in your mouth. I wanted to suck your toes, kiss your legs, slide my tongue deep inside you, nibble your belly, suck your nipples, knead your breasts, kiss your neck, tongue your tongue, as I thrust deep into you. But, wanting isn't doing. I kept my promise, but I didn't realize how hard that would be. You excite me so. I will continue to keep my promise to you until the time is right for both of us. But, for now, I am content just to be with you. I would like to see you again, soon. In a coffee house or my back seat, your choice. And, I promise, I will not step over that line, no matter how difficult it is to resist, because a promise is a promise. But, I will not be able to keep my hands off of you any more than I did last night. You felt wonderful. I would like to touch you in a way that brings you to orgasm. I would love to feel you shudder with desire beneath my probing fingers. I want to look deep into your eyes and watch your face, as you give in to the waves of ecstasy that flow over you from that orgasm. I want to kiss those hot sweet tempting lips again. Just tell me when.

Have a great day kitten, and a great weekend. I'll be dreaming of your touch.

– Henry

PS: Those eyes – wow.

June 9, 2000
Dear Henry:

Although your letters are full of horniness, I don't think that is what is motivating you. It's more than that. I know it is for me. Did you say "suck my toes"? No one has ever done that to me before. I think I might like that. You've got me thinking about that. You are really a good writer. But, I told you that already. - Julie

June 9, 2000
Julie:

Thank you for recognizing that horniness is not what motivates me. I would love to see you again soon. You name the time and place, and I'll most likely be able to make it happen. An after work interlude like last night would be my first choice. Meeting me for dinner, etc., would also be fun. Crawling into my back seat would be even more fun. You name the activity that strikes your fancy, and I'll provide the rest. As to when - my schedule is likely more flexible than yours, so you tell me when. Would you consider a weekend day meeting? We could sneak away somewhere cozy. You could say you were going on a shopping trip. If you could arrange it for next Saturday, the 17th, I could meet you during the day or evening if you like. Or, any evening you would like, or even breakfast. See, I am really very flexible where you are concerned. I really want to see you again, and will rearrange my schedule for any day, except Father's Day, to accomplish that. You fire my blood. - Henry

June 9, 2000
Dear Henry:

I really want to see you again also. As much as I want to see you, and even though my husband and I sleep in separate bed-rooms, every time I go out, I have this guilty feeling. I haven't told him yet that I'm actually seeing other people, but I think he knows. We talked about it. He's in denial and expects that the problems in our marriage will somehow go away.

Henry, being with you was so exhilarating for me. I felt like I was sixteen again and was experiencing sex for the first time. Does that make any sense to you? - Julie

June 9, 2000
Hi Julie:

Your life is so much like mine. Your relationship with your husband is very similar to the relationship between my wife and I. If she knew that I was seeing you, she would flip out, even though she knows that I want out. She too, is in denial. I don't want to hurt her unnecessarily, so I do not intend to "rub her nose" in the fact that I am seeing you. Brief interludes would be good for both of us, so that we don't get too carried away. Smile. But, I would very much like a repeat of last night. That was so very nice. A Sunday AM would also be great. If we met about 6:30 AM on a Sunday, we would have almost five hours together. That's plenty of time to get into real trouble. Julie, as I said in a previous email, you name the time, and most likely, I can be there at your convenience. If possible, I would like to see you during the coming week. I could meet the bus like last night. But, I must admit, those after work meets would be for kissy face, cuddles, and touching. And, I would prefer at least one per week, but I also know that is difficult for both of us and unrealistic. When we meet for dinner, it will be JUST DINNER, and you don't have to be dessert. I want to know you well as a person, and as my friend. It would not be what I want if we based what we have on sex alone. All you have to do is name the day sweetie, and I'll be there. It will be good to just sit and talk with you without heavy breathing getting in the way of our conversation. A walk through the Park, holding hands and looking into your beautiful eyes would also be a great day. Anyway, you pick the time, place, and what you are in the mood for. If it's getting kissed and having your thighs tongued in the back of my car, or a very proper "hands off" dinner – either would be fun for me. So, let me know. How about going to a drive-in movie in Warwick, New York, if you could swing a Saturday night out? We could fondle, touch, and taste for hours, snuggled up under a blanket in the back seat of my car. I would love to fondle you under that blanket. And, at a drive-in, it would feel so naughty – just like a couple of horny teenagers.

So, Julie, did you enjoy last night? Did you enjoy my kisses and my touch? I loved touching you. Your skin felt like satin to my touch. Did I get your juices flowing? Did you want me to do more to you? I wanted to. One day in the future, we will make love for hours in every way that you could imagine. I want to watch you, as you experience my lovemaking. I will do everything I can, or that you would want me to do, to bring you pleasure. I want to fill every one of your sexual fantasies and leave you dripping wet. It would be a dream come true to feel your naked, sweat covered, body pressed up against mine. Based on last night, we both know now that we turn each other on. Sex or no sex, I want to spend some time with you, so please think about when and let me know. And Julie, as always, don't do anything that may make life more difficult for you. Don't take any chances that Don may discover. You don't need that right now. Julie, I will wait for you. And, I am prepared to wait a long time, so don't feel that to keep me, you have to see me, because you don't. It is just that it would be so nice. Well, my dear, I hope you trust me more now than you did. I will never knowingly bring you to any harm. Hope to see you soon, sweetie. - Henry

(The evening we spent in the back seat of my car, I had given Henry a short story I wrote, and asked him to critique it.)

June 9, 2000
Hi there Julie:

I did read your short story, and you are right. There is something missing. I think it's the abrupt ending. I will read it again over the weekend when I can give it more thought. Next Sunday AM would be great to see you, and I will surprise you one night this week for a cuddle. Thursdays, I need no excuse, because it is our late sales meeting night, and I am here until 6 o'clock, or sometimes as late at 8 o'clock, or until the boss is satisfied with our progress reports. But, I need no excuse any day really, because I work unpredictable hours.

We could take a day off and play hooky. You could call in sick. I would love to spend all day fucking your brains out, if you feel you are ready, then anytime would be great. Like ten minutes from now would be OK. I could get us a room at a decent hotel the night before, and then you could leave for work at the regular time and drive to the hotel instead. I could be licking your little love bud at the same time that you usually catch your bus. Next week, I will look for an appropriate hotel. If we do that, I will make you another promise. I will give you orgasms more times in one day than you thought possible. So eat your Wheaties. You know just writing this to you has given me a rock hard erection. Have a good weekend. I'll be thinking of you. – Henry

June 9th, 2000
Henry:

Getting a hotel room now seems a little bit too fast. Let's take things easier. You had mentioned a drive in. That could be fun.

June 9, 2000
Julie:

I meant that I would start "looking" for a hotel. I was not implying that we meet at a hotel right away. We still have a way to go. Not too far, I think, but we are still not entirely ready for that yet. I need both of us to go into this without reservations. That will take a little more time for you to develop the trust in me that you need. Next month or next year is OK. Remember, I don't push, and am content to wait until you are ready.

I was serious about that drive-in date for a Saturday night. I know that is most probably completely impossible, but it would be so nice to have four or five hours with you, close in the dark, as I still have a lot to explore. And, I have something I would like to show you. But, I am afraid that if we do ever make the drive-in, you will have to release me from my promise for that one. There is no way I could restrain myself for that long, with that much privacy. You would definitely go home tingling. - Henry

June 11, 2000
My Dear Henry:

I woke up this morning in an incredibly horny mood. Last night I dreamt about a particular day when we know each other better, and we decide to play hooky. You're always talking about the wonderfully incredibly luscious things you plan to do to my body, but we never talk about what I intend to do to your body. I feel like I know you well enough to at least tell you about some of those things. In an email you wrote to me Friday, you expressed a desire to learn in specific detail what those things are. Did you ever watch the movie, "9 ½ Weeks"? In the movie Kim Bassinger and Mickey Roarke have this incredibly erotic love affair that lasts 9 ½ weeks. I didn't like the end of the movie, but for some reason when I think of "us" that movie comes to mind. There were some things in that movie that I would have liked to try with a lover such as you. Does that shock you? You may not believe this, but it is the absolute truth – I have NEVER said the things I've said, and am about to say, to any other man in my entire life, not even my husband. You somehow bring out the erotic nature I didn't know I had. That erotic foreplay that you did in the back seat drove me crazy with passion. Please tell me that I am not some kind of scientific experiment and that these things that are happening between us are spontaneous and a natural result of finding someone who thinks and feels like you do about things. I see that we are alike in so many ways, yet different too. The things that you have done in your life, and that you do, show me that you are a passionate man about everything. I am that way too. When I do something, it takes my whole undivided attention, and I become so immersed in it, that everything else in the world at that moment disappears. I think you get that way too about certain things. That's why you grow "prized" bonsai, and not just ordinary bonsai. It's one of the things I admire about you.

This morning when I woke up, I wasn't thinking about our walk in the park that we plan to have on some Sunday morning. No, instead I was thinking about a hotel room, and a day of lovemaking. I thought about exploring your entire body with my mouth and tongue, and trailing my erect nipples down your torso very slowly and lovingly. Is your backbone extremely sensitive? Mine is. I will massage each and every vertebra so slowly and carefully. I also think that I will love sucking and licking your penis. I think your tongue will turn me into your sexual slave, and I will crave to do the things I know that will turn you on. When I look at your hard erection, that sacred tool of pleasure, I will lick it, suck it, and think of it, as an ice cream cone. I'll start by licking the head, and then run my tongue along the ridge and across it. I will flick my tongue over the ridge between the head and the shaft. While this is going on, I will stroke the rest of your penis, your thighs, your stomach, anywhere I can, with my free hand. I will slide your penis slowly inside my mouth, let it rest on my tongue and move my head up and down, and my hand will be around the base moving up and down in rhythm. Or maybe I'll just dip your penis into a jar of chocolate icing, and lap it up, sucking every last drop of chocolate off slowly. I'd have to figure out a way to burn off all those extra calories with you. I love the position called "69". I think it's so wonderful to feel your tongue on my vagina, as I use my mouth to get you hard at the same time. Just thinking about you and the things we will do has gotten me so wet and bothered that I have to take things in hand. Henry, I think you bring out all my wild naughtiness. I don't know what happens to this, or where it leads, I'm just going to enjoy every moment of it for as long as I can, and not try to think about it, or analyze it, at all.

- Sincerely,

Your secret friend, Julie

June 12, 2000
Dear Julie:

Oh Boy! I saved your letter to read this morning. Now, I am sitting here with a rock hard erection. I wish you could relieve me of the pressure right now. You are not an experiment of mine, but I must admit that our love making is, and will not be, entirely spontaneous, because I fantasize about you so much. I am becoming obsessive where you are concerned. I, like you, tend to focus deeply on a subject of interest to me, and I become very single-minded regarding that subject. I pride myself on doing things right and trying to do better than anyone else in a given area. That's how I view making love to you. I want to be the best lover you have ever had, and when you are one hundred years old, you will look back on our first lovemaking, and smile that secret smile. I hope that we can go for our walk the park this coming Sunday morning. I would cherish the opportunity to just sit and talk with you. I have attached some 'light reading' for your coffee break. Have a great day, Julie, and I look forward to seeing you soon. - Henry

Attachment:

My Dear Luscious Julie:

I have trouble going to sleep nights. It is difficult to slip into sleep when I am so very hard, because I am thinking of you, and what our lovemaking will be like. The time we spent together in the car enflamed me in a way that I haven't felt in many years. I look into your eyes, and I can see the flames of your passion and desire for me burning there. I kiss you and feel the response in your body. As we kissed you writhed and squirmed in passion. I know you wanted me to slip my tongue into your waiting beckoning pussy. I know you wanted to take my shaft in your hand, feel its warm stiffness in your mouth, suck me, and taste my passion. I know you wanted me to make love to you there in the back of your car. I could smell the sweet allure of your excitement. I knew what you wanted when I licked your ears and felt your nipples harden under my fingertips. I could hear your breathing getting deliciously heavy as I sucked your nipple, licked your breast, and fondled your inner thigh. I heard your rush of breath as I slipped my arm through your legs and allowed the muscle of my biceps to press against the thin fabric of your panties, pushing up against your wet crotch. I knew then, for sure, that we would make love and it was only a matter of time.

Our day in the hotel together will be one of the most passionate you have ever spent. We will make love without any inhibitions that usually overtake and keep people restrained, even with those we have been married to for many years. Even in the most intimate times, we always hold back a little for fear of being judged, or through embarrassment, so we never really let go completely. How many times have you made love, and wanted to touch and fondle yourself at the same time you were being made love to, or been afraid to ask for what you want, but you held back, afraid of what your lover would think? That will not be us. We will explore all those secret fantasies of sensuality that you have denied yourself over the years.

I will suck your toes, caress and lick your legs, up to the tops of your thighs. I will kiss and lick your ears, moving my tongue around the back of your ears, driving you wet with passion and desire. Then, I will move my tongue down your spine, slowly and very sensuously, one vertebrae at a time. When I kiss you, our tongues will explore each others' mouth, tasting each other deeply. I will nibble and lick your neck working my way down to, and across your collar bone, and down into your armpit where I will taste the musky fragrance of your rising desire. As you become more and more aroused, a thin layer of sweat will cover your body. I will suck and lick your nipples until they are rock hard and stiff. I will straddle you, slip my stiff hard erection between those soft cool breasts, and guide your mouth to the head of my shaft, while my hands fondle your wonderful breasts. You will suck me harder and harder until I feel that irresistible urge to let go starting to build in my loins. Then, I will deny you the reward your lips are asking for, and once again begin kissing and fondling you, down to your breasts, across your heaving stomach to the top of your pubic hair – my tongue will trace a path through the dense black hair towards the moist pulsating lips waiting between your legs. I will gently spread your legs as I lick your inner thighs. You will not be able to restrain yourself any longer, and will take my head in your hands, aim and press my mouth to the most intimate part of your body. My tongue will slip inside. You will cry out with ecstasy as the pulsating muscles inside you close around my tongue. I will lick and suck its lips, pulling them into my mouth. My tongue will caress and dance on the little trigger hidden there. My fingers will slip up inside you as you pump your hips rhythmically. You will explode in your first overwhelming orgasm. The love juice will flow out across my lips. I will begin working my way slowly up you, kissing, fondling, touching and licking your body to arousal once more, until I am once again looking deep into the pools of your eyes as I slip into you for the first time. My shaft will be rock hard, ridged, and wanting you. You will lift your hips to meet me, thrusting, pumping fast, then slow, in and out, as my hand caresses your dripping pussy, pulling on the lips, tracing little circles around that sweet pink bud. Rolling, first I am on top, then you, riding me, moaning, your body wanting all of me deeper and deeper inside you. Then, when I get close to unloading, I will stop and begin licking and sucking your pussy again, until I am back in control, then in this way I can mount you again and again until you are overcome with yet another strong all consuming orgasm. I will move you to a sixty-nine position once again, where we will taste each other, and I will give you orgasms again and again. Then we will get out of the elevator, and go into the hotel room. (Smile.)

June 12, 2000
Hi Julie:

How's this for a deal? On Sunday, our meeting will be confined to a meeting of our minds. Your mind is far too delicious to ignore, and I would very much like to talk with you and connect further in that way. However, if it is raining, we can still meet, but then we can cuddle up and steam up the windows of the car. We can let fate decide. So, did that elevator ride amuse you? Did I miss anything? – Henry

Henry:

You didn't miss anything. And, yes, I enjoyed reading about our elevator ride. - Julie

June 12, 2000
Hi Julie:

I will do the sunshine dance, but in some ways, I will be disappointed that we may not get to snuggle in the car, because we should connect intellectually so that you don't think I am just after your body. It's sometimes a bummer to do the right thing. My instincts are to rip off your clothes and cover your body with tiny bites, but I'll behave, unless you want me not be behave, in which case, I want to kiss your bare thighs. So, if you don't want my tongue to be on the loose down there, in such close proximity to your pussy, then wear pants, or you may get a wet probing surprise. But that would not be a wise thing to do, because all day long you will have this big smile, and Don will only question why you are in such a good mood.

As far as Wilma goes, I just told her I have an early meeting on Sunday morning. She is used to that. In my line of work, it is not particularly unusual for me to have meetings in odd places, at even odder times. What time would you like to meet? I am looking forward to seeing you again so much. - Henry

June 12, 2000
Dear Henry:

You are extremely amorous. We will just talk on Sunday and I think 7 AM would be a good time for me if that works for you. Is it too early? We can talk about poetry or whatever else that we think of. I am looking forward to it. - Julie

June 12, 2000
Hi Julie:

Seven AM is not too early to see you. As far as preferring to talk about poetry, etc., no, I would prefer to screw your brains out, but just as long as we can remember that we have connected on a different level is what counts. How do you expect me to keep my hands off you? I can't. I would just absolutely hate it, if you ever thought even for one minute that I was just after sex. I want sex with you so bad, but that is because your mind has enflamed me. And, that's where we connect. Our bodies enjoying each other is just a great and wonderful bonus. I never want to loose sight of who you are, but you drive me wild with desire. I have never felt this way before. I want to make love to you more than any other woman I have ever met in my life. I don't really understand it, but I find you so incredibly sexy and sensuous. I think about you all the time, and when I close my eyes and concentrate, I can even smell and taste you. I have always found small breasted, petite women to be what attracts me sexually, and yet your big luscious breasts are constantly on my mind. I long to hold them in my hands and lick your nipples. They turn me on so very much. I can't wait to feel your erect nipples trailing down my body. I can't wait to feel my shaft between your breasts. I can't wait to touch, kiss and taste every part of your nakedness. You and your body are a complete turn on for me. We will have the most erotic and steamy love affair imaginable. I want you to tell me what you want, with no holds barred, so that I can completely arouse and satisfy you. I look forward to the first time we spend the night together. The thought of waking up next to you after a long night of lovemaking, would be a dream come true. But, just as important to me, I also look forward to the day when we can just be with each other, relaxed and happy. Sitting together on the couch, watching a movie, or playing scrabble half the night or just lying in bed in each other's arms, and talking while we listen to the rain. I would really like sharing that feeling of affection, intimacy and closeness with you, as we both have been without that for so long. I have a feeling that you will make an outstanding lover, and an outstanding friend. I have never given in to these impulses before, but this time I want to ride these impulses and see where they take us.

Fondest thoughts. - Henry

June 13, 2000
Good Morning, Julie:

I enjoy you immensely. I enjoy your writing, your conversation, your intellect, and that great body. Oh boy, that body. I am so glad that you liked the time we spent together in your car. So did I. Only it was over too fast. I would like to spend three or four hours engaged in that kind of foreplay with you. I would so enjoy lighting your fires. But, in many ways, I am glad that it ended when it did. I was having a tough time keeping my promises to you. I wanted to rip off your panties and use my tongue on you more than you could imagine. That is the first time for me "in the back seat" in over thirty years. It was very nice.

When I showed you my art, I didn't bring it all. I have drawings of women of all shapes and sizes. I just showed you some of the ones with the larger breasts. I am not the kind of man that "settles" for anything. I don't know why I am so attracted to you. You got me going long before I saw your "assets". You are the first woman in my entire adult life that I have been attracted to, that does not have a petite build and small breasts. When I was a teen, like all guys that age, I guess, big boobs were it. But, as I became an adult, and my tastes matured, I came to appreciate a small framed woman for a sexual partner. So, where did you come from? And, the same thing has happened to you, where I am concerned. I am not a "biker" type, and I do not have tattoos, but I turn you on. Surprise, surprise. You are voluptuous, and you turn me on in an intense way. I must get my hands on you soon before I go nuts. I will see you this week after work one day, and I am looking forward to nibbling your ears again while you squirm with delight. I know you cannot take much time, but if you could manage just a half hour to allow me to kiss you properly, fondle you, and bite your ears - that would be great. But, I would take a nice big wet kiss; if that's all you have time for. You are so sexy.

I have read the short story you gave me, and I have a couple of ideas that I want to talk with you about on Sunday that I think would improve the story. I will call you during the day today. Did I mention that I am as horny as hell, thinking about you? I enjoyed hearing your voice last night. It fueled my evening fantasy of you. – Henry

June 13, 2000
Hi Julie:

You are right. It is your sensuality and your passion for life that interests me. When I look at you, I see my female counterpart. You are me. Our minds operate on the same frequency. I thought I was alone, an alien castaway on the beach of this strange hot and heavy land. Then, you came along. I have always thought that fate gives us what we need (not what we want), when we need it. I think that at this time in our lives, we came along into each other's lives for a reason. I need someone like you right now, and you need someone like me. We recognize that in each other. We will help each other replace that missing piece and give each other the courage to do what we know in our hearts must be done for us not to drown and survive. I will help to keep you afloat, and I will breathe life back into your existence as you are breathing life back into mine. We have known about each other all of our lives. It just took this long to meet. On Thursday, in your arms, I felt that connection, that closeness that usually takes a long time to forge. It was already there. I am comfortable with you. You arouse me and fill me with a passion that I thought I had lost. I want to explore that passion further. We will make love and it will be fantastic for both of us. I am a free spirit in the bedroom, although I also am not into pain, etc. But, I am a willing lover whose main objective is to bring as much pleasure to my partner as I possibly can. Nothing would please me more than to hear you cry out with pleasure and passion, and to know that I brought you there. I think that the bedroom is a place for fun without rules. If you like it, if it feels good to you, then I want to give that to you. My needs will be satisfied by you having a great time. If you enjoy yourself, then you will respond enthusiastically, and I will reap the benefit of that. I long to kiss you and hold you again, and count the days to when you will lay next to me, naked and willing. Thank you for being who you are. – Henry

June 14, 2000
Good Morning Cutie Pie:

I hope that you are in the mood to be nibbled on. I will see you at the bus stop tonight. Do you know what the Latin phrase "Non-semper ubi sub ubi" means? It would be appropriate for tonight. It will be chilly tonight. Perhaps we had better cuddle up under my car blanket. I guarantee I'll warm you up, especially if you take that Latin phrase to heart. (big lecherous smile) Don't worry Julie; I will still keep my promise. I am looking forward to snuggling up under that blanket with you. But, as I already told you, I would be happy with one long, deep kiss. If you can stay longer than it takes for one kiss that would be a great bonus. My arms are feeling extra empty today. I wish you were in them right now. You have no idea how much I would like to wake up one morning with you next to me. I have an inexplicable need to be close to you, and I'm not referring to sex. A night with you, just holding you close, touching your back, kissing your face, feeling your warm body pressed up against mine, feeling the touch of your breasts against my chest, your head on my shoulder, your lips against my neck, smelling the fragrance of your hair, tasting your skin, and listening to your breathing while you sleep safe and contented, our legs intertwined. Now, that would be a perfect night. – Henry

June 14, 2000
Hi Henry:

I should be at the bus stop around 6:30 tonight. How long do you want to be together in the back seat of your car? I can't wait to see you again, but I don't want things to get out of hand too soon. We never finished our poem. Are you bored with it? I had a poem published today. It won an award. - Julie

June 14, 2000
Hi Julie:

As to how long I would like you to stay tonight – all night would be Ok with me. Actually, as long as you can manage would be fine. The longer the better, but don't get yourself in a jam by staying too long. I am happy to have you to myself even for a short time. Don't worry Julie, I also don't want things to get out of hand too soon for us either. When the time is right they will most certainly be "in hand". I am looking for some longevity with you, so I don't and won't, push you. You will let me know if and when the time is right for us, and I am content with that. And our poem, I most certainly am not bored with it. I am just thinking about the next lines, and I am not quite ready with my turn, but I am working on it. Now, as to your poem, I am so very pleased for you. You deserve the recognition as the poem is very good, and you are a very talented writer. I wish you luck with it. Congratulations on having your work so well received. – Henry

June 14, 2000
Hi Julie:

I checked out the poetry website. You should be proud of your work and it doesn't surprise me one bit that you were recognized by the Literary Guild. I especially liked your poem "The Shell of Our Dreams", and thank you for dedicating the poem "Take me to the Stars", to me. It touched my soul that you would do that for me. How can I repay such a wonderful gift as that? I count myself truly fortunate that I found such a gentle, warm, beautiful and talented person in you. I am counting the minutes until I see you tonight. -Henry

CHAPTER FIVE

On the bus that evening, all I could think about was seeing Henry. I remembered how good it felt to be in his arms and the expression in his eyes when he looked at me. I loved the way he looked at me. It was like he could really see "who" I was, not just "what" I was. He made me feel good. I craved the way he made me feel, and it wasn't about sex. I just wanted to be near him, so I could feel that way again.

He found another area of the parking lot that he felt was more private than the last one. There were several trucks parked there, and it did seem much more private surrounded by empty parked trucks. This time we used the larger back seat in his car, then we started kissing, and it wasn't long before it got uncontrollable once more, but again, he kept his promise, drawing an invisible line that he would not cross. I wonder how long he could have kept that promise. I guess I'll never know, because a security guard came by the car, knocked on the window, and asked us to leave. It was probably the most embarrassing moment of my life. Henry was embarrassed too, but he laughed about it. In fact, we both laughed about it after the guard left. Then, Henry suggested that we go to his office for future meetings. I wanted very much to see him again, and at a place where we could cuddle and kiss. Although his office was private, I was apprehensive about it for a number of reasons. Later, my fears proved to be unwarranted.

June 15, 2000
Good Morning, Julie:

Thank you for last evening. I could smell your perfume all night. I usually take a shower when I get home from work, but your fragrance still lingered, and I wanted it with me throughout the night, so I went to bed still wearing it. Too bad you weren't there too. You are a truly beautiful woman – sexy, sensual, intelligent, fun, a great personality, and those eyes. Oh boy, those eyes. Plus, being with you, I get to meet nice new people, like that nice security guard. You are so pretty when you blush. It is very endearing to see that there are still some things that do make you blush. It's cute. Thank you for that feeling of affection. And, thank you for making me feel alive or the first time in many years. I haven't felt that way in a very long time. When I look into your eyes, something happens inside me that I cannot easily explain. I think I'm in trouble. And, thank you for that. It is good that the guard showed up when he did, however, otherwise...

My only regret in knowing you is that we cannot spend more time together. There are so many things that I want to say to you, and so many things that I want us to do together in and out of the bedroom. I am looking forward to seeing you on Sunday, and hope that you can make it. I am a lucky man for knowing you, no matter where this takes us. – Henry

June 15, 2000
Henry:

Was my face that obvious? I don't know why I got so upset. I mean, he was just a security guard. If I passed him on the street today, I wouldn't even recognize him. There was nothing he could do to us. You can't get arrested for making out in the back seat of a car, can you? Could you see us – me calling Don, and you, calling Wilma, to bail us out? How would we ever explain? Smile. I think my problem is that I feel like such a prisoner in this marriage, that sometimes I blow things a bit out of proportion. I want to have a 'normal' relationship with you.

Henry, you are a married man. I couldn't waltz into your office without half your staff figuring out what was happening behind that closed door. You have to have realized that. Maybe after you are separated, I will come there, and I will just wear a trench coat with nothing on underneath. Then, I'll sit on your leather sofa, and beckon you with my eyes. I will ask you to remain behind your desk as I very slowly unbutton the coat, one button at a time, first revealing my legs, then upwards. And, we will have a conversation about asphalt. You will tell me about the recipes for making asphalt roads. I will ask you to go into intricate detail as to how you build a road. By the time I have totally unbuttoned the coat, you will be as hard as a rock. Then…tune in next week for the next episode of the wild adventures and perilous perils of "Henry and Julie". Are you laughing?

I understand about our deepening connection. I feel it too. I want you to make love to me, and I know you will. We both know it is inevitable, and that scares me a lot. I want to follow my heart and my instincts, but my mind keeps holding me back. Why is that, Henry?

You tasted good too. And what is happening is good and clean. I agree with that. I just need some time to get used to it. I am looking forward to Sunday very much. I'm glad you want to talk about your life and dreams with me. I find that I very much want to know you better. On the other hand, I feel I know you so well already. Figure that one out, Einstein. - Sincerely, Julie

I attached the poem we wrote together in its final version. Although it wasn't a very good poem, it did show our feelings at that time. The indented lines were his, and the other lines were mine.

MAKING LOVE WITH YOU

I feel your scent through the soft whisper of the breeze,
and, with one seductive look, you possess my soul.

> *The hunger in your eyes, electrifies my senses.*
> *I beat with your heart, as it beats.*
> *I follow your soul, where it leads.*

I taste the passion in your lips, and
as your mouth takes mine in a meaningful kiss,
our tongues intertwine, caressing slowly, and so intimately. . .
Your fingertips move down my spine,
making little circles over each vertebrae,
silently and deliberately, telegraphing your arousal,
while they slowly dissolve every bone in my body.

> *I have found my world in your arms*
> *and, I want to possess you,*
> *as you now own me.*
> *Take me, I beg you, and*

please dampen down my fire
before it consumes my soul.
My body pleads with you, to end my torture now,
instead, you fan my flames, while

I strain against the building sensations,
and my body becomes unbearably awake
to every touch, and
my heart begins to pump
like a jackhammer.
I feel the blood stir in your loins
As you press up against my belly,
forcing me to feel your building passion.

Knowing this love, feeling this kiss, touching you,
For this I have waited since the hour of my birth.
And now, my life, my love
You have made me whole,
And my soul complete.
You've taught me not to fear
My last complete reunion with the earth.
For I know now, in that paradise eternal
What it is for that I wait,
It will be you,
Standing there my love,
Waiting for me by heaven's gate.

June 15, 2000
Julie:

I would like that visit very much. Just thinking about you standing before me unbuttoning that coat drives me wild with desire for you and made me hard. And as far as my staff goes - none would question if you came to my office in the evening and met with me behind closed doors. My office is private, and my dealings in it are equally private. My staff would never ever question what was going on. I have many meetings with males and females in my locked office in the evening, and my staff would not even consider interrupting me or question what I was doing. In fact, it would not occur to them to even wonder. Much of my work is of a confidential nature due to my position here, and they are used to that. Even my boss (the owner), would never dream of interrupting a closed door meeting of mine. But, none of this is to persuade you to come, although it would be fun to be "naughty" in my office with you. I suggested my office to you last night, because of the complete and wonderful privacy that it would afford us. We could kiss and hold each other as much as we wanted without being interrupted or nervous. And, on Sunday, we already know each other so well, so what we will share is facts about our lives as we already know who the other one is. I have attached a poem for you that I just wrote that may help you to understand what I feel. I hope it touches your heart. - Henry

Dance the Lovers Dance

For Julie

Tomorrow there is a time for us to dance
Tomorrow needs no excuses
Tomorrow beacons us to come

You are my perfect bloom
You are my breath of spring
You are my reminder of summers long gone but not forgot

With me there is no fear
With me there is no reason to hold your heart
With me life is new again

It is not to me that you are special
It is not to me that you show your longing
It is not to me that you show your heart

It is to yourself that you should be special
It is to yourself that you show your longing
It is to yourself that you show your heart

I say to you what I feel
I look at you the way I feel inside
I touch you as my reward to myself

For me you need no defense
For me you hold the key
For me you bring life

Beneath my touch your skin is fire
Beneath my breath I whisper to myself your name
Beneath this smile there is tenderness for you

Behind these eyes is desire for you
Behind this face is a heart
Behind my time is an old and tired life

Before me is a new day
Before me is the object of my desire
Before me are pleasures yet unknown to be shared

My look is wonder and longing
My kiss is your kiss
My words are truth

Give into yourself
Give into your desire
Give into what you know is waiting for you

Take what is mine to give
Take from me that which has always been yours
Take the piece of me that you already own

I offer you my hand
I offer you my time
I offer you my heart

Give me your hand
Give me your time
Give me your heart

Free me from my torment
Free me from my longing
Free me from my lonely life with just one kiss

Join me in my heart
Join me in my life
Join me in my dreams and in my bed

Let me take you to that special place where only we belong
Leave behind your fear and learn at last to trust
Wrap yourself in me so I can keep you safe from harm

Give you to me as I give me to you.
Become with me that person you have buried for so long
Let us share that special thing that only lovers share

Let me start you burning with a fire that only my kiss can quench
Deny yourself no longer that which you know you want
Throw yourself on to me and drink from my cup

Dance, Julie, Dance with me, Dance the whole night long.

- Henry

Around this time, I had sent Henry another poem that I wrote for him.

CONFESSION

In the base of the night
I wrap myself in a cloak of quiet,
And sit on the edges,
Watching you pull me
In a direction I am afraid to go.

Here,
Alone
In
My
Bed

I can meet you,
And confess to you all the things
I didn't have the courage to say
When we were together.

Now,
As I write down my heart,
And tell you how you can make me
Smile and fear like a child,

And why I feel the need
To structure a defense, because
You treat me so special,
With such tender loving care,
Knowing just what to say, and
Just how to touch my skin
To stir the passion I hold within,
And, in the process
You somehow make me think of

Who
I am.

Maybe it's the way you kiss me,
Or the way you look at me,
Ways I've never been kissed or looked at before;
Or maybe, its that special sparkle
That only I can see in your eyes,
That makes me want to look
Into
Tomorrow
And see your face.

Henry:

I am very much afraid of coming to your office in the quarry.
I don't like sneaking around, but I understand why we both have
to do it. Too many people will be hurt if we don't keep this under
wraps. I'm also afraid of making love with you. I'm afraid of the
feelings I am building inside my heart for you. - Julie

June 15, 2000
Julie:

The poem is very beautiful, and it touched my heart. Actually, my other internet friends are all chained up in my office. I just need one more to complete my set. I am missing a hot blooded Italian, beautiful, sensuous, attractive, brunette, with bottomless green eyes and soft moist lips, sensitive ears that are her erogenous zone, shapely legs, a kissable neck, soft yielding breasts that love to be touched, thighs that long to be caressed, and a body that wants me inside her.

Don't be scared because you know that we are going to make love very soon. What is there to be scared of? Only one thing, and that is that it will strengthen our bond, and allow us access to each other's hearts. And that will give each of us a weapon to hurt the other. But, Julie look into your heart. You already know who I am. Can you truly believe that I have it within me to hurt you? You have seen the way I look at you. I can't hide it. How can that look be faked? You know how it feels to have me touch you. Can that touch be false? You have felt my kisses. Can kisses like that be just lust? All I want is to bring you pleasure and happiness. Your fears will be replaced by unbridled passion, of the kind you have never known. For me, that time will be worth the risk of making myself vulnerable to you. (You see, I am also frightened, because something is happening between us that I don't understand), but Julie, you are worth that risk. You are worth the secrets, worth the sleepless nights, worth the longing in my chest, worth the time I have spent adrift. I must admit that in some way, I was so proud that this unknown security guard caught us. I felt like saying to him, "look what I've got, and eat your heart out." The day will come when I can show the world how lucky I am to have found you. It is rare that a man feels this way for a woman and has that woman feel the same way for him. I want everyone to know that sometimes dreams do come true. I knew exactly and in detail what would happen last night before I even met you. The kissing, the touching, and the way you took me into your mouth. All of this was no surprise to me as I thought about it happening while I was waiting for you, and knew that it would happen that night. I don't know how I know what will happen with us, I just do. I guess because I recognize it is a natural progression of our growing feelings for each other. I also know that very soon we will spend the day making love, and so do you. It is inevitable because it is right, and we should not try to avoid it, because we can't. I will make love to you, it will be wonderful, and it will banish all your fears.

The sentiments in your email are no surprise to me. I knew what you would say before I even got your email, because I saw the look on your face last night. I know that you don't feel right about last evening, because you feel uncomfortable sneaking around. I do also. I know that you are not the kind of person that would sneak into my office for sex (too bad). I know that you have never done anything like this before. Well, neither have I. Julie, if you are uncomfortable with anything, anything at all, then all you have to do is tell me. It will not ever hurt what we have growing. I don't want you to do anything that doesn't feel right to you, because this is too important to me. I have an extremely high opinion of you, and I know very well that the only reason that we were together last night is because of the feelings that are there for both of us. I love being close to you, but our relationship is not based on that. I would miss very much the opportunity to kiss and hold you close, and touch you. I want desperately to make love to you. But, if you wanted a relationship without that, then I will tell you that in my opinion, our relationship will continue to grow, and be just as close and strong without that physical part, even though it would be so very hard for me to be with you without that.

I also got a reality check last night, but of a different kind. Last night brought home to me very clearly that what I have for you is not infatuation, and is not a game, nor is it there because of loneliness. The feelings I have for you are there because of a deepening connection that is growing daily. I like you very much, Julie, and I hope that doesn't scare you too much. I also don't want you to sneak around. I want better than that for you. You deserve better. If I could, I would make love to you today, all day, and every day, but I am prepared to wait and cool off our relationship, if you want. I don't mind if you want to put sex on the 'back burner' until your life is sorted out. I would rather wait for you, than risk loosing you. So, as I have told you many times before, no pressure from me to do anything that does not feel right to you, although it felt so right for me last night. I wanted you to stay all night with me. You fit so perfectly in my arms that I think you belong there. I know that you want me as much as I want you. When and if you feel that we should be lovers, I will be ready. I want you more than I can tell you. You excite me more than any woman ever has, but I will always give you the same advice over and over. Follow your heart, follow your instincts. They will lead you in the right direction. Thank you for last night. Even if it was a little embarrassing, it also was fun to be 'caught'. That hasn't happened in thirty years and it rolled back the clock for me. It is good to feel that young and alive again. You tasted so good, too. Last night or any other time we will be together could not possibly tarnish what is so good. What we do in life really doesn't matter, it is the reason we do it, and the impact on others that matters. The reason we were together last night is because of a connection and need to be with each other. What we did was not wrong in any way. Neither of us is promiscuous. Neither of us is using the other. What happened, and happens, between us is good and clean and pure and right. There is nothing wrong with us expressing affection for each other physically, because that affection really exists. So, please don't feel guilty or embarrassed or uncomfortable. What we did was right. It was the location that left something to be desired, not our actions or motives for being there. I look forward so much to Sunday, and if you want, I will bring pictures of my life. I want to know everything about you and your life up to now. On Sunday I promise to follow your lead. All I ask for is a kiss and a hug from you. You always have the ability to set the ground rules.

I don't want to complicate your life. I just want to make your life more enjoyable and better. Take all the time you need. I am a patient man who expects nothing. And, I also know how to cry and am not afraid to. It is your sensitivity that draws me close to you. Stay sensitive for me. It is your most endearing quality. If you ever cry over me, it will be tears of joy. Enjoy the rest of your day, Julie. I'll be thinking of you.

With deep affection - Henry

June 16, 2000
Hello my green eyed sweetie:

How are you today? I know how to get to the park. I can meet you there as we originally planned. And, of course, I do have a cell phone with me and so will you. So, if either of us is not there at 7 AM, then we can call each other and find one another that way.

So, what's new in Julieville? Do you miss me as much as I am missing being with you? It is actually better for both of us that we are seeing each other on a somewhat regular basis. If absence makes the heart grow fonder, and if I didn't see you for a long period of time, then we really would be in trouble by the time we met. – Henry

Hi Henry:

You always know how to make my day brighter. You have such a way with words. Here's a question I haven't asked yet. What are your feelings about religion? I don't believe in any god. I think that man made god up. God even looks like a man in all the pictures they have of him. Somehow I think you feel the same way I do about a god.

The poem we wrote together could be two poems. You really are a good writer. I love being in places surrounded with nature. I have plants all over my house, even a baby tree in the bathroom. Do you think that's funny?

. I am so looking forward to our morning in the park. - Julie

June 16, 2000
Hello Julie:

If I make your day brighter, that brightens my day. Why did you assume that I was not a religious person? Is it because I have the devil in my eyes? I will bring my walking shoes on Sunday and a blanket. The walking shoes will be used to get to a good spot to spread out the blanket. I often lie on the grass and reflect on the world around me. I use that time to protect my sanity. I especially like to lay on a warm summer's night and look up at the stars. The night sky never ceases to fill me with wonder. I do not subscribe to any form of organized religion, and in fact I think that TV evangelists should be sent straight to jail. I don't like churches, because I think many of the preachers forget that it is the song, not the singer that is important. The ultimate church is all around us. I do see the purpose to it all. Some call that purpose God. If God is there, then I see her as a new bloom on the rose, or hear her voice in the cry of a child, or in the tears of a lover. God is in the stars and God's hand moves the heavens and our hearts. God is within us all. We call that conscience. We are all born knowing what is right and what is wrong. If we are lucky, we fall in love. We can appreciate beauty and create it. All of that is also God's hand. Do I believe in God? I don't know, because I cannot make up my mind. I once was a divinity student, and consider myself 'spiritual', but I cannot truly decide on what I believe. I just try to live the right way, even if God did not exist. I just hope that God does exist. I do believe that we are not an accident. I do believe that if God does not exist, then it is necessary for our sanity, to invent her. The universe is a strange and wonderful place that we pretend to understand. The more I learn of science, the more I think with wonder at it all. I think the entire universe could be described as the breath of God. How about you?

I agree with you. The poem we wrote together could be two poems. Writing poetry is new to me. You inspire me to create. Are you really a muse in disguise? I would not laugh at the baby tree in your bathroom. I have trees all over the house and my office.

Back to our walk in the park. I have a small folding shovel that I always keep in the car in case I run into any cute little trees. Julie, I hope that the day is bright and clear, as what I would really like to do, is lay on the blanket with you, and just hold you close, and enjoy the 'alone time' while we enjoy the song of the birds, the breeze, the sunshine, and just absorb the world, and you. Please, could I also nibble on your ears?

You know, I would love to see you naked in that park setting. I think you would fit in perfectly with the beauty of nature. When it gets warmer in a couple of months, would you like to really be naughty and sneak up there super early (dawn) and go skinny dipping? I have never ever skinny dipped. Just a thought.

- Henry

June 16, 2000
Hi Henry:

I was brought up as a Roman Catholic. I went to Catholic schools all my life, and church every Sunday morning. I was forced to do this. My parents made these decisions for me. All during those years, as I learned more and more about religion, and I learned a lot about it, it became more and more obvious to me that God was something that man created. Not, the other way around. Whenever someone cannot explain something, they can always say, "It's God's will". When people die, they say that person "is with God, now". It's man's way of comforting himself. I don't know if there is a greater intelligence out there, or if what we refer to as "Gods" are really aliens from outer space, as some people believe. I don't think I'll ever know in this lifetime. I could find no proof of, or logical reason, to believe that "God" exists. And, once I was allowed to rule my own life, I stopped going to Church. My children were taught Catholicism, Judaism, and even went to a Protestant (Baptist) Sunday school. I wanted them to learn about more than one religion. I never forced them to attend Church, and they were allowed to make up their own minds about God. They know I don't believe in God, and for some reason, all three of them do. That's their choice. I think I did my part as a parent, by exposing them to all the various possibilities. I've read the Bible, and I believe that it is some form of "history" book. I've read the books of Zola, and find them fascinating and mind boggling. I think that even though I do not feel comfortable practicing any one religion today, or can say I believe in "God", I am more spiritual than most human beings, because I bond with nature. I have a passion for the cosmic beauty around us. I enjoy nature and truly appreciate its beauty. I will show you some of my photography work on Sunday, where I try to capture some of the beauty of nature in my work.

Henry, you are a 'natural' poet. You have the ability to create whatever you set out to do. I know I can write and I can take good photos, but I cannot draw as well as you. I love being creative, and I find it the hardest thing to do. Maybe that's because it's not always logical. It's from the heart, more than from the head. I think creativity is something that people have to develop within themselves. Everyone can be creative. If you strive for something, you will be better and better at it. I went to school for writing. I took writing workshops and classes, every chance I got. My work has been critiqued by Kurt Vonnegut. Kurt was one of my teachers. Henry, you are so smart, you wouldn't even have to go to school, just read a book about technique. I'll give you one of my poetry writing books to review, if you would like to read it. Just let me know.

I think that just enjoying the "alone" time is what I want to do, too. And, you know I love it when you nibble on my ear. You don't have to ask permission. I would love to go skinny dipping with you, but I'm not sure if the park lake is the place to do it. A lot of fishermen go there in the early mornings. If we could find a private lake, I would. I never skinny dipped before either. It would be wonderful! I am looking forward to Sunday morning very much. - Julie

June 16, 2000
Julie:

You always say the nicest things to me. I wish I were a natural poet. You are the one who created the poet in me. You are the only woman I have ever written poetry to. As I said before, you are my muse. I have a feeling that you will inspire me to do some things that I have not even considered doing before. Thank you for opening that door for me.

I would very much like to borrow one of your poetry books. I am impressed – re: Kurt Vonnegut, a great author. I dug "Slaughter House Five". I am looking forward to seeing you on Sunday so much. Although it is not a good idea to discuss politics and religion, they are two subjects that I think I would like to talk with you about, but please, no politics on Sunday. I am more spiritual than religious, because I am a skeptic about almost everything. I think that I am probably more Buddhist than anything else. And, Buddhism is not a religion, but a way of life. I do feel the message of all the major religions is the same and it is a good message - a good way to live your life and a good code of ethics. It is too bad that religion has caused so much suffering in the world, because of its misuse. One of the things that interested me over the years is where the ideas and stories came from, in a historical context. I have done extensive research in that area. I have an excellent book on the subject called "The Power of Myth", by James Campbell. You may find it interesting. I will bring it with me in case you would like to borrow it. It is an unbiased study of the stories in the various bibles of the world's religions, and to where they can be traced. I am impressed that you have been so open-minded regarding your children's religious education. I did the same thing with my kids. They have both reached the conclusion that a divine being is a charming myth.

You said that I don't have to ask permission to nibble on your ear. Do I have to ask permission to nibble on anything else? Please say "no", because I have a particular spot in mind. Smile. Skinny dipping with you would be the ultimate. I am eager for the time when we can spend the entire day together, close and intimate. You have the ability to change my mood, always for the better. I would like to show you the affection I feel for you. Enjoy Saturday, and I will be thinking of you. – Henry

June 17, 2000
Hi Henry:

The weather forecast for tomorrow is rain. I think I will find a way to get out of the house anyway, because I really need to talk to someone who understands what I'm going through, right now. Don and I had a long talk last night. He finally admits that we are both unhappy together, and that we should each try to find our own lives, separately, and try to make ourselves happy. He really wants me to be happy, just as I want that for him. We even got so far as to talk about who is taking "what". I feel this last conversation really made some progress, but for some reason, I feel so empty inside. We both cried and hugged about it, and I think that was good. We needed to get the pent up emotions out. He now knows that if we stay together, we will begin to resent each other, and that would be a horrible way to live. I know we will always be friends, and be there for each other and the kids. I have a feeling that after all is said and done, we'll get along better apart than we did together. I hope so.

How has your Saturday been so far? I bet you worked in the garden today. I am looking forward to seeing you tomorrow. I need to look into the eyes of a friend who cares about me. Henry, I think you came into my life just at the right time. At first, I thought too soon, but I realize now how much I need a friend to talk to. I hope I can do the same for you when you need someone. I thank you for all your kindness and understanding.

Today is my birthday. I'm fifty-one. I don't feel that old. In fact, I don't even feel like it's my birthday. There must be a mistake on my birth certificate. When is your birthday? Do you believe in horoscopes? - Julie

June 17, 2000
Hi Julie:

You have reached the point with Don that Wilma and I are at. It sounds as though you will be able to split amicably, and be able to keep the one man in your life that has been your friend for most of it, as I will keep my wife (I hope), as a dear friend. It isn't that our spouses are our enemies - they have become friends, instead of a wife and husband. I love my wife very deeply. It is just that the kind of love I have for her is not the kind that a husband should have for a wife. I don't want to hurt my wife as you have no desire to hurt Don. I have explained to Wilma that it is me that has changed, and it is not her fault. She also understands that this is every bit as hard for me as it is for her. That is why she is no longer fighting with me, as she does understand that this is not an attack on her. There are real parallels between our lives, aren't there? That is why we are good for each other, and right now is the perfect time for us to be entering each other's lives. We understand so very well what the other one is experiencing and even feeling. We can help each other over this, and give each other the courage and support that we both need. It is so difficult to explain those deep feelings and motivations. It is good to be able to talk to someone who doesn't need an explanation of what I am feeling, as you already understand. We have known each other for such a short time, and yet it has been a true 'quality time' experience, and I think that we couldn't know what is in each other's hearts any better if we knew each other for years. Some things don't have to be said or explained. You just know and feel the other – true empathy.

Happy Birthday! I wish I had known! It is about 11 PM, and tomorrow when I see you at 7 AM, the stores will not be open yet, so I can't even get you a card. Would a birthday kiss be OK? You look way too good for fifty-one. Do you have a painting of yourself in the attic that is aging?

I always read my horoscope. It is uncanny how accurate they are sometimes, and on an emotional level, I guess kind of, sort of, put some store in them. But, my mind tells me very clearly that I do not believe in them. I do enjoy astrology, however. It might surprise you to know that I have an extensive library on the occult, and I have a Wiccan philosophy about the forces of nature. I am looking forward to tomorrow. If it rains, I will still be there, and will wait until 8 AM for you. If you can't make it, there will be other times, but I hope that you will be there. It will be good to see you and talk with you. Good night, and happy birthday again. Your friend, Henry

CHAPTER SIX

When I arrived at the park, Henry was already there. We both arrived early. The night before, I was restless and hardly slept in anticipation of this meeting. It's strange in a way, because we hardly knew each other, and yet, we knew each other so well. That day I found him sitting at one of the picnic tables with his drawing pad, creating a picture of an oriental geisha girl. I particularly liked the subjects he chose for his artwork.

The sky was overcast and rain threatened to fall at any moment. Already, we could feel a slight drizzle, but we decided to go into the park anyway. It didn't take us long to find a tall pine tree to lie under. We crawled behind the branches, felt the ground, which was still dry, as it was shielded from the rain by the long tree branches, and laid out his blanket. We lay there starring up through the pine needles of our tree, breathing in the pine scent, listening to the birds making their homes in that tree, singing and chirping and we talked and talked about so many things. Between sentences, he nibbled on my ears, nuzzled my neck, and starred into my eyes, filling me with wonderful sensations. I don't remember a time when I felt happier or more relaxed in my life. It was such a relief from the constant stress I felt at home. It was good to just lie there, and absorb each other, with all the beauty that surrounded us. Now, looking back on that day, I feel that although we did not say the words, or even realize it ourselves, I think we were already very much in love. We sensed the underlying feelings that we had for each other, and this time together was so precious to both of us. Even to today, every time we are together seems so precious, like a fragile and wonderful gift or reward we give to ourselves.

That day, under that tree, I knew I could no longer hold out. I wanted to fully make love with this man, and each time I saw him, the craving for that kind of closeness and intimacy with him grew stronger and stronger. We devised a plan where we could spend an entire day together. We decided to play hooky from our jobs the upcoming Wednesday, just three days away. Each of us would leave our houses as if we were going to work, then we planned to meet at the 'park and ride' at my bus stop, leave my car there and go to a motel together. He said he would make all the arrangements for a room, get one the night before, so we could arrive very early, and just spend the day together, doing what we were so compelled to do.

The rest of that Sunday morning we spent watching airplanes take off from the private airport that was in the park, and showing each other pictures of our lives, our children, spouses, our homes – glimpses or hints as to what we were like in that other world we both had. I took pictures of the park, and of him. I wanted to capture that look I saw in his eyes whenever he looked into my eyes. We stayed together as long as we dared to stay away from those 'other' lives we each had. Then, parted, and left with the anticipation and excitement of what would happen in three days.

June 19, 2000
Dear Henry:

There are some things I wanted to say on Sunday, and for some reason couldn't quite get the words out. I am shy like that sometimes. Maybe that's why I prefer to write down my thoughts. So, here it goes. You told me a few things about where your life is going, and I wanted you to understand where I see myself going.

When we were watching the planes take off, you told me about how you would just like to be able to go up to your wife and give her a hug, and she rejected such gestures. That brought back memories, and I was thinking, if only Don would have given me little hugs like that, and signs here and there of his affection – it would have made me so happy. I am such an affectionate person, I find it almost *impossible* for someone to care for some-one, and not touch them, and yet he couldn't be that way. I don't know why I never noticed things like this before I married him, but I didn't. We never lived together before we were married, and there were lots of little things I found out afterwards that I didn't like about him. But, you learn to compromise in life. I thought about how many times I would have liked him to walk up behind me, and give me a hug when I was washing dishes. I thought about all the times I would go to him to just cuddle, and he'd brush me off. I used to think that there was something wrong with <u>me</u>, but, later on, I realized it was him. Maybe it had something to do with the way he was brought up, but whatever the reason, you were so right when you said "it makes a person harden". I know if I continue with him, I will get so hard, that I will loose all sensitivity, and I don't think I would like the person I would become. That is why I am leaving this marriage.

I'm sure that if Don or Wilma would suddenly change, and open up to either one of us the way we would like them to, we'd reconcile in a heartbeat, because we have invested over 30 years of our lives into these marriages, and there's some pretty strong glue there, the kind of glue you only get from having a history together with someone. I left Don once before, and 16 months later he convinced me that he had changed, and I went back to him, only to find out that he lied to me and manipulated me. My problem was that I wanted to believe him so much. The change didn't last very long. I am convinced that it's never going to happen with him, because people just don't change, and I'm never going to give him another chance again. This time when I leave, it will be final.

But, Henry, I'll be honest with you. I'm not looking to be free to "play" – as you put it. The first time I left Don I met men and went out with quite a few. There was only one that caught my interest enough to get involved with, and we were together for a while. I couldn't handle seeing more than one man at a time, and quite frankly, I don't want to *play*. I'm looking for someone to laugh with, have fun with, someone to love me, and *make love* with, and be there for me as I would be for him, someone to share my life with, play scrabble at two in the morning with, and just grow old with. I don't know if that someone is you or not. It's way too soon to tell. I do know that we connect on an intellectual level, and there aren't many men out there that I can do that with. Also, there is an incredibly strong physical attraction, and I'm not sure if that's because of the intellectual thing or not. When you find someone like that, you need to see where it leads, or you'll always wonder. There just aren't that many people that either one of us can connect with, Henry. I think you realize that also. "Marriage" is just a word. It will take me probably about two years just to get a divorce. The separation is only the first step. I'm <u>not</u> about to get married again, if at all. I don't need any of the things that marriage offers. I have my <u>own</u> hospitalization and dental plans, I can't have any more kids, even if I wanted them, and I can afford to support myself and buy my own house. I even know how to hang my own pictures. But, I want someone to hold me all night long, to cuddle with, and be my companion, and if he wanted to decorate, that would be one thing less I'd have to think about. And, that's what I'm looking for. If you aren't looking for some of the same things, then let me know now, before we get to the point where you could break my heart. If things don't work out with us, at least I'll feel that it wasn't because I read your signals wrong. I hope that you will maintain your honesty with me. That's all I ask. All I want to do is follow where this leads, hopefully we'll both get lucky. If not, there will be no regrets, only pleasant memories. Just keep honesty in the relationship. That is my one request.- Julie

(With this letter, I also emailed to him the picture I had taken on Sunday of him.)

June 19, 2000
My Dear Sweet Julie:

How can I be anything but honest with someone like you? The way you describe your life with Don and the lack of affection in your marriage, is also a very good description of mine. I know exactly what it is like to be a warm affectionate person, without anyone in my life to show that affection to. I need to touch, cuddle, and hug. I need to make love, instead of having mechanical sex. Wilma can, and does change, but for only very short periods before she slips back into the same old, same old. That is why no matter what she does, or what she says she will do, I know deep in my heart, that the way it has been all these years is the way it will be in the future. I can't go through life without someone who returns that affection in a close way. I need that contact, that feeling of being wanted. If I could press a button or wave a magic wand to make Wilma different, then I would. Thirty years is a long time. It's my entire adult lifetime, and it is so hard to turn my back on someone who has shared that life for so long. I am convinced that if Wilma does change, it will be something that she will give to someone else, because she is just too used to being a certain way with me that I know she will just slip back eventually.

When I said that I wanted to be free and play, I think you misunderstood what I meant. Playing for me is to find someone to share laughter with, have fun with, to share intimate moments with, and to make love with. To have someone to hold close that wants to be held close. I want someone also that will share my life and not try to control it. I also want to have someone that I can spend hours with, just talking and play scrabble with until two AM. Julie, I want someone who I can enjoy life with, who will not smother and stifle and try to control me. Someone that welcomes those impromptu hugs and kisses and responds to the affection I feel towards them. I want desperately to wake up with you in the morning, after being intertwined with you in my arms all night. But, after all these years, I also need my 'alone' time as I still don't really know who I am yet. I need to discover that too. And, I want a life that I can live and enjoy living. It has been so long since I have enjoyed life. We all want someone that will be with us until we grow old. I don't know if I am that person you are looking for, and I don't know if you are the person that I am looking for. We are both coming out of situations that we must leave in order to survive as people. I do know that right now I need and want you in my life, as you have all the qualities that I am searching for. You are that person I thought didn't exist. We connect on so very many levels. We connect intellectually, physically, and our personalities mesh so well. Our lives are so similar and our wants and dislikes are also so similar, it is uncanny. I have a very strong attraction to you. I love just to talk with you. You are honest and say what's on your mind. I dislike people that agree with me because they think I want them to. You have your own mind. A mind for which I have a great deal of respect, and, a body that I want to bring to the peak of physical excitement and fulfillment.

I like you more than 'like'. I do not want to hurt you in any way, and I am not using you as far as I know. My intentions with you are good. If I thought that what I feel for you was driven by lust or loneliness, I would not pursue you any further as I have no desire to bring sadness into your life. I want to make you happy. I want to make you laugh. I want to help you live again, instead of just exist, and at the same time this will also produce all of that in me. It is true that I am lonely and you help fill that void. It is true that I lust after you in a way that I haven't felt in many years, and I hope you can fill that need also. I have an incredibly strong physical attraction to you, and I want very badly to make love to you with complete abandon.

If we parted now, it would leave behind very pleasant memories and I hope a friend I will have the rest of my life. I can make you no promises for the future at this point, and all I can do is tell you the truth. You are too good a person and too sensitive and kind for me to hurt intentionally. I will try so hard not to hurt you or break your heart as that would also break mine in the process. I understand how fragile we both are right now, and we will help to make each other strong again. Julie, be my friend and confidant, and stand by me through this horrible time in my life, and I will do the same for you. That is a commitment, and the only one I can (in good conscience) make right now. Neither of us can predict the future, as we have no real experience of what life will be like for us. Even though you have been on your own before, this is also a new experience for you in so many ways.

I guess to boil it all down to its essence, what I am left with is this. You have great qualities and I like you very much as a person. I enjoy your mind immensely, and connect with it in a way that I have rarely encountered. I want you as my lover. I have not set out to use you or do you any harm. I am afraid of becoming involved with you, because I am so scared that I will break your heart one day, and I am even more scared that you will break mine. Because when you care for someone, you hand them a weapon to hurt you. But, you, I cannot pass by, and I am willing to take the risk of having my heart broken by you, because the potential rewards are so great. Julie, if you want me close, then let's enjoy this moment in our lives, and see where it leads us, one day at a time. If you are afraid to get involved further, I will understand, and remain your dear friend for as long as you'll have me. And, we can use Wednesday to play scrabble if you like. But, sooner or later, we both have to take chances if we want our lives to go forward. I can't think of anyone else whom I would rather take that chance with. Your friend – Henry.

PS: Loved the picture, but how about one of you? It is not often that I see a picture of myself that I like. I like this one very much. Thank you for saying that you think that it makes me look sexy. Just hold onto that thought. I enjoyed seeing you Sunday, but as always, the time was way too short. At least on Wednesday we can spend some real time together, whatever we do. Thank you for being so honest, and for being my friend. There are so many things I want to say to you, but the time isn't right. - Henry

June 19, 2000
Hi Henry:

You always know what to say. Thank you for being honest. I feel much better now, and feel that I now can enjoy Wednesday with a free spirit. I don't want any commitments from you, except one of honesty, and I will always be honest with you. In fact, I want a promise from you that there will be no commitments fore we both are far too unsteady in our lives right now, to handle a commitment. You are a good friend, and good friends are very hard to find. No, you are more than just a good friend. I don't contemplate going to bed with people who are just "good friends". Smile. I also need time to myself to sort out my life, and pursue things I have had on the back burner for far too long. I know we will help each other go through this time of transition in both our lives, and during that time, we will discover what we are or will be to each other. On Wednesday, I don't want to analyze anything – just want to enjoy YOU.

-Julie

PS: You already have a picture of me.

June 20, 2000
Good Morning Hot Stuff:

Yes, I do have a picture of you. It is very small, and most definitely, does not do you justice. I would like one to hang on my office wall, to remind me of what a lucky son-of-a-gun I am, although I know that no picture would ever capture what I see when I look at you.

It's 6:30 AM, and I can't help thinking about what I will be doing twenty-four hours from now. Please confirm the time we will meet. Did you say 5:00 AM? I will stop by the motel on the way home tonight and get the room. Huba huba. It will be so nice to spend the day with you. I am really looking forward to laying down cuddling you, holding you close, feeling your naked hard nipples pressed up against my chest, without the benefit of security guards, or having to look over our shoulders. This will be the first time we can be together without worrying about who will disturb us. It will be an eternity until tomorrow. I can't wait to look into your eyes, kiss your waiting lips, smell your hair, and stroke your soft smooth yielding skin, to roll you over so that I can make love to your back...kissing, licking, and massaging every inch of your spine. I can't wait to nibble your ears, feel you respond to that, to kiss your neck, and trail my tongue down the length of your body to the warm moist place between your thighs, where I will kiss you deeply, rolling my mouth and tongue around, teasing you with my tongue, gently sucking on those swollen waiting lips, and then plunging my tongue deep inside you, and hear you moan with pleasure. Then, I'll pull you on top of me, where we will do sixty-nine, until your body is rocked by the strongest orgasm you have had in years. Now, I'm hard as a rock and can't stand up, so I'd better end before I get too carried away with my fantasy. Later, my sweet. - Henry

June 20, 2000
Hi Henry:

The early bird gets the worm. I think that's an old Chinese proverb. And it is so true. Yes, I did say 5:00 AM. If that is a problem for you, let me know, and I will bring a good book to read while I wait for you. I usually get to the bus stop between 5 and 5:20, depending on what time I wake up. Since tomorrow morning I will want to spend a little bit more time on my shower and hair, most likely I will be there later. But, since all I could do last night is think of tomorrow, and I didn't get much sleep, I most likely, will be there earlier. Don't worry if you can't come that early. Come when you can. I'll be there. Smile. If I had known you would be in the mood you were in when you wrote this last email, I would have told you today instead of tomorrow.

Wink… I miss you Henry, and am looking forward to seeing you again, and playing scrabble with you, while you plunge your tongue into whatever suits your fancy. You did say you could do two things at once, didn't you?

I don't think that putting a picture of me up on the wall of your office is a very good idea. What if I decide to come there one evening? Everyone who saw the picture would know that we are not talking business behind your closed door. Henry, you just can't do that. Besides, I don't have a good enough picture of me to give you. - Julie

June 20, 2000
Hi Hot Stuff:

I miss you too. Why would you want to spend any extra time on your hair as I intend to mess it up by running my fingers through it, right away? Yes, I can do two things at once, but scrabble isn't one of them. I will be there for sure between 5 and 5:30 AM. Eat your Wheaties and take your vitamins. You'll need them. In this case, the early bird gets Julie. I don't think that any photo would do you justice, but I would like to see our face during my day.

You won't think about food tomorrow. You will be sucking, however. I have a suggestion for that book you can read if you have to wait for me. How about the 'Karma Sutra'? I'm going to lick you from the top of your head to the bottom of your feet. No matter what I do, I keep thinking about sucking on your erect nipples and sliding my stiff shaft between your wonderful breasts towards your waiting lips. How do you expect me to work today? By the time tomorrow comes, I'll be a horny wreck. I know I won't sleep tonight. You have no idea how much I want this. I want you so much, it actually hurts. It's almost 9:00 AM. If this would be tomorrow, we would have been making love for at least three hours by now. - Henry

- Henry

June 20, 2000
Hi Hot Stuff:

I had planned on massaging everything very well, including your feet. The anticipation is killing me. Only thirteen hours to go – Smile! I'm on my way out the door to go and pick up the key right now. Have a good night's sleep. Pleasant dreams.

- Your secret playmate, Henry

CHAPTER SEVEN

On the way to the motel I kept asking myself, "What am I going to do with this man for an entire day in a motel room?" I wondered what possessed me to agree to do this. Most of the times I've made love in the past, it was for an hour or two, at most. What would we do for twelve hours? I think we both were wondering the same thing, but we were there anyway. I think that deep inside, something made each of us have to be there.

The first thing I saw when I entered the motel room was the dozen white roses Henry had put there the night before. He bought them for me, and it warmed my heart to know that he thought it was that important. He couldn't find a vase in the room, so he used the trash container to hold the flowers, and those roses in the trash container, sitting on the table, said more than words could ever say. They were so beautiful, filling the room with fragrance, and were just the right touch to what was to become one of the most beautiful and wondrous days of my life.

He lay me down on the bed, and began making love to my lips, then started to tease my neck, and nipped my earlobes gently with his teeth. Then, he caressed my breasts, so lovingly, but with just enough firmness in his fingers, to send waves of pleasure over my body. I was very tense, and his kisses were soft and gentle at first, relaxing me, and gradually easing me into the mood he wanted. I felt his throbbing arousal, and at that moment, I wanted him so much. I became lost in the moment, and I fell into the world of making love with Henry, sweeping every stressful thought from my mind, and letting him encompass my thoughts, encompass my entire being. We could not get enough of each other that day. We made love many times, intensely, intimately, like two hungry souls, trying to fill the wells that had run dry over the years, with new life. We flowed into each other over and over again. I did not know that a man could have as many orgasms as he had, and I came so much, that the sheets on the bed were literally drenched, with the juices of our lovemaking. Every single second of those eleven hours we spent together, was filled with unbridled passion.

Afterwards, we stopped to get something to eat before parting, and I think we both were overwhelmed by what happened that day. Neither one of us expected, or was even prepared, for what was happening between us. The power of our passion scared us, because neither of us was really free to explore all the possibilities that lie behind it. But, we both knew that it was some kind of beginning, and we each felt we had to see where it took us.

That day inspired a poem that I wrote for him, to remind us of that day, because I never ever wanted either of us to forget it.

JUNE 21, Y2K

With one seductive look, you are able to possess my soul.
I taste the passion in your lips, and as your mouth takes mine in
a devouring kiss,
our tongues intertwine, caressing gently, and so intimately. . .
Your fingertips move down my spine, making little circles over
each vertebra,
silently and deliberately, telegraphing messages, while they slowly
dissolve every bone in my body, overwhelming me with desire.

I strain against the building passion,
and my body becomes unbearably awake to your every touch, while
my heart begins to pump like a jackhammer.
Is that your tongue I feel inside my ear, tracing its way
Around the edges, then on down to my neck,
Bringing one erotic sensation after another?

As, your mouth moves lower, your teeth capture my nipple
Nibbling ever so gently, making it swell and stand erect.
My fingers take on a mind of their own, and move down to touch
The hardness of your arousal.
I take you up between the mounds of my breasts,
Then, into my mouth greedily and lovingly.

Your fingers tangle in my hair, and their gentle massaging
motions
Blended with your growing hardness, drives me wild.
I am happy because I taste your salty semen,
As you can no longer hold back your passion for me.
Then, when you move on to taste me,
I feel my blood stir once more.

Your mouth and fingers torch my body into a raging fire.
Lifting me into another galaxy, and I am no longer in this world.
Over and over again, you fulfill my once empty body, with flame,
the bed is drenched from our sex.
And yet, I am insatiable,
because I can't seem to get enough of you.

Each time we rest, you look deeply into my eyes
And reveal a piece of yourself
drawing me closer to your soul.
This day with you, Henry, is a very special present I gave myself.
I will put it into the little book in my heart reserved for incredibly
wonderful memories.
A day of pure passion and sharing, of giving and taking, and
happiness.

June 22, 2000
Hi Julie:

I never did give you that foot massage – not enough time, I
guess. How are you this morning? Are you still OK with yesterday? I hope that you have no regrets. I don't. Did you get the
smile off your face yet? Did you sleep well? Julie, yesterday was
almost perfect (almost, because we didn't spend enough time
with each other.) I am so glad we played hooky, and I am so glad
we played. Being with you was like opening a safety valve for me.
I would have liked to see the maid's reaction to that bed. It is
hard for me to understand why the men in your life haven't taken
advantage of what lays just below the surface with you. What is
wrong with them? I think selfishness. You are sensuous, sexy,
and a willing and generous bed mate. I certainly was satisfied
in that respect, and have absolutely no complaints. You have

nothing at all to be nervous about. Any man would welcome that chance to be with you, if they only knew what was waiting for them. I hope that you were satisfied too and still feel tingly. I must admit, however, that my very favorite part of yesterday was laying with you in my arms, so close and intimate, breathing you in, looking deep into each other's eyes. That was nice. This morning I feel more stress-free than I have in years, and that has more to do with that closeness than anything else. So, did you think of me last night? Even my people here commented on what a good mood I am in. I hope it affected you in the same way. Thank you for a wonderful day. I guess, like me, if you take a day off, then the next day just means two days' work. I plan on calling you later, if you have the time to talk.

Have a great day, your secret playmate – Henry

June 22, 2000
Hi Henry:

Yesterday I went to bed at 8 PM because I was exhausted. I a poem about yesterday so I never forget that day. It was such a beautiful day. - Julie

June 22, 2000
Hi Julie:

After reading your email and poem, I guess that you had a good time yesterday, and that you were so worn out that you were asleep by 8 PM. I'm so proud (that male thing). I hit the sack at 10:30 PM, but only because I had so much to do before I could retire. If I could, I would have been asleep by eight myself. You wore me out. Thank you. I woke up this morning feeling pretty damn good about myself, and more alive than I have felt in a while. I am very happy that I had the same effect on you. You see, the real Julie isn't dead. You just lost her for a while. Now, you found her again.

Don't ever think or believe that you are not an attractive and exciting woman. As I told you yesterday, there is nothing wrong with being fifty. No matter what you do, or how well any of us takes care of ourselves, middle age is middle age, and we cannot pass ourselves off as twenty year olds. So what! Why is a twenty year old body more desirable than a fifty year old body? It's all in the mind. We have been conditioned to believe that only anorexic pubescent women are attractive. It is not so. Don't believe the propaganda. Why is it that we believe a woman gets old and a man becomes 'distinguished'? It's because we are told to believe that. Just because in the past you had regrettable circumstances where certain males have not shown you the attention you deserve, has nothing whatsoever to do with you. It has all to do with them. If you did not respond, or feel with them in the way you responded and felt with me yesterday, it does not mean there is one single thing wrong with you. In my opinion, there are no frigid or unresponsive women, only inept men. I feel very fortunate to have spent yesterday with you. I have had the chance many times to spend a similar time with a variety of women (some of them in their twenties), and have turned down that opportunity, but I spent the time with you. And, I am happy that you chose to spend that time with me. I guess the strong attraction that we feel for each other really is based on something other than being 'alone'. You were better than my fantasies of you. Thank you for making me feel attractive to women for the first time since I was a teenager. - Henry

June 22, 2000
Henry:

Whatever made you think that you are not attractive to women? You are an exceptionally attractive man, and I think most women would want a relationship with you. Like me, you tend to put yourself down. Maybe that's because you have a spouse who tries to make herself feel superior by putting you down, or rejecting your attentions. I think your wife is absolutely crazy not to want to make love with you at every opportunity. You had a little bit of a contradiction in your last email. You said that "there are no frigid or unresponsive women, only inept men". Henry, you are far from being inept, yet from what you told me about Wilma, she is definitely unresponsive, so you might want to rethink that statement.

Thank you for helping me find the "real" Julie. She was lost for a long time. And, thank you for making me feel "special". I haven't felt that way in a very long time, and yes, I know that our attraction for each other is based on something much more than loneliness. I find you to be a very intriguing man with an interesting mind. I would not have had yesterday with you, if you were anything less, no matter how lonely I felt. I have standards, and those standards are very high. There are so few men in the world that measure up. You, Henry, are one that does. I could very easily fall in love with you, and that scares me so much, because when I love, I give my heart away, and I am way too vulnerable now to handle that type of a relationship. Yet, I don't know how much control people have over who they fall in love with, or when it happens. I am going to put such notions right out of my mind for now, though, and just take each day as it comes. – Julie

June 23, 2000
Hello Julie:

How is your day so far? Your last letter was very flattering to me. I do not get approached by women and have not been told that a woman found me attractive since I was nineteen. When I look into the mirror, I see an average looking guy, nothing special. So, you saying the wonderful things you said to me are very welcome. I am glad that you find me attractive. You already know that I most definitely am attracted to you. I know that you have not had many intimate relationships with men in your life. Our time together was very special to me, because I know that you do not give yourself lightly, and I am flattered and honored that you gave yourself to me, especially so freely and uninhibited. If I was a good lover it was you that helped me get there. I really enjoyed making love to you. I also felt totally uninhibited with you. Making love with you was truly a wonderful unforgettable experience, and I am glad it was with you. To know that I gave you that much pleasure pleases me tremendously. I know that I could do better if given the opportunity again. I would like to make love to you that way for a long weekend. To lay naked with you, making love, holding, talking, making love again, passing out, waking up, only to start over again, for two or three days straight would be my idea of the perfect time with you. A woman like you should be made love to, not screwed. What a waste that would be, although there is a lot to be said for the quickie in the back seat. If I could pull that response from you the first time we are together, imagine the response the next time, now that I understand what you enjoy. I loved everything about that day. I loved tasting you - all of you. I loved the change in taste that signaled your climax. I loved the way you moaned with pleasure. I loved the way you were ready for whatever I gave you. I loved the feeling of that rush of wetness, flowing down over me as the waves of pleasure consumed you. I loved the feeling of coming deep inside you, and feeling your inner muscles take hold of me, as you convulsed with orgasm after orgasm. Have you ever come that much in a week, let alone one day? I loved the way you hungrily accepted my semen, and how your lips and tongue sucked to get all of it. That felt fantastic, as did the thought that you tasted me in the most intimate way possible - the ultimate kiss. I loved your full ripe breasts, the taste of your ears, and the smell of your hair -and that dreamy look in your eyes.

I want to do it again and again. I want to feel like that over and over again. We were together in that room, making nonstop love for eleven hours. My passion for you allowed me to climax five times. Each time felt like the first. My only disappointment was with me, as it felt so good, that I wanted to climax, over and over, and coat you with the product of my insatiable endless passion for you. I would have liked to join you in drenching those sheets (that poor maid), but my body would not cooperate with my mind. I wanted many more of my releases to be between your lips, so you could taste me over and over again. I could easily lie back all day while you do that, because it felt that good. Every aspect of our lovemaking was perfect. You were great. The whole day was wonderful. Please, can I have some more??? Julie, there is a letter attached. - Henry

(Attachment)

Julie, Dear Julie:

Your prose touched me deeply. Thank you. That day was also one of the very best of the best for me - a day that has given me a memory to treasure always. As I have already said, there was a great deal more going on in that room than two people enjoying each other's bodies.

I care about you. I will try to do the right thing for you. I want to be with you. Your pleasure, wants, and desires are in many ways more important to me than my own. I am willing to sacrifice for you. I feel loss when you are not with me. I am disappointed every morning when I waken and the pillow next to me is empty of you. I think about you often during the day and night. You recognized what I feel in my touch, and in my eyes, when I look at you. I feel something for you that I have no right to feel, and that I am resisting.

This is a very dangerous time for both of us. If this was a year or two from now, it would be so easy and so tempting for both of us to be swept away by the strong connection that we are forging. You see, I also would find it very easy, too easy, to fall in love with you, Julie. It is not yet the right time for you, and it is not yet the right time for me, I am afraid. Not so much for myself, I am afraid for you. You have such a sweet generous heart, and sweet generous hearts can so easily be broken. I don't trust or understand myself enough to tell you that I will not break yours. I have no intention of breaking your heart, no intention of hurting you. My intentions towards you are only the best kind. But, good intentions – well they say the road to hell is paved with them. You have had enough hell in your life already. So, be careful of your heart. Guard it well. If I broke or hurt yours, I would surely never get over or forgive myself for that. I desire you more than I could ever express to you. I want to wake up in the morning and see your face next to me. I want to repeat the day we spent together many times. I want you as a friend for as long as you care to stay. Julie, I will make no demands on you. Any time that we can be together will be wonderful, and I will be grateful for it.

Hold that piece of you that allows me access to the deep parts of your heart, secure and safe, for now. Maybe when our lives are renewed, who knows? But, one thing I do know. It is that we have something rare that has happened between us, and that I will never regret. Thank you, Julie.

With great affection – Henry

June 23, 2000
My Dear Sweet Henry:

Do not worry about my feelings so much, I want you to guard your own. You have also been through hell and back. This friendship we have "feels" good to me. It feels right. I don't know what it is, but I see something in your eyes, I even captured it on camera – it's the way you look at me.   I am not afraid that you will hurt my feelings. <u>You</u> would never do that, intentionally. We both want to start these new lives we are entering, fresh, without commitments. I never expected to meet you. I really didn't. I was just cruising the internet to see if there was any intelligent life out there. And YOU popped up from out of the blue. I care very much about you, Henry. I couldn't have had Wednesday, if I didn't. Either could you. I know you have deep feelings for me, as I have for you. And, we both are fighting these feelings, because they are not what either of us wants in our lives right now. You're right, two years from now, we might welcome these feelings. Now, we both have some rocky roads to cover. I can't handle more than one relationship with a man at a time. I never expected this. I don't go onto the "personals" websites anymore. I want to see what happens between us. On the other hand, I think you may need to see other women, and get a feel for what's out there. That doesn't bother me. I know that when you start to realize that the phrase "dumb" blonde is really true, and that most of the women our age you will meet, will be bitter divorcees, you will realize how lucky you are to have found me. I'm not like anyone you will ever meet again, and I know that you are not like anyone I'll ever meet again. So, why don't we just give each other what little time we can, and take each day as it comes? If I'm wrong, and you do find someone more special, I will be nothing but HAPPY for you, because I want you to be happy. Henry, you deserve it. I think that your wife tried to control your life so much, that you are terrified of becoming involved with another woman. There are women in the world that would prefer that the MAN dominate the relationship. In fact, most women do. Don't allow the bad experiences in your marriage to distort what happiness you can have with someone else.

When I leave Don, I intend to get my own place, by myself. As much as I hate living alone, I think that I must do this to find my inner self. I hope that you will be a very frequent visitor because I enjoy your company so much. I might even give you a shelf in my medicine cabinet. One of the reasons I went back to Don the first time, was that I hated the loneliness. I know some of the mistakes I made the first time, and will not repeat them. I'm a big girl, Henry, if you break my heart, it will mend. I promise you. I also know that in order to get anything in life, you have to take chances. One of my favorite phrases, "*no guts, no glory*" is appropriate here. You, Henry, have to find yourself too. You need space to do that. I am aware of this, because you are very much like me. And, I do not wish to rush into anything, or make any commitments. But, I think that having each other now, will help each of us make the break from our old lives, that much easier. (And, Henry, if it turns out that you decide to give your life with your wife a second chance, I will understand that too. You have a good deal of your life invested in that marriage, and that should be a consideration for you.) I will make no demands on you. And, I certainly don't want you to make any "sacrifices" for me. I will not play games with you either.

I will just be myself with you. And, I definitely want a repeat of Wednesday, or better still, as you said, I want to wake up in the morning, to your face.

Please don't be disappointed in yourself. You are a wonderful lover, and your body was just fine. Trust me on that one. So, now that we got the gooey stuff out of the way, can we just get on with the good stuff? Look, the only times my cell phone is on, is when I am alone. If you find yourself free for an hour or so during the weekend, call me. I can meet you at the park, if I'm free also. If the phone is off, leave a message. You might catch me between errands, and I can always say the errands took a bit longer. I will not call you, because now I realize that your phone is on all the time, and you may not be alone. So, it will be up to you to take the initiative. And, I do need to see you again, hopefully sooner, rather than later. Of course if we can prearrange meetings, that is always easier. Henry, promise me that you will just ENJOY LIFE AND BE HAPPY. Stop trying to analyze everything. What's to be will be. Your good friend and secret lover, Julie

June 23, 2000
Hi Julie:

I have just finished reading your response to me. I am unbelievably lucky to have found you. - Henry

June 25, 2000
Hi Henry:

I just wanted you to know that I was thinking of you. I woke up this morning remembering last Sunday at this time, when we were under the pine tree. In fact, I have a lot of wonderful memories lately. Ever since Wednesday - I keep seeing myself in some sort of sexual act with you whenever I daydream. I also find myself daydreaming more than normal, lately.

How is your weekend going? The weather yesterday was beautiful. It looks like we will have another beautiful day today. I took my granddaughter to the carnival Saturday night. We had a great time. She wears me out. – Julie

June 25, 2000
Good Morning, Julie:

I also miss your company. When I woke this morning you tiptoed into my thoughts (naked, or course). My son and I went to see Harry Conick, Jr. last night in Scranton, PA. The concert was outstanding. Great weather this weekend. I am off to Stillwater to watch my goddaughter perform gymnastics this afternoon. Did you have a good time at the carnival?

In a couple of more days, I will be suffering from "Julie deprivation". Have to do something about that. Have a great day, Julie. I'll be in touch sometime Monday, but I don't know when, as I must be in Queens by 7 AM for a meeting, and am not sure when I can escape. Be good... - Henry

June 25, 2000
Hi Henry:

Sunday a friend took me on a motorcycle ride through Pennsylvania and my back is sore. The rumbling of the seat brought on my sciatica. Hopefully, it will go away with some rest.

The gymnastics sounded boring. But, I'm sure your goddaughter appreciated your being there. Can you get away on a Saturday night? - Julie

June 26, 2000
Hi Julie:

Sorry to hear about your sore back. Have you tried a chiropractor? If you need one, I know a pretty good one, locally. Perhaps a slow careful back massage after a hot bath would help. No, that's not an innuendo, but a real suggestion. I just returned from driving into Queens. I hate the traffic on the return trip.

The gymnastics was interesting - kind of like watching grass grow. But, I go to give support to my goddaughter, and it's not that bad, though a little long.

As far as getting my wife to agree to me going out, she didn't. I just announced that I was going out one Saturday night, and then went. She was pissed off, but I went anyway. Now, she is still mad when I go out, but has given up on bitching about it. I did not say that I was going to see other people. I told her it was "guy's night out", and I was going with friends. She occasionally goes out with her girlfriends the same night, once she knows I have plans. I go out one Saturday in three, and occasional week nights. I have not yet stayed away all night, but she did. I am not 100% sure that she didn't meet someone when she didn't come home that night. She has never given me an explanation, nor have I asked for one. But, I did tell her what's good for the goose is good for the gander, so if I ever do stay out all night, she has nothing to say about it. Anyway, I would never rub her nose in it, by flaunting a date with another woman, even after we have separated. I don't think it necessary to hurt her feelings more than I have to. Besides, another person is not the reason I want out of the marriage. But, this is something I think we should talk about, instead of writing about it, and the next time I see you, we will talk about this. It would be interesting to me to get a woman's viewpoint on some things, and I think perhaps the same is true for you, so that Don's feelings can be put into better perspective, if you hear a guy's opinion. It's like chicken soup – it may not help, but it won't hurt.

How was your weekend? I missed you. I tried to call you today, but you were at lunch, so I left a dumb message on your cell. I am falling asleep, so I'd better leave for home while I still can. I will be in touch tomorrow. Sweet dreams, hot stuff. Hope your back feels better. – Henry

June 27, 2000
Hi Henry:

How busy will your day be today? Mine isn't too bad, and I go to the acupuncturist at Noon for a treatment. He swears that he'll make me all better by July 4th. So, I'll give him till then. If not, I will ask for the name of that chiropractor.

Henry, I think I misunderstood you from our conversations. I thought that you and your wife both agreed to see other people. Don't you think that just going out, and not telling each other where you go, is as hurtful as being open about it to each other? To be honest with you, I think its worse. That's because the other person knows you are lying to them. I'd rather know the truth, no matter how much it hurts, than be lied to.

Since Don and I have discussed the fact that there is no future in our marriage, it has been difficult living with him. I would never flaunt a date, or bring someone over to the house, but by telling him that I am going out with someone, it gives him an opening to do the same. Do you really believe that Wilma thinks you "go out with the guys"? I don't know many married men who go out with the guys on a 'Saturday' night. Saturday nights are usually reserved for the wives. I don't think your wife is that naïve. Don't you think it would hurt her much more, if she thought that you thought she was stupid? Friday night Don had a sales meeting. These things usually end around nine o'clock. He didn't get home till two in the morning. I never questioned it. But, if he wasn't with a woman, I'm sure he was at some bar with the single guys in his group, looking for one. And, that's OK.

Now, I don't feel so bad when I say I'll be home late. I haven't reached the point where I can tell Don the truth yet, either. Friday night I will tell him that I will be home late, because I am taking a friend who is leaving for maternity leave, out for a few drinks. In actuality, I do have a friend who is taking a maternity leave, but I'm taking her out to lunch on Friday. It'll give me a chance to spend a little bit more time with you. What are you using for an excuse to be with me this Friday night? Don't you think it would be better if Don told me the truth about last Friday, and I told him the truth about this Friday? I'm certainly curious about a guy's opinion on this whole thing.

Well, let me go and do some work, so I don't start to feel guilty about getting paid, too. - Julie

June 27, 2000
Hi Julie:

I told Wilma that I will most likely be home late on Friday, because I have a sales meeting that night, and I will be going out for drinks, etc., with some of the guys from work, afterwards. Yes, I know that it is not the truth, and I also know that I should be honest with my wife, but that would most certainly lead to a major confrontation. I would rather avoid the confrontation. Wilma has resigned herself to the fact that we will not be together next year, and that the clock is ticking. It isn't that she is stupid, but she would rather not admit to herself that I may be seeing a female. There is no reason for me to make her feel worse than she does already, or to tell her the truth, which would start a fight. It would not benefit either of us, and would not change the outcome of our relationship. All it would do is create unnecessary turmoil while I am still at home. Turmoil I am no longer emotionally equipped to handle, as the last couple of years have taken their toll on me, and on her.

I feel very guilty that I am not being honest with her, but sometimes, honesty is not the best policy. It was being honest with her that caused most of this trouble to begin with. I just want to keep the peace while I am there. Also, I would get some major crap from my kids, if I was dating while still married to their mother and living at home. It's only six months or so before I am out on my own. Then, it doesn't matter what I do. Frankly, I know that I am avoiding the issue, but this is the best I can do for now. It has taken every bit of effort to get this far. I just don't want to make life more difficult for myself, and I know that's selfish. If I have to deal with another severe confrontation, I'll snap, as I have more than I can handle right now. I must admit that I applaud your honesty and courage with Don, but it is courage that I just cannot muster, at present.

How's your back? Any idea how you injured it? I am sure we will be in contact later, but I am looking forward to spending some time with you, and a conversation over coffee would be super. A little kissy face would be OK too. Do you have exciting plans for the holiday weekend? And, do you have Monday off? We don't know yet if we do, or not. My holiday weekend will be mostly painting and touch ups on the house, etc., as my son's wedding is getting close, and there is still a lot to do. Talk to you later, sweetie...Henry

PS: Let's try another poem. How about these first lines?

What do I owe for this unasked for gift of love;
that I am told has been mine for oh so long?
Alas, it does not provide wings for my spirit;
Or for my heart a song.

June 27, 2000
Hi Henry:

I got a laugh out of you applauding me for honesty with Don. If I were truly honest with him, I would tell him the truth about Friday night. But, I can't. I also prefer to avoid confrontations. I don't know if it's being fair to him, to lie. I think I'm probably being very selfish. My suggesting to him that we see other people did not go over well. He knows the clock is ticking, and is trying to use every minute to make me change my mind. I don't understand why, because he admitted that he was also unhappy in the marriage. At times, I find myself resenting him, and I don't like what those emotions do to me. I also don't seem to have the courage to be honest. Somehow, I think that telling him would be the right thing to do, and lying to him is wrong. I'm in a turmoil over it. Enough of this confusion…

What do you say to showing me the quarry and this fancy office of yours on Friday night? I'm sure on Friday night no one would be around. I would love to see the prized bonsai tree you keep bragging about, also. My back is slightly better. I had my second treatment today, and I will have another at 7 AM tomorrow morning. I'll be going for treatments every day till Friday. I've never had acupuncture before. I like to try new things. It doesn't hurt when I'm sitting, but I haven't been able to get to the gym all week. Monday, I did three minutes on the treadmill, and I thought I would die from the pain. The acupuncturist told me to take it easy this week. I injured my back by sitting on the back of a motorcycle for a ride of about 100 miles on Saturday. A friend took me for a ride. I had a great time driving through the back roads of New Jersey, but I am paying for it now. This is the second time a motorcycle ride has hurt my back. I think my body is trying to tell me something, here. Why don't I listen to it? Saturday and Sunday I have no special plans. I will probably work in the garden part of the time. If my back feels up to it, I might take my bicycle out for a ride. I want to check out a few houses for sale this weekend.

I will work on your poem, but I have to admit, those lines are excellent, and will be a hard act to follow. - Julie

June 27, 2000
Hi Julie:

Sorry to hear that your back isn't better, yet. But, Julie, you did it to yourself. I understand. It's hard to turn down fun, and sometimes we pay the price. Was the motorcycle ride worth it? I hope that it was. You strike me as a natural where motorcycles are concerned. I would love to show you around the quarry on Friday. I think you would find the entire operation here interesting. And, don't worry. I hardly ever bury people in the mines. Thank you for the praise regarding my opening lines. If anyone can follow one of my acts, it's you.

Take care. I'll be in touch, baby...Henry

June 27, 2000
Hi Henry:

Friday is "dress down" day here at the office. So, I'll be wearing slacks, and will be able to see the mines. But, I won't go into any pits. Smile. I am looking forward to seeing the quarry. I've never been inside a quarry before. It will be exciting for me, and I may even use it as a background for one of the chapters of my book. I really don't mind working on Monday. It's not as if Don and I planned on something to do for the weekend. If I had someone to do it with, I'd take the whole four days off, and go somewhere romantic to play. - Julie

June 28, 2000
Hi Julie:

I suggest that when you visit the quarry, you bring your camera, as there are some great photo opportunities here. How is your back feeling today? - Henry

June 28, 2000
Dear Henry:

I will bring my camera to the quarry. My back is much better, thank you. But, I still have trouble walking around. I don't feel any pain when I sit or lie down – it's just when I walk. I had my third acupuncture treatment this morning. I will not let this get me down, but I definitely will think twice before taking another motorcycle ride. I am seriously thinking of selling the motorcycle I bought. I think that there are just certain things in life that I will never be able to do. Smile. I will have to think of a new hobby, like skydiving, or maybe I'll write a book about all the different ways to make love. Will you help me with the research? - Julie

June 29, 2000
Hi Julie:

I am glad that you are starting to feel better. Don't give up on the bike yet. I think that you could do anything that you set your mind on doing. On Friday, I suggest that you bring both the zoom and the panoramic lenses, as you might find some interesting things to photograph. If you want to do field research on lovemaking, I'm your guy! But, I think I may have done my best work with you, already. Then again, you know what they say, practice makes 'perfect'. Too bad we are missing the sunshine, as it would be a good beach day. Would you like to go romp in the surf with me, Sweetie?

- Henry

June 29, 2000
Hi Henry:

I'm certainly happy to know I have a willing research associate. I will definitely keep you in mind if I decide to write that book. In fact, I'll keep you in mind, even if I don't write it. The back is feeling much better. - Julie

June 29, 2000
Hi Julie:

I am very happy to hear that you are starting to feel better. Now, don't overdo it. Yes, Julie, I do think that you are capable of doing anything that you set your mind to, and I want to be your passenger in the bike parade next year. I have more confidence in you than you have in yourself. See you tomorrow, and have a great night. – Henry

CHAPTER EIGHT

The quarry Henry worked for is one of the largest quarries in the country. I'm still not sure if I wanted to see it, because I was curious as to what a quarry was like, or if I just wanted to see where he spent his days. Regardless of the reason, once there, I was wonderstruck and totally amazed as to the intricate beauty of it all. I saw mountains of different types of stone categorized, and earmarked for various customers. Huge machinery, the likes of which I've never seen before, dotted the landscape. I stood next to trucks that had tires taller than me, and watched them move the stone from one pile to another. The quarry was working twenty-four hours a day. Then, Henry showed me an immense piece of machinery that he helped design that recycled soil, filtering gasoline out of the soil and debris, and turning it back into clean environmentally safe topsoil. This was Henry's world.

He spent close to two hours taking me around the whole complex, pointing out various items of interest, explaining the different functions of all sorts of machinery, and letting me take pictures of things I felt were photo worthy. Here was a world I knew hardly anything about, and he patiently and very methodically walked me through how a quarry worked, and the various components that went into making asphalt.

Then, Henry took me to his office in the technical center. His office was impressive. He had designed the whole tech center and decorated the office himself. One entire wall was devoted to plaques, awards, degrees, licenses, and other various documents commemorating his accomplishments in the industry. I was impressed, not just with his accomplishments, but with his ability to put me at ease, in spite of the fact that I felt like I was in the presence of a true genius. He had a natural innate humility that was part of his charm. Another wall was devoted to pictures of his family and friends, and his artwork. It was here that I spotted the picture he drew which I later used as the cover to my first book of poetry. The picture was a black and white pencil drawing of a girl who was so gentle and delicately graceful, that a butterfly fluttered at her fingertips. It matched a poem I wrote years ago entitled "Butterflies". It was almost as if the picture were drawn to go with the poem. The fit between the two was perfect.

The office was so much like him, everything in perfect order, clean, yet comfortable and inviting. His bonsai trees thrived on the windowsills overlooking the concrete existence around them. They were like a ray of sunshine brightening the grayness. The years of care and love the artist gave to these trees showed through. In my opinion, they truly were prize winners. I could see that a great deal of thought and planning went into making this office the way it was, and at that point, I knew, not only was Henry my intellectual match, but he had the same level of thoughtfulness and consideration that I possessed. He is probably the first man I ever met who came that close.

We sat together on the black leather sofa that graced one wall and talked. It wasn't long before we were cuddling, and I was in his arms again. Memories of our tryst last week in the motel room flooded my mind, and I was swept away in this vast universe of stone and sand that belonged to Henry.

July 2, 2000
Hi Cutie Pie:

Thank you for visiting me and allowing me to show you my world. I am glad you enjoyed the tour. You always say the nicest things about me. I will never look at that couch the same way again. You left me wanting more – a lot more. Enjoy the holiday weekend. Talk to you next week.

How could I possibly let you start your week without letting you know I'm thinking of you? I woke up this morning and you were the first thought I had. Sorry, you have to work. Perhaps with luck, you can get out early. Hope your back is OK. I already know your front is great. Enjoy what is left of your holiday weekend, Sweetie. I'll be thinking of you. Maybe next year we can spend it together lying on a blanket under the stars watching the fireworks before we make some fireworks of our own. Have a great day. - Henry

July 3, 2000
Henry, you're so sweet.

I was thinking of you too. In fact, after Friday, you were on my mind most of the weekend. I will definitely try to spend next July 4th with you. You inspired another poem. I worked on it over the weekend, and just now had a chance to type it. It's not finished yet – just a draft, but I think it's coming out pretty good, even if I do say so myself. You have become my "muse". The first poem I wrote you is now a semi-finalist in a poetry contest, and will be published in a book of poetry. Here is the latest I wrote. I hope you enjoy it. – Julie

HOW I MISS YOU

How can I describe to you
The joy I feel
When my eyes look through your eyes
And, my soul stares into your soul,
Drinking in all that is you.

But, our time together
is swallowed too quickly.
I feel myself tremble in disappointment
when we part.
Each time, more difficult to turn away,
to go home alone, and miss you.

Missing the way you look at me
When you want me,
I miss your hunger;
Your passion for life;
Your passion for me.
I miss that most of all.
It's what I always wanted,
And never had.
Until you.

July 5, 2000
Good Morning, My Dear:

I read your poem. It is rare to run across someone with as much talent as you. You bare your soul to me in those poems. I find it hard to understand why any man who meets you, wouldn't be consumed with the same passion for you that I have. Did you have a good 4th? Hope you caught some rays (I would like to see the tan lines). I was looking for you during the fireworks at Lake Arrowhead. I could feel you there, were you there? - Henry

July 5, 2000
Hi Henry:

Compliments will get you everywhere… No, I didn't attend the fireworks At Lake Arrowhead this year. I was not in a very good mood this weekend. All my children and my mother ganged up against me, and told me what a terrible thing they all think I'm doing to their father. Everyone was sympathetic to Don's needs, and no one cared about my needs. What you probably felt was my need to find a strong shoulder to cry on, and someone to tell me I'm not making a mistake. Regardless, I got through it and I'm OK now.

- Julie

July 5, 2000
Hi Julie:

Any time you need moral support, just call me. I am sorry that you were ganged up on by your family. Believe me; I know what that is like. You only have one life, so considering that it is yours, then you should do with it what you feel is right for you. All of your adult life has been filled with the obligations that you have towards others, now it's your time. If you feel that it is right for you to continue to accommodate the needs of others, then that, or course, is up to you – if that is what makes you happy. But, you are accommodating the needs of others, because they are selfish, and think of themselves, instead of what you want for your life. Then, well you know what to do. Ultimately, the decision is only yours, because the life you have is only yours. How you choose to live it is your right. It seems strange, but the people I find who like to tell others how to live, will not accept interference in their own lives.

Is your back feeling any better today? – Henry

July 5, 2000
Hi Henry:

Thanks for the pep talk. You are so sweet, but I will not call you, because now I know that you may not be alone when I call. It might be embarrassing for you to talk to me if I called and you weren't alone. I managed to handle things as best I could. I know that each one of them had a selfish reason for the attack, and Don is trying to make everyone feel sorry for him. He plays on my mother's and my daughters' sympathies, and of course, they overreact. It's very hard, when you sit at the dinner table and your whole family starts in on you at the same time. I was so angry, that I just got up and walked out. I got into my car, and drove to the park, sat on the bench watching the airplanes land until I cooled off. They didn't expect me to leave, but enough is enough. I haven't changed my mind. In fact, now, more than anything, I want to just move out of there. When I came back, I told them that if they are not going to let me feel comfortable living at home, I'd leave before we sell the house. I told them I've made up my mind, they will not change it, and I did not want to discuss it again. That didn't go over too well, but they finally let it die for now. I'm wondering now if Don will try to turn my children against me.

My back is all better, thank you. And thanks for the words of wisdom. Deep inside I know I am doing the right thing for myself. It feels good to know that I'm not the only one who thinks so. - Julie

July 5, 2000

Julie, regardless of which direction your life takes you, I hope to remain your friend, no matter what, as I also hope that you will remain mine. In the long run, it doesn't really matter what direction your life takes, just as long as you are the one who decides where it will go. Hang in there. I understand what you are going through. Remember, you are no longer out there swinging in the breeze. I will do everything I can to help you land squarely on your feet, if that's into your new life or back to the old one under new terms. I'll be rooting for you and supporting you. At least you are doing something about changing your life, so better days are coming. They don't understand that one day you just woke up. It doesn't mean that you don't love those around you. You just see the world differently now. Too bad your independence threatens everyone else. Makes you think, doesn't it?

Talk with you soon - Henry

July 5, 2000

Henry, I also hope that we will be friends for a long time, regardless of which direction either of our lives takes. I enjoy your company, and there is a certain chemistry I won't deny between us. But, even if there weren't that chemistry, I would still like to be your friend, because we think the same way on so many issues, and I like conversing with you.

My independence threatening everyone is very scary. I tried to bring up my children to be able to support themselves independently. My son succeeded, but for some reason, my daughters need much more support from me. I have a thirty year old daughter who is afraid to get her own apartment and live on her own. And, my twenty-eight year old daughter, who is a mother herself, cannot make ends meet. I don't mind helping them out financially from time to time. They know I still will do this. But, I keep thinking about what will happen if I die – what will they do? And, my Mom is so afraid that Don won't help her move into her new house because I'm leaving him. He told her that he will still help her do whatever needs to be done. It's hard for her to see me as a single woman. She's an old fashioned Italian lady who thinks that women should cook and clean and be cared for by a man. She doesn't realize that I'm the one who put most of the food on the table for the past twenty years.

This isn't new. Every so often, my family feels that they have to say something about what I want to do. I remember the last time I left Don. It will be worse after I leave for a while. But, I think in the end, everyone will see me happier, and hopefully Don will be happier also, once he realizes that he doesn't need me as much as he thinks he does. It's this time before the move that has me in a state of Limbo. We lowered the price of the house again. The realtors say the whole market is quiet. I guess I'll just have to wait it out.

How are your son's wedding preparations going? When is it exactly? I bet everyone in your house is excited about it. How does it feel marrying off your first son? I remember I felt as if I was loosing my son when he married. He went off to Virginia, and now, I only see him a couple of times a year. I miss him so much. Daughters somehow stay closer to home than sons. - Julie

July 10, 2000
Good Morning Julie Sweetie:

How was your weekend? Better than last weekend, I hope. Are your kids still unhappy with you? And, how do you feel? I just wanted you to know that I was thinking of you. – Henry

July 10, 2000
Good Morning Henry:

My weekend was OK. No, the kids kept to themselves this weekend. I was offered a new higher position at my firm. It is considerably more money and much more responsibility. I am looking forward to the challenge.

Henry, something is wrong. You are different. After June 21st, I've noticed that you seem to be sending me email that is, I'm not sure how to describe, but different. Not as intimate as before that day – not really responsive. I think you are trying to distance yourself from me. I hope that's not the reason. I am not complaining, but please, be honest with me. I don't want to be out there chasing rainbows. - Julie

July 10, 2000
Julie:

Your insecurities are showing. There is no problem, except lack of time and preoccupation with the wedding. We will make up for lost time, I promise. Distance is the one thing I never want between us. I want to spend many days closer to you than we have been. That emptiness inside of me is not as empty as before I met you, and it is growing smaller each day. I would like to see you sometime this week. I miss you, Julie. Dear friend, you are no longer alone. And thanks to you, neither am I.

I have been super busy. Work is gaining momentum, due to the weather getting a little better (rain hurts us), and home is nuts, mainly because of the wedding. My son is getting married on the 29th of July, and they are arriving from Texas on July 21st. I will have an additional seven people staying at the house for two weeks. I have been scrapping and repainting the front of the house, and cutting the hedges (those bloody hedges). Due to all the rain, they are real hairy again. Starting next weekend, we will boil the interior of the house. Understand, Wilma is German, so you could lick the floor, but there are a couple of things that still must be done. My job is to wax the floor of my bedroom, and completely clean the basement recreation room, which is the entire basement level (my part of the household chores). Then, I must hang the garland outside around the gazebo, and put up all of those wedding decorations around the garden, etc. Plus, we have to set up the hall for the reception.

This past Saturday night was Wilma's 50th birthday, so we all went out for dinner to the Black Forest Inn. The food was good, and the time wasn't bad either. We have gotten to the point where we don't fight anymore, so things are easier.

Is your mother all moved into her new place now? Any bites on the house? And, how is your back? All better, I hope.

So, tell me about your new position. I bet you are also very busy, setting up everything the way you want it to run, but I know it feels good to be handed a new challenge, and know that the folks there have such a high level of faith in your abilities. I miss seeing you. - Henry

Hi Henry:

It sounds like she's really got you going. I never heard of giving your husband "chores". That would never happen in an Italian household.

My new position is very challenging. I have a lot to learn in a very short time, but I'm doing the best I can. I've got a new larger office and am in charge of twenty-two people who report directly to me. I hope I can earn the "faith" my employer has in my abilities.

Are you trying to distance yourself from me? - Julie

July 11, 2000
Hi Baby:

Thank you for seeing me the way I would like to be, rather than the way I am. I do and will try to be a good and impartial friend, but sometimes it is hard to be truly impartial, because I can't help but let my own feelings seep in. As far as your comments on my 'chores' goes – well now you know how structured a life can be. Julie, I feel very close to you and care about your life, because you are a kindred spirit. I just hope that in some small way I have added some joy to it. Don't ever read anything into any email or phone call that is not said directly, as I would not do that to you. That isn't fair. If I want you to know something, I will not hint around. I will tell you straight out – good or bad.

Expect to see me waiting for your bus one evening this week, as it is difficult to go for two weeks without seeing you.

I am sure the time will come soon when we won't have to sneak around and hunt for a time to see each other. I am looking forward to that. I would like to do the normal mundane things with you, take in a movie, walk hand in hand through the mall, go for a picnic, and lay on the beach. These are the things that I look forward to the most with you. It would be great to spend a quiet evening with you just sitting in front of a fireplace, sipping sherry, and exchanging ideas. Then, as the embers die and night cloaks the sky, I will pull you towards me and make love to you in front of the hearth. You asked if I was trying to distance myself from you. I want to be close enough to you, so that when I look into your eyes, our breath is shared, and our sweat blends into one musty, sexy aroma of lust and lovemaking. To have you wake in the morning, and have you open your eyes to the first sight you see – me. Does that sound like wanting to distance myself? You have been without being wanted for too long. It shows. Have a great day, Sweetie. - Henry

July 11th, 2000
Hi:

Henry, I never thought that one person could make another person feel so good before I met you. I used to believe that we made ourselves feel good or bad, and that we make our own happiness. And, I still believe that this is true, but you make me happy too. I want you to know that.

How I see you is how you are with me. You are a beautiful and sweet man. You say that you would be honest and open with me, but Henry, you are such a compassionate person, and I know you would have trouble saying something you thought would hurt my feelings. I know this, and that is why I asked you outright if you were trying to distance yourself from me. I knew you would answer a direct question.

You gave me an idea. Do you think if I asked Don to do "chores" that he would leave me? That was a joke.

I hate sneaking around. I am not a sneak. I think that is a problem with us. Yet, there's no other way right now. Neither of us wants to hurt Don or Wilma in such a way. They don't deserve to be hurt. It will be hard enough when I start to pack and move out. Every time I look at houses that are for sale he wants to come with me. It's not that I don't want him there, it's just that I don't want his tastes and needs to influence any decision I make for MY house. My whole life, I've done what other people wanted me to do. The next house I buy will be strictly what I want. But, I don't have the heart to ask him not to come with me.

You have given me a lot of strength. I think just knowing that another man still finds me attractive at age fifty-one, is what helps the most. But, also your common sense and logic reinforces my own thinking. Sometimes things happen that give us doubts, and uncertainty creeps up on us. We wonder if we are making the right decisions. My son called me last night and asked me if Don and I would go to the Caribbean with him and his wife this fall. He already knows that Don and I are separating, but I think his father put him up to this. I told him I can't do it. As much as I want to be with my son and his wife, I don't want to be in that close proximity with Don. Then, my son told me that I was making a terrible mistake. I don't know how to convince him that he is wrong. I asked him if he wanted his mother to live with an alcoholic for the next twenty-five years. He knows that his father has a problem, and he didn't know how to answer that. He said that I will be alone for the rest of my life.

Now, on a lighter note – I would love to make love with you in front of a fire. I don't drink sherry. After dinner I prefer sparkling wines like Asti Spumanti. They help you to digest. And, speaking of movies, I saw "The Patriot". It's a great movie. I think you would enjoy it. It's playing locally. Check it out, if you have the time. Some day we will go to a movie together, and we'll sit in the last row and smooch during the boring parts of the movie. And, if the movie is very boring, well, anything can happen in the last row...

– Julie

July 11, 2000
Hi Julie:

Don't be too hard on your son for trying to "set you up". He may be misguided, and it may seem as though he is maneuvering you, and he may admonish you about your plans, but always focus on the one thing that you know for sure. He wants the best for his Mom and Dad. - Henry

July 12, 2000
Henry:

Thanks for the letter and phone call. You're wonderful, and I don't know what I did to deserve such a good friend like you. But, whatever it is, I'm glad I did it. You were so right when you said the time we spent together was a 'tease". You left me horny as hell. I didn't get enough kisses from you, not nearly enough to quench my appetite for you.

When we were together, for one brief second, I looked through your glasses, deep into your eyes. Your guard was down, and I saw more than you wanted me to see. And, you saw in my eyes the same emotions mirrored back to you. Then, reality hit, and we both blinked away – scared, unable, or maybe unwilling to deal with it. Do you remember when that happened? And,

Henry, I'm a writer. I always bare my soul when I write letters, poems, etc. That's what writers do. Does it bother you?

You talk of going to movies, laying on the beach and picnics. But, all I want to do Henry is fuck your brains out. Smile. Last night was too brief. - Julie

July 12, 2000
Dear Hot Stuff:

I enjoyed your 'visit'. Hope you didn't' get home too late. How are you today? Our time together was great, but as usual, nowhere long enough. Although I would rather be with you in better surroundings, I must admit that being 'naughty' in my office does have its fun side. . . kind of like playing in the park, or at the drive-in. You are so hot. Sooner or later a weekend will become a must. It was lonely in bed last night.

I was so horny when I left you. Yes, I want to go to the movies, lie on a blanket and go for a picnic. Then, fuck your brains out. In fact, to hell with the movie, let's just fuck our brains out together. But, I need some warning so that I can work out and take my vitamins and eat my Wheaties, because next time I want to really fuck your brains out. Last time was just a warm up (foreplay). Smile. I was being easy on you. There I go, bragging again. Last night, I had an erection all the way home because of our time together. If I could, I would have made love to you right at the bus stop. I would love to slip my tongue in your ear and suck on your nipples. I like the way your hard erect nipples feel in my mouth. And, I like the way you respond to my tongue in your ear when you caress my swollen shaft. It's swollen now, just thinking of you. You can make me so horny with just a look.

You are so right. Yesterday, you did catch me with my guard down. It's so easy to let my guard down with you, and you did see something in my eyes. It was the same as what was in yours. Softness, caring and affection creates softness, caring and affection. But, I think if one word were used to describe what is between us it would be 'empathy'. We tend to instinctively feel what the other feels. That's why you feel so horny around me. It is safe to bare your soul to me because I will never use that exposed vulnerability against you. If all the other things between us are boiled away, the lust, the affection, the caring, the need to be together, what will always be left, is our close friendship and understanding, and that is a rare and wonderful thing. To find someone who in such a brief time can become such a close and caring friend, without expecting anything in return. I value you, Julie. Have a great day. - Henry

July 14, 2000
Hi Henry:

I had a wonderful time with you last night and wish it could have been longer – much longer. We timed it right, and I got home just before Don. Even if I were later, I have a right to go out if I want to. He goes out whenever he wants to. Maybe in August, I will tell him I have to work on a Saturday, and we could spend a whole day together. Would you like that? Could you manage that? I doubt if I could do a whole weekend until I'm out of there, though. Then, you can come to my place for the weekend. I will unplug the phones, and lock the doors, so we won't be disturbed, and we could cuddle all weekend. I really like cuddling, especially with you. - Julie

July 14, 2000
Hi Julie:

I agree with you. I think the cuddling is actually the best part of a bunch of nice things when I'm with you. Yesterday was really nice. A Saturday would be great, regardless of what we do. - Henry

July 14, 2000
Hi Henry:

Maybe we can go to those oriental gardens on a Saturday. But, we have to leave plenty of time for cuddling, too. If we start with the cuddling, we'll never make it to the gardens. If we start with the gardens, we will wiz through them quickly, so we can have more time to cuddle. Do you see the problem? How would an engineer solve this problem, Henry? - Julie

July 14, 2000
Hi Julie:

We could find some bushes in the gardens and cuddle there. - Henry

July 14, 2000
Henry:

I see you are not going to be satisfied until we actually get arrested. – Julie

July 14, 2000

Hey Julie! You said you wanted some spice in your life. Live dangerously. It's more fun. Maybe they'll let me strip search you. - Henry

July 14, 2000

Henry, did you mean –
Turn around,
Bend Over,
Spread my cheeks….?

You realize that you have to search all the body cavities, don't you? Why don't you go over and take a wiff of the middle pillow on your office couch…that'll make you smile. – Julie

July 14, 2000
Julie:

I have had my face buried in that middle pillow on and off all day. You do know that you're bad. Almost as bad as I am. – Henry

July 17, 2000
Good Morning, Julie:

Just a note to say "hello". How was your weekend? Mine was super busy. My kid is arriving on Friday, and we were boiling the house all weekend. Any bites on your house, yet? Would you like to lay in bed with me and listen to the rain? - Henry

July 17, 2000
Hi Henry:

I can't think of anything I'd enjoy more than lying in bed with you and listening to the rain. My weekend was super busy also. On Saturday, we moved my mother to her new home. My brother and his wife came over and we rented a truck and filled it up. She still has lots of stuff that we couldn't fit in the truck. I'm going over there next Saturday to help her unpack and organize everything. I'll probably spend the night and go into her pool also. Sunday, I worked on refinishing a chair I've had for about twenty-five years. I enjoy making old furniture look beautiful again. Can you tell me what type of fertilizer you use for your orchids?

One couple did come to see the house on Sunday. But, nothing materialized. Is your house all disinfected and boiled out yet? I bet you can't wait to see your son again. I know I miss my son very much. It's always good when he visits.

So, when do we get to lie in the rain? I'll start to do a rain dance now. - Julie

July 17, 2000
Hello:

I hope that when you moved your Mom, you missed the rain. I also enjoy refinishing old furniture, and have redone all my bedroom furniture. In fact, my ivory art deco bedroom dresser started out life as a very gothic buffet cabinet. Next, I plan on reupholstering a chaise, also for the bedroom. I am looking for a suitable fabric.

I use Peters powder fertilizer 20-20-20, on my orchids, with very good results, as I get lots of new foliage and almost never ending blooms. I understand Osmocote is also good. It is time-released.

My house is all disinfected and boiled with the exception of my bedroom which I will do Wednesday, and the garage (yes, even the garage gets done). Then we will be done. My son plus his new family arrive at Newark Airport on Friday, but I won't be there to pick them up. Wilma will have to do it. I am taking a good friend to a Moody Blues concert at the Garden State Arts Center for his birthday Friday night. It should be fun. I have had the tickets since before my son even announced his wedding plans.

When the wedding is behind me and the smoke settles down, which should all happen by the second week of August, I will begin searching in earnest for a suitable house. Also, I will finally have some time to myself. Perhaps that would be a good time for us to lie in the rain. So, you would like to get laid in the rain...I mean lie in the rain?

- Henry

July 17, 2000
Henry:

It's amazing how many of the things you like to do that I also enjoy. Where do you buy the 20-20-20? Most stores don't carry it. And, yes, I'd love to get laid in the rain. **Big Grin** - Julie

July 17, 2000
Hi Julie:

I'll get you some fertilizer for your orchids. It'll be my treat. I am not surprised by the things we have in common any more, as they are just too many. So, does making love on the lawn in the warm summer rain, turn you on? - Henry

July 17, 2000
Henry:

Making love with you anywhere, rain or shine, turns me on. It's the person who you are making love with that matters, not where you do it, silly. - Julie

July 18, 2000
Good Morning, Julie:

Beautiful morning…the sun is shining, birds singing, there is a cool breeze, and the temperature is perfect. Too bad we have to work. What a day for the beach. How are you today, Julie? Would you like to start a new poem with me? - Henry

July 18, 2000
Good Morning Henry:

You always manage to put a smile on my face. Do you like the beach? I do. Whenever I go to Virginia Beach to visit my son, I always get a room with a balcony looking out on the ocean. Don and I used to rent a house on Long Beach Island for a week during the summer when the kids were younger. Did you ever do that? It's fun. I haven't done it in years. I'd like to spend a long weekend at the beach with you, Henry. Maybe some day we'll get a chance to do that.

Last night my family attacked me again. I asked Don to put out his cigarette because the smoke was in my face, and my daughter accused me of being mean to him. She said that I never ask her to put out her cigarettes, only him. Therefore, I am being mean. I didn't think the statement was worthy of a reply. I just left the kitchen and went to my room. I can't handle the nonsense any more. So, when I got your email this morning, my whole world brightened up. - Julie

July 18, 2000
Hi There Julie Babe:

I am a beach person for sure. We used to also go to Long Beach Island, but I haven't been there (even a drive through) in over twenty years. In fact, I haven't even been to the beach in at least ten years. I would like to spend some time at the beach with you, but I just heard that the nude beach at Sandy Hook has been closed, so I guess we'll just have to get naked in the hotel room. Maybe someday…

It is too bad that our kids feel the need to get involved in our marital difficulties. I don't feel that anyone who doesn't have a perfect life has any right to advise anyone else how to live. I find that the people who are the most free with advice are the ones who have a less than perfect track record in their own lives, and that includes our kids.

- Henry

July 19, 2000
Hi Julie:

It's good to hear that you are feeling better. The attack was from Wilma. It was the usual, either get under her control or get out. It is starting to really wear me down. At least the wedding is only a week or so away, and after that… - Henry

July 19, 2000
Hi Henry:

What do you mean by "get under her control, or get out"? That's pretty strong language. What kind of "control"? With the wedding so close, and all these people coming to stay at the house, I would imagine that she is pretty stressed out. She probably wants to make a good impression on her new daughter-in-law. Maybe she came on stronger than she meant to. I could be wrong, but I know that when I have a lot of stress going on in my life, I tend to be a bit frazzled.

If it gets really bad, just move out. You don't have to wait to buy a house – rent an apartment. I had a dream about you last night. In the dream you were making very passionate love to me. The dream was very vivid. I think it's a sign that I miss you. - Julie

July 20, 2000
Hi Julie:

Having sex dreams about me, ah! Great. Besides, why should I be the only one who has those dreams? I miss you too. Hope your day is going good. I have a real busy week coming up. My son arrives tomorrow night, the wedding is next weekend, and our septic just quit. It never rains, only pours. But, once the wedding is over, you and I just have to get together. I will see you for sure one night at the 'park and ride' during next week, if only just to say "hello" and give you a big sloppy wet kiss. The only question is where would you like me to give you that kiss (you get to pick the spot)?

- Henry

July 20, 2000
Hi Henry:

You got me smiling again. I really didn't think I'd see you again until some time after the wedding, and your houseguests return to Texas. So, don't worry about me. If we can get together, great, but I do understand what you are going through right now. I've been there and done that. Besides, you know we can never stop at just one sloppy kiss. Just drop me an email or call, every now and then, and let me know that you still think about me. Are you taking vacation days next week?

What a time to have a septic problem. You've got to stop eating those prunes. Smile. I hope you're able to get it fixed before your company arrives. Don is planning a golf junket Labor Day weekend. He will be gone at least two nights. Does that give you any interesting ideas? Grinning now. – Julie

July 21, 2000
Good Morning Hot Stuff:

I hope that I always can bring a smile to your face. If not a smile, a lecherous, lustful grin would be OK too. Not see you until after the wedding? How could I go almost three weeks without seeing you? Of course, I will meet your bus one night - at least one night.

Unfortunately I can only take one or perhaps two vacation days next week, but I do plan on spending as much time as I can with my kid and new family. And, although we now must bring a porta john trailer (with bathrooms, sinks, washing machine, carpeted, etc.) actually it's pretty nice. It looks like a Winnebargo and it's brand new. I am sure the day will still be fine, and the wedding will go just great. The septic guy can't rebuild the system for another two or three weeks. What a great time for this to happen. Besides, if I didn't look on the bright side, I would have thrown myself under a train years ago.

So, Don's going away Labor Day weekend. Yes, that does give me one idea. Can you guess what I'm thinking? If you can, then you are very very bad. - Henry

July 21, 2000
Hi Henry:

Last night on the bus going home, I wrote another poem for you. I like this one a lot because it's short and to the point. I think that by the time you're done with me, I will have written you enough poems to fill a book. I will entitle the book "Henry's Poems", and one hundred years from now, when they write about the greatest writers of the 21st century, and they come to my work, everyone will wonder "who" Henry was, or will they know?   I'm glad you can't go three weeks without seeing me. When we get it down to three hours, I'll be happy. Smile and be happy today – it's Friday! – Hot Stuff

Hot

I want to be hot, damp, and exhausted,
tangled in your arms and legs,
listening to the rain with you,
and thinking about how
your tongue keeps finding new ways
to arouse my
body.

July 21, 2000
Hi Julie:

Loved the poem. I wrote a quickie for you too this morning. It is attached.

- Henry

You

Your letters make me want to see you
Seeing you makes me want to touch you
Touching you makes me want to smell you
The smell of you makes me want to taste you
The taste of you makes me want to make love to you
Making love to you makes me want more of you.
But, more of you is never enough.

July 21, 2000

Henry, I love it. Enter it in a poetry contest. It's a winner. Whenever I find myself missing you, I'll take out that poem and read it. – H S

July 24, 2000
Hi Henry:

Just a note to let you know I was thinking about you. How was your weekend? Are you enjoying your visit with your son and his new wife and family? And, are you starting to feel like a Grandpa yet? How is the portable septic working out for you? Look at it this way – it'll be the wedding that everyone remembered. - Julie

July 24, 2000
Hi Julie:

My weekend was OK, thanks. My ten year old new grandson is calling me Grandpa. I don't know whether to kiss him or slap him. Went to a concert Friday night at the PNC Arts Center with my best friend Mike for his birthday. The old fart is fifty- three. We saw the Moody Blues. They were as good as ever - a great show. As you can imagine, things around here are nuts. People everywhere. I actually think of work as a hiding place – that's how many people are at the house. The portable septic gets delivered Friday. Until then, we pump ours out every two days. How was your weekend, Sweetie? I look forward to seeing you soon. I'll be in touch tomorrow. Sleep tight and think of me. I'll be dreaming of you. - Henry

July 24, 2000
Hi Henry:

I feel sorry for you, but I know that you are enjoying all those people too. Smile, Grandpa – grandchildren are the bonuses we get in life. Try to remember that as you wipe the drippy chocolate ice cream from the back seat of your car. I lay out in the sun for an hour on Saturday at my Mom's pool. But, I spent most of the day helping her organize her new house. I put up pictures, and put together her stereo for her. I actually got her believing that she doesn't need a "man" around the house. Then, Sunday I finished the chair I've been working on. It turned out darned good, even if I do say so myself. Miss you - Julie

July 25, 2000
Hi Babe:

I already had my share of drippy chocolate back seats from my own kids. Actually there are pluses to having grandchildren that I have discovered. Like spoiling them rotten, then giving them back full of sugar at ten PM. And, I get to watch Saturday morning cartoons - guilt free.

So, your Mom's all settled. That's good. Did you get any new tan lines at the pool for me to check out or trace with my tongue? Also, I wish I could see that chair. You will just have to show me how to reupholster as I would like to redo my chaise. I hope to see you soon, as I am missing you too. Have a great day Julie, keep the faith – Henry

(I wrote this poem for Henry, and sent it to him on August 1st.)

THE EFFECT YOU HAVE ON ME

Your eyes, full of lust and love,
drown my heart
with your sweet passion.

Your fingers stroke my secret places
coaxing me gently
into submission.

Your lips tell a story without words
allowing me to feel
your thoughts.

Your arms hold me close, wrapping
my body and soul
into your web of fire.

You lure me into
giving so much back, and

I give, because
I need to

as my body quakes feverishly
and the blood roars in my head.
I open myself to you,
exploding over and over.

Yet, I ache for
more.

August 1, 2000
Hi Julie:

I am sorry for my long silence. I couldn't even get close to my home computer as my house was full of kids and family until last night when I dropped them off at Newark airport. Today I am back at work, as I took most of Friday and yesterday off, and have just opened and read your poem. What can I say, I loved it and it flattered me so. You are a talented poet, Julie. Keep it up. And, you have talent in other areas too – Smile. I will call you if you are going to be around tomorrow, and see how you are doing. The wedding could not have been better. Unfortunately, I must close this now as I am using a customer's computer to send this, as I am at Pier Seven at the end of Atlantic Avenue in your old neighborhood, Brooklyn, and if I don't leave now, I will get stuck in that awful traffic. I did spend a little time on Canal Street today (lunch). I would like to go back when I have more time. Thirty years ago, I went to Chinatown all the time, but would you believe, haven't been back to just walk around and enjoy the shops, except for an occasional drive through, and one or two very brief stops, in over thirty years. Anyway, I've got to go. Thinking of you, and again, thank you for that wonderful poem. There are only a few people who care about how I feel and how I am doing. I am so glad you are one of them. Have a great day, Hot Stuff – Henry.

August 1, 2000
Henry:

You already know that compliments will get you everywhere! I'm glad you liked the poem. If it gave you even a little bit of plea-sure, then it was worth sending to you. For some reason, when-ever I am with you, afterwards, when I reflect on the encounter, I get poetic. No other person has ever had this sort of effect on me. Don't you think that's strange? In fact, just about everything about our relationship seems strange to me. Anyway, I'm glad that you are OK. I really was worried about you. I worry about the people I care about. I can't help it. And I do care about you – a lot. You sounded surprised that I would care. Why? Do you think that I would make love with a man I didn't care about? Don't you know me by now? Too bad you didn't have your lunch today in midtown, I would have joined you.

This weekend, I have been looking for, finding, and editing, some of my early poems to put into a book of poetry I've decided to publish. I found more than I realized I wrote. I have to limit the book to twenty pages. If you still are willing to allow me to use your drawing of the woman and the butterfly on the cover, please scan it into your computer, and email it to me. I would like to insert it into the cover page on the disk I am sending the publisher. By doing that I can save $175 on the cover artwork. If you changed your mind, I understand. I will give you the credit for the drawing. I will be using a few of the poems I wrote you. Don't worry; I'm not dedicating them to you in print. I'm not suicidal. But, you'll know, and I'll know. I know that using your drawing may be a little bit risky, but I think I can explain it away, and besides, your work is too good not to use. So, it's your call whether or not I use the drawing. The book is just going out to family and friends, and also a few poetry book contests.

One more thing – you don't need an appointment to call me. Please feel free to call me anytime during work, and on my cell, most days from five to six thirty, when I have it turned on. I miss you and want to see you soon. – H S

(He started calling me Hot Stuff. I began signing my emails to him "H S".)

August 2, 2000
Hi there Julie Love:

I am very pleased that you are collecting your poems to put together in a book. The examples that I have seen are something that should be shared, as they stir deep thoughts and emotions, and give the reader insight into the author. You have a good heart, Julie, and I consider myself lucky to share a piece of it with you. And, actually, I think I know you pretty well.

If I were not involved with you, and were giving you advice - after being told how our relationship is, if you were having it with someone else, there are some things I would ask you to consider. I would ask you to recognize that you are extremely vulnerable right now, and have not experienced any affection, or been shown much attention, for a long time. And, perhaps, those deprived and lonely feelings have more to do with how you feel, than the man you are involved with. I would caution you to protect your heart. Having said that, I miss you too, and for me, seeing you and being with you is an immense joy that I cannot easily explain. I like you too, Julie. You are fun, you are smart, and I enjoy your personality and mind. We are very much alike, you and I. And, we are experiencing much of the same thing on the home front.

I think we both recognize how lucky we are to have each other's support and concern. I too, would not make love with a woman I didn't care about, and I cared about you, long before I even met you. How lucky, that we also find each other sexually attractive – an added and unexpected bonus to our growing friendship.

You are welcome to use any artwork or poems of mine that you feel have merit. Even if you didn't have any direct input in a given piece, I assure you, that you were the inspiration for all of it, so you must share in its ownership, even if you never put a pen to paper, for without you, it would have never been written anyway. Of course, you can use my artwork. I am flattered that you think it that good. Also, I am honored that you would use my art to present your work. Thank you. I have attached a scan of it. If you have any problems downloading or opening it, let me know, and I will forward it to you in different formats. As far as giving me credit, I have no problem with it either way, and will leave that up to your discretion, just as long as I get a signed copy of the book from the author, and a night of wild sex.

I am going to try real hard to call you today, although it might be after you are on the bus. Hope to hear your voice later...see you, hot stuff – Henry

August 2, 2000
Hi Henry:

Thank you for the compliments on my poetry. So far, you have only seen my "passion" poems. I've written poetry about many different subjects. The book will give you even more insight into the real me. I don't think my poems are that great, but they're mine, and I get pleasure from them. And, isn't that what counts? I think I need to discuss "deprived and lonely" feelings with you for a minute or two. What are you cautioning me about? I'm confused by your statements. In one sentence you say you care about me, and in the next, you "caution" me. Should I not take you seriously? Is what we've developed together just a "passing fancy" to you?

Henry, it's not just because we're going through similar circumstances, or have reached similar crossroads in our somewhat parallel lives, or that we feel "empathy" for each other's emotions. It's much more than that. I'm not going to short change it and call it something *less* than what it is. Before I met you, I was starting to think that I was the only person in the world who gave unconditionally, without wanting something back from the people I cared about. But, you are that way too, and more. With you, pride and ambition are overweighed by love and generosity. You'd cut off your arm before you'd cause hurt to another person. And, cut them both off, before you'd cause a moment's pain to someone you cared for. In fact, there are so many similarities I see in you that I see in myself. It really is scary. You are such a rare and special person that I didn't think you existed. But, I understood exactly what you were like from the very beginning, in your emails, before I ever set eyes on you.

I picked you over more than forty others, to actually start up a friendship with and meet. If I was just lonely, I would have met at least ten, or more. But, I didn't, I narrowed it down to you. I'm not a teenager, although at times you make me feel like one. I've been around the block a few times, and know what and who I want in my life. I am not in love with love. I am not in such a vulnerable time in my life, that I don't know what I'm doing or feeling. I can see through the stars in my eyes, and I see what goes on in your eyes. I know exactly what I am doing and feeling. So do you. I find you so incredibly sexy – no other man comes close to you. I miss you when we are apart. I find your mind is one of the most complex and interesting minds I've come across in years. You actually "think" and question things. You don't just take what you see at face value. You look beneath the surface. So many people are happy just existing as couch potatoes, allowing the television to fill and control their existence. They live on the timetable of their favorite sitcoms. That's so sad, it's pitiful. To think that the majority of this great country is reduced to watching a square box in their living room, on any given night - scares me. But, you and I are not like that. Your imagination is so creative and alive. It's wonderful and I found you. Now, I know what the apple must have tasted like when Eve took the first forbidden bite - succulent, so unbearably delicious. Nothing else ever tasted so good, nor would be quite as satisfying again – and I am lost in the flavor of you.

Henry, when I am with you, I am so happy. It's more than "happy" – it's pure joy to be with you. You may think things will boil over, and the emotions we feel for each other will die. Or, at least you said something like that to me once. I don't agree. I'm old enough and smart enough to know that someone like you doesn't happen to me every day, and may never ever happen to me again. You are a gift that I will cherish for as long as you let me. I'll take you any way I can get you, on any terms, even stark naked and starting from scratch. You told me once to follow my instincts. My instincts tell me that I am in love with you. Does that scare you? Is this uncharted territory for you? It is for me. I don't love easily. And, now that I've lowered the shields, and it took every ounce of courage I had to say that, did I make a mistake to tell you? I don't think so, because if you're just playing with me, you'll end it. If not, at least you'll know how I feel. I can live with disappointment. I can't live with someone telling me something is not what it is. That would be degrading my feelings.

As far as my book goes, I do want to use the picture. When you see the poem that is on the cover, you'll understand why. I need it to be in JPEG format.

Smile...I bet you can't figure out how to answer this one, Einstein. – H S

August 2, 2000
Hi Julie:

First, I am not scared off. I knew very well what you were beginning to feel. As your friend, not as your lover, I wanted you to reflect on those feelings. You see, I do care about you, and your welfare, so I must put on the "friend" hat, and ask you to reflect every once in a while, so that at least you are sure, and recognize what is happening, and then decide if that is where you want to go, and what your motivations are. The last thing in the world I want is to bring any more negativity or downside to your life, even inadvertently. I also want to protect my own heart from more pain. I know you are an adult and know what is up, but there are times in our lives that we are not adult, because our heart begins to rule. There is an old Arab saying: "when the stomach speaks, you forget your brain, when the brain speaks, you forget your heart, and when your heart speaks, and you forget everything." My comments to you had nothing to do with our "romantic" relationship. It had to do with that part of our relationship that is platonic and unbiased – a good friend's advice. I still believe that if I were only your friend, hearing how you felt, I would advise you to be cautious, because I know you have been so unhappy for so long, and I care about what happens to you. Just because I am the man involved, I still have a responsibility to you as a friend, to protect you from everything that I can, including me. I have no intention whatsoever, of hurting you, leading you on, etc. I just wanted you to reflect and be sure, that's all, because in the long run, the friendship will endure. You can trust me to give you an unbiased appraisal, even if it hurts me personally. This is not just a fling to me. I am also so very happy and carefree around you. I am happy to be with you whenever we can be together, because even limited Julie, is better than no Julie at all. I will call you later, but I wanted you to read this first. I hope it makes more sense to you than it does to me. – Henry

August 3, 2000
Dear Henry:

I know you're busy and don't really have time for this, so am I. But I think it's important enough to make the time. Last night I didn't get much sleep. Unanswered questions kept wandering through my mind. Our eight-minute phone call yesterday didn't begin to cover all I wanted and needed to say to you. How does anyone talk intimately with someone you care about while riding on a crowded bus? You just don't.

The first time you tell someone you love them; you should say it in person, face to face. I guess I shortchanged you there. I'm sorry I told you in a cold piece of email about my feelings, but when we're together, sometimes my tongue gets all tangled up, and I can't say what I want to say. You most likely weren't ready to hear it anyway. But, your email to me yesterday made me so angry; I just blurted it out, along with all the rest of what I said. I was furious with you when I wrote that, because you were trying to tell me things, and acted as if I didn't think about them and ponder effects, etc. You were trying to tell me that what I think I feel is something else. I didn't like that. Are you trying to convince yourself that what you feel for me is just your "vulnerability" reaching out to someone? Empathy? Do you feel this way about the other women you go out with? Look, this wasn't supposed to happen. I had my life all planned out. I was supposed to sell my house, have a nice clean separation, buy my own place, decorate it, get my divorce, finish my novel, then, and only then, think about finding someone to grow old with. That was the plan. But, you had to answer my email. Didn't you? You had to meet me, didn't you? You couldn't just pass me by, could you? I think I fell in love with you the very first day I met you, when you started opening up your mind to me, and I discovered your wonderful imagination, and there's something in your eyes, I don't know how to explain it. Anyway, I tried to fight these feelings. I really did. You know I did. So what do you want me to do? Here is the way I think you would approach the problem. I think I have two choices here, first, I could put you on the back burner until I do all those other things and stick to the plan, and if I'm lucky, I could take up with you again in two or three years, or secondly, I could follow my heart, and see where it leads, and modify the plan. Of course, I can call it quits, and then I go back to the original plan without you on the back burner. Is that logical enough for you?

No matter what happens, know this: I care deeply for you, and that's not going to change. I will never give you any pain or hurt you in any way, shape, or form. I care about you too much. Are you so insecure with yourself, that you think I couldn't love you? Henry, take a look at yourself in the mirror - many women would want you. I will never ask you for anything, I will make no demands on you, and expect no commitments or promises. I'll see you on any terms you want. If you want me to see other men, I will. I think it's a waste of time, but if it makes you feel any better, that I've had enough experience to make an "educated" decision, then I will. You mentioned something about "using" me. I didn't quite understand what you meant by that. Our spouses are the users. Not us. Why do you think they cling to us? Love? I don't think so. Both of us give ten times more into our marriages than we get back. Don is the one who is using me. Do you have any idea how my six figure salary enhances his lifestyle? When he walks away from this marriage, he will have a much stronger net worth figure than he ever could have had on his own…thanks to me and my working for the past twenty years and investing our money wisely. He doesn't want to loose that, and all the other things I do for him. The way I look at it, I can put out the garbage pails myself. I'm tired of being used. You couldn't use me, because when I'm with you, I get as much as I take. I never had that before, and I don't want to loose it. So, Henry, what do you want from me?

If you still want to see me on Monday night, I'd like for us to have dinner together, if that's OK with you. I find that when we are in public places, we can keep our hands off each other long enough to have some conversation. I know that if we are alone together, all we will do is make love and cuddle, and the questions go right out of my mind. I really need to have some questions that have been puzzling me, answered. I want to know more about your situation at home. If you'd rather not tell me anything, then that's OK also. But, I think if I knew, I would understand better what you are going through, and how I can help you as a friend. It seems that Wilma has you on a very short leash. Why do you allow that? Why is moving out predicated on buying a house? Is it a financial issue? Maybe I can help. What are all these "attacks" about? Why don't you just get an apartment, and buy a house later on? How are you able to live with someone after you've told them you are leaving? I find it very difficult and uncomfortable, myself. I don't have a choice in my situation. The monthly nut on this house doesn't allow me the luxury of moving out like I did the last time I left Don, otherwise, I would have left already. But, I've told him that I will be seeing other people while we wait for the house to sell. I'm so tired of sitting home on Saturday nights and watching him drink beer in front of the television. I want to go out and get away from him as much as possible.

Well, Henry, now I've gotten everything off my chest. Maybe I'll sleep tonight. How you deal with what I said is anybody's guess. - H S

PS: I love the drawing. She's so beautiful. I've inserted it into the cover page of the book. I am emailing you the entire first draft. It's almost finished - just some touching up and editing remains. Your acknowledgement is on page two. I think you will especially feel an affinity with a poem I wrote years ago called, "The Sunshine of Freedom". It won a prize, and made me think I was a poet. You might also feel some emotion when reading the poem "Breaking Up". As far as the cover goes, if you could think of a way to make it better, please let me know. After all, you are the artist. I wanted to make the picture the whole page and impose the text onto it in white, but I didn't know how to do that on the computer. Also, I think the butterfly needs to be a stronger shade of yellow since it will be the only color on the page. I don't know how to do that either. Maybe the publisher can do it. Do you think so little of your work that it's only worth <u>one</u> night of wild sex? I would have given you at least ten for it! Thanks again, and enjoy the book, even if it is only the first draft.

August 3, 2000
Hi Hot Stuff:

As far as the picture goes, I can enhance it with my computer. First, I will increase the contrast so the black is really black, then using "Picture it Express" which is a utulity program in Windows '98, I can resize and recolor it, no sweat. I am truly honored that you chose it to present your work. As far as you offering ten nights of wild sex for it – Ok, but one night with me, baby, is worth ten nights with someone else. Smile. I had a terrible night last night, as my wife chose it for her regular "attack Henry" night. But, it did strengthen my resolve to be on my own soon.

Your letter was interesting. I truly didn't want to anger you in my letter to you. It was written with a sense of caring. So, please look at what I was saying, not what I said. I care about your welfare, your emotions, and you as a person. I don't like to see friends hurt, so I only wanted to point out the possibility that your feelings were influenced by your situation. I did not want to imply anything negative. We both have hearts that have been broken by long suffering marriages, and are both looking for someone that we know will fill that missing piece of our souls. We are lucky that we discovered each other, but I would like you to be sure of your motives, that's all. You are apparently more mature than I, and know your own mind better than most. But, you are talking about changing your life plan because of me, and that scares me, as I don't have my own act together yet, and the responsibility of effecting someone else's life to such a degree, at this time, is unsettling, as I want to do the right thing towards you, and I am not sure if I am able to do that, yet. Give yourself time to really get to know me. I am not perfect, and am a constant disappointment to myself. I don't want to end up a disappointment to you.

What I want from our relationship is to care enough about the other person to make their welfare at least as important as our own. If we do that, as we have done so far, then our relationship will be a beautiful thing, and something that neither one of us has experienced for a very long time. I want to be in your company, as I enjoy it very much. You are a vacation from a very unhappy situation, and are very dear to me. Please, don't be angry any more. I meant no harm, but only good for you. I will meet you for dinner, if you want, on Monday, but I would like some cuddle time, if you are still so inclined. (I'll behave.) It is very hard to put into words all the things I want to say to you, and all the things I feel. All I can tell you, is that being the custodian of someone's deep feelings is an awesome responsibility, because when someone hands you their heart, what they are doing is handing you a potent weapon against them. Thank you for having that much trust in me. I know what is in my heart, and you have to trust what is there. So, Julie, when you give your heart, be sure it's to the right person, and for the right reasons. That's all my letter said, and I still think that's good advice.

I would very much like to spend more time with you, in and out of the bedroom, and very soon that will be possible, as I am about to slip my leash. And, incidentally, I appreciate the offer of possible financial help, but I will never do that. You see, I know you want to help me, but I can only let you help just so far. If you have one major flaw, it is that you are a very good, kind, and giving, person. That kind of person sets themselves up to be hurt. I will never intentionally hurt you, but your good heart makes you a vulnerable person, even if you do sometimes act tough. I know what is inside of you, and I suspect that when you are alone, you cry for yourself often. Anyway, please don't think harshly of me for just trying to protect your heart.

If you have any questions you want to ask me on Monday, no problem, I have no secrets from you, and will answer any questions you have as honestly, and as clearly, as I am able. I am really looking forward to seeing you. Julie, be at peace – Henry

August 4, 2000
Good Morning, Hot Stuff:

I hope that you are OK this morning. Still angry? I hope not. I will only be here at work until 1:00 PM. After that, I won't have access to a computer until late Sunday night, but will be in touch then, so you can catch up with me on Monday morning. I am looking forward to our having some time to talk. We seldom have that opportunity. It will be nice. But, this time when we are at the table, I would prefer to sit across from you, so I can look into your eyes more easily. Because your eyes say it all – they always did. At least since the childhood fever that made them turn green. Maybe if I fire you up enough, they will change again. Smile – Henry

August 4, 2000
Hi Henry:

Winston Churchill had nothing on you! Henry, you are a great diplomat. Smile. I'm not angry any more, and you know I'm not. I blow off steam quickly, then go on. I have to see if I've got this straight, though. Now, you want me to look for your imperfections, huh? Henry, do you think I care if you remember to put the cap back on the toothpaste tube, or put the toilet seat down after you pee? Wilma may care about such nonsense, but that kind of stuff doesn't bother me. Besides, any man who has had thirty years of boot camp, can't be that bad, can he? Laugh!

Henry, I can see that you have a lot of mending to do. You have a very low opinion of yourself, and there is no basis that I can see for that lack of confidence. If you continue to hang out with me, I will make you feel like you can conquer the world, Ceasar! You can, you know. You really can.

Thank you for saying that you think that our relationship is a "beautiful" thing. I know it is. I also know that you have my best interests at heart. I can see that you are not used to sincerity and honesty from women. Maybe that's because there aren't many women who speak freely of their feelings as I do. You've given me good advice and made me see things in three dimensions. I thank you for that. I disagree with you on one piece of advice you gave me. I don't and never will consider my being kind and generous as a "fault". On the contrary. I may set myself up to be hurt, because of it, I agree there, but the positives outweigh the negatives. I will give you an example:

When my Dad had the stroke and I saw that my Mom could not cope with the situation, I had this house I'm living in now built. I sold my other house, and moved them in with me. I hired a nurse twenty-four hours a day, seven days a week, to care for my Dad. It was the only solution to keep him out of a nursing home, as I did not want him to suffer the abuses of such a place. He didn't deserve that. Though my parents have some money, this was a huge expense for me, both financially, and in my life. No sooner is my Dad buried, my Mom decides she wants to live in her own place again. That hurt. But, nonetheless, I helped her make the move. Now, I'm sitting in a home I don't want, and am in a situation I'd rather not be in. Was it worth it? YES. The two and a half years I had living with my Dad, were the closest years I'd ever had with him in my life. I discovered so much about myself during that time with him. I would do it again in a heartbeat. So, you see Henry, generosity is not a fault. It's all in the way you look at things. And, if I'm vulnerable in some ways, I'm strong in others. But, you are wrong about one thing – I don't cry for myself very often. You really don't have to worry about me.

And, another thing, Henry, I didn't hand you a potent weapon you could use against me. I gave you the most beautiful gift I had to give. You can't help but cherish something like that. I miss you too, and can't wait to see you again. – H S

PS: Here's a poem to make you laugh:

SIXTY-NINE
My body shivered,
when I felt your tongue in my ear,
never expecting such fervor
from an engineer.

Feeling your fingers,
my skin comes aflame.
Desire shot through me,
and I cried out your name.

My hand wanders down
your response to hold.
You swell even more
as my fingers cajole.

Feelings shine from your eyes
as my mouth grazes down.
My tongue flicks the ridge
between the shaft and the crown.

I feel it grow,
exploding arousal.
Taking it deep into my throat
I almost swallow.

Then, your cock throbs
And, you beg for mercy
I continue to suck, as if
it were a Hershey. J (I wanted to find something to rhyme with
"mercy")

Not able to handle
what your mouth does to me
My body convulses,
and I plead, "Fuck me!"

You look up and smile
hunger fills your eyes
And you move to position
thighs upon thighs.

Feeling your need
as you slide in my heat,
my legs wrap around you
and I press down with my feet.

With each thrust you bring me
higher and higher
then you ease, with a tease
prolonging my desire.

Inner muscles urge you
to ride me hard,
as you build momentum
and, come off guard.

Over the edge
faster movements increase
bringing us ecstasy
with one final release.

August 4, 2000
Hi Hot Stuff:

You really are Hot Stuff. That sexy poem was not only very good in a literary sense, it also gave me a heck of a boner. So, you want to be sexy today, do you? OK.

There you are, standing, facing the mirror, naked, and breathless, and I stand behind you, fondling your breasts and licking your ears and the back of your neck. You feel juices beginning to stir deep within you. Your nipples become ridged and sensitive beneath my fingers, and you push back against my stiff arousal. You feel my passion pushing hard. You watch, breathing heavily, as my hand caresses your body on it's way to your thighs, and you quiver involuntarily with anticipation, because you know what I am going to do. My fingers stroke your wet soft outer lips, coaxing them to open to reveal your trigger. You feel your knees going weak as I roll your love bud between my fingers. You reach back to fondle my hard and waiting shaft. You push back with your palms against the wall to support yourself as I pull your hips towards me and slide into your waiting wetness from behind. You are fascinated, and cannot pull your eyes away from the mirror, watching every thrust of my hips. Watching me thrust in and out of you, you come for the first time. Rivers of love juice run down over me, down your legs, and onto the carpet. You pump your hips faster and faster, coming a second and third time, in rapid succession. Each time stronger, juicier.

I turn you around to face me, and slip my tongue deep into your mouth, exploring your tongue, as my hands fondle and caress your aroused body now trembling beneath my passionate embrace.

"Fuck me, fuck me hard." You whisper, as you pull me towards the bed. The desire within you, makes you loose control, and you push me down on the bed and straddling me begin to impale yourself onto my love tool. I feel your fluid cascade around my loins, warm, sexy, pungent. I roll you off, and hold your knees high in the air, as I plunge my tongue into your waiting throbbing passion. You instantly come, as you feel my tongue exploring you, fast, slow, hard, and gentle. As my tongue begins to work overtime, I slide a finger into you, pumping to the rhythmn of my tongue. The bed is soaking wet, and yet you continue to come again and again, as my tongue works that magic that only a tongue can do. Your back aches and you convulse in the throws of deep abandonment to passion. You must taste me. You begin sucking my stiff shaft. Running your tongue around the rim, then nibbling, licking. Your hand caresses my balls, as you feel the head swell in your mouth. You can faintly taste a salty sample of what is building inside me.

I pull out from between your lips and slide between your ample breasts, as you hold them together. I pump and thrust between them. I am beginning to breath heavier. You grab my hips and draw me closer, licking the end of my shaft, sucking on the head. You take me in your hand, and begin pumping me slowly at first, then faster and faster - Short strokes concentrating on the rim. You can feel me build. "Oh, my God!" I yell, and you wrap your lips around the head as your mouth coaxes a mammoth release. I French kiss you and can still taste my passion in your mouth, and you taste yours in mine. Our tongues and tastes mingle as one as I slip into you again. With you, I know no limits to my desire. We ride that crest until you feel my entire body stiffen, as I come deep inside you. Your inner muscles suck on my shaft, closing around, and holding on, you come with me. You roll over on top of me looking down into my face.

"How was that?" You ask. I pull your face down to mine and gently kiss your lips and eyelids. You have your answer. – Henry

August 4, 2000
Henry:

Fuck me now, fuck me deep, I want the kind that makes me weep! I'm suddenly no longer interested in dinner Monday night. How do you expect me to do my work after reading your last email? It's bad enough that my pantyhose are dripping wet. Smile. Henry, if you were here this very instant I'd fuck your brains out! – H S

August 4, 2000

Julie, If you prefer to skip dinner on Monday, I still want to eat...you. And, you can use me as a lollipop any time you want. Hope you have a great evening, my internet passion pit. - Henry

August 7, 2000
Hi There Hot Stuff:

So, what do you have planned for tonight? Dinner? A short talk? A long talk? A cuddle in my car? Getting naked in my office? Ladies' choice...Gee! I would just love to suck on those nipples of yours tonight and feel your bare breasts against my hairy chest regardless of what else we do. But, as I said, it's ladies' choice, Sweetie. See you later. - Your little buddy, Henry

August 7, 2000
Hello:

After reading your email of Friday only 47,673 times this weekend, I'm not hungry for dinner. My plans for tonight lend themselves more toward going to your office for some hot and heavy sex. I do want to have a chat, so I am going to hold you to your word about being "good"...Smile. We will talk while we cuddle – I hope. - H S

PS: Did you have a bowl of Wheaties for lunch today?

August 7, 2000
Julie:

Now, my hot little Italian Babe, I will pick you up at the bus stop, and we can come up here to my office. It will give us a quiet place to talk, and if you want, all we have to do is talk. But, if you would like, I will be happy to lick whereever it would give you the most pleasure. I was serious about feeling your breasts against my chest. I would really like that and miss it a great deal. It will be up to you how much more happens, if anything, but I just gotta have dem boobs, babe... - Henry

August 7, 2000

Ok Henry, you say what we do tonight will be up to me, but why do I feel that it is more up to you, and that you have complete control over the situation? The "breast/chest" thing is a definate. What happens after that will depend on how adept you are at nibbling my ear...Grin... - H S

August 7, 2000

Well, I'm just about the best ear nibbler in the world. So, get that little pink thing ready to receive my exploring tongue. You'll be moaning with delight tonight Sweetie, as my lips suck in that little pink bud, and my tongue flicks it into orgasm. - Henry

August 7, 2000

Henry, did I ever tell you that you have a one track mind? When you promised to be good, I didn't know you meant that good. We'll have to leave the windows open all night, just to air out the scent of our lovemaking! Somehow, I think I should have stuck to the dinner plan. The "food" dinner that is... - H S

CHAPTER NINE

That night, I met Henry at the bus stop, as planned. We went to his office to be alone together, made wonderful passionate love, and for a few hours, we were able to block out the rest of the world and the stress in our lives. When I got off the bus, he was there patiently waiting for me, and it was like we couldn't wait to be inside each other's arms. There seemed to be this underlying hunger inside each of us to be with the other, a hunger greater than the will to defy it. We were drawn together, and all we could think about was satisfying this craving urge we each had, with all our consciousness focused on this need we had to feed off each other. The sex was incredible, but even better, was the cuddling, and feeling each other's body, chest to chest, naked, warm, and up close, yet not able to get close enough, thinking that each moment was a gift, and knowing that we may never get this chance again.

After the loving, we lay there together, entwined in each other's arms and legs, on the leather sofa in his office, talking about our lives and feelings in the most intimate way. I was amazed at how much he seemed to understand me, and how logical and objective he could be with his comments. He empathized with my sadness, and I with his. It was obvious to both of us that we were in love, and each time we were together, we fell deeper and deeper. We were surprised and shaken by the enormity of such an extraordinary intimacy that either of us had ever known, and it was as if our souls merged to become one entity. But, I knew that he was very confused about his marriage, and what he still felt for his wife. I also knew that his feelings for me were confusing him even more. I didn't want to do this to him, and I couldn't help it.

August 8, 2000
Hi Henry:

I'm very busy today. I just wanted to make sure that you didn't have any problems last night when you got home, and to let you know that I'm thinking about you.   - H S

August 8, 2000
Hi There Julie:

Wilma was waiting, or should I say, lying in wait for me, when I got home last night. We had a very long talk, and I didn't get to bed until three AM, so I'm tired. She tells me now that after a year and a half of torturing me, and telling me she wants a divorce; she has decided that she wants a reconciliation. Now, I am more confused than ever. I have so many mixed emotions.

Thank you for a wonderful evening. Time with you is about the only stress-free time I have in my life. I will never look at that couch the same way again. - Henry

August 8, 2000
Hi Henry:

I think she wants to reconcile, because she feels that she is loosing you. I could be very selfish and tell you that you'd be crazy to do it, because I know from experience that people don't change. They are what they are, but on the other hand, it may be what you really want deep inside your heart. Maybe I should stay away from you for a while, until you sort out your heart. I don't want to influence you to do something you'll regret later on. Listen to your heart, Henry, and don't reconcile for the wrong reasons, as I did in 1994. I'm not going to contact you again, unless you contact me. I think you need some time. Just don't make "finances" a reason to stay with her. Stay, because you love her enough to accept her as she is. Remember, I'm here and thinking of you. There's a whole world of opportunity for you outside of that marriage. When you make your decision, either way, let me know what you decide to do. I think I may loose you, and that makes me sad, but if it's the right thing for you, then when I get over the sadness, I'll be happy for you, and I'll never regret a single moment I spent with you. - H S

PS: I emailed my book of poetry off to the publisher this morning. I'll send you a copy when it's printed. Thanks again for the picture.

August 8, 2000

Julie, you are probably one of the very few people in my life that actually cares enough about me to put my feelings before their own needs and feelings. I believe you love me, because of your reaction to that email, more than any other reason. Julie, you are my friend, my lover, and I owe you so very much. I will never turn my back on you. You are a wonderful warm human being, but I think you are right in one regard. I am confused, and need to think things through. I wish I was all grown up like you. I will be in touch. I do care for you very much, but I also do need some time to think. – Henry

August 8, 2000
Henry:

You are right, in that I do love you, more than you know, but you are wrong in that I am not so grown up...take all the time you need – you are worth the wait. – H S

August 8, 2000

Julie, you know that I love you too, and that's what's so confusing for me. Thank you for being the way you are. - Henry

August 8, 2000
Henry:

I had to write you one last letter. I promise that after this, you won't hear from me again. I mean it this time. But, I wouldn't be able to sleep, if I didn't say these things. I feel that I left too much unsaid. I've got a knot of emotion clogging my throat, as I try to blink back the tears that threaten to fall, because I know the last emails I had from you were "goodbye", and I feel the pain of it. And being the person that I am, I can't just walk away without telling you some things. Things I saw in you and observations I made, although I warn you that they may not be too objective.

I always knew – from the very beginning, that this friendship was dangerous. I mean, you belonged to another woman. She had so much of you, for so long. You were her other son. And you liked and hated it at the same time. You knew there was a whole other world out there, and you reached out to grab it. For twenty years you were unhappy, and now she suddenly gets a *whim* that she wants to reconcile, and you are going to throw away the rest of your life, keep the chains around your neck, and live on an allowance for the next 25 years, it you don't commit suicide first, although I think sometimes people commit suicide even though they are still alive. I know because I did in 1994. And, I'm not saying this because I want you, and I do, I'm saying it because I care enough about you to try and make you understand what you're doing to yourself.

You came to me, pursued me, and bonded with me in the most intimate way a man and woman could be, and all the time, warning me, while you made me fall in love with you. And, maybe I should have listened to your warnings, but I couldn't, because all the wonderful things I've told you about yourself pulled me closer towards you. Now, I feel like my happiness rests on her whims. She wanted you to leave, so you were going to leave, now she wants to reconcile, so you will do that. Just think of all the money you will save on a divorce lawyer while you bury yourself. I'm sorry if I'm sarcastic. But, you couldn't get your car out this summer because it wasn't in the "budget", and she charged over $20,000 at J.C. Penny. Is that "love", Henry? Somehow I don't get it. Ask Don if there was anything he ever needed for his car that he wasn't able to buy whenever he wanted it. Henry, I make $120,000 a year, and that's just the salary. I have enough money to support both of us, with some to spare. I'm selling a half million dollar home. Where do you think you'd be better off financially? When you talked about your finances you sounded a bit worried. Please don't do it because you feel she'll strip you financially. Whether it's me, or someone else, most women have a lot more in assets than you think. Can you honestly say that she wants what's best for YOU? Or, does she just want to make sure that her little kingdom stays in tact? I say kingdom, because from the way you described her, she is a king, and you are the loyal subject who pays the taxes.

When I met you, you were so unhappy. You found something in me, and I in you, and we bonded. And, I don't care what you say; I know that you were happy every minute you spent with me. I probably never should have told you how I felt, because I know it scared you. But, you know what - it scares me too...especially, tonight when I feel so lost. I'm not blaming you. You are doing what it is you feel you have to do. Just don't do penance because you feel guilty for wanting to have a life; because you want to draw; because you want to listen to opera and go to museums; because you want to cuddle and hold a woman who cares about you. Whatever you do, do it for the RIGHT reasons. Henry, don't throw away the most beautiful thing that has happened to your life in a long time. That's all I've got to say, now you really won't hear from me again, until I hear from you. - H S

August 9, 2000
Hi Julie:

I read your letter, and it made me cry last night. It is making me cry as I write this to you. I have hurt you, but don't be hurt. Those letters were not "good bye". Please, don't cut yourself off from me for my sake. Do it only if you need to for your own sake. That, I would understand. You are so right in all you say. I know that Wilma is manipulating me, but I am not sure why. Is it love that makes her do this, to keep me, or is it a fear of being alone, or the need to keep all of her "stuff". I am not really sure. There are things that I am sure of. I am on a fifty/fifty split in my life – at a true crossroads. That crossroad wouldn't be there if it were not for you. You have given my life a choice. A choice I didn't have before. You have shown me that there is still a chance for me for true love. Please, don't think for one minute that it has come down to a choice between you and Wilma, because that's not it. The choice is a life choice, and one that I have to think through. I do still want you to see me, but for the sake of your heart and feelings, I will leave that up to you. If you do still want to see me, it will be on your terms. As a friend and confident, or as a kissing friend, either way, I can't just let you go. I want you as my close and dear friend, in any capacity, for the rest of my life, if you will have me. I can't go through my life without your warmth, your honesty, and your uncompromising friendship. You have inspired me to think in a way that I never did before. With you, I have always been happy. I still desire you more than any other woman I have ever met, but will forgo any romantic relationship with you, if I could only keep you as my close dear friend. We are so much alike, you and I, that even though I find it so very difficult to explain myself, I feel you know what is going on in my head, probably better than I.

I was resigned to the fact that Wilma wanted a divorce. You are right. She has always called the shots, and still is calling them. I know that. But, Julie, this is a thirty year investment in time and life, and this truly is the last shot. If I don't give her a chance to show me that she means what she says, I will never be happy, if I leave. This is the test that will give me a clear conscience, if I leave. And, I swear to you, that if she doesn't do the right thing by me, I will leave, and not look back, and will not give her another shot at me. I am not choosing between you and Wilma, so don't you ever think that you are my second choice, because you are not. What I am doing is following my conscience to do the right thing, and I was raised to believe that the right thing is to play it out to the end, and make absolutely sure that there is really no hope, before ending a thirty year marriage. You have been there, so you know how hard it is to cut that one last string. Well Julie, this is that one last string for me, and I realize that more people than just me will be affected by what happens in my life. I am afraid - afraid of losing my children; afraid of the future; afraid of taking the wrong direction. I know that I could be happy with you. And, I know that this doesn't make a whole lot of sense, but I just feel I need this one last look at my life, because I truly don't know what to do. I don't even know what to think. I am so very confused and so very unhappy. If I leave Wilma, it is true, that I may have you, but I will be loosing so much that those thirty years took to build. On the other hand, I can't loose you after finding so rare and beautiful a person, and friend. And, I can't loose the dream of the future, so full of freedom and growth that I will no longer have. Deep inside, I want to go, but fear of something, I am not sure what, keeps me there. I am not the man who you think I am. I am a child and a coward, who can't make up his mind. I guess I just don't want to accept the consequences of my own actions. I am not very happy with myself right now, because I see myself loosing out, no matter what road I may take, and it scares me so much.

I know very well, that between us, there is enough money for me to come out of this smelling like a rose. I could live off you, and escape, but finances are not what is keeping me there. I make more than $100,000 a year myself. I won't have much left after the bills are paid, but my paycheck is good, and I'll catch up. If I decide to go, then I don't really care if I live in a cardboard box under a bridge, I will leave. And Julie, do you really think that I would take money from you? It has nothing to do with false pride. I just would never ever take money from you, because if we were together, I would want you to know without question, that I was with you because I wanted you, and not your money, or the security that you could offer me. In matters of the heart, money only complicates things.

Bottom line, Julie, is that what started out as just fun for you and I has become something of beauty and value, and that has complicated things in my life very much. I wish that I was just using you, and you were just a toy. Then my choice would be clear, fore I wouldn't give a damn about how you felt, so if Julie gets hurts, so what. But, that is not the way it is. I care for you, Julie. And, I care very much if you are hurting. I can't loose you, as my friend. I just can't. I still want to see you, if you will have me. I will see you in any capacity you want. We don't have to have a physical relationship. I need you in my life in any way I can have you. If you don't want to see me, to protect your own feelings, then I would understand that, and will not bother you again. But, I will miss you so much. Your gentleness, your compassion, and your empathy - these are things that I will not see again from anyone else in my lifetime. This I know for sure. Why did we have to meet now? Why did you have to be who and what you are? Julie, don't you see that I love you too, but I have to do this. If it is in my fate to be out of this marriage, then I must do this to cut the final cord, or I could never find true freedom and happiness. I must give her, me, and this marriage that has lasted for so long, this one last chance. In my heart, I don't think that she will change, but I must be sure.

- Your devoted friend, Henry

August 9, 2000
Henry:

I have been crying inside since 3:13 yesterday afternoon when I received your email, telling me that, "she wants to reconcile". I cry because I see that you are being manipulated by a cruel and selfish woman. You, who are so kind and gentle, and you are a victim of vindictiveness. You say she is your "best" friend, yet you claim she tortured you for the past year and a half. Henry, I don't have any *friends* that torture me. Wake up and smell the roses. Look at your life. You live in a Victorian decorated house that <u>you</u> paid for, have a choker chain around your neck, and live on an allowance. What's wrong with this picture, Henry? You said yourself that if it weren't for your sons, you would have left her a very long time ago. You've invested 30 years in a dream that somehow became dysfunctional. Are you going to throw another 10 or 15 years into this dysfunctional dream? People don't change, and you've been unhappy long before she said she wanted a divorce. I'm going to quote from a letter you wrote to me – "on your deathbed, you'll look at your life, and will you feel sad for the lost opportunities?" That's something how it went. This isn't about me and you. This is about you and your marriage. And, maybe I have no right to say this, but I think that caring about you, gives me some rights. I would never say something to hurt you, or try to make you do something that will hurt you. It's just that I see so much inside of you that yearns for freedom. Read my poem the "Sunshine of Freedom", even though it's about society, it could be you. You can stay, and always dream about freedom, or you can be free. It's as simple as packing a bag and walking out the door. Why don't you tell her that you want to get an apartment and live on your own for a while? Maintain the payments on the house, and live by yourself for a while. See if you miss her. If you do, you can always go back. But if not, after 18 months, if you are still separated, go for a no-fault divorce. During that 18 month period, I will have, for sure, sold my house, and I will get a temporary apartment myself, until I find a house to buy. If it turns out that we want to live together, when I buy the house, you can move in. If you want to, if you do move in with me, you can pay something towards the expenses if it'll make you feel better, but I would never ask you to. As much as she says she won't trust my judgement, she will agree to you moving out. And, if you decide you want to go back, she will take you back, also. She really doesn't have a choice, Henry. During that time period, you will find yourself. You need that time. Right now you are too close to the situation to make a decision, and I'm afraid you will make the wrong decision.

You've already played it out to the end, Henry. You just don't want to face it. Moving out isn't cutting a string, it's giving both of you some desperately needed breathing room. You can't have me, and live with her. It doesn't work that way. She would never tolerate it, and I need more of you than I would ever get. Look at it this way; if you were to meet her today, knowing the way she is, would you even consider having a "love" relationship with her? If you can answer "yes" to that, then I'm missing something, and I'm all wrong. I can't be just a friend to you, Henry. I want a "love" relationship with you. I want to grow old with you. I'm sorry, but that's what I want. Maybe we will see each other over the next 18 months, and decide that possibly, we are not what we seem to be to each other. I don't think this will happen, we're both too pragmatic for that, but if it did, you still will have kept the door open to go back to Wilma. You are NOT a child or a coward. Decisions like the one you are making are not easy ones to make. Don't be so hard on yourself, and you don't have to decide anything right away. You need to live on your own, desperately. I can see that. Don't short change yourself.

Here's a poem I started to write from yesterday's emotional trauma:

CONFUSION

I don't understand why loving me confuses you.
You recognize that you love me,
but instead of that being a joyous and wondrous

feeling, it is tarnished by perplexity.
Where is the logic in that?
How could we have been as close as we were,
and not understand each other?
I wasn't prepared for the jolt of pain I felt,
when you said you were confused.
Now it throbs in my gut
every minute of the day, and
a constant knot of emotion
clogs my throat with an ache so deep,
I cannot describe it.

I guess I'm just the "other" woman.
Strange, but I don't feel that phrase fits me.
But, your confusion made me believe it.
Funny as it may sound,
I always looked at your wife as the "other" woman.
I'm the muse for your poetry;
with me, you are always happy;
I encourage you to pursue your dreams;
you say that I inspire you to think in a way you
never thought before;
that you desire me more than any other woman you've met;
I know that I'm the one who lights the fire in your loins.
and, that we are so very much alike, you and I.
Is that a description of the "other" woman?
Maybe your confusion stems from my not being
like any woman you have ever known before.

How could you have known in the beginning,
that you would become so immersed with me,
on so many levels inside yourself?
Is this really confusion, or are you just surprised
that you might need someone so much,

that it scares you?
You are afraid of what you feel for me.
But, if it is not fear, and really just confusion,
I won't be able to swallow back the tears
your confusion brings.

Like I said, I just started writing it. It needs some work, but the ideas and feelings are there, and you will be able to understand them. The poem is for you.

One more thing, Henry – you shortchanged me, too. I want you to tell me you love me, to my face. Can we see each other tomorrow night, or is "twice" in one week too much to ask? An hour? I need to look into your eyes after all this.

- H S

August 9, 2000
Julie:

I know what you are saying is all true, but... And, that's the problem. I don't even understand what the "but" is. Of course, I will meet you on Thursday. I will be there, I promise. - Henry

August 9, 2000
Hi Henry:

I wasn't going to try to influence you, but it seems that I am doing exactly that. It's just that, I don't want to lose you now that I've found you. You must know that you could never truly reconcile your marriage, and have a relationship with me. How could you possibly expect me to stay in your life, if you stay with her? It wouldn't be fair to me or to Wilma. And, on the other hand, what's right for you? I can't answer that. Maybe, neither one of us can.

Take the emotions out of it for a few minutes, and analyze the problem as an engineer. Make two lists. One will have all the things you will lose if you leave, and the other will have all the things you will gain. And, I'm not talking about "things". I am talking about such items as "freedom", "self-respect", "opportunities you haven't even imagined yet", etc. Then put the lists on a scale, and see which one weighs more. What can't you live without, and what can you forego? Do you really believe that you will loose your sons if you break up with your wife? I don't think so, Henry. Your sons love their father, not their mother's husband. They are too old to allow themselves to be manipulated by her. I can tell that you have a solid relationship with them on your own. In fact, without their mother in the way, you might even get closer to them.

Take my own personal experience into consideration. In 1994, I gave Don one last chance. That was six years ago. Of course, if my Dad hadn't have had his stroke and become my top priority for three of those years, it would have ended sooner, but can you really afford to throw away so much more time? If you are talking another chance, you are talking "years". You do realize that, don't you? I will help you, if you like, but you must realize that I cannot be objective. And, don't be afraid of new things and new people. It's so easy and comfortable to stay with something or someone that is familiar. Try to figure out the "but". It's not like you to not have the answer. Somehow I feel that your decision is already made up, and that I'm wasting my time here trying to convince you otherwise. I can feel it. Are my instincts right? Have you already decided to try with Wilma again? Please answer that honestly. - H S

August 10, 2000
Dear Hot Stuff:

My problem is that I am always as honest as I know how to be with you. I would like to be able to lie to you. That way, I could have you sail through my life oblivious to reality with me, and that way I could have you as part of my life, and enjoy you without worry. But, I value you, respect you, and my heart has a big chunk that is owned by you, so I tell you not only what happens in my life, but what I am thinking, and what I am feeling. Perhaps I shouldn't seek the council of someone who is so affected by what I do with my life. I know it isn't fair to ask you. But, you are one of the few, the very few, people that I trust to tell me what they think, and who cares what I do. I would never ask you to play second fiddle to Wilma, or to be my 'mistress', and I know very well that I cannot have the both of you.

Until you came into my life, it was a mess and fairly uncomplicated. But now, for the first time in my life, I have a choice of two alternatives, because I care for you so very much. That caring for you is what is making things so difficult for me. Before I met you, I would have grabbed at a chance for a reconciliation with Wilma without doubts. I would have tried again, and again, and again, to make things work, but now, I am not so sure that I want them to work, because of you. You, Julie, are the "but".

On that imaginary scale, is a relationship, good or bad, that I have had for all of my adult life, full of lots of good things and bad, as life usually is. It has my children, the memory of a beautiful love that I had for my wife when we were young; the years of struggle together that make people bond, in short – thirty years of my life. And on the other side of the scale is a relationship I have had for only a few months. The relationship with you, although so short, means as much to me, as all the good that the long time in my marriage has given me. And that's how important you are to me. To have that much of an impact on me, and on my heart, in so short a time, is hard to understand. But, I know how you did it. You did it with your caring, your honesty, your warmth, your beauty of body and soul, as well as spirit, your intelligence, your ability to inspire our love and with a connection that is almost mystic.

I realize that you want me to "fish or cut bait", and you are right. I realize that I am at a very real risk of losing you by my indecision. God, I wish I were able to clear my head and think. I just can't think. I wish I could see my life as clearly as I can see into the lives of others. I would never end my own life, because I want to live it, and not miss out on it, but I understand why people do end their lives. It is to escape their inner agony. The kind I am now suffering. I cry every day, because no matter what course my life takes, I will loose something important to me. I will be waiting for you tonight. You may say angry terrible things to me, or you may say gentle kind things to me. You may slap me, or you may kiss me. I don't know what your reaction to me will be, but I want to see you, and hold you close, and I will fight back the tears that want to overwhelm me when I think of you not being in my life. I don't think you even realize how much you have to offer, as a friend, as a lover, as a trusted confidant. I look forward so much to seeing you tonight. Your devoted friend, Henry

PS: I wrote this poem for you:

What is this thing called love?
Where does this feeling from,
That causes so much joy and so much pain?
It is the thorn on the rose
It is the sting from the bee
It is the shadow of deep sadness behind the smile
It is the sound of being lonely in laughter

It is the warmth and comfort I feel, when I smell your sweet fragrance
It is the pit I fall into, called despair, when you are not there
It is the caring for more than myself
It is the need for me to have you find happiness
It is the taste of promise on your lips
It is the promise of a future yet discovered
It is the secrets yet to be uncovered.

If only the world were different
If only the world would go away
If only you and I were left
Then I would know my way
Then perhaps with you I could always stay

Joy, sorrow,
Pleasure, pain,
Courage and fear,
Fulfillment and disappointment
Laughter and tears in equal amounts, which is what love is.

We know not what the future ultimately holds
What path our feet will tread
But when my light grows dim then flickers, before going out
As I close my eyes forever, and prepare to close the book
I swear, I will think of you, and your deep green eyes, full of love
And the last thing I do on this earth will be to cry before I die.

August 10, 2000
Dear Henry:

Your poem made me cry, Henry. Why do you think that when you die, you will think of me, and "cry"? Is there no hope for "us"? Have you already decided to end the most beautiful thing that ever happened to both of us? I haven't given up on us? Why have you? Please call me, Henry. I want to hear your voice, and tell you that I love you. Your poem is so very sad. It also is an excellent poem. The best you've ever written. Why is it that the best in us always seems to come out when we are going through such emotional traumas? - H S

August 10, 2000

No, Julie, I haven't given up on us. It's just that great emotion brings tears. And, I won't call you during the day today because I want to see you tonight - see your face and look into your eyes, when you tell me that you love me. – Henry

August 10, 2000

Just got off the phone with my publisher. She loves your art-work and made a point of mentioning it to me. I want to see you tonight also. – H S

August 10, 2000

Julie, I am very flattered by that. Thank you. I take it as a very great honor for you to be using my artwork in your book. Believe it or not, that piece was a doodle I did sitting at my desk one night while on the phone. I almost threw it out, as I never thought that it was that good. I only hung it in my office because it was black and white and fit the décor. I can't tell you how surprised, thrilled, and delighted, I am, that you see merit in it. But then again, you see merit in me, also a surprise. - Henry

August 10, 2000

That must have been quite an interesting phone conversation, for you to come out with a doodle like that! Smile. Come on, Henry, you knew it had merit the minute you finished it. I'm sure you don't frame and hang up all your black and white doodles. That happens to be a very good – no . . . excellent, doodle. How come I can't doodle like that? And, it fits so well with my cover poem. Maybe some day it will be worth something. Do you know how much Picasso's doodles sell for? **GRIN** Do you have any more doodles lying around? I'm really starting to believe that you honestly don't know how much talent you have. Have you ever done anything in oils or water colors? If so, I'd love to see the work.

I searched through the emails you sent me. I keep them all, you know. They are so very special and precious to me. There was one in particular I was looking for, and I found it. It was written in May, before we even met. Anyway, in this one particular email, you gave me very good advice about my marriage. I made a copy of it and will give it to you tonight. I think you need to take some of your own advice right now. In that email you said so much to me. In fact, maybe that's when I started to have feelings for you. You wrote from your heart to a perfect stranger. It was one of the most beautiful letters you sent me, and I could never "top" it, as far as advice is concerned. I think after you read it, your own words, you will know what you should do about your relationship with Wilma.

I also have struggled with my relationship with my spouse. But, maybe Wilma has more to offer you than Don has to offer me. I made my decision and will not change it because of guilt or obligations. I only have a few years left for happiness and Henry, I don't care what it takes anymore – those years are MINE. I paid my dues to him and then some. I'm not going to do penance for a commitment I made thirty-two years ago, anymore.

I know that we've known each other a very short time, but sometimes when I'm with you, I think that you are the other half of my soul, and that I've known you all my life. I know I'm complicating your life. I don't want to do that, but how do I stop? If you asked me to, I would walk out of your life, but I couldn't do it on my own. But, then again, it was a long time before you met me that you were unhappy. You were searching for someone like me – why else would you have put an ad in the personals on the internet? You put that ad in before you met me. You don't have to make any decisions now, or tomorrow, or the next day. I am not giving you any ultimatums. Why do you put such pressure on yourself? Give yourself a few more months, or years – if you need them, Henry. But, just get Wilma to loosen the leash a bit, so you can at least have some freedom to see me more often. The more I see you, the more I want to see you. (Your words) When I finally sell this house and move out, I know that I will not want to live alone as long as you are in my life. I will want you in my bed, holding me, every single night, whether or not you want to live with me. I want that now. I think I told you that I had a very lengthy affair with a man during the 1980's. That affair saved my marriage, because he gave me what I wasn't getting from Don. But, Henry, with you, it's different. I wasn't in love with that other man. I cared for him, yes, we were very intimate, but there wasn't this strong attraction that I feel for you. The affinity you and I have is so strong.

You won't loose me that easily. As long as you want me, I will be there for you. As much as it may seem that I am trying to get you to see yourself inside your marriage, as I see it, I also want you to be happy. I know that with me, you will be happy. I can "feel" it, because I would always put "us" before everything else. And, maybe with Wilma, you will be happier...but, she already had thirty years, and you're still not happy. Even if she does everything you want her to do, which you know she can't do, will you be happy, then? You really must read your own words to me. In fact, tonight, I will read them to you.

I am looking forward to seeing you tonight also. Very much so, and all I want to do with you, is hold you, and be intimate with you. I have your jasmine plant in my car. Its sweet scent filled the car on the way to the 'park and ride' this morning. You will love the plant, and I hope that it will remind you of me every time a breeze comes through your window and moves the scent around the room. I hope you put it in your bedroom. Smile – H S

We cried together in each other's arms that night. We were so close, and we talked so much about our feelings. We didn't make love, just cuddled in each others' arms. We made plans to meet early the following Sunday morning for a jog around the park.

August 11, 2000
Good Morning Hot Stuff:

It looks like it's supposed to rain on Sunday – boo. So, how are you this morning? See how good I can be? I almost kept my hands off of you last night. And, almost, is quite an effort for me. Julie, I must thank you for being so empathetic and understanding. I love my jasmine plant. Now, whenever I smell jasmine, I will think of you, for sure.

It has been a very long time since I went jogging, so you will have to take it easy on me. Don't make me chase you. Even if it does rain on Sunday morning, and we can't go jogging this weekend, we could make it a regular thing when the weather is nicer. I would get in shape, and I would also get to see you – a double bonus. And, it would give me some more stamina – a bonus for you. Smile. As far as my doodle – thank you for saying that I am talented. Perhaps you are biased in your opinion. I think my art is OK, but far from professional quality. I am strictly an amateur, and I wish I was as good as you think I am. I do a whole bunch of things half-ass, and almost nothing really well. I would like to try acrylics (oils are too hard to clean up), and I would like to paint you. If it is any good, then you can hang it over your fireplace. Would you be willing to pose for some photos that I can use to construct a portrait? I don't copy photos when I draw or paint, but they are good to use to get an overall 'feel' of the subject. What do you think of a bare breasted portrait? You have such beautiful breasts; they should be immortalized on canvas. You don't have to pose bare breasted for the photos. I can do them from memory, and feel my way. I could even include a nipple hickey. Actually, all kidding aside, I would like to paint you, and capture your softness.

Julie, almost all of what you said to me last night rang very true, and has given me a lot to think about. Although Wilma and I are no longer fighting, I feel she is moving in on me. I have gotten too used to my privacy, and that's gone now. It is amazing how quickly I got used to it, and now I hate to give it up, but…

From a philosophical point of view, I would like it if our problems went away. Deep inside, I still want to live alone. I feel that "trying" is the right thing to do, but I must admit that I know that I will loose something of my freedom, not to run the roads, but freedom to allow my creativity to bloom, and I will miss that "alone" time that I have come to value so much. I was drawing every day, but I haven't put pencil to paper since before my son's wedding. I just don't have it in me right now. What good is it going to do me to try and change, if I am the only one trying?

But, if I try and even if I fail at trying, at least my conscience will be clear. Hope to see you real soon.

Affectionately, Henry

August 11, 2000
Good Morning, Henry:

I didn't suggest jogging because you needed to get into shape or needed any more stamina. I love you just the way you are. There's nothing wrong with the way you look or your stamina, right now. I suggested jogging, because I thought it would be a good excuse to get out of the house, and I jog anyway, so it's easy. Besides, it will be a chance to do something else with you that is fun and 'physical'. We will get lots of laughs out of it. I just want to see you again – soon. Unless it is pouring rain, with thunder and lightening, I will be there Sunday morning.

And, as far as last night goes, my only regret is that I didn't rape you. I was very horny when I got home. Henry, your art is good – better than good. You are talented, and it will be a shame if you don't do something with that talent. I don't know about letting you paint me, though. Why don't you try drawing me first, and if that comes out good, you can do the painting. But, I am disappointed that you don't want me to "pose" for you, and you would prefer to do it from memory and photos. I am also very flattered that you want to do a picture of me. Thank you.

I know that you want to live alone, Henry. That's because your wife has been smothering you for so long. Not all women smother their partners. But, I wish you were living alone, instead of living with Wilma. At least then, I could call you when I felt lonely, and invite you over "every" night. GRIN. I like my privacy too. It's not that I mind people living with me. I like…no, enjoy, my own company. Sometimes I just like to read or write without interference. I don't want to have to answer to anyone, and just want to be able to do what I want to do. Don doesn't even sleep in the same bedroom, and manages to crowd me anyway, almost all the time. It drives me nuts. Maybe I just don't enjoy his company any more. I don't know what it is.

Henry, your creativity will bloom. Sometimes it's not the fact that you're alone. It's just having the right setting, or being with someone who realizes that you need your own space, and doesn't feel threatened every time you do something, or have friends that don't include her. Wilma needs to find things that she enjoys doing, and things that will make her feel good about herself. Should we take her jogging with us? Smile. Try to encourage her to do something that she's good at, if you possibly can. I've encouraged Don to golf, and it has developed into an enjoyable outlet for him. He's very good at it. It gives him confidence in himself, and gives me some desperately needed "alone" time. I've never met Wilma, but from what you told me, I can tell that she has little confidence in herself.

I'm glad you love your jasmine plant. It's my favorite fragrance. Whenever I feel like splurging on myself, I buy this expensive perfume, "Bulgari" that is made from jasmine. I got a kick out of the look on your face when I said that I wanted to make "babies". You didn't realize that I meant baby jasmine plants. You won't have to worry about that, Henry, I had my tubes tied over twenty years ago, and couldn't have any more babies, even if I wanted them.

Love you – H S

August 11, 2000
Hi Julie:

You always seem to have 20/20 insight. I enjoyed last night very much. I must admit, I promised myself that last night's meeting would be sex-free, and that we would just talk to each other, and be with each other, and when I got home I also was very horny. I can't be with you, or hear your voice, without wanting you physically, no matter how hard I try. Maybe I am looking for a surrogate mother, because I have never felt more at peace, secure, safe, and content when my head is nestled between your breasts, and I can hear your heart beating.

I wanted to draw you from photos, because if you pose, it would be difficult to sit for that long, and also I could use the photos when you are not around to work on the drawing. I also enjoy my own company, and the peace and quiet. Without my alone time, I go nuts. Wilma invariably never leaves me alone, and doesn't understand that constant company is stifling to me.

I have to see you at least once a week, and even that isn't enough. And, I hope we do get to see each other Sunday morning. - Henry

August 11, 2000
Henry:

You feel peace, security, etc. when your head is nestled between my breasts, because when you are in my arms, Henry, you are home. At least I feel that way when I'm with you. I define "home" as a place where there are people who love you, not a building, or necessarily the place where you sleep.

The next time I see you, I will show you some photos I have of myself, and see if you can use them for your picture. If not, we can take more, but I warn you, I am not very photogenic. I never like the way I look in photographs – and, in the drawing, I expect you to knock at least ten years off my face. Smile.

I want you to keep a great big smile on your face for the rest of the weekend.

Love, H S

CHAPTER TEN

I never asked Henry how long he thought about leaving Wilma. I know that it took me years to reach a decision about leaving Don. When I left him the first time six years ago, I had been thinking about it for over two years prior to actually leaving, and I waited until after my son joined the Navy before moving out. I moved into the city to avoid the commute. Don somehow thought I planned on staying in the City from Monday to Friday, and I would be home on weekends. I don't think he wanted to face the fact that, for me, it was a full separation. It wasn't until I started dating, that he realized I wasn't planning on coming back.

I don't really understand why I did go back eighteen months later. I think I felt sorry for Don, because he was always so sad when I saw him. He made our children think that it was my fault. It was easy for him to do that, because I was the one who walked out. Everyone in the family made me feel guilty. They plotted against me, time and again. For example, leaving me stranded on Thanksgiving, so that I had to spend the night with Don. Or maybe, to me, my life didn't seem that much better without him than it was with him, at that time. For whatever reason, or combination of reasons, I did go back, and it took me six years to get up the courage to decide to leave again.

I think that Henry was very insecure about his decision to leave Wilma. I'm sure he was going through much the same agony that I went through six years ago. I think to anyone who has been in a long term relationship, the scariest part of leaving is the uncertainty of whether or not you'll miss that person who lived through so much of your life with you. As much as you don't want to hurt that person, even more, you don't want to make a mistake where your own life is concerned. That person, right or wrong, feels very comfortable to you, whereas, you might never get another relationship where the other person feels as comfortable. And, that's important. You wonder if you are capable of getting "close" to another person again, or even if you want to. Everyone needs to share some part of their life with another human being. The intimacy that two people who are close feel for each other, is the most satisfying feeling I've ever felt. When you no longer can feel that way with someone you felt that way in the past with, you wonder if it's you, or if you can ever feel that way again. I felt Henry's pain and guilt, and knew that there wasn't much I could really do for him, except be there when he felt the need to reach out.

Maybe at the time, I should have walked away and shut him out of my life. I know that I must have influenced him to move out. He'll say I didn't, but how could I not have? Yet, I valued what we had together. I knew how rare it was, and how fragile it was. I didn't want to risk loosing it, by leaving him when he needed my support more than ever. Intuitively, I knew he needed my strength to help him do what his instincts were telling him he must do to survive. Not breaking away from him now, was probably a big mistake. I set myself up to be hurt, yet I couldn't do anything else, because I knew that if I had someone like Henry in my life six years ago, I would have had the strength to stay away, instead of putting myself through another six years of stagnation, and having to put Don, myself, and my family, through this pain once again, to save my soul.

August 13, 2000
Hi Hot Stuff:

How are you this evening? Well, I hope. Somewhat inclement weather we are having, don't you think? At least we don't have to water the flowers today, mainly because they are actually in the neighbor's yard, and heading south as I write. I hope you and the house survived the storm. I heard on the news that parts of Essex and the lake had some flooding. I'm worried about you. Frankly, my dear, during the thunder and lightning I kept thinking that it would be fun to lay with my head on your naked breasts, watch the storm, and listen to your heart beat at the same time.

Well, after watching the weather forecast for tomorrow, it looks like we will be canceling our jogging date in the morning. Too bad, but I guess we don't have to set the alarm. As far as Thursday goes, I am still going to congratulate you and Don on your wedding anniversary. I am sure that over dinner you both can look back together at some very happy and joy-filled times. May those be the memories of each other that you will always carry with you. You have three fine children to be thankful for, and for the love that made them happen. Congratulations for that. I have a late sales meeting on Wednesday. It ends at six PM. How about that? But, with your anniversary the next day, perhaps you would rather go directly home. I would understand that.

It really is too bad that the weather has gone nuts. It would have been nice to see you first thing in the morning again. And, I certainly could have used the exercise. You have a peaceful night, Sweetie. I wish we were together – Henry

August 13, 2000
Hi Henry:

Thank you for worrying about me, but where I live, flooding is not a problem. How about you? Did you loose electric power? I did get caught in the rain though, because I drove down to visit my Mom and on the way home it poured. It took me four and a half hours to drive sixty-three miles. It was bumper to bumper all the way. It was raining so hard, I could hardly see out the windshield of my car. I'm not used to driving in such weather.

You wrote the letter I am responding to at one AM. I'm so sorry that you had to go to that much trouble just to write to me. The rain stopped this morning actually, but everything is so wet, jogging might not have been so much fun after all. Wednesday night will be OK, but Wednesday is matinee day in New York, and traffic is always heavy on Wednesdays. We'll be lucky if my bus hits the 'park and ride' by six thirty. My dinner with Don is Thursday, so Wednesday is free. How are things on the home front? I thought that Wilma was going to give you a little bit more space. It doesn't sound that way. You seem to have to account for every minute you are away from her. Henry, how do you stand it? It looks like you are the one making all the changes, not her. I feel for you. I know that if Don were that way, my marriage would never have lasted as long as it did. I'm starting to think that maybe I should let you go now, and wait till you break free of your current prison, instead of what we are doing, sneaking around all the time. Yet, I can't think of life without you in it, even if it is just for an hour here and an hour there. Somehow getting you all horny so you can go home and have sex with your wife is not my idea of a relationship that will last. I'm sorry, but right now I am feeling a little bit sad, Henry. I wish you were here so I could look into your eyes and see the love you have for me. Love – H S

August 13, 2000

Oh Julie, I am so sorry that you feel sad. I don't like this sneaking around, either. It doesn't do justice to either one of us. Although my intent (if I can get away) is to be with you, I hate not having a 'normal' relationship with you. Little wonder that when we do see each other, we can't get enough of each other. Julie, I am not happy either. You know that. Some things have got to change soon. This is not the way it's supposed to be. Our original aim was to give each other support. You have been doing that, Julie. Without you, I would have gone over the edge more than once. I am pulled in so many directions at the same time that I think I am going to just blow up one day. But, one thing I feel, is that in many ways, I am letting you down too. I know what you want out of life, and although I feel this passion and love for you, I have not been coming through for you very well. Try to smile for me Sweetie, - Henry

PS: We are OK here, we didn't drown, but Oh boy, did we get rain. Sleep safe, Sweetie.

August 13, 2000
My Beloved Henry:

I am not going to put any pressure on you. That's not me, and not what I'm about. Instead, I'll take whatever you are able to give me. Don't worry about it. I know that we both are in an impossible situation that we are trying to sort through. Believe me; I am going through much of the same agony as you are going through.

Did I tell you that you are the most beautiful man I have ever met? Your beauty overwhelms me. And, sometimes, I wonder if you know how much I think about you. Memories are such a tease – like a stripper disappearing behind the curtain with a smile. You can look, but don't touch. What happens when you need to touch? Hunger breeds a strange appetite. And even if I couldn't face the sneaking around any more, I could never really leave you. What do you want me to do? Tell me, and I'll do it. That's my feelings all laid out for you. Just don't be sorry, because you couldn't help my falling in love with you any more than you could help yourself falling in love with me. It is what it is. I'm not sad. I think it's just loneliness. But, I'll be happy again on Wednesday. Smile. Love, H S

August 13, 2000
Julie:

What I want you to do is do whatever it takes for you to be happy. That will make me happy. See you on Wednesday. You are a wonderful person. I don't deserve you. Smile for me Julie. I love you – Henry

August 14, 2000

Julie, it looks like you may be cut off, as all the roads seem to be blocked or closed due to the storm. I am in the same position. I am going into work real late – maybe 9:30 or 10 AM this morning, as I hope the roads will be open by then. Drive safely, if you try for work. Wild weather. Missing you... Henry

August 14, 2000
Good Morning, Henry:

All lanes on Route 35 were open this morning, and I had no problems driving to the bus stop. In fact, I was ridiculously early, as I anticipated problems.

Lots of "stuff" happened on the home front this weekend. I guess we caught the 'rainy day in the house crazies', and all hell broke loose. I managed to somehow calm things down, but I am seriously thinking of leaving, even before the house is sold because Don is becoming impossible to live with. We lowered the price on the house again. The house is a "steal" at the current price. Even the realtor was surprised when I told him to go down again. I just need to end that chapter of my life and go on, and you can't put a price on your well-being. I think Don does too. He knows that our interests are as far apart as they ever were, and that staying together in a bad marriage is unhealthy for both of us. I feel like I am at such a turning point in my life now, and I'm so afraid that I might make the wrong decisions.

All this rain knocking out the roads and bridges will have you very busy at the quarry, I assume. Think of me as you mix those asphalt recipes. Smile. I miss you, too. You are the one ray of sunshine in my life right now. - Julie

August 14, 2000
Hi Julie:

First, let me tell you how glad I am that you are OK, and didn't have any trouble with the roads. Many of the smaller roads around my house are closed, so it is difficult to get to Route 35, but I also found it OK, once I got there. No traffic at all. I am sorry that you had a hard time this weekend, and that all hell broke loose at your house. When tempers flare the truth comes out. At least you are talking with each other. As you know, I understand when you say that you are afraid of making the wrong decisions.

I am a poor one to give advice in that matter. But this I would say to any close friend, and I say it to myself also. One thing I know for sure, only you can make up your mind as to what to do, because only you know the entire story, and only your heart feels all of the pain. You know that I will be here to help you in any way that I can, but these decisions of yours are life altering, and you must take the time you need to make them. Please don't give up on any aspect of your life, unless you have considered it very carefully. You may not know what you've got, until it's gone. But, if you can see no other way to make yourself happy, then don't be afraid to leave.

Yes, I do say these things to myself. I just don't take my own advice very well. I worry deeply about you. I will always be here for you, and be your friend, Julie. I truly wish from the bottom of my heart that your life takes whatever turn it needs to for you to find happiness and contentment.

Smile, Julie, the sun is coming out. - Henry

August 14, 2000
Henry:

I want you to stop worrying about me. As you say, the sun is coming out. If there's one thing my father taught me, it was to analyze every aspect of a situation before making a decision. I am not as emotional as the majority of women. I don't "think" with my emotions, or at least I try not to. It seems that I am more concerned about what my decisions are doing to other people, than what they are doing to me. That is a fault I am aware that I have, and if I allow it to control my decisions, I will be doing myself irreparable harm. Its one thing where there are help-less children involved, and another, when the parties involved are all adults with their own free will. I cannot allow myself to take responsibility for Don's happiness or unhappiness. He is responsible for his own happiness. And, I am not going to throw away my life so he can be happy. I told him as much this weekend, and gave him some things to think about. Henry, I gave him thirty-two years, now I've decided to take back my life. He knows that I will always be there for him, if he needs me, but I no longer want to be his "wife". I want to be his friend. I told him that I am seeing someone else that I care about, but no details. I couldn't lie to him any more. I do not like to deceive people. He is not happy about it, but he knows that he cannot tell me what to do. In a way I am glad that it is out in the open. I feel much better about it now, and it gives him freedom to go out himself. Be happy for me Henry, because I think I am mak-ing progress. - H S

August 14, 2000
Julie:

I am glad that you are so sure of your own mind. I wish that I was as together as you. It took a lot of bravery to be that up front with Don. I admire you for it. After telling him there is someone else, that pretty much closes the door for him. I am happy for you that you are on the way to starting a new life, and will find happiness that way. At least you will experience freedom and the chance to discover yourself at last. But, I am also sad to see a thirty-two year marriage end, regardless of who is involved, or the reasons for it ending.

I can't help worrying about you, Julie. I worry about everyone I care about. When I write to you, or tell you that you need to think things through, I am being your devil's advocate. Everyone needs one. Better days are coming, Julie, because things just can't stay this screwed up and unhappy. I am looking forward to seeing you, if we are still on for Wednesday evening. You are still the bright spot in my day. Just to hold you close for a little while is better than nothing, and it is like a vacation from life for me. Those brief times are some of the few times that I have when I feel content. - Henry

August 14, 2000
Henry:

I don't know if I'm all that "together", or so brave. I just did what I felt was the right thing to do. I can't tell you what the right thing is for you. Only you can do that yourself, in your own time. You will know when the time is right. For me, the time seemed right now. I know that by being honest with Don, I am also allowing him to get on with his life. Now, he can think about what he wants to do with the rest of his life and plan accordingly. In a way, at least for me, not telling him was the selfish thing to do. By not telling him, I was leading him on under false pretenses. Whether or not this relationship I have with you will last, it certainly is not fair to Don to go on with it, and keep deceiving him about it. I know that if the tables were turned, I'd want him to be honest with me. If I've made a mistake, then I will pay the consequences, but I know in my heart that deceit is selfish and cruel. Somehow, I know that lying to save him pain; will eventually hurt him much more. And, yes, I do still want to see you on Wednesday night, and I just want to make mad passionate love to you – not talk. - H S

August 14, 2000
Julie:

After reading and rereading your letter, and seeing how honest and caring you are, lets me see what it is that I love about you. So, you want to make mad passionate love to me, and not talk. OK! I can say so much more to you with my hands and lips than I can ever say with words. So, Julie, are you going to rape me? I am so defenseless with you. Are you going to tear off my clothes, throw me on the couch, and lick and suck me into submission? I hope so...

I can't wait to taste you. Can't wait to slide my tongue deep inside you...can't wait to feel my nakedness against you...can't wait to feel your hands on my body. Why do you drive me so crazy? Why do you have this ability to make me instantly horny? I want to make love to you long and hard. I'll eat my Wheaties for breakfast on Wednesday. And, it doesn't take much to motivate me where you are concerned. - Henry

August 15, 2000
Henry:

I knew it wouldn't take much to motivate you. Must be all that testosterone! I suggest the Wheaties for both lunch and breakfast. Grinning. And, you've got it a little bit backwards. I'm going to let you tear my clothes off, and I will do whatever it takes to motivate you to lick and suck me into submission. And, being the executive that I am, I really know how to motivate people. I have something "special" in mind for you! And, I know exactly how you "talk" to me with your eyes, lips and hands…you manage to say so much more that way. Great Big Grin – H S

PS: I think I'd like to play chess with you. I've attached a board that you can open in Excel. You are the red, and can make the first move. Now, Henry, I never play chess unless there are stakes involved. In this case, I think the stakes should be very high. How about – the loser must be a "sex slave" for the winner for eight hours straight the next time we actually have eight hours together? This way, in case you're a better player than I, and beat my panties off, I kind of win anyway. Don't forget to turn the font to red on whatever box you move into. Of course, if you're afraid to play me, I can understand.

So, what are you working on in Brooklyn? Are you analyzing the potholes? - H.S.

August 15, 2000
Hi Hot Stuff:

Or course I play chess. So glad you do too. I just got into the office. I was out in Brooklyn all morning. I'm glad to be back. How are you today? As far as looser is the sex slave of the winner – actually that's a no loose proposition. I wouldn't mind being your sex slave for a day. I have very little male ego to bruise in the bedroom. I just like to have fun, so sex slave is OK. Would you like to win by default? Now, as far as you being my sex slave…same, but more of the same, perhaps. Either way, sex with you is great fun and uninhibited, and I'm ready right now, baby. Can't wait to lick your ears and get you horny. I love how your nipples get hard when I kiss your ears. Anyway, I'd better stop thinking like this. I'm getting hard myself – so I'd better sign off and open that chess board.

August 15, 2000
Ok Hot Stuff:

So, you want to put your pussy on the line? Here's my first move...

August 15, 2000
Hi Again, Hot Stuff:

I'm working right now on the piers in Brooklyn. The piers are the pits. I hate all the traffic and noise – but, it's a paycheck.

I think that if I win this chess game you will be real busy. You would make an awesome sex slave. I have some ideas right now. I bet you can guess them all. Anyway Hot Stuff, I'll see you tomorrow. Can't wait to see you and can't wait to get my hands, along with other body parts, on you, etc. - Henry

August 15, 2000\
Henry:

Tell your boss I said he should hire you a chauffeur. You deserve one. Henry, if you ever finish your novel, you might just make enough money from it to be able to give up that rock breaking job. Who am I to talk? I'm only a third of the way through my novel. But, I try to do a little bit every day. Do you? Just remember that many science fiction novels end up as movies.

Don't be so sure that you will win the chess game. I see that you started off rather aggressively, but I know a little something about this game. My moves tend to be more subtle. Actually, I think you are the one that will make the very awesome sex slave! In fact, just thinking about it is making my mouth water and my juices flow. See you tomorrow. - H S

August 16, 2000
Hi Henry:

Did you sleep well last night? I don't understand why, but whenever I know I am going to see you the next day, I have trouble sleeping the night before. For some reason, I am in a particularly horny mood this morning. Did you know that certain times of the month, women are hornier than other times? You probably knew that already. I think that you have studied the female body in depth, and have probably read everything ever written about it. Haven't you Henry?

I noticed that you moved your queen out early in the game. I like aggressive men. Are you this aggressive every morning, Henry?

Last night I read in the newspaper about some of the damage in your town done by the rain. I didn't realize that you got hit that badly. Did your home suffer any damage? - H S

August 16, 2000

I always start my first game with someone the same way. It allows me to learn how they play. Actually, I don't necessarily expect to win this game as I usually don't underestimate anyone especially, someone like you. But, as you pointed out, even the looser is a winner – considering the stakes.

If you would like – I can attempt to cure your horniness in about seven and a half hours. I do know of a way that might do that. I really want to get my hands and mouth on you. And, I can't wait to feel your hands and lips on me. Now, I'm all hot and bothered.

We did get quite a lot of damage in town. Bridges and tunnels are on the edge of collapse, and some roads have washed away. But, I am high and dry, and even my basement stayed dry.

I have brought with me some of my "under construction" drawings for you to see. Just remember these are preliminary drawings, not yet finished artwork, but I would like your opinion. For some reason, all my drawings of women seem to have ample bosoms lately. I wonder why. - Henry

August 16, 2000

I am looking forward to Dr. Henry curing my horniness condition in about seven and a half hours, if I can hold out that long. I am also very much looking forward to seeing your drawings. I am flattered that you are interested in my opinion. You always manage to say something to make me smile.

Henry, you've got me on the defense already! And, I'm not going to let you check mate me in the next move, Henry. You can learn a lot about a man by the way he plays chess. I see you are not the soft spoken, mile mannered, and sweet, calm man you portray yourself as. Instead, when faced with the 'highest' of stakes, you are a formidable opponent. I see I will really have to watch myself carefully while playing chess with you, if I want to keep my sexual freedom in tact. Too bad we're not playing this game in person. I could use a few diversionary tactics. - H S

August 16, 2000
Hi Hot Stuff:

I'm impressed. Most people miss the fact that I could mate them in the next move. Even experienced semi-pro's have fallen for that particular gambit. So, if I can't mate you one way, then I'll just have to mate with you tonight. Huba Huba! See, even chess turns me on, when you are involved, and I can't resist a pun or innuendo. I think that you are about to give me a run for my money. Although you said only one move a day, here's tomorrow's. Just don't look at it until then. It is the only logical move for me, so you probably know what's coming anyway. See you later, Hot Stuff. Be prepared to have your thermostat turned up a notch, you sexy thing...

August 16, 2000

Huba huba - three and a half more hours to countdown! And, you are not really impressed, are you? That three move opening thing is the oldest move in the book. Any amateur would have seen it. You are too much. I still wish I could use those diversionary tactics. I have a really good one involving your genitals and my mouth in mind. Speaking about thermostats. . . I suggest that you turn your office's thermostat to freezing, so we don't melt as we usually do. Smile. I can't wait to see you. - H S

CHAPTER ELEVEN

August 16th was an incredible evening. Henry confirmed my belief that he is a highly perceptive man of considerable courage and acute passion. It wasn't just the lovemaking that drew me closer towards him, it was the man. He opened up his heart to me that night. He told me of his fears concerning the breakup of his marriage, and of his passion for drawing, and his need to continue growing. He told me of how he was torn between doing the right thing, or what he thought was the right thing, concerning Wilma, and wanting to pursue his own goals and desires. He described his life at home with his wife as one of unhappiness and pain. My heart reached out to this man, who I saw as someone who would never intentionally hurt another human being, and yet if he didn't hurt some people, he would sentence himself to a life of unhappiness. I could feel his inner conflicts and his need to do what he felt was right. I understood his terrible guilt, because all he wanted was to be happy. I wanted to help him, and yet, I knew that his relationship with me was only complicating his life even more.

August 17, 2000
So Julie:

Is it still necessary to finish the chess game after last night? After all, I am your sex slave already. Smile. I see you didn't move yet. Did that old "three move mate" get you thinking? Or, did last night's three mate move get you going?

I wish we had more time together last night, but the times we do have are so concentrated, that we seem to pack in what most people take all day to do, we can do in an hour. We always seem to find the time to be intimate and close physically, and still talk and share ideas and feelings at the same time. We are so fortunate that we can do that so naturally and easily. I feel as though I can be truly honest with you and just expose my feelings and show you what is really there. You are the only person that I trust enough to show my true heart to. Mess, isn't it? But, all the confidences, and all the kisses and hugs in the world, won't get you off the hook. Let's play chess. There's pussy at stake here. Have a great day, hot stuff. - Affectionately, Henry

August 17, 2000
Good Morning, Henry:

I have been doing a lot of thinking about us, and I composed the attached letter to you. I hope you understand where I'm coming from concerning this, but I guess I also tend to overanalyze things at times. Also, here is my chess move as well. - H S

(Attachment)

Dear Henry:

There are times that I feel I should end our relationship. Not because I don't want to see you anymore, but because I do want to see you, so much more. Can you understand that? Last night I was so happy, and felt so alive, so loved, and so at home in your arms, that I forgot about things like "time". When you said that it was getting late, it dawned on me that maybe I'm the only one of us feeling this way. Then, I thought about some of the things you said about the other "friends" you have, and that you love. I know that you have had, and may still be having a *sexual* relationship with those women you spoke of. And suddenly, I realized that maybe your relationship with me isn't "special" to you, the way it is to me. You can have sex with many women during the same period of your life, and love them all, whereas I can only have sex with one man at a time, and I feel that I must care deeply for him to have sex with him. I have male friends that I would always be there for, but I don't go to bed with them. I find that my sexual relationship with you, although it's not nearly enough, does fulfill my physical needs. I don't need other men, or want them in that way. And, I know I will need a man in my life who feels the same way about me. I don't think I can settle for being one of *many* lovers to someone. For practical reasons, there are too many diseases going around, but even more importantly, I need to feel intimate with someone who can give me the same level of intimacy that I give to him. I don't want to be intimate with a man, who is intimate at that same level, with other women too.

I guess what I'm saying is that while I know that you have other friends who you care about, and have a history with, as do

I – I'd like to feel that I am the only one you make love to. I know that you can't avoid sex with your wife, just as at times, I can't avoid it with Don, although now that our relationship is taking on a new identity, that may have changed. But, I don't *make love* to him. There is a distinct difference.

As I have told you, I am looking for someone who cares for me with the same depth and level of feeling that I have for him, and who wants to grow old with me, and who I want to grow old and spend the next 25 to 30 years of my life with. Someone to travel with, wake up with, share ideas with, challenge my mind, push me when I'm lazy; someone who won't take less than the best I can give him, who has the same passion for life as I have. I think that you are all those things and more. But, I feel that you may have other plans for your life, and that's OK. But, a few hours a week will never be enough for me, once I am living alone and am truly free to have a relationship with someone. We may end up just being good friends (which may be impossible with you), and I may grow old with someone else. If that happens, I doubt I could continue as we have been, because I will feel a sense of loyalty to whoever I do end up growing old with. But, I want you to know that if I had a choice, you'd be it.

I think I may need a break from "us" to sort out everything you've told me and to put our relationship into it proper perspective. So, it's good that I'm going to LA. Whether or not I see you again before that trip will depend on how you answer this, I guess. I hope you appreciate my frankness, and understand my need to be frank at this point.

Love, Julie (aka 'hot stuff')

August 17, 2000
My Dear Julie:

I have read and reread your letter several times. When a letter is written in such an honest, frank and open-hearted way, it deserves to be answered in the same way. One of the things I have always admired about you is the fact that you do speak your mind. You are honest with me, and that deserves honesty in response.

I also sometimes feel that we should end our relationship, not because I don't want to see you, but because I know that what you want out of life is something that, right now, I can't even address, let alone promise. It is out of selfishness that I want to keep you, because not seeing you would be very hard, as I have developed a deep abiding affection for you. You remain the most exciting and interesting woman, no – person, that I have known for many years, and I would hate not to have that in my life. We obviously share a physical attraction that is hard to resist. Sexually, you excite me like no other woman. Being sexually intimate with you is not forced, has no boundaries, and is the way we wish all our relationships would be – perfect, when we are together. And, long lasting relationships are based on so much more, and we do have more.

I have other women in my life. I am not sleeping with anyone else, and although there are times when I cannot refuse my wife, sex, I still make love only to you. But, there is one fundamental difference between us. You have made it very clear that you are looking for a life partner, but I am not. That doesn't mean that I don't have love for you, or that the love I have for you isn't real. But, it does mean we want different things out of life.

I thought I had found my person to grow old with thirty-one years ago, and now I think that she isn't that person. I honestly believe I am not capable of looking that far ahead in my life. Although, I, like everyone else, eventually want that stability and plan for the future, as no one wants to go it alone, or die a lonely old person who is unloved, I honestly am nowhere near making that kind of commitment, even to myself. I am not a promiscuous person, and don't have a slew of girlfriends – you're it. I make love to you, because I love you. But, Julie, if you truly want someone to share the rest of your life with, I can't tell you that I'm that guy. I just can't risk, after going through this nightmare of a marriage, another long term relationship coming to an end. If I go through this again, next time I think it will kill me, for sure. I just can't leave one thirty year commitment and go straight into another. I would rather have no one, than risk this level of hurt again. And, because of that, I will most likely always hold some part of myself back. I am gun-shy. The very best I can promise you, is that I will always care for you, and want always to be your close and trusted friend, regardless of what our eventual relationship becomes. Even if you do find someone who can promise you the next thirty years, I will still always be there for you, caring about you and your welfare. I don't have to have sex with you, to love you, or to be your friend.

If you are having any second thoughts, then Julie, my advice to you, as your friend, is to watch out for yourself, and think this through very carefully. If you need a break from us to think, then take it. I understand. I will never be upset with you for following what you believe is the right path for your heart, even if that path no longer leads to me. You are too important, and your eventual happiness is too important to me, for me to not wish you all the happiness you can get. If after reflection, you feel that you want to end or modify our relationship, I won't argue the point, or become upset with you, because you being happy is more important to me than you will ever know. I will always be thankful for what we have had so far. It's been wonderful, and has made me feel young again.

You have been unhappy too long; I see the deep sadness in your eyes, even when you smile. You deserve a second chance in life, with whoever you can count on to be there. For now, you can't count on me for that. If you do end this, then I will always be grateful for you showing me love and affection, for listening, and for being my friend and lover. It has been wonderful, full of life, and I will always remember the wonderful times we shared with a smile and warmth, and how beautiful you are, both outside, and in your heart. I just wish we had met a year or two from now, when both of our lives had sorted themselves out. Please, one request, don't close the door on me. I make a better friend, than I do a lover.

With love, from your lover, your chess and poetry partner, your admirer, you're confidant, and most important of all, your friend – Henry

August 17, 2000
Dear Henry:

I thank you for your honesty. I know that you are always honest and frank with me. And, I appreciate that quality in you very much. You told me what I already know about you – that you cannot plan your future. Everyone should be able to dream about their future, Henry. Sometimes, those dreams aren't very realistic, and sometimes they are. I am going to say some things to you that you may not like. I am not saying them to hurt you, but because I care so much for you. I don't want you to continue to live in such sadness and pain, and maybe, something I say will help you to find your way.

Henry, you have shut yourself off from dreaming. I feel so sad for you. Dreaming is very important. It gives people a sense of hope. I think that's what I feel you lack most of all – hope. You live day to day, in a relationship that is dominated by dishonesty and deception, and somehow you rationalize the dishonesty to yourself by saying that you can't bear to hurt Wilma when in fact, you are a victim of a very abusive relationship. And, the abuse has gone on for several years. Your wife plays control games with your mind, and has given you so much emotional abuse, that it has affected your self-esteem and your ability to plan your own future. Instead, you live day to day, taking spurts of happiness wherever you can, whenever you can, thinking that these little spurts will somehow hold you over. Victims, like you, end up committing suicide. They don't grow old with an abuser. I don't want to see that happen to you. If such a thing were to happen, the world will have lost someone very special and unique. Abuse, very typically alternates with declarations of love and statements that they will change, providing a "hook" to keep the partner in the relationship. Answer me this – if Don were an abusive husband, and hit me, which he doesn't, what would you, as a friend, tell me to do? Would you tell me to try to reconcile every time he says he is going to change, or would you fear for my life, and tell me to leave him? I know that Wilma doesn't physically harm you, but what she does to you mentally and emotionally, is life shattering.

I found something beautiful in you. Something so precious, that I can't just walk away from it. I know that you will eventually find your true self, once you realize that your marriage is a lost cause, and has been for many years. It's a long uphill battle to sanity. If I thought that there was even a slight chance of your marriage mending, I would definitely walk out of your life – not because I don't love you, but because I do. I don't want any commitments from you, Henry. I don't understand why you think I do. Love is a commitment in itself. Don't you know that? I don't want to get married again either. I don't have to live with you. What I need is some kind of mutual understanding that you would be there for me, if I ever needed you, because I would be there for you. And, I already have that. You know that we cannot be just friends. We can't keep our hands off each other. I am glad to know that you are not having sex with other women. From the way you were talking last night, I kind of thought you might be. But, then, the way you respond to me, makes it difficult to think that.

I want to go jogging with you Sunday morning. I hope you are able to keep our date. I can't end something that seems so "right" to me. I need your friendship and affection, as much as you need mine. I just hope that you will one day soon see what is happening to your life. If all you can give me is two hours a week, then most likely, when I am living alone again, I will see other men, because I'm human and need companionship. I am too sensitive a person to live on two hours of affection a week. I don't know if I'll get involved with any one else on a romantic level, but I might. I will never deceive you about it. But, you should know, in case you want to spare yourself pain down the road. It has never been my intention to hurt you in any way. I do not want to stop seeing you. I can't. Am I making any sense to you, or confusing you more?

- H S

August 19, 2000
Good Morning Henry:

While riding on the bus today, I was thinking of you and wrote another poem. You are becoming my absolute best muse! I think that this particular poem is one of my better ones. What do you think? And, what happened to your chess move? I miss you. – H S

LIFELINE

I heard your cries,
made with such little hope
remaining in your weary soul.
But, I can barely see you there,
So deep, in the pit of despair.
You are bleeding, hardly alive,
looking up through the one ray of sunshine
you managed to find
with such tired eyes.
It would be so easy for you to just
die.

I will not let my friend go.
You, who have so much to offer,
and, have given me back my life
in so many ways.
I threw down the lifeline -
do not fear,
fore the rope is strong,

woven with threads of love, and
it will not break
from the weight of your perplexity.

Tie me around your waist,
make sure the knot is tight,
hold on,
and let me pull you up,
out of the storm.
I will share my rainbow with you,
and once you feel the sunshine on your skin,
and the beauty of my soul within,
you will never again fall
into the darkness of
despair.

August 19, 2000

Julie, I read your poem. I am fortunate indeed to know a person with the heart and soul to write such a poem and have such insight. Thank you. And, yes, you do confuse me sometimes, but I also know that feelings are powerful motivators. I understand exactly what you are feeling. It's like being addicted or eating chocolate. We know that some things are not always the sensible choice in some respects, but we indulge anyway. At least that's how I feel sometimes. My good sense tells me that my life must be a certain way as I have obligations, etc. to fill, and the status quo could be lived with, and that is what the world and convention expects me to do. It is also the easy way. Then my chocolate side tells me that it's my life to live, so start eating, and to hell with the zits and expanding waistline that the candy brings.

But, over the last few months I have developed this wicked sweet tooth. Ah! Julie candy – it's so sweet! - Henry

August 19, 2000
Henry:

I read your last email twice, and I'm still trying to figure it out. First off, what obligations do you have besides the usual financial? Your kids are grown. I don't know if you noticed this or not, but Wilma is an adult, and is fully responsible for her own actions. She's over twenty-one, and can take care of herself. She is not an invalid. I assume she knows how to drive a car, use the washing machine, and fix herself dinner. Besides the fact that for the last eighteen or twenty years she made your life miserable, stomped on your ideas, and turned you into her own personal slave, what is your obligation to her? Maybe there is something that you haven't told me.

And, I have news for you. The specifically formulated "Julie Chocolate" does not give you zits or expand your waistline, but it does taste so good, doesn't it? Grinning....You can indulge without worrying about the calories. So, are we jogging Sunday morning? - H S

August 19, 2000
Dear Candy:

Now, who's confused? My chess move is attached. As far as Sunday goes, it's too early to tell right now. I'm waiting to see if we are going to the Liberty Science Center on Sunday. I'll let you know. And, incidentally, your kind of candy actually works off the waistline – grin – and you do taste so good, and you are addicting, Julie. - Henry

August 19, 2000
Henry:

Don't use an excursion to the Science Center as an excuse not to jog! You know I'll make it worth your while. You'll be home before nine AM. The Science Center is open all day long. I'll ponder the chess move over the weekend, and give you mine on Monday. Smile - H S

August 21, 2000
Hi Henry:

Are you still alive? I was thinking about trying not to think about you, but if I don't hear from you soon, I'm going to start calling all the hospitals in the county to see if you're listed as a patient. Please let me know that you are OK. I am worried about you. You haven't answered my last few emails, and I didn't hear from you at all this weekend, and that's just not like you. What's going on? - H S

August 21, 2000
Hello Hot Stuff:

Sorry that I made you worry, but I've been laid up with a vicious migraine. I took today off and have spent it in bed. I feel a little better now, and at least I can see again. I don't get them very often, only a couple of times a year, but Friday afternoon it started up, and I did go to the Statue of Liberty yesterday, but by mid morning, I just had to head back home, as it really hit with a vengeance. I'll be OK, thanks, and by tonight

I am sure I will be almost normal again, or at least what is normal for me. Thank you for worrying about me, but I am OK, really. How are you? I missed being able to communicate with you. When are you going to LA? I think you said Wednesday. I would like to see you, if only to say "hello" before you go. I miss you, Sweetie – Henry

August 21, 2000
Henry:

I'm so sorry to learn that you have been ill. I don't get headaches, but I know someone who also gets migraines. There are specific herbs you can take for them. I will look up the cure in my herbal health books, and have the remedy for you tomorrow. There is no reason why you should suffer when the solution is at your fingertips. Sometimes when people are very anxious about things or worried about something, they get tension headaches. Maybe I should massage the knots out of your neck. I give one hell of a massage. Did you ever have your scalp and head massaged? It is the ultimate feeling of relaxation. I can do that quite well.

I wish you would have somehow let me know that you weren't going to be there on Sunday. I went to the park just in case you'd be there Sunday morning. Whatever made you decide to go to the Statue of Liberty? Did you climb the steps?

I missed you too, and if you're able to slip your leash tomorrow evening, I would love to see you; since tomorrow is the only evening I am free this week. I leave for LA on business, Thursday morning, and will not be back until late Sunday afternoon. Henry, if you can't get to a computer, please call me on my cell phone and leave a message. Although the cell is only on when I'm in transit, I pick up my messages every morning and evening. At least I would have known that you were OK, and wouldn't have gone to the park to jog alone. I waited almost an hour before beginning my jog. Is there someplace in your home where you can have some privacy when you are on the computer?

Let me know about tomorrow, and feel better. – Love, H S

August 21, 2000
Hi Julie:

I will be there to see you tomorrow night. I wouldn't miss it. I have no privacy when I use my computer at home, unless I am home alone. I am so sorry that you waited for me on Sunday. Please accept my apology. It didn't occur to me to leave you a voice mail. I will know for the future. I didn't think. You are right; it is tension and stress that gave me this damn migraine. It actually makes me sick to my stomach when it cooks off like this. I have some stuff to take. I find that Excedrin Migraine works really well, and I can't complain, as I only get one or two a year. Again, I can't tell you how sorry I am you waited for me at the park, you must have felt like **$#@** standing there waiting and not knowing. I have done that – it sucks. I'm sorry. I just hate the thought of you standing there alone, waiting, and I didn't show. I owe you one (what would you like?) Now be good. I went to the Statue of Liberty, because in all these years, I had never gone there before.

I need to lie down and get some sleep, so I will end now. I will be in contact for sure tomorrow. Stay well Julie, until tomorrow, Love, Henry

August 22, 2000
Dear Witchy Poo:

Or, is it Goddess of the Earth? You know it wasn't that long ago that witches were burned at the stake. You would have made a great witch. Not the stereotypical kind with the black hat, broom, and wart. But, the real kind – the one with the gift of understanding the forces of nature, the spell binder, for you have me bewitched. Did you cast a spell on me? That would explain so much. Smile.

So, Elvira, how are you today? I am tired, real tired. Thank you for your concern about my migraine. It actually is better now. I think I just need a vacation from life for a week or two. I am looking forward to seeing you tonight. What would you like to do? I looked over your chess move this morning. I'll have to think about that.

Did I tell you that you have great legs? I hope your day is going good. See you later Hot Stuff, and thanks again for the concern. With Love, Henry

August 22, 2000
Henry:

I can see that you are getting back to your old self. Smile. There is no such thing as a witch. Utter nonsense. I have studied about the forces of nature, but I certainly cannot put spells on people, etc. Maybe that's why I'm so intrigued by it. I have some pills that will give you some energy if you need them. I usually take them before I work out, but they definitely will perk you up, if you are tired. Hold off on your chess move until you are feeling better. I wouldn't want you to say I won because you weren't back to your full self. I prefer to win the old fashioned way.

I got a kick out of you asking what I would like to do tonight. Henry, you are a laugh a minute. Since you are so so very tired, I think we should just go back to your office, and I will give your head that massage I told you about, and your head will start to feel really good, and maybe I'll even give you some head, if you think you can stand the strain of it. But, if you feel that is too much activity so soon after your migraine, we can just lie down in each other's arms and talk for a while. Maybe I'll even smoke a joint with you. But, then we might forget the time again. Henry, do you have an alarm clock in your office? - H S

August 22, 2000
Hi Dr. Hot Stuff:

I am just plain beat – real tired. I think the last few weeks have finally caught up with me, and I am looking forward to the weekend so that I can just put my feet up and snooze away half the day. I agree with your diagnosis doctor, a head massage is exactly what I need. Which head were you planning on massaging? The little one, I hope. You can massage it with your lips and tongue until I come. That will most definitely make me feel better, and I do reciprocate. I really enjoy you squirming under my tongue as I slide it in and out of you.

Let's just go back to my office and relax. I don't plan on sex, but then I never do. It just seems to happen with you. It must be that spell again. And, don't try to deny being a witch. I know better. . . because you do most definitely have me bewitched. There is nothing wrong with being a witch. When I was younger, my friends used to refer to me as the "Wicca Man", because I was "in tune" with the earth. I have always, even as a child understood the magic of nature. I understand and appreciate the forces of nature and actually believe the planet to be alive. Not just the things living on it, but the planet itself. But that's a philosophical discussion for another time, but one I would like to have with you. It is what the Buddhists believe also. I always have weed on me, and would be happy to get "stupid" with you on the way up to my office. We can go on a tour of the quarry, and I'll change your state of awareness. Sex while stoned is fun, and much more sensual.

I have attached my chess move. This is getting interesting. Look forward to seeing you tonight. Have a good day, Hot Stuff. - Henry

August 22, 2000
Henry:

You took my knight, huh? I think you might be a little bit too aggressive for me. I knew you would take it, but I had no other move that made sense to me. I will have to ponder over my next move once I get out from under today's work load.

Henry, I prefer to get stoned in your office. I don't like driving and getting high at the same time. Is that OK with you? If you're afraid that the guy in the lab might smell it, we can do it another time. I don't need to get high to get sensual, as you already know this.

When I was discussing the head massage, I was talking about the big head. You know the one that had the headache...However, if you feel the little one needs some massaging also; I could be coaxed into doing it. ** GRIN** Now, for the rest of the afternoon, I will be thinking about what you said your tongue would be doing to my body. Thank you for the distraction. Why do you do this to me, Henry?

And, Henry, I am starting to wonder about you. How come every time I say something that I am into, like nature, it turns out that you are, or were, into it also? I think you are just saying these things. Let's see if you even know the five forces of nature. Can you name them? Got ya! (I hope.) I have a line to start a new poem with you on – see if you can pick it up:

The years that we have left to live
Will be the best that life can give

Also, when are you going to send me the first paragraph of our short story? I have been thinking about it, and put together something I think we can use in it. I will bring it tonight. That is, if you are still interested in pursuing this story. You got me all excited about it, and then left me at the edge of the cliff. Well, it's back to doing what I get paid for, and I'll see you tonight. - H S

August 22, 2000
Hello Julie:

How's the day going? Are you almost ready to go home? Do you really think that I just agree with you, or say I'm also into some of the things that you are into, just to make a connection? I hope not. I haven't said anything that I did not believe when I said it. As far as being "into" nature – well yes, I am. I think that I can answer your question regarding the five forces of nature, but I am not real sure if you mean forces or elements. If you mean the Chinese five elements as used in Feng Shui, then they would be Wood, Fire, Earth, Metal and Water. The Celtic or Wiccan five elements of nature would be Earth, Air, Fire, Water and Akasha (which is all the other elements combined and none of them). So, did I get you?

See ya later, toots... Henry

August 23, 2000
Good Morning, Henry!

I feel absolutely wonderful today, and it's all because of you. I just wanted you to know that. I'll give you my chess move a little later on in the morning, after I do a couple of things for my employer. And, no, in answer to your question, I don't think that you agree with what I say just to make a "connection". It would certainly explain a lot if you did, though. But, I know better. We think alike, and we feel the same things. Scary, isn't it? But, it's also wonderful to find someone who is as nuts as I am!

I looked quickly at the museum exhibits for the Labor Day weekend. There is so much, I don't think we could see it all in one day. There is just so much for you to see, Henry. When you see all the culture that is so close to you, you'll wonder why you never went to these places before. We're going to have a great time. I'm getting excited about this excursion we are planning, and it's so nice to have something to look forward to.

Love ya – H S

August 23, 2000
Good Morning, Julie:

I am so happy that you feel good this morning. I always enjoy your company in the evening (clothed or unclothed). I am really looking forward to our trip into the city. It will be fun to spend some real time together. And, incidentally, I was very impressed by what you had written so far towards our story. The writing style was concise and entertaining. You really are quite a talented and very descriptive writer. By the time you get back from LA, I will have the opening on paper. I'll be back in touch before you leave today, for sure. Affectionately, Henry

August 23, 2000
Henry,

We always spend real quality time together, no matter what we do. I also am looking forward to that day, and to seeing the expressions on your face as you experience all the paintings and beautiful works of art we will see together.

Have a good day. I think I will be leaving early – about three, if I can break away, because I have so much to do at home tonight before I leave for LA. Get some rest this weekend. I'll be thinking of you tomorrow as I watch the California sunset over the ocean. Here's my chess move. - H S

August 23, 2000
Hi Hot Stuff:

I have attached my chess move for you to ponder over on the plane. Have a safe trip, enjoy the break from the daily stuff and I'll look forward to seeing you on your return. Take care, Love – Henry

August 23, 2000

You are NOT going to checkmate me in the next move, Henry. I moved my knight from F3 to D4. You can be the one pondering over the weekend. I'll be reading a good book on the plane, not thinking about chess. I miss you already. Love, Julie

August 23, 2000

Very Slick! Have a great time, Julie... - Henry

August 27, 2000
Welcome Back Hot Stuff:

So, how was LA? Jersey was emptier without you. Hope you are not too tired. It is good to have you back. Have a great day. I'll check in during the day on Monday.
Hugs and Kisses – Henry

August 27, 2000
Hi Henry:

It was so nice to read your email this morning. It makes me think that you thought about me once or twice while I was away. Smile. California was wonderful. I got my two meetings out of the way on Thursday and Friday, and then was free the rest of the time. I drove ninety miles per hour on the California freeway, blasting oldies on the radio while watching the California sunset over the Pacific. I didn't have anyone at all to answer to – only me. Jealous?

My audit of the branch went well. I'm very good at what I do. My visit to the U. S. Penitentiary was an experience I'm not sure I'd want to repeat, but my friend was very happy to see me and the visit went well, or as well as one can expect under the high security conditions in which he is allowed to have visitors. Back in LA on Saturday night, my cousin gave a little party for me. I thought it was wonderful and it was especially interesting to see his diverse group of friends.

So, did you get a chance to work on our little story this weekend, or did the monster hedges consume all your spare time? I wrote a poem on the plane, but I haven't had a chance to type it up yet. Later today, I'll send it to you. Whose move is it in our "Chess for the Genitals" game?

I missed you too and love you – H S

August 28, 2000
Hi Hot Stuff:

Glad you're back. I did miss you, and yes, I am jealous. I have attached my chess move for you to look over. I am glad that you got to see your incarcerated friend. Did you enjoy your time with your cousin? I have some interesting news for you regarding my family. I just heard from my cousin, Julia, who moved to Australia fourteen years ago. I haven't heard from her in thirty-three years. How about that? I am pretty excited about renewing old family ties. I thought that I was the only one left. Are we still on for Saturday? Be in touch later... Love, Henry

August 28, 2000

Henry, when you put a person in "check", you are supposed to say so.

I think it's fabulous that you were able to contact a long lost cousin. Is this from your mother or father's side of the family? You should plan a trip to Australia and visit with her, or have her come here to America to see you. Life is too short to let this go. Being Italian, I was brought up to believe that "family" is very important. Since my Mom's parents had nine children and my

Dad's parents had eleven children, you can imagine how many cousins I have. Too many to count, and I have a special relationship with every one of them.

Here is the first draft of my new poem. Although it's not really about you, because I too have some of these problems, I was thinking about some of the things you told me when I wrote it. In fact, I think everyone can identify with this poem one way or another.

As far as I know, we are still on for Saturday, unless you back out. Are we still on, if it rains, or will your excuse of going to the shore loose some of its plausibility on a rainy day? Why do I feel that this is going to be too much trouble for you? What would happen if you just told her the truth? Doesn't she know about your other female friend who's going into the hospital? And, if you go out shopping with your goddaughter's mother, who she knows you slept with, why couldn't you go to the museum with me? Henry, it must be such a strain on you to live with such deception. How do you do it?

- H S

CHOICES

Sleep eludes us while we drown in our own tears,
as we struggle to make decisions threatening
to intrude upon our lives.
What do we owe to ourselves
as we stand at each crossroad of life?
If we have the courage to choose
the road that dares to go forward,

*will we be forever haunted
by what we left behind,
or
if we back off from the edge of new worlds,
and allow the fears inside us to win,
will we be forever haunted
by the roads not taken,
and fall backwards into the pit of cowardice?*

Choices . . .

*forever altering our lives -
what might we have had
from the creative framework of our minds, and
what will we never get back
from the past that has served us so well?
Or has it?
Awake to the challenge of a future unbound by limits,
or
numbed by the convenience of the predictable and familiar?
Alive with promises of the future,
or
buried in the casket of the past?*

*If only it were easy to make
choices . . .
and, if this poem could give us answers,
fore the world spins constantly, ever changing,
leaving the future destined
by our
choices.*

August 28, 2000
Hi Julie, Sweetie:

If you don't back out, I'll be there Saturday. I didn't, and never will admit to Wilma, that I had any intimacy with my god-daughter's mother. I don't like this deception either. It truly goes against my character. I told Wilma that on Saturday I was going down to my buddy's boat at Manasquan, rain or shine. I did tell her that I would be spending the Saturday (September 22nd) at the hospital when my friend, Elizabeth, has her surgery done. Wilma isn't happy about it. But, I'm going anyway.

I didn't read your poem yet, but will as soon as I get offline. My cousin saw my youngest son's name on a punk rock web site that she got onto after she put the family name into her computer's search engine, just to see what turned up. When she saw my kid's name, she wrote to him to ask if he knew if there were a family connection, and that's how the ball got rolling. I haven't seen her since she was seven or eight years old, and I was about seventeen at the time. She will be visiting in a year or two to see a friend in Rochester, NY, and we will hook up there. I can't wait, as I am very excited about it. I also have a male cousin (her brother), and a bunch of little ones I never even knew existed. Oh, and the chess game – check (don't sweat it; you're going to win anyway). I guess I'll just have to resign myself to being used for my body. Miss you... Henry

August 28, 2000
Hi Henry:

I moved my knight. You didn't leave me much else to do. You haven't won yet, Einstein.

Well, at least you are truthful about one of your friends. Smile. I don't know how you do it, Henry. Did you ever think that the "dishonesty" is the real reason for your confusion, and not Wilma? She is what she always was. You're the one who has changed. I probably shouldn't say anything, but it's just that I see you so "lost" sometimes. I want you to be happy and carefree. You deserve to be.

I think it's amazing that your cousin just happened to find you, thanks to computers. If it weren't for the internet, she never would have found you. I NEVER WOULD HAVE FOUND YOU. It's wonderful. I will be able to see you on Thursday evening. I miss you too, and need that "Henry fix"! What did you think of "Choices"? Your opinion is very important to me. Got to get back to work. Take care – H S

August 28, 2000
Hi Sweetie:

You are right, or course. I don't like being dishonest. I am not proud of myself for it. I have lots to tell you about my cousin when I see you next. I was hoping to see you sometime this week, if that's OK with you. But, if you're busy, that's OK, because I do get to spend time with you on Saturday. That will be great. I am very busy for the next day or two. But, I do have a few hours free Thursday evening. Anyway, HS I will be back in touch tomorrow when I return from Brooklyn. Have a super day.

And, Julie, I thought that "Choices" was too close to home. Excellent. I think that it would strike a nerve in anyone who reads it. Be in touch tomorrow. Have a great evening.
With Love, Henry

August 31, 2000

Today is the first day of the rest of your life! I don't know who wrote that, but I love that phrase. Anyway, Good Morning to you, Henry. I hope your trip to Brooklyn was enjoyable. Bring me back some spumoni. Some day I will take you to the Spumoni Garden in Bensonhurst where you will taste the best spumoni you ever tasted in your entire life – home made, from a secret family recipe.

I love the opening sentence to our short story. It's great! I'd like to play with what we've got so far, if that's OK with you? If not, I won't. But, I think I can flush it out a bit, while still using all your thoughts and ideas. Will you trust me with that? Would you rather I just pick it up from here with a paragraph or two, or do you want to do more first? Let me know. I have to go over this outline with you a bit on Thursday. Some of it doesn't make sense to me. Did she loose the child or not? How does the government find out about her? Henry, we need to work on it a bit, but it will be good when we are finished.   – H S

August 31, 2000
Good Morning, Julie:

Good news and bad news. First the good news – I can for sure make it on Saturday, if you still want to get together. And, the bad news – I can't make it tonight. I have to be working at Newark Airport from 1:30 PM through about 11:30 tonight. I just found out. Bummer - but we can make up for it on Saturday. I hope you can still make it as I have wanted to spend some time, not just the two hours per week we usually see each other, with you. So, how is your day going?

I have so much to tell you about my long lost family that I am discovering. And, Julie how did you know that spumoni is my all time favorite type of ice cream? I'm not kidding. I fill the gap with mint chocolate chip because I rarely find good spumoni. So, I am going to take you up on that Bensonhurst trip. I haven't been in the office in the last couple of days, as we are very busy, and I have a lot of projects to visit. I was in Allentown PA all day yesterday otherwise I would have emailed you.

Be in touch later, hope you can confirm Saturday. Love, from your part time playmate and full time friend – Henry.

August 30, 2000
Henry:

You are doing it again – spumoni is my favorite ice cream flavor, not yours!

I'm totally devastated about tonight. I was looking forward to seeing you so much. I will have to make do just on Saturday, then. I hope I can get all my kisses in that day. Where would you like to meet me on Saturday? Do you still want to go into the City, or would you prefer to do something less taxing? **GRIN**

What kind of roads are you building in Allentown? Are you preparing the asphalt for the new parking lot at Newark for Continental? Parking there right now is disastrous. When will they finish? What do you do there until 11:30 at night? I thought that you just made the recipes. I didn't know that you poured the asphalt also. You know you don't have to make excuses up for me, Henry. You can tell me the truth if you are just too tired, or need more time with Wilma. Please don't be dishonest with me, Henry. I don't think I could stomach that. I did some work on our story, but will wait till you answer my questions about it before sending it to you. - H S

August 31, 2000
Hi Hot Stuff:

I am also very disappointed about tonight. I am not making up excuses. Although I am the chief materials designer here, I am also the technical director, so on many projects, I do site trips during installation of the material to avoid technical problems.

Much of our work is conducted at night so that we have a minimal impact on traffic. Yes, we are doing work at Continental, but I am going to the airport on a taxiway/refueling area evaluation that is not the Continental area. The Port Authority is conducting some in place testing on the area, and I am going down to assist them with that structural evaluation. You know that I am a pretty good engineer and the Port people value my opinions and expertise. We are working at night because of the flight schedules. We cannot close the area off in that loading area. The work in Allentown is on both the Lehigh Valley International Airport and the road off of Route 22 known as Airport Road. I am rebuilding the entire access road to the airport, and it will be a two year project that has already started. I am also rebuilding several piers at Brooklyn's Atlantic Avenue for the Port Authority.

What do you mean, "I'm doing it again"? I don't make this stuff up. Spumoni is my favorite ice cream flavor. I also like Terramassu. All these coincidences and similarities draw us together. Weird, isn't it?

I would like to BS with you about our joint venture story on Saturday. As far as Saturday is concerned, my main interest is just spending time with you. If that is going into the City, that would be great, but I would also be happy just sitting next to the lake at the park with you, just as long as I get the chance to spend some time with you. What would you like to do? I am game for just about anything. In any event, anything we do will be fun, as far as I'm concerned. - Henry

August 31, 2000
Henry:

I'm sorry that I made you feel that you had to go into intricate detail to explain yourself. I am curious as to the things you do, because I care about you, and am interested in everything you are involved in. But, sometimes I feel insecure, and wonder if you lie to me the way you lie to Wilma. I'm sorry. I was definitely wrong. Are you going to spank me? When? Soon, I hope.

I have a hankering for some spumoni right now. How about Saturday, we go to the Botanical Gardens in Brooklyn, and then if you want to, we can go to the Spumoni Garden in Bensonhurst? Would you like to see where I grew up? It really has the best spumoni in the country. Almost as good as, if not better than, the kind they make in Italy. Or, we can do some research in Central Park and check out the museums in New York City. Henry, I just want to be with you and don't really care what we do as long as we are together. So, if you have a different idea, that's good also. I think I can be ready by eleven AM. Does that time work for you?

I'm sending you what I did to our story. It's only three pages, but I'd like to know what you think of it. We don't have to use it, if you don't want to. I gave our character a name. Don't laugh – "Dat". I thought a one syllable word would be best, and the sound of "DA" is the first and easiest sound that a baby makes. So, I came up with "Dat". Henry, I just couldn't keep calling her "she". Are you working tomorrow? - H S

August 31, 2000
Hi Sweetie:

You know that you don't have to apologize for anything. And, yes, I am working tomorrow. Seeing where you grew up would be cool. I'd like that. You and spumoni would be a great combination. How about I lick it off of you? Eleven AM would be fine with me. Would you like to meet at the park and ride, or anyplace is OK with me.

I have to go to the airport now, and will be in touch tomorrow. I've downloaded our story and will read it through tonight. Love H

August 31, 2000
Henry:

The park and ride at eleven Saturday works for me. I'm going very casual. I most likely will be wearing jeans. Leave a message on my cell if anything should change. I will do likewise, if that's OK. See you then. And, I like what you said you will do with the spumoni. We should definitely fit that in. I can't wait to see you. - H S

August 31, 2000

"Very casual" – does that mean no underwear? - Henry

September 1, 2000
Henry:

If you had a choice of doing anything you wanted to do with me tomorrow, what would that be? You do have that choice, you know. And, please don't give me a bullshit answer, like "it doesn't matter what we do", because it does. Just to let you know – I don't have to prove to myself that I could have a great time with you "out" of bed. I know I would. I know what I would like to do tomorrow, and it's not going to the museum or eating spumoni in Brooklyn. Although, if that is what you really want to do, we can do those things and I would enjoy them also. It's supposed to rain tomorrow, anyway. I have something else in mind. Do you feel the same way? And, what did you think of what I did to our story?

- H S

September 1, 2000
Hi there cutie pie:

Actually, this is not a bullshit answer. Anything we do is Ok with me, because I just enjoy your company. I also know that we can have a great time "out" of bed. But, if you would like to spend the day screwing our brains out, well, that's OK too. I definitely know that we would have a great time doing that. Actually, that sounds like a whole lot of fun...wanna? I would most certainly not turn down an offer like that. You know what an animal I am when it comes to you, Hot Stuff.

If you would like to go into the city, and are just not in the mood for some nookie, then we will have a great time in the city. You know you are pretty hot stuff. Would you believe I just got a boner writing this to you? That's anticipation for you. Seriously, it's been a long time since we were able to spend some time making love. Some time when I didn't have to watch the clock. It would be nice to cuddle up and relax, but truly, it is your choice. Either way, would be fun, just as long as you are there. - Henry

September 1, 2000
Henry:

You know what I "wanna" do. **GRINNING NOW*** But, where? - H S

CHAPTER TWELVE

That Saturday was the second full day that we spent together. Henry took one look at me, and I at him, and we knew that the only thing we really wanted to do was make long luxurious love in a cozy little nest somewhere. So, all our grand plans about going to New York City and browsing around museums, or the Botanical Gardens and eating spumoni in Brooklyn, flew right out of our heads. It was great to be so "in tune" with someone that you instinctively know what they want, and even better when you both want the same thing.

Henry managed to find a motel that allowed us to check in before Noon. And, as soon as we were alone in our room, our hunger for each other took over. We made love so many times – no one was counting, and when we weren't making love, we talked while cuddling in each other's arms. This was the part I liked the best – talking and cuddling. I never had that before. It rained, and we watched the storm from the balcony outside our room. It was a pretty sensational day, and just not long enough.

Both Henry and I are the kind of people who can be very comfortable alone within our own heads. But, I needed to feel connected to someone and to share my life, and not just share bits and pieces. I needed love in my life. He, on the other hand, feels that he needs to go through life alone. I think he was terrified of our relationship, and the feelings he had for me. He was so afraid of getting hurt. I knew where those feelings were coming from. I was there myself once before. In fact, it was so bad before I left Don the first time that I fell into the trap of thinking I couldn't make it on my own. Henry had been abused by Wilma in the worst sense of the word. For thirty years, his wife systematically chipped away at his self-confidence, his self-esteem, his courage, and his choices. She did it so skillfully that these things were gone before he realized what was happening. He was a victim, and she exploited him, because she needed to feel superior. It's not easy to rebuild those things she took away from him, and Don took away from me. But, something about being together made us both feel "normal" again. We were doing what we had to do to get away from the negative energy our spouses were exuding. We were fighting for our lives...for our sanity...for what was left of our souls.

Henry has this personal code of honor that means more to him than any rules of society. I knew he would have to overcome his guilt first. Then, he will have to work on rebuilding all those things he lost before he could come to terms with what we were starting to build together. I think I meant more to him than he thought anyone could mean to him, or than he even realized, and he didn't want to mess up my life with his baggage. But, I also had a long road ahead of me. I had baggage too. I don't think anyone over fifty who is "normal" doesn't have baggage. I love him so much. He had the ability to arouse and sooth me at the same time. That love we have for each other gave me the strength to do the things I knew I must do. It gave him strength also. We fed on it. Without it, I don't think I would have been successful in the breakup of my marriage. I will always be grateful to Henry for that.

September 3, 2000
Hi Henry:

Happy Sunday! I'm a little bit worried about you, and just wanted to know if everything was OK when you got home last night? If you get a chance to email, let me know. If you need to talk to someone, I'm here for you. I'm still recovering today from yesterday, but tomorrow morning I plan to go jogging. Interested? I had such a good time yesterday. I will be smiling the rest of this holiday weekend. Now if only the weather will cooperate. Hopefully, we'll get some sun tomorrow. - H S

September 3, 2000
Hi Hot Stuff:

Are you still tingling? What a great day. Yesterday will be one of those days I will smile about when I'm one hundred years old.

Wilma and I drew up a property settlement today. So, it looks as though this time I really am on my way. Enjoy the rest of the weekend.

Sleep well and keep smiling – Henry

September 5, 2000
Hi There Hot Stuff:

How was the rest of your weekend? My Saturday was great...

I have been looking for homes to purchase. I found a nice stone ranch in 'move in' condition in Montague. It's on a two acre lot. It has two bedrooms, a two car garage, a paved driveway, fireplace, solarium and basement – all for $139,000. Next stop is the bank this week, to see what kind of mortgage commitment I can get. So, are you still tingling? - Henry

September 5, 2000
Hi Henry:

Were we supposed to get together tonight? I thought you said something about it on Saturday. Maybe I'm mistaken. Tonight is probably the only night that I can see you, because I expect to be working late the rest of the week. The house you described to me sounds like a dream. But, Henry, you just started looking. Don't you think you should investigate the market some more before making such a large commitment? If you decide you made a mistake, houses in Montague are so far out, they are very hard to sell. How long has this house been on the market? Have you done comparisons to other similar homes in the same area? (Also, you'll be so far away, I'll never get to see you.) I thought you were planning on renting a house from your company for a while. Did you change your mind about that? - H S

September 5, 2000
Hi Julie:

I am planning on meeting your bus tonight. The house in Montague is the first one that interests me, although there are several others I plan on seeing. There is also one in Vernon that seems as though it could be OK for $119,000. I plan on finalizing all my financial stuff with Wilma tonight (I hope), then according to my bank, I need some kind of legal document to delineate who pays what as far as the debt is concerned. If I give them a copy of that document along with a list of the debt that I will carry, then they will give me a mortgage commitment. I think that about $135,000 is my top limit on a house - $120,000 is more realistic. I haven't decided on any particular house so far, and very well may rent one of the company houses, but it doesn't cost to look. So, if I find a good one, then I will go for it. I still plan on an early spring move, unless something changes. At least, according to the rough numbers worked up by the bank, I don't have to live in a rat hole. If I need to drive a little further to work, if it's the right house, and the right money, then I'll do it. I know that Montague is further out, but I can get so much more for my money that way. I'm just looking at what's available in my price range right now, and I am pleasantly surprised by what is available in the $120 – 130,000 range.

See ya later, Toots – Henry

September 5, 2000
Hi Henry:

I thought I heard you correctly. Great. I will see you later. I hope everything works out well with your bank. I know people in the mortgage business. There are ways you can play with your paperwork so that the bank is happy. Smile. Although you may get more house for your money, the further out you go makes it that much more difficult to sell. Remember that a house is an investment, and the resale value should be one of your biggest considerations. Montague is like - the middle of nowhere. Nobody outside of the County has ever heard of it. Find out the average amount of time that a house sits on the market in that area. I've bought and sold houses, both personally, and as a realtor. I still have my real estate license. Henry, let me help you with this. I won't steer you wrong in spite of the fact that I hope you live closer to me. - H S

September 6, 2000
Good Morning Overworked Hot Stuff:

How's your day going? Mine is shaping up to be very busy. The Fall is panic time in this industry, as everyone is scrambling against the cold weather clock to get the projects done, and because we had so many rainy days this Summer, we are behind about twenty percent. Tomorrow and Friday I will be at Newark Airport almost all day, but I will find the time somehow to email you a "hello". Incidentally, last night I noticed that you lost some weight. I can see it in your face. Don't work too hard, and have a great day. – Henry

September 6, 2000
Hi Henry:

Hopefully, I am changing shape for the better. The way I look at it, there is no reason why at fifty-one I can't have the same figure I had when I was twenty. It's just a matter of mind over hunger, and lots of exercise. I think it's all this wonderful luscious sex I'm having with you that is making me sleep late. I think that's also what's contributing to my weight loss. When someone is as happy as I am now - it's just that I'm no longer depressed. I feel wonderful all the time! And, it's all your fault. I'm smiling all the time, lately, too.

I hope you have a great day too. I'd like to see you over the weekend, if possible. We're having great jogging weather. The endorphins will fill your brain, and I promise you will feel absolutely wonderful afterwards. And, jogging does make me horny.

Are you going to look at those houses this weekend? - H S (Love you!)

September 7, 2000
Hi Hot Stuff:

I finally got home from the airport. Oversleeping just means that you needed the rest. Did you catch up? How is the rest of the week going for you? I will be back out at the airport tomorrow from early morning until about 2:00 PM, and then I have a wedding to go to so I think that I will be able to contact you tomorrow. But, just remember, you are in my thoughts. I will let you know about jogging Sunday morning. As of right now, all I want to do is go to sleep, so this isn't the best time for me to give you an answer about jogging.

Tuesday night was great. Every time I am in your company for any reason, it's great. Hope you have a great day today, and don't work too hard, just hard enough. Remember you can only do what you can do. And yes, I do see a difference. You are starting to change shape. Sleep well, kitten. - Henry

September 11, 2000
Good Morning, Julie:

I hope this week is better for you than last week. How was your weekend? I spent mine waiting for the septic guy, who never came. Things here are about the same. No time for anything lately between work and what I must take care of at home. It seems that I have no time left for myself. Wilma and I have reached a workable property settlement, and I expect to get a formal version of it in the next day or two. Then, it's off to the bank with it to get a mortgage commitment. I expect to be in my own place sometime in January. I am definitely still looking for just the "right" house. If the weather permits next Sunday, I will definitely go jogging with you, if you are going. How did the weekend work out with your Mother? Good, I hope. Well, Julie, you have a great day. I have to start my fourteen hour day. It's off to Maryland this morning, but I will have access to a computer most of the day. Take care, Hot Stuff.

Miss you. - Henry

September 11, 2000
Hi Henry:

Sorry I didn't respond sooner, but I was working in my new office all morning and my computer is still in the old office. I will be spending the next week or so changing offices, so watch what you say in the email, since I may not see it right away. Keep it clean, please. Smile. I've got a much nicer and bigger office than before. It's just that I have this fancy pedestal desk that shows my legs and a window wall, and since I like to wear short skirts, everyone gets to see my legs. I guess that could work in my favor when it comes time for a raise. Grin.

You sound pretty busy yourself. After reading your email, I got the feeling that you won't have any time to spend with me this week. Did you see that house you liked this weekend? I spent Sunday looking at open houses. I saw two in Newton that were very disappointing. My Mom cancelled on me this weekend, but I think I'll visit with her next Saturday. I haven't decided yet.

I doubt if you will join me for jogging next Sunday because you've made an excuse every week I asked you lately. I think you are afraid that you won't be able to keep up with me. Every time you think I'm ahead of you, you stop. Like the chess game.

333

I haven't gotten your next move in over a week. Are you afraid I might actually win? Henry, I can let you win, if you like. And, when we're jogging, I'll slow down when you do, so you don't feel that I'm in better shape than you. How's that? I hope you know when I'm teasing you.

So, what are you doing in Maryland? Are you staying there overnight? That's a long drive to do back and forth in one day, isn't it? I'm working late myself. Tonight I'll take car service back to the 'park and ride'. When I leave the office, it will be too late for the bus. If you get lonely on the drive from Maryland, call me. I always have time for you. I'll be in the office until about seven tonight. By then I'll be totally pooped out, since I started before seven this morning. It's a busy time for me, too. I miss you, too. This is no way to have a relationship. Henry, I think we've got to do something about this, before we give up on each other. - H S

September 11, 2000
Good Afternoon, Julie:

Don't you dare let me win at anything. That's selling yourself short, and it does me an injustice. Besides, what makes you think you can beat me at anything? Smile. Although I must admit, when we are alone, you do take me to the limit, sometimes. Actually, I think that you are giving me a run for my money in the chess game, too. And, I know for sure, you could run me into the ground jogging. I feel that you would be a formidable competitor in any field. I meant it about this coming Sunday. I really think that if I got to bed early for a change, I could make it by 7:30 AM Sunday, if you are still game. Don't work too hard, now. And, as far as that window wall and pedestal desk showing off your legs, goes – they are worth showing off, so you should wear shorter skirts.

Enjoy your larger office, but don't work too hard. Have a great day, and I will be back in touch tomorrow as I am leaving Maryland now and heading back. Take care, Sweetie – Henry

September 11, 2000
Henry:

I never sell myself short! If you set your alarm clock, you can probably make it on Sunday. I noticed that you are afraid to go jogging with me, so I assume that you are afraid we'd race. I'm pretty fast. You might feel threatened by a woman who can run faster than you. I still think you will find a reason not to jog. It's not your thing. That's OK. I'll still love you!

I won't let you win the chess game without a good fight. It's just that if we were playing in person, I could distract you with a low cut blouse or short skirt. But, playing chess via email doesn't give me any advantages at all. I have to really "think" about my moves. Smile. And, when I "think", I usually win. Some men feel threatened by a woman as smart as I am. I wouldn't want to loose you over a measly chess game. You are too important to me for that.

So, what's on the agenda this week? Is there time for us to get together? Or, should I just work late every night and 'dream' about making love with you instead? Sometimes those dreams are pretty good, actually. But, I always prefer the real thing. I have enough work to last me through the next year. How come you evade most of my questions? Take care – H S

September 12, 2000
Hi Sweetie:

I'm in Maryland again, and will most likely stay a day or two as the commute is rough. Are you all moved into your new expanded "boss type" office? I tried to call you last night at six thirty, but the office phone didn't pick up, so I called you on your cell, but only got your voicemail. Look forward to seeing you, Julie. I will be there Sunday for sure, if it doesn't rain. I miss you - Henry

September 12, 2000

Henry, what are you doing in Maryland? I got your phone message, but I was still at the office. I expect to be working late again tonight. You have to call my direct number after five thirty. There is no one to answer the switchboard after that. I know that when you're out of town, it can get pretty lonely in that hotel room. Give me a call, and I'll cheer you up, if you're feeling down. I miss you too.

I hope it doesn't rain on Sunday. - H S

September 13, 2000
Hi Julie:

I didn't get your email until this morning. I will call you today to say "hello". I am working with the FAA people in Baltimore, and helping them redesign the main runways. So, how are you? Still showing off those beautiful legs? Gee! It's so hard to keep this "clean". Instead of writing what I'm thinking, I will just let your imagination work a little. Smile. Any bites on the house yet? How come you are working so late? Talk to you later. - Henry

September 13, 2000
Hi Henry:

I miss you – miss us. No bites on the house as yet. Maybe soon, I hope. Henry, everything you do at work sounds so "intelligent" compared to what I do. I mean, helping to design a runway and all. You should be proud of yourself.

I'm working late because I'm changing the whole department around. I need to make things more efficient and I'm moving four people to different locations. I inherited some problems that I am wrapping up now, and just found out that the paper backup for our institutional equity composite was never generated for the last two quarters. On top of that my operations manager quit on me, and I hired another middle level compliance person to pick up the slack. I'm in the middle of an NASD audit – do you want to hear more, or do you get the picture? Smile. I'm used to pressure. In fact, I work better under pressure. That's why I get paid the big bucks. The work gives me a good excuse not to come home, and I really don't want to be home any more in the evenings. It's unpleasant. I look for any reason to be out. There's only so much of my energy left, and Don is slowly draining every single drop of it out of me.

Take care, and please call me. I want to hear your voice. - H S

September 14, 2000
Hi Julie:

It was so good to hear your voice yesterday afternoon. Well, I'm back in New Jersey, at least for the rest of this week, although it looks like I'll be away a day or two next week also. It isn't that the work I do is so "intelligent"; it's just that it's different from the world you inhabit. Our work is actually quite similar. You have financial rules and regulations to follow, and I have engineering rules and regulations to follow. We both use rules to perform our work, research and compile data, make decisions based on that data, and we must both comply with state and federal guidelines, and worst of all, we must both be administrators, which means we must deal with people. The main difference is you're prettier than I am.

I know it's tough, but try to have patience with the house. It will sell, but be prepared to wait until spring. We are entering the slow season for house sales. I understand what you mean about Don draining away your energy. I am in the same situation. My stress manifests itself as fat. In the last year, I have gained fifteen pounds. I just get so depressed sometimes, and food is comforting. I must stop. I can't give in to this feeling of being drained of energy and spirit. I'm going to loose my extra weight by chasing you through the woods. What are you going to do about this drained energy? I suggest that you let me catch you. That will help. Smile. My chess move is attached.

Be in touch later, Hot Stuff – Henry

September 14, 2000
Good Morning, Henry:

I'm glad you are back in New Jersey. I know what a pain in the ass these overnight business trips can be. I hate them myself. Henry, don't make believe that the work you do is "less" than what it is. You're dam good at what you do, and you know it! So am I.

You are not fat. I like you just the way you are. Don't put yourself down. The only way to eat less is to replace the pleasure you get from food with other pleasures that are just as, if not more, satisfying. When we're together, we don't care about eating food, Henry. In fact "food" is about the last thing on our minds. See how good I am for you! If you want to loose weight, you'll just have to see more of me. And, as far as drained energy goes, I am going to replace that energy with more energy. I'm going to hang out with people who don't drain my energy, and who give me energy as I will give energy to them. People just like you! And, I don't know if I'll let you catch me until we've done at least three miles. Smile. I suggest that you wear long sweat pants instead of shorts. Because, when you jog, you will sweat, and sweat attracts mosquitoes. So, unless you want the mosquitoes to have a picnic on your legs, wear long pants. Smile. It really is a lot of fun. In fact, the jogging will give you a higher high than pot. – H S

September 16, 2000
Henry:

My computer was down most of yesterday afternoon, so I don't know if you emailed me or not. I am just going to assume that you'll be there on Sunday morning at 7:30 as you said. I'm looking forward to it since I haven't seen you in a while, and I always enjoy a good jog. I'm in my new office now and it's cool. I've got spotlight lighting over beautiful original watercolors and all kinds of neat things. See you tomorrow. – H S

CHAPTER THIRTEEN

During our jog that Sunday, Henry and I talked a long time about his marriage and the property settlement he made with his wife. He was giving her so much money each month, there was hardly enough left over for him to live on. I knew that the settlement was influenced by his guilt, and she was playing it up to the hilt. I felt so sorry for him. Yet, what could I say? It really wasn't my business anyway. Perhaps as a friend, I thought I could at least advise him, or say something to make him realize what he was doing to himself. It wasn't just the financial settlement that would hurt him - it was the whole thing with the house he owned with his wife. I didn't understand why a house would be so important to him. Or, maybe it wasn't the house so much, but the inability to "let go". The way they were arranging things – if either one of them marries another person, that one forfeits his or her interest in the house.

Perhaps, deep inside, they really wanted to hold onto each other, and this was their way of doing it. I knew if that were the case, my relationship with Henry was doomed. I didn't stand a chance against someone who he spent the last thirty years of his life with, the mother of his children, and the joint owner of his house. It made me wonder why he even bothered with me. Was he using me to make Wilma jealous, or for the sex, what was his reason for even seeing me? I loved him and somehow I put all those doubts and questions out of my mind. Instead, I concentrated on how I could help him, fore he was a friend first, and a lover second.

September 18, 2000
Hi Henry:

I enjoyed our jog yesterday. I'm sorry that I left so abruptly. I was distraught by your willingness to suffer financial devastation because you feel "guilty" about wanting some happiness in your life. I guess I was angry, and I didn't want to say anything I might regret later. It's probably none of my business, but as a friend, I feel obligated to try and make you see what that property settlement will mean to you. Henry, you did nothing wrong. You don't have to do penance the rest of your life, because your wife drove you into the arms of another woman. She's using emotional blackmail to insure her future with little regard for you. And you think she loves you? Right! I have another friend who is in pretty much the same boat as you. He was married for twenty-two years. He and his wife couldn't agree on a property settlement, so the judge did it for them. She got three years' alimony and the house with the mortgage. The judge gave her sixty days to refinance the mortgage for a longer term, utilizing the alimony as income to get the new mortgage. My friend got his name off the deed and the mortgage. Why would you want to be tied to a house that you don't live in, but have to constantly fix up every time something breaks? What if you decide to move to Arizona...do you hop a plane and run over there if the roof leaks? No judge would ever give a woman lifetime support unless she was disabled. Your wife is capable of holding down a job and supporting herself. Don't be a fool because you think you hurt her. She hurt you too. I wrote a poem about all this. I couldn't help it. When I get angry, I get all frustrated, and poetry comes out. I warn you. You will not like this poem, but when we first started emailing each other, we did say we would help each other, and boy do you need help. Please, Henry, see a lawyer and get yourself a property settlement that at least allows you enough money to buy yourself some dinner now and again. Smile. Don't worry; you can always bum a meal off me. I mean, what are friends for, anyway? - H S

HENRY'S NEURAPATHY

Your blood no longer circulates through your body,
and you never felt it,
when Wilma sliced off your toes.
Now, she's working on your feet.
You've become a piece of salami
she slices away at,
and I see you shiver
so cold, that
your lips have turned blue.
I try to warm you,
but I become frustrated,
because the cold has made you numb.
I feel so helpless,
unable to shield you, my friend,
while I watch her throw another stone at you
she's thrown so many, that
you've stopped feeling the pain
as they hit your body

over and over again.
I don't understand why
you allow her
to smother your passion.
What happened to the fire that burned
in your heart...
the fire that you let me sit beside one day?
Has she doused that as well?

And here you sit, now
doing her bidding
taking care of your executioner -
no toes
no feet
lips blue
numb
afraid of pain
alive
without a life!

September 18, 2000
Hi Julie:

I wondered why you left the way you did. I thought that perhaps I said something to upset you. I enjoyed the "jog", although it is clear to me that I am sadly out of shape. I couldn't keep up with you. Also, my thighs are sore as hell today. I guess I need more practice. Thank you for the poem. It did hit home, of course, and I thank you for your honesty and concern. This is a very difficult and confusing time for me, but it is coming to an end. I know that the property settlement is "generous". Better days are coming. Don't be too mad at me. It seems that everyone

I know is angry at me for something. Some for giving Wilma too much and some that feel I am screwing her over. Julie, you take care and again thanks for your concern.

Hope to see you soon. - Henry

September 18, 2000
Hi Henry:

I'm glad you're still writing to me, after my "down to earth", and hard hitting poem. Henry, I just hate to see you get taken advantage of. You are such a good person, and it's so easy to take advantage of people like you. I'm not much better. But, I wouldn't give Don so much that I wouldn't be able to live myself when I retire. And, if you think that you will be able to rene-gotiate this thing, with inflation adjusted dollars – you will get nowhere. I think that's what friends are for – to let us know when we are being ridiculously generous. That's why we help each other. Cheer up; you can always become an "escort" on the side. I'll be your pimp. You'll make a fortune with those hands. We'll advertise your services in my mother's retirement village newspaper. I hope to see you soon too. When? I have to really plan these dates for the next few weeks until I get over the hump. I want to see you very much. More than I've been seeing you. Henry, absence makes the heart "insecure". I promise I won't say a word about your property settlement again. I said enough already. I'm not angry with you. If anything, I am probably the one person who understands why you are doing it. That's why I wanted you to see yourself through the poem. I purposely made it strong, because Henry, you are sitting right on the edge now. I don't want you to fall off. – H S

September 18, 2000
A poem for you, Julie.

> *Roses are red*
> *violets are blue*
> *what would I do*
> *without a friend*
> *like you?*

Henry

September 20, 2000
Good Morning, Julie:

How's compliance today? Are you enjoying your new office? My aching muscles are OK now, and I am ready for another run. Are you game? I miss seeing you.

- Henry

September 20, 2000
Good Morning Henry:

It's not just compliance anymore. I'm Director of Compliance, Client Services and Administration. Didn't I tell you that I got a promotion? I thought I did. Anyway, I feel like I practically run the whole place. That's one of the reasons why I've been working late so much.

Did you find a house you liked yesterday? I have a feeling that you didn't get my last email to you. Let me know when you want to get together again? I haven't looked at the chess board as yet. I'll send my move to you later on in the day. – H S

September 20, 2000
Hi H S:

I'm free Thursday evening until about eight or so. Or, we could hook up for a jog on Sunday AM, as I am free until around nine that morning. So, how's the day going? I haven't found a house yet, even though I look almost every night. Tonight I will be taking a test drive out to see a couple of places in the Poconos. At least I will be able to judge the commute from there after this evening. - Henry

September 20, 2000
Hi Henry:

What's wrong with Friday night or Saturday? Do you have plans? Thursday may not work for me, because of a project I am working on at the office, and I may have to work late. It depends on how much we get done during the day. I could probably meet you later, after eight, if you would like, because I usually don't work past seven. But, lately I've been pretty tired after working twelve hour days. At least with Friday night dates, I get to sleep in on Saturday mornings, and can stay out later. If not, we can always go for a jog on Sunday morning. But, let's make it at six-thirty so we can watch the sun come up. Or is that too early for you? Henry, can't you see if there is a way we can get together on Friday or Saturday? I really miss seeing you, and I'm starting to feel really insecure in this relationship. Do you understand what I'm saying? You have so little time for me, it makes me nervous. - H S

September 20, 2000
Hi Julie:

    Don't feel insecure. It isn't that I don't have time for you, it's just that my schedule is nuts, and I don't have much time for anything. Friday I will be at the hospital all afternoon and evening as a friend is undergoing surgery. Saturday, I have appointments with realtors, and Saturday night I am having dinner with some friends here at the house. Sunday at ten I am meeting old friends here. So, you see, I am not avoiding you at all. It is just my full schedule. I looked at a house this evening. I am pretty sure this is the one. I will tell you all about it when I see you. Don't overwork. At least I will see you Sunday morning. Hugs and Kisses - Henry

September 20, 2000
Hi Henry:

    I can't help but think that you are avoiding me. It's not just your schedule. You never even emailed me yesterday, and all your letters to me are really short. You hardly respond to anything I say. If you can't get to a computer, you can always pick up the phone. But, you hardly ever call me. You stopped being responsive to me. I don't know why, but you did. You have no idea how busy my schedule is, and yet, I always find the time for you. But, then again, I'm not juggling three boyfriends like you are with three girlfriends. Or, at least three is what you told me about. I understand that I am a very small part of your life, and I appreciate your honesty with me, but I don't know if I want to continue a friendship with someone who doesn't care enough to make the time to see me. I think you should examine your own feelings about me and make a decision whether or not I'm worth the trouble I seem to be putting you through. Maybe we should both examine what we're doing here. I know this isn't coming out right, but this is how I feel. I want to spend more time with you. The relationship is becoming frustrating for me. I mean, I would go with you to look at houses or into the City. You just never ask me. It hurts, Henry, when you tell me about all the things you do without me. If you want me to be part of your life, you will have to make me part of that life. Otherwise, what are we doing? What we had was so beautiful... - H S

September 21, 2000
Hi Julie:

I'm sorry if I upset you. My schedule is really crazy right now and it isn't in the least that I am trying to avoid you. In fact, I have been busy trying to reschedule my time so that I do have more time for you. I don't have three girlfriends. I can't handle you, so what would I do with two more? I would like very much for you to see the house that I am considering, and to go house hunting with me, but I didn't ask, because you told me that you are working so hard and long, and that your own schedule is tough. I didn't ask you to go to the city with me because that was the weekend that your mother was up. My friend's surgery is scheduled for the morning on Friday, and I want to stay until I can see her in recovery, but if the surgery goes as scheduled, I will be able to see you Friday night if you still want to. I understand how you feel, and I truly am sorry for making you feel that way. It is true that I am not giving you the time you deserve, but please understand that I don't have time for myself either. Life for me right now is so hectic and difficult, but I hope to change that soon. Julie, if you feel that you don't want to invest any more time in me, I will understand without any hard feelings. You are and have been one of life's gifts to me, and I will always treasure the time we have had so far, but I know that you want to get on with your life, and wouldn't blame you in the least, if you choose to do just that.

I care about you, Julie. Make no mistake about that, but I may not be able to give you what it is that you want from me. I am trying so hard to get my life in order, and I need time to do that. I hope that we will see each other on Friday evening. It will give us both a chance to look into each others' eyes as that says so much more than words, and cannot be misunderstood or misinterpreted. Please don't sound so hurt and upset. Put a smile on your face for me. As for me, I also would like to see you more and I miss you too, but I look at things differently than you. What I see is that we spend time together, and I am grateful for the time we can have together, no matter how short. I see my glass as half full, not half empty, and the time we spend is a beautiful experience that I would not have had if I hadn't met you. Of course, I would like more, but for now, I am grateful for what I have. Julie, you need to do what your heart and instincts tell you to do. If you elect to dump me, I will always care for you, and be there if you need me. I hope your days get better. With love, Henry

September 21, 2000
Hi Henry:

Thank you for your kind email. I definitely do not want to "dump" you. I just want to feel that I'm important to you. That's all. I feel good when we are together, and I want to feel good more often. In fact, my times with you are probably the only times I do feel good. You told me that you had three girlfriends – myself, Elizabeth, and Sophia. I didn't make it up. If they are not your girlfriends, then what would you call them?

I would love to spend time with you Friday night, but I don't want to take you away from Elizabeth, who is going through surgery right now. I would imagine that after the surgery, she will be sleeping most of that day. If you feel you can do it, then let's get together. Don't assume that I can't make it somewhere with you. Ask me. I'll tell you if I'm busy. OK? And, I can go house hunting with you on the weekends. It would give me an idea of what to expect when I'm out looking myself. I would like to see the one you like also.

Henry, how do you know you can't give me what I want, when I'm not even sure of what I want myself? Let's just take each day as it comes, and see what happens. But, if you enjoy being with me as much as I enjoy being with you, then, let's make an effort to see each other more often. My instincts tell me that being with you is healthy for me. Both our spouses know that the marriages are over, so it shouldn't be a surprise to either of them if we are out of the house more often, should it? - H S

September 21, 2000
Hi H S:

"Girlfriend" is an overused, misunderstood, and ambiguous word. I have my dear friend Sophia, who is the mother of my goddaughter, and who I am not romantically involved with. She is just a good dear friend. I have Elizabeth, who is undergoing that surgery, who likewise I am not sleeping with, and who I like very much as a person, and who I do sometimes have lunch with, but I am not romantically involved with her either. Then there's you…that's it. So I am not the Don Juan you give me credit for. You're the only person crazy enough to sleep with me.

In a week or two at the most, my plate should start to empty and then if you want, we could spend a Saturday together and start seeing more of each other. I would like to have you see the house. How about next Saturday? I called the real estate agent today, and put in an offer on the house, and I called the bank to get a mortgage preapproval, but they haven't returned my calls as yet. I really want this house as it is exactly what I have been looking for - a contemporary ranch home with high cathedral ceilings with a fireplace and a garage. It was built in 1993, so it is fairly new construction, and a pretty unique looking house. It has the "feel" inside like a townhouse – wide open space, lots of light, big windows and skylights – a very airy and light feeling. It has three bedrooms and two baths, a large open living/dining area and kitchen. The property is a very nice size, about 1.08 acres, wooded and super private, a screen house sits on the back deck. It is in a closed private gated community that you need a special pass to get into. The house looks as though it belongs at the shore. I think you will like it. It reflects my personality, and is in 'move in' condition. It comes with all the appliances, fully carpeted and a large fireplace in the living room. The exterior is stained gray textured siding and is very attractive.

For Friday, probably it is best if I call you on your cell phone, and we will see if we could hook up. If not, there is always Sunday morning jogging. And, if I didn't care, why would I get out of a nice warm bed to go jogging with someone at six-thirty on a Sunday morning (the one and only morning I can sleep in)? Just so I can see you, and if I have to get up early and jog to do that, then I go jogging. You are worth it. Anyway, I hope you are feeling better. See you soon. - Henry

September 21, 2000
Hi Henry:

It was great talking to you on the phone today. You sounded so excited about your future house. I hope it all works out for you. I really do. I want you to be happy. Now, to answer your email. If these women in your life are not your "girlfriends", then what would you call them - "dear" friends? And, what would you call me – "mistress"? So, you think I'm crazy to sleep with you, and all the other women are sane, because they don't want to "bed" you. They don't know what they're missing. Your true charm comes out when you're undressed. Do they know about me - the one crazy enough to sleep with you?

I don't expect to be working late on Friday. I make it point to never work late on Fridays. If you need to be with Elizabeth, I understand. You don't have to see me. I really don't want to go home Friday night, that's all. I hate being there with him. I don't know if you can understand that. You may not have the same problems with Wilma that I have with Don. I'm having another open house this Sunday, so maybe this week the house will sell. I hope so.

I'm looking forward to our jog on Sunday. This time I will bring the camera. The mist coming up from the water, the lone boat, and the sunset, could make a great photo. I know that you enjoy jogging also. You just have to get into the spirit of it. After a while you'll just love it. This week we'll pick up the pace a bit. I didn't even work up a sweat last week. Didn't you feel totally invigorated when you went home last Sunday? Love you, H S

September 22, 2000
Hi Julie:

No, I haven't told anyone about you, or our relationship, yet. Once I move out or get a divorce, whichever comes first, then I don't care who knows. We'll put up a billboard, if you like. Smile. And, who said that my 'female" friends don't want to bed me? I said I wasn't sleeping with them. I didn't say that they didn't want to, but then again, I don't know for sure, because I didn't ask them if they want to. And, you are not my "mistress". You are my playmate. Actually, I'm really not sure what you are, except a kindred spirit, a good friend, a great lover, and a confidant and support system to me. So, what one word describes all that?

My little buddy, Elizabeth, had her surgery and they performed a total hysterectomy. Thankfully, she does not have cancer as the low white cell count turned out to be caused by a low grade infection in one ovary, but the condition of the surrounding tissue persuaded the surgeon to save her any future problems, by removing all that was there. She doesn't plan on having any more kids, so, in the long run, she will be much better off. I did ask her when she was in the recovery room, I mean, seeing that she was in bed and all, if she felt horny, but she said that she wasn't in the mood, just then. I will go and visit with her again at four, and stay an hour or so. If you let me know what time you expect your bus to be at the 'park and ride', I will meet you there. I would like to go over and see that her kids are all OK for the evening before returning home, so I would like to be out of here before nine, if that fits with your schedule. If not, then I'll see you for sure Sunday morning, and I'll be there. I have friends arriving at the house at ten on Sunday morning so I have to leave in enough time Sunday to get showered, cleaned up, and ready for their visit. I think a camera would be a great idea as that morning mist against the trees would make a super photo. Maybe I could take a picture of you. Hope to see you later. Take care of yourself Hot Stuff – Henry

September 22, 2000
Hi Henry:

I have little time to answer this in detail, but I will meet you tonight. Call me on my cellphone, and I'll let you know when the bus will arrive. Why don't we go out to dinner – you know, do something conventional? I'm glad that everything is OK with your friend, Elizabeth, and hopefully, she won't spend too long in the hospital. See ya later – H S

September 25, 2000
Hi Henry:

Just a note to let you know that I'm thinking of you. Did you buy any good antiques yesterday? Are your legs sore from our jog? Any news on the house? I've been thinking about it, and I think it might be a good idea to look some more in the Poconos before rising to the bait too quickly. Our conversation on Sunday inspired another poem. I think you'll appreciate this one. Although this poem reflects my feelings about my life, I think you will be able to identify with some of it. You always seem to bring out the poetry in me. You are just a big muse. Smile – H S

Dreamcatcher

dreamcatcher, dreamcatcher,
   catch my dream . . .

      as the sun sets
      over the ocean,
      I can see my love,
      and I'm sitting in front of him -
      between his legs,
      entwined in his arms
      my head resting on his chest,
      and the sound of his heartbeat fills my senses
      as we watch gulls swoop down
      to find their dinner,

> *we hear the waves*
> *break the shore,*
> *and the salt of the ocean,*
> *touches our skin,*
> *bringing a chill, making us*
> *seek each other's heat,*
> *the warmth of his body generates to mine;*
> *our eyes speak emotions that we can't explain.*
> *and we connect,*
> *on a level far beyond*
> *passion. . .*

> *dreamcatcher, dreamcatcher,*
> *catch that dream.*

September 25, 2000
Hello H S:

Thank you for the copy of "Dreamcatcher". I got a call from the real estate agent this morning, and I told her that the counter offer, even at $119,000, was too high, that there are other houses around that I like just as much for less money, and that I would need to see the house again before giving her a response. I think she will go back and tell her client that, and I am hoping that they are desperate enough to sell, that they will rethink the offer, and come down in price. It's worth a try. I really want that particular house as I like its vibes.

Even if I did have to get up way too early on Sunday, it was worth it, just to see you. Thanks for a good start to the day. My antique shopping went well. It was nice to spend time with my buddy, Mike, as I don't get to see him often enough. I only bought a picture frame for five dollars, but I had fun looking at other people's junk. I like to play a game of appraisal with myself, to see how close I can guess at the price, before turning over the ticket. I'm getting pretty good at it.

How did your Sunday turn out? Did you get any bids on the house yet? I hope that you enjoy the rest of your day. Don't work too hard. – Henry

September 25, 2000
Hi Henry:

That was a smart move on your part. I think you should look at other houses anyway. You need to familiarize yourself with the price range of the area. Although this particular house may be exceptional, there may be others just as nice, but cheaper. Remember also, that it is a very long commute compared to what you are used to. You'll be adding two additional hours a day to your travel time. Think about what that free time is worth to you. I know that you think you'll be close enough for your friends to visit and all, but I know that every time I come visit you, it will be a major trip, and after factoring in all the travel time, how much time will we really spend together? I'll probably not even be able to come and see you when it snows. I hate driving in bad weather. One thing that is very important to anyone who is going through what you are going through is to have close friends that you can lean on when you're feeling sad. Why is it so important to you to own a house right away? The worst thing you can do to yourself in your situation is to plant yourself out in the middle of nowhere, far away from everyone who cares about you.

The open house turned up a possible renter for our house… not very encouraging. But, even so, it might allow me to get on with my life. - H S

September 26, 2000
Good Morning, Henry:

How are you today? I have been questioning in my mind for some time now – what is it about me that you find attractive? Last night I think the answer came to me while reading a book of poetry. You don't evade my boundaries, and yet we can still be intimate. Everyone draws a circle around themselves. This is "my" territory. Yet, at the same time everyone yearns to be intimate with another person. In a way, it's a contradiction – but it doesn't have to be. I think you and I have discovered through bitter life experiences that you don't have to invade another person's circle to become intimate with that person. We each enter the other's circle when invited, and we each, instinctively, know when to leave. Instead of trying to sneak into each other's circle, we respect each other's circle, and wait for an invitation. Is any of this making sense to you? Henry, I don't think you have to move into a gated community to maintain your boundaries, but I understand how badly those boundaries have been bruised, and I understand your need to protect them. Trust me with that knowledge. I won't disappoint you. I'm not as bad as you, though. I'm not "afraid" to say, "I love you". You say it all the time with your eyes, but you have trouble mouthing the words. I do understand.

Now, on a lighter note – I miss your email. You hardly write to me any more. Why? We used to talk about poetry and philosophy, and whatever happened to the story we were working on? I am always busy at work, but I still make time to answer your email. You make me smile during the day, and bring sunshine into my office, which I really need since I don't have a window. Imagine working in the trade center and not having a window to look down at the view. I have to go to the conference room to see the view sixty floors down.

I moved my pawn to A4 on the chessboard. It's your move. Can't wait till Thursday night! – H S

September 26, 2000
My Dear Hot Stuff:

How are you today? You are a very bright and talented person who needs to spend more time being creative. My life tends to smother my creativity and I hope that when I am living alone, that my creativity will have the chance to finally express itself. As far as living "up in the boonies" – I have always been a very private person, and I am so tired of people, not you, trying to run my life for me, that I desperately need to get away to some seclusion and privacy which is the main reason for my picking that particular location. It is absolutely a beautiful peaceful tranquil area, and I can see myself being happy there. It feels right. It is not as far as you think. I will be adding only one hour extra time to my travel per day. It's not so bad. I need a sanctuary as much as I need a home. You, of course, will be welcome there. If you decide to come up, I will come, get you, and deliver you home, so you don't have to drive all that way.

I understand very well what you are talking about as far as boundaries are concerned, and both of ours have been stomped on for years. I am not even sure where mine are anymore. I do recognize that I am overly sensitive to intrusion, however. Even a well meant suggestion from most people, raises the hair on the back of my neck, as I will not tolerate any manipulation from anyone again. I need to do what I want to do for the first time in my entire life, and I am looking forward to the opportunity to do just that. Julie, you are one of the very few people who I do not resent telling me what they think would be a good course of action for me, because I know that you say it with only my best interests at heart. Most others have what is best for them as their primary reason for their suggestions. I will always respect your boundaries, as I know you need to be free also. We are starting a very unique relationship. Although we care for each other, we also respect each other's privacy, feelings, and wants, before our own. That's nice, but it is also very rare.

Yes, I do have some trouble admitting to loving you, or any-one else, other than to say I love someone without the roman-tic connotations. I love my kids. I love my friends (male and female), but I am not "in love" with them. You are talking about being in love, not loving someone. That's different. I am in love with you, and I do love you. The reason I have trouble admit-ting to it, is actually quite simple. You and I have been in a very repressive relationship for many years, and we both need to try our freedom. I am not talking about dating all kinds of people and sleeping around. I am talking about true freedom. Neither of us knows who we really are, or at least, I don't. I need to find that out. I hold back from saying I am in love, because I want you to have that freedom too. You know I love you. I can't hide it, but I also cannot leave one long commitment and begin another, because I know deep in my heart, that if we go at this full force, it will fail. I don't want it to fail, as I want you in my life for a very long time. I guess the point of all this is that we both need to be out of these dreadful marriages before we can even discover what it is we want out of life. We both think we know what we want, and what we will want when we are finally free, but we don't, or at least I don't know for absolutely sure until I am free. You see, I have never lived alone, ever. This is the first time, and I need that "alone" time or that "down" time, to get my head straight. I am so grateful to you, and for you, as you have helped me get through this thing more than you will ever know. Julie, at one point, I had actually considered suicide, as I thought that I would never find anyone who would love me. Then, I met you, and you changed my mind and raised my self esteem more than you could ever know. Thank you for that.

I hope you can understand what it is I am trying to say. I do love you, Julie. My life is in a horrible turmoil right now, and I need the dust to settle before I can truly feel comfortable loving you, without restraint, and that will take some time, because I am so badly hurt. I don't know how much time it will take before I can be clear about the direction my life will take. I am happy for any time I get to spend with you, as time with you is so low key, so happy, and so stress free. I intend to spend a lot more time with you when I finally move out, which should be the first week of December. I also have your very best interests at heart, and want you to be able to experience personal freedom too. Just remember that I care for you very much, and don't read anything negative into this letter, as nothing negative is meant. I am scared, that's all. I'm frightened by commitment, afraid of being alone, and frightened by being in love. Anyway enough of that before I say something that may be misunderstood by you, or might upset you. I am really happy that you will be seeing me on Thursday. I value you so very much, and want you in my life very much. See you soon, babe, and please view this as a good letter, as nothing bad is meant or implied, so please try to see what I mean, and not just read the words. Have a good day. Love, Henry

September 26, 2000
Hi Henry:

I wish I had more time to answer this properly. There isn't much to be said, really. I know exactly where you are coming from. I really do. Know this – I will always respect your privacy, as I know you will mine. We both are going through such turmoil right now. Sometimes I wonder if I'll make it. I never thought about suicide, but I did think about just disappearing – packing a suitcase, starting a new life, and just chucking it all. But, I love my kids too much to do that. So, I know a little bit about what you mean by wanting to commit suicide. Don't ever do it, Henry. I would miss you terribly. I want you to understand that I am not asking you to make a commitment. Neither one of us could handle that right now. And, don't you dare feel guilty about that. Just know that there is no one else I would let get as close to me as you have gotten to me over these last few months. We both let each other into our hearts, and that's good because we each invited the other in. I hope to visit you often at your new "digs". But, I would never come without an invitation. I don't take people for granted, especially the people I love. But, I do feel a need to be closer to you. To see you more often, interact more with you, because I really like being with you. I have fun with you. We were like a couple of kids Sunday morning, running around the park. I don't remember when I've had more fun. With you, I can be all sweaty, hair a total mess, and not worry about the way I look, because you see beyond my face. Henry, it's OK to be scared. Just trust your instincts. I was going to make this short. Love, H S

September 27, 2000
Hi H S:

I'm so glad I chose someone to be a friend that understands. Julie, I also had a wonderful time with you on Sunday at the park, and I really enjoyed our dinner together. It is not often enough that we have the opportunity to really just hang out and talk, and I would like more of that. I enjoy your company.

I was at my wife's attorney's office yesterday afternoon. The property settlement is now signed and we have reached several understandings. Although I want to leave and start a new life, it is still emotionally difficult to leave someone who I have been with for over thirty years. This will be the first time ever in my life that I will have the opportunity to do whatever I want to do. I consider that a privilege in some ways. How many people can truly say that they can do whatever they want to do, whenever they want to do it? I have learned from this experience that the best laid plans don't always work out and life throws curve balls every day. But you, Julie, I want to know you for as long as I can...forever would be fine with me. To have you as a close kindred soul is important to me, and I do make a pretty good friend in return. You inspire my creativity in a way that it hasn't been inspired before. You encourage me to write, draw, etc., but more importantly, you make me want to do it. In the future I intend to surround myself only with people that enrich my life, and that, of course, includes you. Freedom means different things to different people. I hope you find your freedom soon.

Your friend, Henry

September 27, 2000
Hi Henry:

I also enjoyed our dinner on Friday. Would you rather just "hang out and talk" the next time we are together? GRIN . . . I know we are getting together on Thursday night. Are we also seeing this house on Saturday, or was I mistaken? I need to know so I can plan for it.

I see that you didn't take my advice and consult your own attorney before signing that property settlement. Don't worry about it Henry, as I said before, you can always bum a meal off me when you're hungry. Actually, you can get a meal off me every single night if you like. But, you may not be able to tolerate my cooking.

Don't be afraid to start your new life. It's long overdue. Besides, since I met you, you've gotten taller. . . much taller. Smile. By the end of the year, you'll tower over Wilma. I'm sure of this. And, Henry, when I was in California I felt that I could do anything I wanted, and it was the most wonderful feeling. In fact, every time I am away from the homefront, and every time Don goes on a business trip, I get this exuberant 'free' feeling that is so wonderful and feels so right. I can't begin to describe it. It's not that he discourages what I do. He makes me feel guilty anytime I do something that doesn't involve him. That guilt smothers whatever I am trying to do. Almost all single people have the freedom you speak of, and the married ones who respect each other's privacy. You see this type of freedom a lot in second marriages when people seek out a soulmate that has the same feelings. Since being on the internet, I have found many people who feel smothered – mostly our age, who got married for the wrong reasons, or who have grown in the opposite direction of their spouse.

Henry, I don't really inspire your creativity. It just seems that way, because I take an interest in what you are doing. Also, I recognize talent when I see it. I think you enjoyed our time in the park because you have a natural affinity with nature, and it gives you a chance to smell the pine and become intimate with nature again. I would like to hear your thoughts on this theory. I know that you have this affinity with the earth, because of your interest in growing plants. I have the same interest and someday I will show you my collection of plants that I keep indoors. I may even have more plants than you have. Love, H S

September 27, 2000
Hi there Cutie Pie:

I will be happy doing whatever you feel like doing on Thursday. I do enjoy nature and I feel a bond with it, but being with you on Sunday is what I enjoyed the most. The 'being with nature' was a bonus. You're right about one thing – plants and animals love me. I am the guy who the dog that goes to no one comes to, and plants that others give up on, thrive for. It's people who I have trouble with. After reading what you said about feeling smothered just because you know Don's attitude towards what you are doing, really hits home. See, you do understand what I am talking about, and what I am feeling, as you hit the nail squarely on the head.

I am not completely naïve regarding the legality of what that document represented. I have an associates' degree in law which is just enough to make me dangerous, but at least I understand the language. Although I know very well that it is a very generous settlement, and that it is way more than a court would give her, it is actually what I want to do. I will have sufficient funds to live my life, and I really won't be all that bad off. I know that I painted a pretty grim picture of me being broke, but you know 'broke' is a relative term. I will be living in a beautiful environment that is a manageable commute, and I will have enough money, really. But, I'll do the cooking if I bum a meal. I am a fairly good cook, and I would just adore the opportunity to cook for you.

As far as this Saturday goes, unfortunately I have other commitments that I must fill, but I would like to take you up to see the house on a Saturday soon. I'll talk to the realtor and see if I can set something up in the next couple of weeks. I just can't wait until you see the place. I hope you like it. It feels like home to me and I get great vibes from the place. I'm sure the house was meant for me. I think that I can be happy there as the house has an atmosphere or a presence that fits with my personality and just "feels" right. So, don't worry about me. Things will work out fine for me, and I really don't have to bum meals, but sharing one with you is always a pleasant experience, and cooking for you would be fun. Once I move and decorate the place, and settle into my lifestyle, then you will be able to see the 'real' me. Gee, I hope you like it. See you soon. Don't work too hard – Henry

PS: Chess move attached. Boy, am I going to kick your butt.

September 27, 2000
Henry:

In your email of September 21st, you specifically asked me to spend Saturday with you. I double checked it to see if I was mistaken. Why did you do that if you had plans? I specifically left the day open to be with you. It's OK. I'm not angry. A little disappointed, but I'll just do something else that day. Did you get the house? If it makes you happy, I'll like it.

You don't have trouble with people – just the ones that take you for granted. And, do you really believe that being your own lawyer is a good idea? You may save a legal fee, but in the long run, it might cost you more, much more. I know you'll be OK in the long run. I also know that some day you will regret this property settlement. But, it's only money and on the scale of things, money isn't very high on the list of priorities – at least not on my list. I did notice one thing about you. You are not very astute when it comes to your own finances. Maybe that's because you have more important things to think about. I'm sure that Einstein didn't know anything about finances either.

I already know the 'real' you. The way you decorate isn't the 'real' you. It's just what you like to have around you. I'm sure that you are an excellent decorator. Most artists are, and when I begin to decorate my new place, I will seek your advice.

My chess move is attached, and you are NOT going to kick my butt. - H S

September 27, 2000
Hi Julie:

Yes, you are right. I did indeed invite you to go this Saturday, but unfortunately, something else came up that I simply must deal with. I am sorry for changing our plans, but this really is unavoidable. But, there will be lots of Saturdays ahead for us, and I will make it up to you.

The house negotiations stand at my offer at $115,000 and they have countered at $122,500, but I am pretty sure that their final price will be $119,000. I plan on countering at $117,000, just to see what they do, but I am prepared to go a bit higher.

Don't try to enlist my aid in decorating until you see what I do with my own place. You might hate it. The best part about my decorating my new home is that I get to do it using my own ideas. Oh, I'll take advice. I'm not that arrogant, but I will enjoy allowing my artistic expression full reign for the first time ever. The only other decorating I have ever done on my own is my office and my bedroom, and I like them both. As far as you liking the house, of course, your opinion means something to me, so I still hope you like it as much as I do. Taste is a very subjective thing, and I think by looking at the way a house is decorated does indeed say volumes about the person living there, so in many ways that house will show the real me to anyone who is perceptive, as I know you are.

Anyway Toots, I truly hope that you are not mad about Saturday, and again I apologize for disappointing you, but I will make it up to you. Hey! You could be my first overnight guest. Would that help?

Have to run now. Have a great day and I am looking forward to seeing you on Thursday. I am going to leave what we do Thursday night up to you, because I have a one track mind, and it involves getting naked and cuddling, but even doing the mall would be fun with you. So, I am open to anything. Take care – Henry

PS: As far as kicking your butt in our chess game goes – you do remember what the stakes are. So, I am trying really hard to win...

September 27, 2000
Hi Henry:

I'm working late again tonight. It's OK about Saturday, really...but I don't know if I will ask you to make it up to me by making me your "first" overnight guest. I just thought about that, and does that mean that you are going to have "many" overnight guests over? Female? Maybe I don't want to be the "first" of all these overnight guests...Smile. Somehow, I think you being 'single' will mean lots and lots of female overnight guests. I don't know if I want to be part of a string of different women, or part of your harem. If you are wondering why I said that, it's your use of the word "first". Maybe I'll decide what we do Thursday night after you wiggle your way out of that one, since you are allowing me to decide about Thursday. Doing the mall could be fun. But, since I'm not in the mood to shop, I'd prefer to do what I'm in the mood for. What I'm in the mood for will depend on how well you know my erroneous zones.

I really like the way you decorated your office. I'm sure you are an excellent decorator. - H S

September 28, 2000
Good Morning H S:

OK, OK…so you don't have to be the 'first'. Boy, how that takes the pressure off, as I plan on getting one of those machines for the house that they have at the deli – you know, the kind where you pull a numbered ticket out, and the clerk will say your number, and then you hand him the ticket to be served. Now, at least that will keep everyone on a first come, first served, basis, if you know what I mean. God, I have so many floozies and so little stamina. – Henry

September 28, 2000

Henry, somehow I don't find that very funny. Try creatine. That's the supplement that the body builders take before they work out. It'll give you all the stamina you need. Why don't you have a pajama party, and invite everyone at the same time? We could all play strip poker, and the looser gets to go to bed with you first! The others get to watch and play with each other – funky…smile. - HS

September 28, 2000

The looser sleeps with me? Did you say the 'looser'? I moved my knight to C3 and took your pawn. - Henry

September 28, 2000

You caught that, huh? Well, the way I look at it…never mind. Just smile. I hope you realize that I was teasing you.

Moved my bishop to A3 - H S

September 29, 2000
Hi Henry:

Last night I looked into your eyes, and saw such sadness. It's like a bottomless sorrow is filling your heart, and you grieve for what you believe you lost. You grieve for a thirty year investment of flesh and bones that went sour. I see so much loneliness and fear. It's so easy to stay with what's familiar. It's comfortable and predictable. If that's all you want, then take the easy road. But, if you want more, it takes courage to be able to meet yourself over and over again. No matter how much you like your own company, you will still long to merge completely with another person in deep intimacy. But please, don't be with someone just to avoid being alone. Do something just for you. Step outside this business we call life, for a minute, and look in. Try to remember a moment of real solitude…a moment when you were with yourself, and felt yourself at the center - when the world was spinning around you, and you felt joy and peace. Do you recognize a hunger for something beyond just continuing? Do you crave a deeper connection with yourself? Don't settle for less than your soul needs to nourish. Don't let your life become "less". Don't anesthetize yourself. Find yourself, and open yourself to living intimately with the world. Do what I suggest to you to do in the attached poem, that had to be written, and wouldn't let me sleep last night until it was down on paper. Then draw, paint, sculpt, write, grow beautiful trees, and truly enjoy the essence that is purely Henry. Because, Henry, that essence is so beautiful, it will take your breath away. And, when you can truly be alone with yourself, and love the company you keep, you will be ready to share your wonderful life with someone. I love you, Henry. And, I am beginning to "need" you in my life. But, I need you happy and at peace with yourself first. I want to help you get there. But, in order to do that, you have to stop resisting happiness, and begin to heal, and become whole. You need time. You need a Christmas tree, and you need love. You need me just as much as I need you. And, boy, do I need you. Because, I too am struggling, and with you I am well loved, and that slippery wetness that pours from between my thighs is a sign of the power of the love you hold for me. Don't be afraid of it. Embrace it, and enjoy it. Let's see if we can find an hour or two Sunday afternoon to be together. I'll be back from my Mom's some time mid-morning, I'm sure. I could call you on your cell when I return, if that's OK. Let me know if that's possible. - H S

solitude

smell the air on a crisp autumn day –
see the leaves as they fall from the trees,
and let your eyes really absorb
the sensuous colors of nature;
bury your fingers deep into the soil,
and feel the rich earth that feeds life;
stand naked in a storm,
and let the rain pour over your body,
and laugh,
because it tickles;
cherish the essence that is inside of you;
nourish your soul,
by growing aware of the world spinning around you,

and embrace the physical sensations
that call you to live -
joining your body with your soul
in a beautiful erotic experience,
that once tasted,
you will hunger for, over and over again.

September 29, 2000
Good Morning, Julie, my friend:

I am so sorry that my troubles kept you up last night. Thank you for the poem. I haven't read it yet, and I will when I get off line. It is very thoughtful of you to be concerned about me, but you have your own troubles. This is a very difficult time for both of us, and hopefully, it will lead to a better life. Julie, you have been of immeasurable help to me. To have a shoulder to help bear the burden and a sympathetic ear, and the encouragement you give me, means more to me than I could ever adequately explain to you. Thank you. I know that it seems as though I have been procrastinating and vacillating regarding my split, but I also know you understand that thirty years is strong glue, even if they weren't the happiest of years. I have been married, as you have, all my adult life, so I know nothing else. The thought of starting my own life, living alone, and finding out who I am and what I can do, does scare me, because we are talking about unknowns. Can I make it alone? I hope so, but who knows? I guess I have to try and find out. I know the strong feelings that you have for me, so I know that I am not alone in the world, but this I must do alone, without too much help, because I have to prove something to myself. The help you give me is support and understanding, and I cherish you and am grateful to you for that. I will learn to find my own way if I can surround myself with friends like you.

You are there for me, and I am there for you. I will help you in any way I can. You know that. So, our relationship will never be one-sided, and I hope that we remain friends forever and a day.

My only trepidation is that I wish that I were truly the man you believe me to be. Being with you makes me want to be a better man. I have told you from the outset that I am not sure if I can be what it is you need and want, and that is because I haven't truly discovered yet who I am. Thank you for trying to help me find out who I really am. You have infinite patience. I have never been filled with self doubt before this whole experience, and I hope to regain my confidence. I am working on it. You are truly one of the most giving and beautiful people I know. What a soul you have. I am truly lucky to know you.

I would like to see you Sunday afternoon for a couple of hours, as you suggest. Perhaps I could leave you a message on your voice mail on Saturday? Please don't change any plans in anticipation of seeing me, but if it turns out that we are both free Sunday afternoon – that would be great.

Since you stayed up anyway, it would have been nice to have been able to spend a little more time with you last night. But, I am not very demanding, and I will never question your schedule. I am just happy with the time we have together, whether that is an hour or a day. It is always quality time. You may disagree with this. In fact, I am sure that you will, but I think that our relationship is perfect for the circumstances we are in. I get to see you, and that's wonderful, and we still give each other the time and space we both need. Frankly, if I saw you more often right now, I would tend to use you for a crutch, and I do not want to do that, both for your benefit and for mine. But, don't read into that, that I am avoiding you in any way, as I see you as often as my schedule and time allows. It is just an observation. When we are both free and out on our own, we will have many years of close friendship to share and the time to do it. I don't know why my life seems so hectic. I am not doing anything different from before, but it does seem as though I have no time any more. I have found that I catch myself sometimes just sitting and staring for hours, but my brain seems to need that "down" time, and it is eating into my free time. But, this too will pass. Julie, better days are coming for both of us. I will help you hang in and you will help me hang in. We will make it.

Love and thanks, Henry

September 29, 2000

I'm pressed for time right now, Henry, but I wanted to respond to your email. This has to be short. You are mistaken about your wonderful qualities. But, that's OK. Once you find yourself, you will admit that I am right. And, I did not make you jump through hoops yesterday. You were the procrastinator. All I wanted to do was make love. You were the one that wanted to call out to the female ducks with that special "mating" call you had. Smile. Leave a message on my voicemail on Saturday for Sunday. If I don't hear from you, I will assume that you couldn't make it. If you can, we could meet at the park and find a place to put down a blanket and lie down with nature for a while. Grin - H S

September 29, 2000

I just read your poem. It's good and full of encouragement. Thank you. Have a great weekend. Treat yourself to an ice cream. You deserve it. Lying with you on a blanket in the park sounds wonderful. I hope I can make it on Sunday. - Henry

CHAPTER FOURTEEN

The next few months passed with Henry and me seeing each other about once a week, which was as often as we had the time to give to each other. Even then, we each usually had to make the time. Each time we met, we felt this incredible craving to make love. This chemistry drew us together, like a magnet. Each time we made love, it became more and more intense. He gave me a sense of fulfillment, and yet, I felt that something was missing. Each of us had this whole other life, with family and obligations we had to maintain. If I didn't have the same pressures he had, I don't think I would have been able to understand, but I did understand – only too well, what he was going through, and I knew each time he saw me, he'd have to lie about it to his wife, because telling the truth would hurt her. I knew because sometimes I did it too. Don knew I was seeing other people, but I didn't want to throw it in his face. And, usually Don's mood each time, dictated to me whether or not I'd tell him the truth about what I was doing. I think Henry felt the same way. Neither one of us wanted to grab happiness at the expense of someone else, yet, there really was no other way. If we didn't see each other, and fill up on each other's energy, I don't think either one of us would have survived that period of our lives.

We emailed each other just about every day. We learned more and more about each other, and grew closer and closer. The more I knew about Henry, the more I liked about him. There were times I wanted so much to just be able to pick up the phone and call him…to hear his voice with that distinguished British accent that I had grown to love. But, while he was still living at home with his wife, and Don was still living with me, we couldn't talk on the phone from home in the evenings. Too many people would be hurt if we were to give in to it, so instead, we spoke on the telephone during the day while at work, or in transit on the way home from work. But, at work usually I was so busy, and so was he, so email was our main means of communication.

Finally, Henry bought that house he wanted, and moved out on his own. Henry's house was very much suited to him. The ceilings were very high and he had big windows that filled the rooms with sunlight. The living room, dining room, and kitchen were open and airy, adding to the feeling of spaciousness. Glass sliding doors led out to a deck and a screen house. He had a beautiful large wooded back yard where the deer and other little animals came often. His closest neighbor was far enough away that he could run around his yard stark naked, if that's what he wanted to do. It was his little piece of heaven, and when I came to visit, I felt like I was in heaven too. I looked forward to going there and seeing all the changes he made since my last visit. The best part of it was that he was so full of enthusiasm to turn the place into what he wanted. There must have been over ten projects he had planned for the house. Once Henry moved, the evenings that Don was away or busy, I was able to call him. I enjoyed our little conversations late at night without the office distractions in the background. Shortly after he moved, I began spending my weekends there. Living at home with Don became more and more difficult. Henry's home became my sanctuary. It was a place to escape to, and so much more. The love I had for Henry grew deeper. We were starting to build on our relationship, or at least that was what I seemed to be doing. The times we spent getting together, then parting, then together again, inspired a poem I sent to him.

VOLTAGE
connect . . .
disconnect . . .
connect . . .
disconnect . . .
when together,
we are like two empty wells
that need to be filled,
and we join,
pull energy from each other
for one brief wondrous moment,
then disconnect . . .
push each other away into darkness –
afraid of the emotions that explode,
scared to allow another person
close enough to hurt us -
then, the wells drain dry,
and when we feel we need
that thing we do for each other,
we connect again,
allow ourselves to plug in once more,
your voltage fills my void,
and my energy flows into your soul,
then, we disconnect . . .

and when I'm alone in my head,
disconnected from you,
sometimes I find myself floating
in the s p a c e between us,
and wondering if
that space will always be there.

October 9, 2000
Hi there HS:

Your poem is great. You are not my friend. "Friend" doesn't describe our relationship well enough. Yes, we are friends, but also so much more. "Voltage" is a good poem because it describes the way we recharge each other's batteries, and make each other better equipped to deal with the down side of our lives. We show each other that we can still have fun, and that a relationship can be free of demands and controls. That's what it is about you that I find so attractive. You make me feel young again. You give me low pressure times filled with fun. Sunday was really fun. Just being able to enjoy each other's company made the day so right for me. You fill a void that I didn't even know I had. I like our low key, low pressure, strange, and wonderful relationship. That kind of openness and honesty I used to believe didn't exist anymore. What a wonderful carefree relationship we have, where we can talk about our plans openly without fear of the other's reaction, gives us both a freedom that I never experienced before. I adore being with you. I adore your company, your intellect. I adore the fact you want me to be just – well, me. You give me the space I need, and don't feel slighted. You understand me, and I think I understand you. We both care for and about each other without expecting anything in return. What a gift you are. What a pressure relief valve you have been for me. I hope this strange and wonderful relationship will be part of my life for a very long time. Have a fun day and thank you, Sweetie, for just being there with a sympathetic ear and an open heart, and for sharing yourself and your life with me.

Love you – Henry

October 9, 2000
Hi Henry:

And how are you on this fine and beautiful day? I think that "friend" does describe our relationship. What else would you call it? Maybe your definition of "friend" is different than mine. I think of a friend as someone who you can open up to, who doesn't criticize you, who cares about your life, and who will tell you when they think you're wrong, even though they know it's not what you want to hear. A friend will make you chicken soup when you have a cold, and visit you in the hospital in the middle of winter in a storm, because they know that you would be feeling lonely. A friend is also someone who you like to be around, hang out with, and see often. The only thing I do with you that I don't do with my other friends is "make love". And I am "in love" with only you, not my other friends. I love them, but am not "in" love with them, and have no desire to make love with them. Our relationship is very special to me, Henry. The only time that this would be something more than friendship to me is if we made a commitment to each other and neither one of us is ready for something like that, even though I couldn't think of anyone else I'd rather make a commitment with. I love being with you too, and I try to see you as much as I am able to. I know you feel the same way. Why else would you get up at six AM on a Sunday morning to jog in the park?

I give all my friends the "space" they need. I don't believe in taking more than someone has or is able to give. That's the way I am with everyone, including my family. (But, I will always press you to be the very best you can be. That's the mark of a true friend – someone who won't let you cop out on yourself.) I noticed that you are that way too. You don't push, and never ask for anything I couldn't give. And, thank you for being you, and not pressuring me. You are a true friend. Remember, I told you once that I have very few true friends. There aren't many people who I give the label "friend" to. You are one of them. – H S

October 9, 2000

You are a beautiful friend, but so much more than that to me. That's why "friend" is not a strong enough word to describe you, Julie. I value your friendship very much. Regardless of where our lives take us, your friendship will mean as much to me in the future, as it does today. I know your heart, and I know you. I like what I have learned about you and your character. You are a rare and underappreciated person who I value very much. Stay the way you are, Julie, so full of life. And you are right. I get up early on Sunday mornings to be with you, not to jog. The jog is just an added bonus. Seeing you on Sunday mornings, and spending that short time with you out in the woods surrounded by so much beauty and nature, makes me feel very happy and stress-free, and in touch. I had almost forgotten how to do that. Thank you for showing me the way. You are such a babe… - Henry

October 9, 2000

Henry, your compliments make me feel good. I hope you really believe everything you say about me. I think you're a nut, but I love you, because you're not like other people I know. You are unique and have a great untapped talent that you are just beginning to discover in yourself. I value your friendship too, and Henry, our lives will take us wherever we want them to go.

We make our own destinies, and can do just about anything we decide we want to do. We both are discovering what it means to be truly free. When we jog together in the woods, like we did yesterday morning, during that time, both of us were truly free, and that's why we felt so good. Those moments are sacred to me, and I will always treasure them in my heart. Isn't it wonderful to have such beautiful memories? - H S

November 21, 2000
Hi Julie:

Just one more week before I move... I want you to think of my new house as your sanctuary from the world. You can even stay there when I'm away, if you need to ever be alone by yourself. Thanks for the offer of groceries, but I have almost everything I need. I'll know better once I'm in. I look forward to seeing you on Saturday morning. I'll email good directions to you before then, if you want to drive up yourself. I'm looking forward to seeing you baking in my kitchen.

So, what would you like for breakfast? The only thing I've ever seen you eat for breakfast was Special K. Hey, you know what you could bring that I could really use – your sweet smile...
Henry

November 21, 2000
Hi Henry:

Special K with skim milk, along with a cup of tea will do nicely. If you don't have Special K, that's OK. I'm not a big breakfast eater. Maybe a hard-boiled egg could substitute for the cereal. Actually, there is something I want to eat for breakfast, and you already have it. Smile. Don't buy anything special for me. I can eat just about anything. – H S

November 22, 2000
Hi Henry:

Don't tell me what you're making. Instead, surprise me for dinner on Friday night. I love surprises. I wish I had more time to see you, but with the Thanksgiving holiday and all – I'm running a bit behind. You are in my thoughts every day, even when I don't hear from you. Keep that in mind.

Smile – H S

November 26, 2000
Dear Henry:

Probably, the one thing I was looking forward to more than anything else in this world was spending the weekend with you. Being with you is my sanctuary, not being at your house, but just being anywhere with you. When you said in one of your emails that I should consider your house a sort of sanctuary, and that I can go there whenever I need to, even if you're not there, you didn't realize that I considered *being with you,* the sanctuary, not the house. There would be no reason for me to go there when you are not there. Henry, some things have happened within the last two days, that will prevent me from coming Saturday, and I think you deserve an explanation. I know it meant a lot to you too. It's not easy for me to talk about my problems. But, there are times I need to write out what's in my heart and head to help me decipher where I'm going. You are one of the very few people in this world who can understand my pain, and I think I can trust you enough to let you in to see the center of my sorrow. I know I cannot save myself or those I love from the sorrow that is part of life. There are times I ache for the freedom I had before I became a mother, and before I became a wife. Right now, this is one of those times. Just remember this – listening does NOT make you responsible for alleviating the pain. There is nothing you can do to ease it. Right now, I am a very tired woman and in need of some emotional support. I don't expect you to perform miracles – just be your usual understanding self.

When I gave birth to my children, I said to myself, if I got through labor, I can get through anything. Maybe the pains of labor are something we need to learn to raise our children. And, when our children hurt us, we draw on what we learned. And when the pain is large, and I cannot pull enough out of myself to hold it, I send out a simple prayer "help me", and allow myself to relax and be held by something larger – a true "friend" who has also learned to sit with pain, who can hold me, and listen to my tears, and help me to forget that impossible ideal of perfection that keeps us from the wisdom we need to live fully with our own humanness. I think you're that kind of a friend, and wish this very moment that you were here listening, instead of my writing all this down to you. I wish I could see the empathy in your eyes, and feel your comfort. But, I can't, and so this letter to you is in a way a comfort in of itself. I will try to explain as best I can.

I have spent the last few days (Thanksgiving evening) holding my daughter, Maria, in my arms, day and night, as she detoxified herself from a $100 a day heroine addiction. I sat through the chills, the spasms, body convulsions, fever, and the horrible relentless pain, and suffered it with her. It has been agony, but somehow through it all, I managed to convince her that she must choose life, and to live, and that she must go into a rehabilitation program on an inpatient basis one more time. She has had a substance abuse problem since she was 16, and has been in and out of rehabs several times over the last 12 years. The first few times I wanted to save her, to restore her to what she was. That belief is now an illusion. I know better. To think I could make things right if I simply tried hard enough. The truth is, all my work cannot ensure immunity from tragedy, and for so long I pretended not to see the truth of it all. But, I have to give her that choice she made – life. And, I am the only person who can help her now. She will be entering rehab today. While she is in rehab, I will be taking care of my granddaughter. This coming weekend, Don will be away, and I must stay home and take care of her. I'll be free next weekend, as Alice will help. Her mother, Maria, will most likely be away for about a month. The holidays will be hard this year for us. After she's released, I hope she will be able to once again take care of her own responsibilities. But, if she doesn't try again, and if I don't do what she needs me to do, she will surely die, or worse. Five years ago, she was in rehab, and afterwards, somehow managed to stay clean for four years. Then last year, she went out with the wrong man, and when he cheated on her, she started using again. It wasn't his fault. She just couldn't handle the emotional side of the relationship, and the problems it caused. She supported her habit by stealing from me and other members of my family. She only started using again a few months ago. And, it has cost us already over $5,000. I could press charges and literally have her locked up, but I know she needs help, and she won't get the kind of help she needs in prison. I only hope that this time, it works. So many times I have tried to think back that maybe there was something that I could have done differently when she was little, but I don't think that any more. Her addictive personality is somewhat hereditary from her father, though I don't want to blame him. Somehow I partly do. If only he could have been stronger – a more responsible father. He's dropping her off there now, and I only wish he also would check himself in, but he's still in denial concerning his own problems.

I will do what has to be done, because that's the way I am. Although I would like to escape, and right now most likely need to escape for a while, life is not allowing me this luxury. And as

I try to breath through the ache in my chest, I will think of you, and your sanctuary, and hope that when I am once again able to come, that the door will still be open. But, I don't blame you if you decide to close the door on me, because this problem I have is too much baggage. I guess I need you to see through the flames encircling me, and throw some water on for a while. Smile. (You did say you were a fireman.) Right now, you are going through some earth shattering moments yourself. I know the strength you must have had to muster up, as you packed each box getting ready to move into your new world. I'm sure you are somewhat afraid as much as you are anxious. I wanted to help you this weekend, to just be there for you, and help you see the rightness of your choice, and cry with you, if that's what you need. I am truly sorry that I cannot be there for you. I will make it next weekend, if the invitation is still open.

This challenge I have right now will pass. Henry, I don't want to loose you, who have been such an uplifting factor in my life. I feel happy when I'm with you. I need the strength that I feel when your love flows into me. It will sustain me through this trial. See, I am destructible. I'm not nearly as strong as you think I am. And, I do need you, but not in the traditional way that a woman needs a man. I need to take some energy from you every once in a while. I need to get my battery juiced up. Right now, it's running pretty low. I'm afraid that it's not a "die hard". I love you, and I miss you so much right now. Remember that this Saturday when you feel lonely. If you give me your new phone number, I will call you. I would like to hear your voice. These emails don't have the same warmth as your voice has. And if you give me your new address, I will send you a Christmas card. . .something funny, to make you laugh. And, please, please, buy yourself a Christmas tree.

Sincerely, and with my warmest regards and deepest love, - H S

November 26, 2000
My Dear Julie:

How do I answer that letter? It was heartbreaking to hear of your sadness. Nothing can wound us as deeply as our childrens' suffering, because nothing in this world is as important as those to whom we have given life. I feel your pain, seeing your child in so much trouble, and torment. Julie, you are doing what needs to be done, and I truly wish you luck in that. At least she is going to rehab, so she has given herself another chance on life. Don't give up on her, Julie, and of course you won't.

Please don't worry about seeing me or coming up to the house right now. Although I would have liked to spend time in your company, I will be extremely busy unpacking, etc. so I have plenty to keep me occupied. I will forward my telephone number to you when I get my phone installed, but you can always reach me on my cell phone or by email, until then. If there is anything I can do beyond moral support, then all you have to do is let me know. My heart and my thoughts will be with you, and of course my door is always open. Bless you Julie, and your family, I only wish the very best outcome for you.

Your friend, Henry

November 27, 2000

Thank you Henry, for being so very understanding. I think I was having a "self-pity" party when I wrote that letter. I'm sorry for putting all this on you, but I felt you should have an explanation about Saturday, and it felt good to just let it all hang out. I wanted to come and help you on Saturday, so badly. You have no idea how disappointed I am. Right now, just knowing that I have your shoulder to cry on is more than enough. In the meantime,

I am finding out what it's like to be a mother to a ten year old again. I much rather truly prefer being the grandmother. It's so much easier. I just hope that this time Maria somehow manages to resolve her problems, because I can't take too much more. And, make no mistake about it – if that door is still open when this is over, I will be coming through it. I miss you, Henry, and really need to spend some time with you, even if it's only an hour or so. I need to feel those arms around me, so warm and loving. I will call you on Saturday night, even if I can't be there, if you like. – H S

November 27, 2000
Hi Julie:

You're sounding better, and there is nothing wrong with a little self-pity, now and again. Being a mother to a ten year old does have its advantages. It will help keep you young. You think too young and act too young to be a 'grandmother' anyway.

And again, Julie, don't worry even a little bit about me. I am sure we can squeeze in an hour or so, and there will be other Saturdays for you to visit. Your time will be much better spent taking care of your family. There will always be time in the future for us to be together. Even if I don't see you, you know that I will be thinking of you, and you know my best wishes are with you every day. Take care, Sweetie. I'll be in touch as soon as I can. – Henry

December 4, 2000
Hi Hot Stuff:

Thank you for bringing warmth and a smile into my new house this past weekend. And, thanks for the little Christmas tree. I'm glad you got home safely. Next time you see the place, it will be a little more together. It was real nice that you were able to get away with all your problems, and my first night alone in the house wasn't alone. Thinking of you. Enjoy your day, Sweetie. – Henry

December 4, 2000

Henry, your house is already warm. You're in it. Heat radiates from your body. Smile. I've attached a poem I wrote about this weekend. It was written just for you, and I doubt if I will ever publish it, because it's yours and yours alone. Print it out, fold it up, and save it in your night table drawer. Then, when you lie awake at night feeling lonely or sad, take it out and read it, so you know that there is someone in this world who wishes she were there with you, at that moment, looking at the stars in your eyes. I will always savor the memory of Saturday night, Henry. Yes, it was THAT good! It was a beautiful night, and you are a beautiful man with so much love to give. Why are you so afraid to get really close to me? I would never hurt you. I'm not like anyone else you ever knew, or will know again. Don't you know that by now? I think I said too much... Have a great day! - H S

December 2, Y2K

When the pain
became bad, I sought your help,
and you pulled me out of the flame
that threatened to consume me,
soothing my burns with your touch,
welcoming me with your smile,
serenading me with your eyes,
cradling me in your arms,
pleasuring me with your warm body,
and the magic of your gentle fingers,

and all through the night,
within the sanctuary of you,
I drew from your strength,
and the tension melted away.

Lying in the web of
warmth and safety that
you wove around me,
while Orion's Belt
faded into the clouds,
we watched the sky
turn from black to gray, and
a glimmer of sunshine
tried to break through
the shadows of tall trees
outside your bedroom window,
then, you pleasured me once again,
so thoroughly loving me
with such intimate tenderness,
that tears back up in my throat
each time I remember the intensity
of what we shared
and gave to each other, and
I ache for so much more.

CHAPTER FIFTEEN

We emailed each other Monday and Tuesday, but the following Wednesday was the first day I hadn't had a communication from him in months. I was so accustomed to hearing from him in some way or other every single day, that when I didn't hear from him, it felt strange. I started to think that perhaps I felt much more for him than he did for me. During my weekend visit to his new home, although it was wonderful, in a way I felt that I wasn't the only woman that Henry was intimate with, besides his wife. There were gaps – times I didn't hear from him, or when I just felt that he was involved with someone else, not a regular friend or a family member, but another woman that he was intimate with. I knew that his friend Elizabeth was also very close to him, and knowing that he gave her the same part of himself that he gave to me, made it so much less on his end than it was on my end. I think that perhaps having two women that he was involved with, was his way of protecting himself from hurt. Yet, he had no idea how much it hurt me, and most likely, her, as well.

That weekend in his house, I felt another woman. I don't know how to explain it, but she was there, a part of his life. Surprisingly, I wasn't jealous. It was just that I thought he was in love with me. How could a man be "in" love with more than one woman at a time? It seemed that he allotted just so much time to each of us. I felt that he wasn't being entirely honest with me. When I visited him, he didn't answer his phone. I thought that was strange, and he could never set a date in advance for the following weekend. It was as if he had to check what someone else was doing first. I always arranged my schedule to accommodate his, and as a result, perhaps he put me off until he had a better handle on what he would be doing with "her". Perhaps I was wrong about that, but it was how I felt, yet I didn't know how to ask him about it without putting him on the defensive. I wanted to believe that I was the only woman he was intimate with, and so I did, but I knew in my heart that the real reason he couldn't give into the relationship the depth of feeling I gave it, was his involvement with another woman. He further confirmed my feelings by his attitude the following week.

December 6, 2000
Hi Henry:

What happened to you today? I didn't get any emails or calls from you. Is it something I said or did? I spent such a beautiful weekend with you, which inspired a beautiful poem, and it's like this past weekend never happened with you. It's so unlike you, too. I'm sorry if I can't keep all my feelings hidden deep within my soul. I'm Italian, and we Italians tend to wear our feelings on our sleeves. Did I read your eyes wrong? You used to write me poetry. You haven't in a very long time. You don't express your feelings any more either. Don't you think I deserve an explanation? - Julie

(Before I wrote the above letter, I received a greeting I didn't know Henry sent, because Henry sent it to my office email after I left for the day. The above email was written that night. The greeting he sent was a card showing a picture of a little devil with his tongue hanging out, that said "I was just thinking about you, Hot Stuff: It's almost the end of the week. Don't overwork. When you get this card, take a break, have a cup of tea, look in the mirror and smile, because you deserve to see a beautiful smile.")

December 7, 2000
Hi Julie:

I hope you noticed that I sent you the card before I got your last email. Some days (like yesterday) I hardly have time to go to the bathroom, let alone take the time to go on line. My nights are filled with work at the house, and I rarely go to sleep much before one AM. The holidays are right around the corner, and I have shopping to do. And, living alone, I have no one who is there to help take up the slack. I have way too much going on in my life right now. So, Julie, please, if I missed one day (which I really didn't, because I sent you that card as soon as I got home), why did you get so upset?

You know that I have so much on my mind that my creativity is on hold. That's why I don't and can't take time out to indulge myself in my art or writing, but don't think that I don't think of you. I have attached a quickie for you to read. I hope you like it. The weekend was not what I wanted, because it was over too soon. It was a joy for me to wake next to you, and to hold you in my arms all night long. We waited a long time for that. But, I can't promise you more time than I give you, because I give you all that I can. I am so sorry that it isn't enough. You try and have a good day, Julie

A long black hair curled around the drain in my shower
Lingering jasmine perfume on my pillow
Half a grapefruit still wrapped in plastic
Remnants of a visit to my inner sanctum
Evidence of a night of passion
Shadows of a day well spent

A twelve inch Christmas tree in a silly bear pot
A mouse pad and a coffee cup written with love
These tiny things keep you on my mind.

December 7, 2000
Hi Henry:

You misinterpreted what I meant, or maybe I didn't say it right. Either way, somehow the translation got lost. Your poem was nice, but unnecessary. I can tell when you write something just to satisfy my ego, and when you write something from your heart. Your eyes tell me one thing, and your lips say something else. Your crossed signals confuse me. Somehow I thought that when you were living alone, I would hear from you more - more phone calls, whatever. It's like you haven't really left your old home. Please don't make an excuse for yourself to me again. It somehow degrades the relationship. I don't want to cause you any stress. I am sorry if I did that. It's just that, Henry; I don't know where I stand with you. Sometimes I wonder if you never heard from me again, that it would even matter to you. Maybe I'm just insecure, but I don't think that's the case. And, as far as your comment about living alone, and not having someone to pick up the slack goes – where are your priorities? If fixing up your house becomes more important to you than your personal relationships, then you will most likely have a beautiful, but very cold and empty house. However, if personal relationships come first, then maybe your house won't be exactly the way you want it, as soon as you would like, but you will be rich with love and warmth. Which would you prefer? You may be British, but you're not that cold!

Your card was cute, and I am glad you at least thought about me yesterday, but somehow an animal with his tongue hanging out is not how I pictured you after last Saturday. It gives me the impression that you only thought the sex was good. I hope I have a little bit more substance than that. Smile (I'm trying to.) – H S

December 7, 2000

Gee Julie, I guess there is just no pleasing you. I tried. I told you a long time ago that I was afraid I would hurt you one day, and that I may not be what you are looking for. You are important to me Julie, and I cherish the time we spend together, and the sex is great, but sex can be gotten anywhere very easily. It is the sharing of affection that made it great. Our relationship would be good even if we never had sex again, and I would still want to see you. You are very perceptive, because you instinctively know there is a part of me that I cannot share with you. It just isn't there in me anymore. I had it once, and I hope one day it grows back, but for now, this is who I am. I cannot be in a relationship that I must constantly feed, because it is just not in me to do it. I very well may be destined to go through life alone. Better that, than hurt someone as sweet and caring as you are. What I have gone through in the last couple of years has wounded me deeply, and I will need time to let that heal before I can give you what it is you are looking for. It isn't that I don't want to, and it isn't that I don't care about you, because I do love you. I am just not ready to be what you need every day. I have been in a relationship all of my adult life that closeted me and stifled me, and I desperately need time just for me, or I will surely go mad. Perhaps when I cease to cry when I am alone, then I will be ready to give you what it is that you want, but that day may very well be far off into the future. If you decide that I am a dead end for you, then don't be sad for me. It has been wonderful, and I will always love you for the joy you brought into my life, and I will always count you as one of my very closest friends. And, I will understand, but Julie, believe this, I have not taken advantage of you, and I have not lied to you, and I have done my best, but it seems that in one respect you agree with my wife, that my best is not good enough. And, I did write that poem from my heart. – Henry

December 7, 2000
Henry:

You are not a dead end! No pleasing me? Your best is not good enough? Henry, where are you coming from? I don't know what I'm looking for. I wish to God, I did. If you think I'm worth the time, I would like you to explain to me about the part of you that you feel you cannot share with anyone. Henry, I love 'who' you are as I perceive you to be. I never said, nor believed, that your best isn't good enough. How could you say that about me? Right now I am very angry with you, because you put me on the same plane as Wilma. That hurts, Henry. It really does. I am absolutely nothing like her. But, when you love someone, you try to contact them, or call them, or see them more than once a week. I don't want you to constantly "feed" me with compliments or whatever it is you think I need. I never asked for that. In fact, I have never asked you for anything. I also have been wounded deeply through my own marriage. You have no idea how deeply, or maybe you do know. Maybe I am a bit gun shy, and need some reassurances now and then. I don't want you to call me if it's not what you want to do. But, gee Henry, you hardly ever call me. It makes a girl begin to wonder if she means anything to you at all. If you really believe that you have to constantly "feed" me, then you don't really know me, and don't even bother answering this email. Don't worry about hurting me. I've been hurt before. And, I can take anything you dish out. I'm a big girl, Henry. But, please don't put me down and compare me with Wilma. That's a rotten thing to do, and a blow below the belt. I don't deserve it. - Julie (Suddenly, I just don't feel like HS any more.)

December 7, 2000
Julie:

I don't know how or why we reached this point. I just don't understand how things could go from so right to so wrong – almost overnight. I know we see this situation differently, and I think perhaps it is a misunderstanding that got out of hand somehow. This is the way I see it. We had a great weekend. The first thing that I saw that let me know something was wrong was your letter asking me what you had done wrong. You took me completely by surprise. I thought that everything was just fine between us. We had corresponded every day except Wednesday during the day. As soon as I got home I sent you that card just to say "Hi", and let you know that you were on my mind. Then your mail arrived from your home computer about an hour later. I was stunned, and responded the best that I could, and whatever I said just seemed to make things go from bad to worse. I didn't know what you were talking about. You saw it as me ignoring you. I saw it as me taking time out from a horribly busy day to sit down and send you a card to let you know I care enough not to let a day go by without at least saying "Hi". You were apparently even annoyed at the card. I thought I was being cute, and I thought you would get a chuckle out of it. I told you that you had a beautiful smile. Even that upset you.

Even though I was terribly busy and truly could not afford to take any time from my work, I did take about an hour that I could ill afford, to write you a poem. And, even that didn't please you. I don't understand. If you are so angry, would you please calm down enough to tell me what it is that I did wrong to set this off? I don't want to loose your friendship. It means a great deal to me. I am sitting here writing this with tears in my eyes. Please don't do this to me. If you are so mad that you are on the verge of ending our relationship, you owe me nothing, Julie, but please if you are considering that, then at least don't do it over something that may just be a misunderstanding. Think it over, Julie. If our relationship ends, then it will sadden me greatly, but I will never have hard feelings towards you, and I could never be angry with you. You see whatever it is that sparks the emotion of anger in me doesn't work, as the only two emotions I am still capable of feeling are affection and deep sorrow. I don't know what to say to you, and Julie, to me, you will always be "Hot Stuff". – Henry

December 8, 2000
Hi Henry:

Did you get much snow? There was a lot of snow on my car this morning when I left for work. I must have read and reread both your emails to me yesterday over and over again. Tears were in my eyes too. I do not want to end the most beautiful relationship I ever had in my life. I don't know how to explain things to you, but I will try. On Monday, when I was driving home and got that call from you, I was so happy. If a bomb were dropped on my car that instant, the smile would have never left my face. It was all because you called me - a little thing like one simple phone call. "Speaking" to me was important enough to you to call. Did you know that I am literally "afraid" to call you? You built these boundaries around yourself with signs all over that say "no trespassing" that I'm afraid I'll get shot if I even dare to put one toe in your territory. You said some pretty awful things to me. I don't know when I made you feel that you had to "feed" me, or when I made you feel 'stifled', or when I made you feel that your best wasn't good enough. Apparently you feel I did all those things.

I never asked you for anything. I thought that your creativity was flowing from the sheer joy of our relationship, as mine was, and if you can't see me, that's OK, as long as I know that you "want" to see me. And you are dead wrong – 'sex' as we have experienced it together, is impossible to get again. It's not "easy" to get. I don't want the easy kind. I can't get off with the "easy" kind of sex. You remind me of a race horse, running with blinders on, running your heart out, with sweat dripping all over your body, and running in a purseless race. I don't want more than you are capable of giving. But, you have to stop thinking that because your relationship with one woman was so stifling, that if you dare to feel some passion with another woman, that she too will stifle you. Wilma and I are like night and day.

I loved the poem you wrote yesterday. It was damned good. You have so much talent, Henry. (Did I really leave a hair behind?) Smile. And you please me as I have never been pleased before. But, don't make assumptions about me, because that was what you experienced in the past. Judge me for myself, not for what you had in the past with someone else – please. I would never come to your home uninvited, or overstay my "welcome". And, don't get mad at me because I love you so damned much that I just wanted to hear your voice. Just talking to you makes me happy. Wednesday, I was going to send you a "good morning" email, and I stopped myself, just wondering if you would be the first to initiate a communication that day. Sometimes, I feel like you only send me email in response to one I send you. When you didn't send anything, or even call me on your way home from work, I wanted to call you, but I was afraid to. Why do you send emails to my office when you know I'm not there? Why didn't you send that card to my home email address? If I had gotten your card Wednesday night, it would have made such a difference. This may sound silly to you, but that day, I needed to hear from you. I wrote you a poem on Tuesday, telling you how I felt, and it was as if it meant nothing to you. I thought, 'is that all my feelings mean to him?' I know that you are currently just about incapable of allowing yourself to love a woman the way you want to love again. I also know that I am not ready to commit to anyone myself as yet. That's OK. We're both slightly dysfunctional. Please stop making excuses for yourself. It's not necessary. I am not Wilma. I just need to know that you "want" to see me again, even if you can't. That's all.

And I want so much to be your "Hot Stuff" again. I really do. Just pick up the damned telephone once in a while, Henry. I don't think that's asking too much from you. If it is, then maybe you're right. Now, that I wrote down my heart to you again, please don't get on the defensive. Instead, accept my feelings as I accept yours, and be "nice" to me, because you can so very easily, just with words, hurt me deeply again. And, I'm just not as strong as you think I am. I have feelings, too. - H S (wannabe)

December 12, 2000
Hi Hot Stuff:

Well, I'm glad that is behind us. Now, I think I understand you a little bit better. I am sorry if you felt neglected. Of course, you can call me anytime. The truth of why I don't call you often, and that my phone calls are always short, is that I want to hear your voice, but I hate the telephone because my hearing isn't that good. I have tintinitous. It's a constant ringing in my ears, and

I miss a good deal of what you say. The telephone in my office has a volume control, and I leave it on max, but still only take the occasional call as I get my staff to do the phone contact. But, my cell phone and the phone at home do not have the volume control, so if I talk to you, please bear with me if I ask you to repeat yourself.

Julie, of course I want to continue seeing you, but I did warn you that I tend to be a bit of a hermit, and I have always been a reclusive person. I need three or four days a week to be totally alone with my thoughts, otherwise I don't function well. This is something Wilma never understood. I am sorry if I upset you with my comments. I don't think you are like Wilma. It is just that I try and do the right thing, but seem to miss. I have never been very good with people. You know Julie, we need to communicate better so that the kind of misunderstanding that happened yesterday, never happens again. I know I become defensive and sometimes say inappropriate things, but I have got into that habit because of the way I have lived for so long. Please try to understand and forgive me. I need time to become 'normal' again. I do hold back, and I know I do. It's nothing to do with you. I have a deep abiding affection for you. But, I am afraid that my personality has been warped, and it may take some time for me to be able to really open up. It's not that I don't want to. It is because that part of me isn't there right now. I have been hurt so badly, and am far from over that pain. But, at least our friendship is back on track. Thank you. I will call you this afternoon when the smoke clears a bit.

Would it be possible for me to see you, even briefly, the week of December 18ᵗʰ? I do need a Christmas kiss. When the holidays are over, and your schedule lightens up, I would like to start spending more time with you (snow permitting). I still want to do all those 'dating' things, like going to the movies, dinner, or dancing, etc. I had a wonderful time that Sunday when you came to see the house and we stopped by the waterfall. It was one of my all time favorite days.

Anyway, have a great day, Hot Stuff – Henry

December 8, 2000
Henry:

Why didn't you tell me about your hearing problem? That explains so much. My Mom also suffers from tintinitous. Eventually you may need a hearing aid, but they make them so small these days, that you won't even know you have it on. I'll try to remember to "shout" the next time we talk. Smile. I really am 'afraid' to call you. So, if you don't call me, I won't hear your voice. Maybe it's good that we had this misunderstanding and clarified some things. You understand me better, and I understand you. Henry, if you need time with your thoughts, that's OK with me. I also need time alone, and there will be times that I also will seek solitude. I like my own company, and when I concentrate on a project, I get so involved in it, that everything else around me disappears. When I can 'focus' like that I do my best work and I've done some pretty amazing things during those times. So, I do know where you are coming from when you say you need time alone just to think. I accept your apology for saying inappropriate things to me. As long as you know that I wasn't trying to crowd you – just love you. You are right, Henry, we do need to communicate better. Some things are harder to communicate than others. Henry, your personality is not warped. Don't think that.

As far as the week of the 18th goes – that's a tough week for me. However, my office is having their annual Christmas party on the evening of the 20th. My company will pay for a hotel room for me in the city that night, if I want it. I could take a vacation day the following day, also, if I want to. GRIN... I can't bring any guests to this Christmas party, but it's usually over by nine o'clock, leaving me the rest of the night free. It wouldn't cost any more if I had someone with me in my hotel room. If you could take the next day off, we could go Christmas shopping in the city together the following day. We could view the tree in Rockefeller Center. I'm sure whatever hotel I pick will have parking. You could drive in that night and drive us back home the next day. It would be a lot of fun. Does that appeal to you? Let me know, otherwise, I'll just take car service home like I do every year from the party. Let me know. – H S

CHAPTER SIXTEEN

When we met in New York City after my Christmas party, Henry gave me a beautiful gold necklace with one solitary pearl. I loved it. I wasn't expecting anything like that, although he had told me that he bought me something for Christmas. It made me feel special that he thought enough of me to purchase a piece of jewelry for me. I always felt that jewelry was something you purchased for the very 'special' people in your life. He later told me that Wilma had found the store receipt for the jewelry he bought his friends, including myself, which deflated my bubble, since I thought he had purchased the pearl just for me, and I realized that he didn't buy anything special just for me, at all. Somehow knowing that he bought jewelry for other women too, spoiled what it meant to me. I wish he hadn't told me that. It made me feel cheated somehow. Or maybe it just brought me down to 'reality'. Either way, I will never think of that pearl again the way I thought about it the very first moment I saw it.

My Christmas gift to him was a signed copy of my poetry book, and a very special poem written just for him that had taken hours of my time to write. He also gave me a portobello mushroom cookbook and we laughed over it. That, at least, I knew was special just for me. That day we had a wonderful time walking around the streets of New York. We played with toys in F.A.O. Schwartz, bought funny looking hats that made us look like court jesters, and just enjoyed all the wonderful Christmas decorations and activities that New York City had to offer. I always had such a good time when we were together. There never was enough time for all we wanted to do when we were together.

My Christmas poem for Henry:

SEARCHING
Your words touched my heart,
and together, we wept
for the parts of our lives
that we lost along the journey
of growing up.

Your door cracked open,
just an inch, and
you let me take a peek
at the insides of your soul.

I saw a man
with a big heart,
but lost and alone,
searching to find
the pieces of himself

that can make
his smiles come alive
once again.

Merry Christmas, Henry

Love, Julie (12/25/00)

I also wrote a poem for Henry over the New Year holiday that I sent him.

LET

Let the winds
learn our friendship
as they blow through our hair.

Let the sky
bring brightness
to outshine our sadness.

Let the stars
blind those eyes
that see without kindness.

Let not a rainy day go by,
without the thoughts of two people
dripping happy tears.

Let the sun
carry our friendship,
even though we're not near.

January 4, 2001
Hi:

Julie, I read your poem. Like all your poems, it touched me and inspired me. I have attached a poem that I wrote a few minutes ago that was inspired by your poem. It is the first poem I have written in a long time. I hope you like it.

Henry

> *When the world is cold and dark*
> *When winter's icy fingers encircle my heart*
>
> *When the songbirds no longer sing and refuse to fly*
> *When my eyes' only use is to tear up and cry*
>
> *When the wind whispers my name across the frozen ground*
> *When the pale moon's only friend is the mournful bey of a hound*
>
> *When the trees stand naked, and snow blankets the earth*
> *When I feel all alone, and without any mirth*
>
> *When the fire no longer warms up my soul*
> *When I am feeling weak, all alone, and old*
>
> *When I can no longer recall summer nights long past*
> *I hear in your voice the promise of spring at last.*
> *For Julie*

January 4, 2001

What do I say to a poem so beautiful?

Your poems arouse me,
your love surrounds me,
and yet I feel alone.
What's missing, Henry? - H S

January 5, 2001
Good Morning, Julie:

First, thank you for your compliment regarding the poem I wrote for you. Finally, I can write again after a very long dry spell. It only took me about ten minutes to write it. It just flowed out so easily. See how easy it can be when you inspire me.

As to your question as to what's missing – I gave that a lot of thought, most of the day, and it was on my mind all night. I don't know what is missing in your life, Julie, but I am very sure that if you become introspective, you will know. Perhaps you already know, but don't want to face what it is you lack. You have a hole in your soul, Julie. I can see it in your eyes every time I look at you. Even when you laugh, your eyes are sad. It is a deep sadness that you will live with until you recognize that missing piece, and take steps to repair that hole. And, only you can answer what that missing piece is.

Julie, dear friend, I care very much about your happiness and well being. Please, find that missing piece and be happy. I'll be in touch later. Smile, it's good for you.

Henry

January 5, 2001
Henry:

You are a very talented writer. I think I fell in love with your mind long before I met you. I think I do know what's missing in my life, only I can't seem to talk to you about it, because I don't think you would understand or take it the right way. Don't take this the wrong way, please. I know it's not coming out right. It's just that there are certain things I can't seem to discuss with you, without you putting up a wall. I've seen this happen before. I am not sad as much as lonely. There is a difference. You can be surrounded by people and still feel lonely. That's as much as I can say. Maybe some day you'll understand, or open yourself to discussing it. - H S

January 5, 2001

Julie, thank you for seeing me as the man I would like to be, rather than the man that I am. You can say anything to me. You may not always get the response you would like, but at least you will get honesty. Have a great weekend, Sweetie. – Henry

January 5, 2001
Dear Henry:

Oh, but I do see you as the man you are. I know your flaws. It's just that I have priorities different than most women, and in my book, your pluses very heavily outweigh your minuses. I know I always get honesty from you. It's just that there are things you'd rather not face, and neither one of us is capable of dealing with at this time, anyway. I think we're trying to be sensible, but every time I see you, I fall deeper and deeper in love with you. When I tell you things like that, you put up that wall and remind me that you want to spend your life alone – Jeremiah Johnson, one man against the elements. How's a girl supposed to take that? Or, you tell me that I should date other men, which I think is totally ridiculous. And, I don't expect to hear ridiculous statements coming from your mouth. So, you see my problem. – H S

January 5, 2001

Yes, Julie, you are right and I understand. I am sorry that it hurts. There are two reasons for that wall which is there involuntarily. First, you are still in your marriage, and I want you to arrive at what to do with it without any influence from me. I know that our relationship does not enhance your chances of fixing your marriage. I know we have something special between us, and I know you will say that your decision to leave Don has nothing whatsoever to do with me. But, you must not allow my existence to influence you at all. That wouldn't be right. Although your support helped me keep what is left of my sanity, I truly wish we had met a year or two from now, when all the turmoil in both of our lives is behind us. Your family is upset with you first for the breakup of your marriage, and even more significantly for the fact that you are dating while still married. So, you see, I am causing you some problems at home, and making things worse. Even though you tell me adamantly that you would leave Don anyway even if I were not in the picture, my presence takes away any chance of reconciliation. Julie, I just want you to do what is right for you to do, without any consideration as to the part I may play in your life.

Secondly, I am just out of a thirty-two year relationship myself, and recognize that I still carry so much baggage from it. That baggage may be with me for a very long time. I cannot give myself completely, until I am baggage-free, and that isn't fair to you. But, I value you so much and would find it difficult to loose your friendship. I love you as much as I am able, but I tend to be either emotionally flat or very depressed most of the time, and need desperately to get over that before I can truly find my emotions again, as they have been so badly injured. I hope that they are just injured, and not gone. So, you see, it isn't you. Any man would be very lucky to have you in love with him, as you are a wonderful person with great courage and an incredible capacity to love. I hope one day to be worthy of the love you have given me, and I hope one day to have the ability not to need to be alone. Then, I will be ready to share my life the way it should be shared. But, for now, Julie, dear sweet Julie, I need to be the way I am to heal my spirit. All the advice gurus say – stay away from a recently divorced or separated man, this is the reason why.

Just remember, I will always be here for you, Julie, and will always care deeply for you. I am sorry that our relationship brings you any sorrow. You deserve happiness from it as you invest so much of yourself into it. Be at peace, Julie. We are very lucky to have what we have. - Henry

January 5, 2001
Hi Henry:

I understand what you mean about not wanting to influence any decisions I make, but those decisions were already made long before I met you, and long before I went onto the internet to try and find a soulmate. My relationship with you is probably the only thing in my life that truly gives me pleasure. I enjoy myself when I am with you, and I am stress-free during those times. The relationship we have is very rare, and it is not often that two people find as much as they do in each other as we have found. Something like that should not be thrown away lightly, because we may never get it again. It's way too precious. You are not the cause of my problems. You are probably the prescription that keeps me sane. Do you really think that I would need any "influence" to leave a man who is drunk every single night?

Henry, you and I will carry baggage for the rest of our lives. That's what happens when you have thirty plus year relationships. The baggage doesn't go away – it just gets put into its proper perspective. Right now the baggage may seem to you to be overwhelming, and it is, but you know what…I may be just a little bit more understanding than you give me credit for. Your baggage can never hurt me. I don't look at it as any more than what it is – baggage. If you wait until you are "baggage-free", you'll be eighty years old, and your whole life will have passed you by. You'll look back and see all that you missed, because you thought that going over to Wilma's house as often as you will need to go, would have made a difference to someone else you loved. Do you see how dumb that is? To most women, that might be a problem, but things like that would never bother me. That's because I'm sure that I'll be doing some crazy stuff on my own with my own baggage. If you didn't have any baggage, I probably would not love you, because it would show me that you are uncaring. The more baggage you have, the more I realize that you are a man who cares about the people in his life, and will do the things that need to be done. So, I think you should reassess your feelings about being "baggage-free".

And, you are not emotionally flat. Yes you are depressed, but I'm working on that. At least you don't put me in a depressed state of mind – just the opposite. And, our relationship doesn't bring me any sorrow – the opposite once again. But, I just wish you could see that you could be with me, and still have all the space you need. I'm not a space invader. I respect your need to be alone. Can't you see that? By now you aught to know me pretty well. You are just so used to a woman making demands on you, that you don't know what it is to feel absolutely free, and still be with someone. You do me a disservice, when you don't judge me for myself, but instead assume I am a certain way, because that's what you've been taught to believe about women by a paranoid dysfunctional wife. Have I ever done anything that fits such a mold? Maybe you're right and there is no hope for us ever being more than what we are to each other right now. Wouldn't that be a terrible shame? I'll think about all that you've said, and try to reassess in my own mind what's going on here. I'm sorry for even bringing it up, because I always get the Berlin Wall when I do, but I don't know if you keep up with the news – there is no Berlin Wall any more. - H S

January 9, 2001
Good Morning, Henry:

How are you on this fine warm day? It was like a spring morning. I even wore a light coat. I didn't need my gloves. I hope the weather stays like this for a while. Thank you for allowing me to visit next Saturday. I will bring dinner. You are not to buy any food. I will bring it all, and I'll even cook. You did say you had a "strong" stomach, didn't you? I really need to get away from all the bullshit, and I miss you terribly. I wish I could get a hug from you right now.

I have some good news to share with you. The International Society of Poets wants to give me some kind of an award at their poetry convention in Orlando, March 2nd – 4th. I remember that you mentioned wanting to go to Orlando also. Any chance you can coordinate your dates to finish up your own business down there that weekend, then join me? I don't think I could get up and read my poetry in front of over a thousand people without your wonderful face smiling back at me from the audience. I'm sure a lot of other poets are also getting an award, but there are also going to be a few workshops and a few famous poets there also.

I've sent copies of my book out to friends and relatives. You have no idea how many cards and letters I got back from people who are telling me that the poems make them cry, or they gave one of the poems to a friend who is having a hard time with something. My cousin read some of the poems to her children. Would you believe that? It makes me feel so good that I was able to touch someone else's life like that. Well, you have a good day. – H S

January 9, 2001
Good Morning, Hot Stuff:

How is your day going so far? And how was your commute home last night? I got in late this morning after shoveling the driveway again. Gee, I hate snow, and the cold. Orlando sure sounds great and is getting greater and greater, the colder it gets. I am so proud of you for being up for an award. You are the first person I know that has had their poetry recognized. It is getting rave reviews from all of the people I have let read your book. Many identify with much of your poetry. This weekend is going to be fun. I visited that Old Lumberyard antique store in Milford this past weekend, and was disappointed as the place is virtually empty. Would you like to visit the Glen Falls indoor/outdoor flea market instead? They have antiques and junk in the buildings. Also, there is a good candle outlet just down the road. We could stop and have breakfast on the way if you would like or lunch on the way back. Also, this weekend I would like to sketch you from life if you are willing. Wouldn't you like to have a charcoal of your boobs to take home as a souvenir? - Henry

Henry and I spent more time on the telephone this week than we did writing, but here are a few emails that followed the incredible weekend we spent together.

January 15, 2001
Hi there Hot Stuff:

Julie, I had a great time with you this weekend. Thank you so much for sharing your day (and your night) with me. It was very special to me that you sought out my company to get away from it all. I don't know why you said you couldn't cook as the meal was wonderful and I enjoyed your cooking for us. I always feel so renewed after being in your company. You make me smile as soon as I see your face, no matter what kind of lousy mood I'm in before I see you. I enjoyed our walk and I hate to get any exercise, especially in the cold. But, walking with you was an absolute pleasure. I enjoy everything we do together. I will work on your charcoal this week. Thank you for posing for me, and I hope to have it finished for you the next time we see each other. I hope your day went well today. I miss you. Be happy. - Henry

January 16, 2001
Dearest Henry:

You always manage to say the nicest things to me. I also had a wonderful day on Saturday, and I can't think of any other place I would have rather been, than your place. As I've said before, I find myself falling deeper and deeper in love with you with each encounter. But, there are things I don't understand, and I am puzzled about, and I hope that you can find the words to clarify these things in my mind. Please, don't evade these questions, and just answer them honestly with your thoughts and feelings. I just need to understand some things. Don't make more of it than it is.

Why is it that you seem to have all your weekends planned way in advance, but never have any plans with me, except the ones I seem to set up? Like this last Saturday, which we wouldn't have had, if I had not asked to come. Why is it that you told me I could not spend more than $15 for a house gift for you, yet you allowed Elizabeth to buy you that expensive fairy statue? I don't understand why you don't want me to meet Elizabeth (who supposedly likes my poetry), or why I couldn't go to the movie with you on Sunday with your goddaughter. I would not have embarrassed you in front of your friends. These are people who you told me do not associate with Wilma, so I just don't understand what harm it would have done. You say that these relationships with Elizabeth and Sophia are platonic now, but my instincts are telling me something different. I am not "jealous" of these women, but I am just trying to understand a little bit better, your relationship with them. Henry, just so you know, in case you didn't already, I have not slept with Don in over two years, and you are the only man I sleep with. I am very careful about who I involve myself with. The reason why I feel comfortable with you is because you were in a 30+ year relationship, and I feel reasonably safe that you are not in the position of transmitting any sexually contracted diseases, such as HIV. Most likely, if I did not feel comfortable with you in that way, I would have asked you to take a blood test before we made love. I guess what I need is some reassurances that you are not going to give me any germs that will make me regret this relationship some time in the future. I could probably handle a broken heart a lot better than I could a devastating illness. I need my health to stay strong when all else fails. I don't want to have a sexual relationship with a man who is having sex with other women at the same time he is seeing me. If you need more time with me, just ask. When have I ever turned you down? I could give you all the sex you could ever possibly want. I hope you do not take this in the wrong way, but I am confused.

I told Don that you were going with me to the poetry convention in Orlando. He said that he was happy that I have someone to go with who will enjoy the convention. He knows that he would have hated it. I think he has resigned himself to the fact that he and I will not be together much longer. He accepts the fact that I go to your place overnight, because I always come home smiling, and he is starting to date. All these things are good. Now, I just wish you'd give me a shelf in your linen closet, so I wouldn't have to lug my hair dryer, toothbrush, etc., back and forth, whenever I come to visit.

Back to your letter, I am looking forward to seeing the completed version of that charcoal you are doing of me very much. But, I want you to make me a copy of it, and hang the original in your bedroom. That would make me very happy. And, I celebrated Martin Luther King's birthday by going on a shopping spree. I bought myself a new bed, and finally had a Monet print

I had in the closet for years, framed. I spent a fortune on the frame, but it should look wonderful when it's finished.

Henry, don't take what I am saying the wrong way. I am just trying to understand the perspective you put our relationship in. That's all. If you feel that the questions I asked are not appropriate then tell me. Our relationship is precious to me, and I do not want to loose it, and if I am making more of it than what it is, then I want to know that too. I have one request, and if you can't honor it, I need to know that. During the time that we are sleeping together, I want to be the only woman you sleep with, because you will be my exclusive sexual partner during that time. Maybe I should have discussed this with you months ago, but somehow I got some strange vibes this weekend, and this is the first time I felt the need to say it. Now, smile and write me an honest answer to this long drawn out letter. – H S

January 16, 2001
Hi Julie:

I have read your letter, and it certainly deserves an honest straightforward reply to some questions that I would rather you had not asked. I would like some time to think about the letter and would like to answer it line by line, honestly and truthfully. Julie, I care about you, and I care about your feelings very much. I promise that my letter to you will contain the absolute truth. Please give me time to write it right, so please bear with me for today, so that I can spend time on it tonight. I am sorry to make you wait for a response and I know it isn't fair to do that, but I want to really think about what I am going to say, so that it comes out right. You are always in my thoughts, Julie. You have brought not only friendship, but affection and love into our relationship when I didn't expect either. - Henry

January 16, 2001
Henry:

You called me "Julie". Now, I know I'm in trouble. Just write from your heart, Henry. It's not all that difficult. I didn't intend for you to sit and write a book about it. What's there to think about when you write the "truth"? You aught to know me well enough to know that I will not, nor ever will, judge you, and I don't want you to have a "stress" session over this. I already know that you haven't been entirely truthful with me about other women (instincts). Although I wasn't entirely sure until this past weekend… But, this is the first time I've told you what I wanted, and about my fears with sexually transmitted diseases. They are fears that every responsible adult should have. I think if you have to "think" about what you want to say to me, that you'll probably not be entirely truthful with me. Please don't make this more than what it is. – H S

January 16, 2001
Dear Hot Stuff:

And, you will always be "Hot Stuff" to me. You don't have to worry about STD. It is just that I need to answer you from my heart and get down on paper exactly the way I feel, and to write feelings is hard, as feelings are felt and cannot always be put easily into words, and I need to tell you why I feel that way without any misunderstandings. I have thought about this conversation more than once, and I do need to think about what I need to say to you, because I care about you. I know what I want to say, the trick is to say it so that you read what it is I mean without any ambiguity. Your friendship means a very great deal to me, because I think of you as a kindred spirit and I truly don't want to screw that up. I have a wonderful record for screwing up what

417

I value most in the world. I am sorry for leaving you hanging like this, but if you want a truthful straight answer, then I need to have tonight to write it. No matter what your reaction, and no matter what may happen in the future, no matter what you may think or believe, believe this one thing of me – I do love you and I only want the best for you.

Your friend and lover - Henry

January 17, 2001
My Dear Julie:

I had a blood test for multiple sexually transmitted diseases a couple of months ago, and I am sure that you will be relieved that I am negative in all respects.

What is difficult about this letter is not just the content, but how do I start it? You see, I want so much not to hurt you, or anyone else. I have to start from the beginning so that you have the best chance of understanding, not condoning, not excusing, but maybe just understanding.

Three years ago, after thirty years, I began to admit to myself that something was wrong with my marriage. I knew that Wilma loved me, but she was incapable of giving me the affection that I needed. I don't mean sex. She would consistently refuse a hug, would never sit close to me on the couch while watching TV, and in the evening, she hardly spoke to me. I loved her so much, my heart was breaking, and I felt so alone. I tried over the years to talk with her about it, and she would most often reply "that's just the way I am". She laughed about it to our friends and family in front of me saying, "Poor guy, never gets laid", and she would make a joke out of it. Even the kids made jokes about when I tried to cuddle her on the couch, and she pushed me away. It was all very funny and a big joke to everyone, but to me. I felt humiliated. It left a big hole in me somehow that I needed to fill. I endured this for twenty years or more. I would look in the mirror and think to myself how very unattractive I was, and that I could never appeal to any woman. After all, even my wife, who I desperately loved, wasn't interested.

I finally turned to a close friend, Sophia, the mother of my goddaughter. We had always been close and I had known Sophia at that time for about twenty-five years. About twenty years before, we had a one night stand. We were alone on the 4th of July. She was single, and Wilma and the kids were down at the shore. I was to join them on the 6th, because I had to work on the 5th, so I stayed up in Hackensack where we lived. I innocently invited Sophia over for some barbecue on the 4th, as we were both alone. She innocently accepted my invitation. Well, burgers, lots of booze, and we were both alone. One thing led to another. But it was three hours, and just one night. We both enjoyed it, but spoke of it only once about two weeks later, but not since...a twenty year old shared secret. That did explain some of the closeness I guess. Anyway, fast forward to three years or so ago. After courting her, and filling my conversations with her with sexual innuendo for about a year, she finally agreed to meet me in a hotel while she was away on business in Philly, ostensibly to have dinner with me as we never saw each other often, and were going to use the opportunity for a long conversation, just to catch up. I spent the night. It was the best night I had in many years and one about which I had fantasized about for many years also. The next day I felt fantastic and like a stupid teenager, fell in love with that feeling, and thought that I was completely in love with Sophia. I told her that I loved her, and she did not encourage me. On the other hand, she didn't discourage me either. I wish now she had either encouraged or discouraged me, because my reluctance to reconcile with Wilma had a good deal to do with the fact that I thought Sophia was out there waiting. I tried real hard to arrange another encounter with her, and wanted a full-blown affair as 'I was in love'. We never met in private again. After a year of this, one day I met her for a very rare lunch. When she kissed me goodbye at the end of the meal, it was as though she were kissing a brother, and in many ways she was. The affair that never happened was over. It was strange, but I was instantly out of love with her, as though she had thrown a switch. That kiss happened about a year and a half ago. Sophia and I are back to being friends, very close, but just friends. You see, I understand her side also.

During the time I was mooning over Sophia (about two years), Wilma, who is not stupid, was reacting. Our marriage became increasingly difficult and as you know, she ultimately kicked me out. I never admitted to anything happening between Sophia and me, although I did say that she was very important to me and had become an adopted member of my family, and that I loved her a great deal. Wilma accused me of being my goddaughter's father (which I am not), and on and on...

So, about a year and a half ago, I started cruising the net, and reading the personals for fun, not to find anyone, but I was curious.

I placed an ad on Yahoo and Elizabeth responded. We began a two month gab session. Not real erotic conversations, but certainly full of sexual innuendo. During this time I was corresponding with several females, some to whom I had responded. You were among these women. I didn't intend to get "involved". I was just having some fun and meant no harm to anyone. Quite the contrary, I began to care what was happening in two of these people's lives…you and Elizabeth. Every word I wrote to you and to her was straight from the heart. We were not face to face, so I could be honest and say what I wanted to say as you didn't know me so that gave me freedom to be me. Eventually, Elizabeth and I decided to meet for dinner. I don't think that I was looking for a "girlfriend", but I did think it would be fun to go out to dinner with a strange woman. Also, Wilma and I had deteriorated to the point where sex was pretty much nonexistent, and in fact most of the time (at least 6 nights out of 7), I slept alone. So, sex only happened during very rare truces, maybe once in a couple of months. Anyway, Elizabeth and I were attracted to each other right away, and besides, we knew each other from many emails. It wasn't long before we were sleeping together. But, we both understood it wasn't love, it was just 'fun'.

It was about this time that you and I met for the first time. Neither one of us was expecting to enter into an affair that day, or even a one nighter, but we were both so curious about the other. The chemistry between us was and is still unbelievable. It was like you exuded an aphrodisiac, and you know where that went. I had no intention of either of us falling in love with the other. This was going to be fun. We didn't meet for the first time at the 'park and ride' because we were in love, we were in lust. I wasn't unfaithful to either you or Elizabeth, because for all three of us, it wasn't a serious thing, then. This was just some harmless fun that seemed to be doing everyone involved a lot of good. By the time I realized what was happening and what I had done, it had already happened. You told me you loved me. Elizabeth also talks of love. I should have stopped right there, but I didn't, and I am ashamed of that. You see, I never lied about my feelings to anyone. When I tell someone I love them, I mean it. I feel it. I don't mean to take advantage of anyone either. I can't explain myself why I am so destructive to you when I truly care for you...stupidity, lack of moral character, lack of experience, or just being a shit. I don't believe I could have caused this mess, but I allowed our relationship to grow while still involved with Elizabeth. I love you, Julie. Make no mistake about it. You are incredibly important to me. I am so sorry if this hurts you and I know that I have fucked up. I did try so often to warn you that I was a lousy bastard, and I wanted to tell you early on, but I just took what I thought was the easy way, and allowed you both to think that there was no one else. That was wrong. I am very ashamed of myself, especially as I have used two people who I truly want as friends. But, now I may loose everyone. I am not sorry for the wonderful times we have had together, but I am sorry for getting them under false pretences. Please forgive me for withholding the truth for so long. I just couldn't face hurting someone else, and I couldn't face loosing you. - Henry

January 17, 2001
Dearest Henry:

I don't know what makes a person wake another person up at 5 AM, but I guess I wasn't feeling like being too thoughtful about others this morning. I'm sorry for that. But, I'm in pain. I wonder if by dying you can make the ache you feel in your chest every time you breath, go away, and if so, is dying better than living? If only I could die and loose the pain buried in my heart right now...I didn't realize anybody had as many tears in them as I cried last night. I cried because I felt I lost you somehow, and I never wanted that to happen. It took me 51 years to find you, and now I have to rethink every single moment we were together, and try to figure out what you were really feeling, and to decide whether or not, my imagination made me believe what I wanted to believe, and not what was really there.

Did I "imagine" what we had for the past eight plus months? Did I misconstrue what I thought I saw in your eyes when we made love? I guess that I need you to look me in the eyes, face to face, and tell me that you don't love me. And, if you are incapable of doing that, then you owe it to yourself to pull me into your life, before it's too late for that to happen. I don't believe in your analysis that it's "too soon for you or me to become involved with another person". It happened. This isn't a textbook romance. We are adults and we know what we are feeling, whether you want to face it or not. Since, you seem incapable at this time (and that's OK) to tell me how you are really feeling, I will tell you how I feel about you, and about us. I crave you, thirst you, love you...love you deeply. When we are separated, I spend my days searching for pieces of you. I have changed because of you. You have helped me extricate myself from the emotional prison I was in. I wonder if you know how much I think of you. I could spend every hour of the day lost in memories of how we are together. You are the most beautiful man I could see, or ever hope to see. You struggle with me, lean close to my words, respect our differences, honor my mind, and challenge my ideas. I have no idea how I can live without your smiling face in my life. What do you want me to do? Tell me, and I will do it. It's not easy to trust your heart, and I cannot say "goodbye" – that word "goodbye" is meaningless to two people who have loved each other with the passion we had for each other. I know I will miss, most of all, the passion you had for me.

You made me feel beautiful. I'm not talking about sexual passion. I'm talking about a different kind of passion. . .the kind that develops when you meet someone who is truly on your wave length and who gets excited about your ideas. I will miss the way you nod your head when you are listening to me. You always made me feel brilliant. I want to spend what little time I have left in this adventure we call life with you, so I could go on feeling wonderful and happy all the time. Now, I think that you have decided to punish yourself for some unknown reason, and are willing to settle for less out of life than you deserve. Henry, if you don't do another thing in this life, be true to yourself! You deserve to be happy. You've earned that right. What you did to Elizabeth and myself is nothing compared to what you are doing to yourself right now. Yes, I hurt, but it wasn't as if I didn't know what was going on with you. I guess I was hoping that I was wrong about how you felt about her. I could not believe that someone who felt the way I thought you felt for me, could also feel that way about another woman. I wanted to believe your lies so badly. But, there were so many little hints that told me otherwise. And yet, in spite of everything you told me, I still don't believe that you love her anywhere near how you feel for me. If you truly felt something deep for her, you never would have started up with me in the first place. Henry, when we are together, we are REALLY together.

I don't want to go to Florida without you in March. In fact, if you change your mind about going, I will not go. I need to use this opportunity to finally expose my poetry to the literary world, and yet, I can't do it without you there listening and smiling while I read my work to the world. You are a part of my poetry, and I need you there, just as I needed your drawing on the cover of my book. I need you in ways other women don't need you, and I don't need you for the normal stuff like financial support. The ways I need you are much harder to give, and maybe I expect too much, but know this – I am probably the one woman in the world who can truly give you what you need in this world, and I am willing to give you that in exchange for what you give to me. Don't throw it away.

Henry, one last thing – there are no second chances in life. If you don't want to look back at your life when you are on that deathbed in your future, and cry about the life you let slip away, then grab onto this rainbow that we started to build together, and take me to the stars!

Always and forever,

Your Hot Stuff

CHAPTER SEVENTEEN

I guess I put it all on the line that day. I took a big chance in telling Henry that if he were going to have a "sexual" or "romantic" involvement with someone other than me, then it would be over between us. I felt that if he were also seeing someone else the way he was seeing me, then he really couldn't possibly sincerely mean the things he said to me. I was falling more and more in love with him. I felt it was better to get hurt now than to expose myself to a deeper hurt later on. His need to lie to me about his relationship with Elizabeth all this time disturbed me. If I felt the need to see someone else, I would have told him about it up front. And, he was lying to her also. It was so obvious that he was also romantically involved with her. I really didn't believe his lies about her coming over for the weekend and it being purely a platonic relationship. When I pushed the issue, he said I was asking questions that were putting him "on the spot", and he really didn't want to answer them. Of course, he didn't want to answer them. That would have meant he'd have to tell me about what he was doing with her. Yet, in spite of it all, I felt that he did somehow feel love for me. I think he was very much afraid of giving his heart to anyone again. By keeping two girlfriends, he thought that he was somehow insulating himself from that type of involvement. I don't think he could handle being hurt again. He still was healing from all the abuse Wilma put him through. So perhaps, that was the reason why I seemed to be so tolerant of it all.

I think he was mistaking love for empathy in his relationship with Elizabeth. When he described her, he described her as a struggling mother of three with no one to help her, but himself. I think she was playing on his sympathies a good deal of the time. She used his credit card to purchase a computer, which is not exactly a necessity, and he had to chauffeur her to the airport when she took a trip, and to her father's house in New York. He took care of her dog for her when she went away. He even played surrogate father to her sons during their karate matches. In a strange way, I hoped that he was getting something back out of all he did for her. I think she recognized that he was a very generous human being and took advantage of that fact. I would never impose on him the way she did. He didn't see it as an imposition. These things made me see that his relationship with her was much deeper than he had led me to believe.

I thought that he would surely break off his relationship with me, and keep things going with her. She seemed to need him. I didn't need him. I wanted him and loved him. I was very much surprised when he did the opposite.

January 17, 2001
Hi Julie:

Tonight I am going to tell Elizabeth that I can no longer pursue a romantic relationship with her. I know that this will hurt her deeply, and I will most likely loose her as a friend. Friends are important to me, and I love her as my friend, but doing what I am doing to both of you isn't fair, so I am going to tell her it is over.

I am so sorry that I have hurt you. I cried last night. I feel so guilty and ashamed of not considering everyone else's feelings, and for being so selfish. I thought that if I didn't see only one person, then I would not become involved with anyone. I was wrong. I didn't stop to consider that I have developed a respect and affection for both of you that I just didn't expect to happen. I do love you, Julie, but even that isn't fair, as I am still tied in so many ways to Wilma. I want to continue our relationship, as it is too important to me to loose. But, you must know that my feelings for Wilma are far from over. I used you and Elizabeth as a buffer against the hurt I was going through, and am still feeling sorrow over the loss of my marriage.

I will end it with Elizabeth tonight. But, do you really want to continue with a man who cannot give you all of his heart, because some of it still belongs to his wife? Do you want to continue to expose yourself to possible future pain with me? That is what I meant when I said that it was too soon. You are like no one I have ever met, and my love for you is real, but I still cannot make a commitment to you. I want you in my life, but you must decide if I am worth it, because I do carry so much baggage.

How can I tell you how sorry I am that I made you cry? How can I tell you how sorry I am that I am not a better man? - Henry

January 17, 2001
Dear Henry:

I cannot tell you what to do with Elizabeth. I can only tell you what's in my heart and my own feelings. Why couldn't you end the "sexual" relationship with her, but maintain the friendship? You managed to remain friends with Sophia. Why not Elizabeth? I am not jealous of either of these women or Wilma, but I cannot have a "sexual" relationship with a man who is sleeping with other women. I only ask that you have a sexual relationship with me exclusively for as long as we have one, and I hope that's forever (wishful thinking). I have no problems with your friendships, and in fact, I would like to meet your friends, because if you like them, I know I will also. I do not have any problems with your 'baggage' from Wilma. I know that you have had a long term relationship with her, as I have had with Don. I also know that you are not "in love" with her. You love her as you would a good friend or sister, and you will always take care of her. I also know that if something were to happen to her, you would be the very first person at her side, as I would be for Don. Coming from the same type relationship, I fully understand what obligations you have, and will continue to have, and I can respect that. In fact, one of the reasons why I love you so is the fact that you do feel these responsibilities.

I know you love me very much. You have shown this to me in many ways. I also know that it is very difficult for you to hurt the people you love and care about, as it is for me as well. If you were to go back to Wilma - which can happen, I know it will be for the wrong reasons, and because I love you, I will try to talk you out of it. Not just for myself, but because your "happiness" is important to me. I've never met her, but from what you told me, I am convinced that she will give you nothing but misery if you were to return to your old relationship with her. However, I will never stop you from doing what you believe you must do - just try to convince you otherwise. I really don't care if you get a divorce or not, as long as I can come over often to be with you. I figure I have about another six months, at most, in my current situation. During that time, I can spend as many nights as I like, away from home. After that, I will get my own place, but I also hope that when that happens, you will come over frequently to spend the night with me. I know that we must maintain separate addresses, but I also hope that we will see each other much more often than we currently see each other. I believe that good things are worth waiting for, and although I cannot make a commitment to you either, I know that if I could, and if I can in the future, there is nobody I would rather make a commitment to. There is no "better man" than you, silly. And, don't be sorry for being human. You don't ever have to say you are sorry to me. - H S

January 17, 2001
Hi Julie:

It's about eight PM and I am home. I ended it with Elizabeth this evening. She didn't take it well. Not angry, just very distraught...how I hate hurting people. I have much to answer for. I hope I haven't hurt you too badly. I am contrite. Please forgive me for what I have done to you both. I am such a shit. I hope that you are still in my life, but I wouldn't blame you one bit if you weren't. Please, sleep peacefully tonight. I know I won't. Call me, please, if you get the chance. Even if it is five AM.

Henry

January 18, 2001
Hi Henry:

Good Morning. Are you feeling any better today? I did sleep well last night, and I even went to the gym this morning. You did the right thing, even though you hurt some people now, it would have been worse later on. I'm glad that you chose to keep me in your life.

I didn't know that you had no plans for the weekend. You told me that you were supposed to be some kind of a chaperone for a teenage pajama party on Friday night, and that your son was coming up Saturday night. So, I just assumed that you didn't want to see me this weekend. The bed I bought on Monday is supposed to be delivered some time Sunday morning. I had made plans with Don to go to Tannersville Saturday, because I need to buy some full-sized bed sheets for my new bed, and I wanted to go to the Springmaid factory outlet store there. I don't think Don really wants to go, because he doesn't need anything there, and was going to back out of it anyway. If he decides not to go, then I'll come over Saturday morning, but I'll have to leave very early Sunday morning so I can be there when my new bed comes. Next Saturday my brother and I are taking my Mom to Atlantic City for her birthday. But, I am free the whole weekend of February 3rd, and would like to spend it with you, if you don't have any plans. I am telling you my plans so that you can try to mesh your schedule with mine, and hopefully, we would be able to see each other more. I know that your family is planning on spending your birthday weekend with you on the 10th, so maybe if we get together on the 3rd, I'll bake you a birthday cake, and have a little birthday celebration for you then. I'll even put candles on your cake and sing Happy Birthday to you! Smile.

I really feel I need a hug from you now, and a chance to talk after all that has happened this week. So, I must find some time to be with you this weekend. Is there any chance you can get out of the chaperone job on Friday night, or maybe see me afterwards?   Love you, H S

January 18, 2001
Hi Hot Stuff:

I cannot back out of Friday night chaperone duties, as I have already backed out of Saturday. John will be coming up next weekend, because he will be busy this weekend, but he needs to confirm that. It is the same Saturday that you will be in Atlantic City with your Mom. As far as this weekend goes – I'll be home Saturday and Sunday all day except if I go shopping locally. If you can come, great. If not, then don't sweat it. We will see each other soon.

Thanks for the offer of help, but I am only going to cut up a couple of small trees, weather permitting. That should take me no more than a couple of hours, and then I will be working in my garage to straighten out some of the mess. This is the first weekend since I moved in, that I will be home all weekend, and have time to do some chores. Incidentally, February 3rd sounds like a plan to me. So, you sing?

The weather forecast is calling for some really crummy weather over the weekend, so you may not get to Tannersville after all. But, if the weather's too bad to go to Tannersville, it will be too bad to drive up and see me also. If Don really doesn't want to go, and backs out, then if you do elect to come up on Saturday, I will drive you down to Tannersville, if you like, if the weather holds. But, please don't cancel any plans you made with Don, even if he seems reluctant to go, let him back out. You don't need to rock the boat at your house any more than it already is. If you are real busy, don't rush your day to get up here. If you come, I want you to be relaxed and comfortable, and not watching the clock. Have a great day, and I'm glad you slept better. - Henry

January 18, 2001
Hi Henry:

Thanks. I wouldn't cancel with Don after already making plans. It's just that I really don't think he wants to go, and was just saying so, because he had nothing better to do. Henry, it's OK to say that you would prefer to be alone, if you like. I would understand. I really would. I thought you might be feeling in need of some warm and loving company after this week, and quite frankly, I was hoping to see you tonight, but because of my car problems, I most likely will have to pick it up, or if what is wrong with it is covered under the warranty, I'll get a free rental car, and I will have to pick that up too. I guess, what I want to do is look into your eyes and feel your arms around me after all the emotional upheaval we had this week. And, I don't' know if I can wait until the 3rd of February to do that. Thank you for the offer of driving me to Tannersville. I certainly will take you up on it, if Don backs out. Smile. - H S

January 18, 2001

Well Julie, my door is open to you this weekend, if you like. If you can make it, great. If not, then I will see you soon. Good luck with your car. - Henry

January 22, 2001
Good Morning Hot Stuff:

I am so glad that you made it yesterday. It seems that whenever I see you, the time goes by so incredibly fast that I don't get a chance to show you things that I want to, or talk to you enough. I was just getting used to you being there, and it was time for you to go. I think that it would take a week or so of us being together just to hit the high spots. But, I guess you follow that golden rule – "always leave them wanting more". Thank you again, for coming. You made digging the snow out of the driveway worthwhile. Have a great day, Sweetie. - Henry

January 22, 2001
Hi Henry:

I'm glad I came early and found you sweaty and unshaven. I like that side of you – very manly and sexy - **GRINNING**

I know that the time goes incredibly fast when we're together. I didn't leave early purposely to leave you "wanting more". I left early so I wouldn't have to drive back in the dark as I don't like driving on unfamiliar roads in the dark. I expect to work late tonight. Another twelve hour day, but then there's nothing I have that I want to come home to, so what difference does it make? Take care – H S

CHAPTER EIGHTEEN

The next few weeks were wonderful. For his birthday, I gave Henry a rug to match his bedroom that I hooked myself. It took me months and countless hours to make that rug, and when his eyes lit up as he opened the box, I knew he loved it, and that I had given him the perfect gift. It had an oriental design, and was the perfect size to fit in front of the fireplace he made for his bedroom. It was even the exact colors of his bedroom – French blue and white. I was so proud of it, and it pleased me so much that he loved it instantly, as soon as he saw it.

The times we spent together during the month of February - cooking for each other and cooking together as well. We made fancy dishes like soufflé and shrimp oreganato. Our soufflé tasted better than what I've tasted at the finest French restaurants in New York City. We discovered that cooking was something we both enjoyed, but both our spouses had taken over the kitchen while we were married, and neither one of us really ever had a chance to be creative in the kitchen until now. I made him macaroni with home made sauce from scratch, and he made me fabulous salmon with grilled Portobello mushrooms. We experimented on each other with new dishes. It was truly a "fun" time for both of us.

We saw each other as much as we could, and February was a month we really got to know each other in ways we didn't know before. When we were together, we mostly hung out at his house. It was cozy, and he always had a roaring fire going in his fireplace. It was the only truly private place where we could go and be together.

There was only one time I got upset, and that was Valentine's Day. Everyone I knew was spending Valentine with a loved one, and I was spending it alone, because he said he had a business dinner meeting. That seemed strange to me because even his business associates had wives and girlfriends. I thought that they would want to spend that evening with their loved ones. I thought he might have really been spending the evening with someone else, and just told me the business dinner excuse, as opposed to hurting my feelings. But, that evening I found a bouquet of roses that he left in my car, and the next day he and I did get together. He gave me the greatest Valentine gift. I will never forget it.

February 15, 2001
Hi Ya Julie:

I'm glad you liked the roses. I am only sorry that I couldn't give them to you in person. The meeting went OK. Of course we had to feed them too, so I didn't get back to the quarry until after ten thirty, and I didn't get home until about twelve thirty AM. The roads were so foggy that I had to drive slowly. I'm tired today. The negotiations on the project are far from over, so I will have to go back several times to the project over the next week or two, but I am sure the job is ours. We are working on the monorail system for JFK. It is a joint enterprise between the Port Authority and The New York State Dept. of Transportation. I am looking forward to seeing you this evening. I do have a small gift for you for Valentine's Day. It's something that you would never ever guess, but very romantic. It's the kind of gift that Romeo would have given Juliet, if he had the chance. Don't work too hard. See you later - Henry

That night Henry gave me a tool box full of tools for Valentine's Day. It was original, so very like him, and I loved it. I remembered complaining to him that Don planned on taking all his tools in the separation, and how I wouldn't have any tools to use to fix things once he left. The tools Henry bought me were good tools and I knew that I would use them many times in the future. It was the "perfect" gift; I will never forget his thoughtfulness, and it was so much better than a heart shaped box full of chocolates.

On February 19th, we went to our first movie together. It was a real date. Prior to that, our time together was so short, that we didn't have time for things like movies, etc. It was nice to be able to do something conventional, and in a way, it proved to me that our relationship wasn't just about sex.

February 20, 2001
Hi Henry:

Last night in the theatre, when your fingers were making love to my fingers, it was the most amazingly erotic experience I ever felt. It made me horny as hell. And, it was much more satisfying than eating popcorn with those fingers. Then, during dinner, your eyes made love to my eyes all during the meal, and I wanted you so very badly. Henry, I really believe that normal dates, like movies, etc. will be very difficult, if we can't end such nights in bed together. At least for me, they will be. Do you feel the same way, or is it just me? - HS

February 20, 2001
Hi Hot Stuff:

I also enjoyed your company last night. I liked sitting in the movies on a "normal" date, holding your hand throughout the movie. So, you saw the way I was looking at you. It wasn't your imagination. I like looking at you. Every time I do, I see something different and new about you. I had a great time. As far as getting horny last night – after our time together, I was "hornied out" by the time I saw you. But, a cuddle/fondle/grope in bed would have been real nice, and during dinner, I wanted to grab those luscious boobs of yours, and just bite right into them. If you had worn a short skirt and no panties in the movies, you and I would have made sure that you left the seat wet. I find it difficult to sleep with anyone as I am now used to sleeping alone, but I like being in bed with you as long as we don't expect to get any sleep. You looked good last night. Thank you for a great weekend, great time at the movies, great time at dinner, and I am looking forward immensely to our time in Florida.

Have a super day, Hot Stuff – Henry

In the beginning of March, Henry accompanied me to Florida where I read one of my poems at a poetry convention. It was a wonderful trip, and we went to Disneyworld, swam in the pool, visited art galleries, and just spent good quality time together. I enjoyed that trip so much, in spite of the fact that he called his wife several times during the trip. He never mentioned to her in any of those calls that he was with someone in Florida. The following week, Henry went on another trip. This time it was to Tampa, Florida. He said he went alone, but somehow I felt that he may have been with someone. That's because the whole time he was gone, he never called me. I tried to reach him once, but his phone was turned off.

I wrote a poem about our trip to Disneyworld which says it all.

DISNEY WORLD MARCH, 2001

I can still feel the tingly sensation of your warmth
As I think about this wondrous time we spent together.
We listened to the lectures and the poems, and
you said all the things about my work that made me feel good.
You made me laugh, and we made love,
So passionately, and so very thoroughly...

We saw Epcot...
And walked around the world
visiting countries we always wanted to see.
Then, I discovered some of the secrets of science,
as the powers of your mind opened up to me.
Then we made love, and you fucked my brains out.

We got lost Downtown Disney,
experienced Planet Hollywood,
then you made love to every inch of my body.

We paid obscene prices for breakfast,
and fed it to the birds,
and, we made love, slowly, deliberately, and so generously.

We enjoyed the hot tub,
and you even tried to teach me to swim,
then, we made love again, playing with each other's body,
like two children with new toys.

We played chess while listening to the rain,
talking about anything and everything,
then we made love, over and over again.

We laughed together at all the funny things,
and we cried together for what we found,
and what we are so terrified of loosing...
Then we made love, wanting to get so close, as one,
deep inside each other's soul ...

Sometimes when I went to Henry's house for the weekend, he'd get calls from his wife or from his friend Elizabeth and I'd have to endure his sometimes lengthly conversations with them. The weekend before he went to Tampa was one such weekend. Henry took a call from Wilma at 7:30 AM, and of course she was being evasive, trying to create some mystery and wanted to see him about something that she couldn't talk about on the phone. It's bad enough that she woke us up, but all the other nonsense was just too much. He didn't see what she was doing. I had enough and just decided to leave after that call.

March 19, 2001
Hi Ya Hot Stuff:

It was a great weekend. My conversation with Wilma went well. I did go to see her. In fact we went out for breakfast. She made me a very nice offer. Under our agreement, I cannot use the house for collateral for loans, etc., but she suggested that I get a small $8,500 ten-year home equity loan on the house to pay the taxes I owe. Considering that she plans to put the house on the market next year, and the debt would be paid out of my end, it will disappear next year. It really takes the pressure off.

And, you left your panties at my house. Now, I have a trophy. I think that I will frame them. The best part of the weekend for me was falling asleep in front of the fire with you. That was nice. Let's make a date right now for next Tuesday eve for soup night. I'll miss you. - Henry

March 19, 2001
Henry:

Why couldn't she tell you that it was OK to do the equity loan for the taxes over the phone? Or last weekend when she saw you? She woke us up at 7:30 in the morning just for that? I think it's very generous of her to offer you this wonderful opportunity, but isn't that house already mortgaged to the hilt? Maybe I misread some past email, but that's what I thought. I guess I'm a bit pissed off because if it hadn't been for that call, I certainly would never have left as early as I did, but after that call, your whole personality changed. I just felt that it was on your mind, and the faster I leave, the sooner you'd be able to handle whatever she had to say. In case you didn't notice, I was out of there in less than an hour after she called. If I didn't need to take a shower, it would have been sooner. So, in a way, she ended up ruining my Sunday morning. It would probably be good for both of you if she decides to sell that house, but she won't, because then what would she have to hang over your head? I thought she really had something requiring a life or death decision to talk about with you. Also, the fact that you ran over there, like a puppy whose choker just got pulled, tells me a lot about your current relationship with her. – H S

March 19, 2001
Hi Hot Stuff:

I would like to see you the weekend after my trip to Tampa if you are free. And you didn't have to run out of there that fast if you didn't want to. I never said that you had to go. I just assumed that you had stuff to do. - Henry

March 19, 2001

I know that you never said that I had to go. It was the feeling I got after you took that call from Wilma. It had to do with your anxiety level, and I know you were concerned about what she wanted to talk to you about, and my presence was preventing you from finding out. I think I know you well enough to understand your moods. I felt that you definitely wanted me out of there once you got that call. I wasn't upset about it. I will never overstay my welcome. If Wilma hadn't called, I most likely would have stayed until noon, at least, and you wouldn't have been able to have breakfast with Wilma. I still would have had enough time to get everything done that I needed to do at home. And, I would have most likely cleaned your dirty oven for you, and then made mad passionate love with you again. Smile. I would have enjoyed doing it. Both the oven and you. You, a little bit more than the oven. I think...Although I can really get into doing ovens. I'm bringing a can of Easy Off with me the next time I come. Maybe you should disconnect your phones the next time I come, too. It seems that whenever you get a phone call, I somehow get upset. I don't mean to, but I'm so sensitive that if I detect the slightest disappointment at my being there, I'll leave. I usually take things the wrong way, I'm afraid. Maybe that has something to do with the fact that in one way, I'm in your life, but I'm not really in your life. I mean I even felt that I had to ask "permission" to leave my hair dryer and toothbrush there.

I actually left my deodorant and perfume also - four things of mine. I guess that's pretty awful for someone who is supposed to be the only person you're sleeping with. Maybe we should have a talk about this, or as I'm sure you would prefer, just table it for the next ten years or so. (Sorry, but I'm still in a sarcastic mood, but not as bad as earlier.) I will come on the weekend of the 31st, only on the condition that you let me clean the oven. I want to leave my "mark". Smile - HS

March 19, 2001

Julie, Julie...You did misinterpreted my mood this time. You said that I definitely wanted you out of there. That isn't so. I was concerned with what Wilma wanted to talk with me about, but I did not want you out of there. I'm sorry if I gave you that impression. And, you can leave any stuff at my house that you want to, if it makes life easier for you. – Henry

March 19, 2001

OK Henry, if you say so, but you can't blame a gal for feeling a bit insecure at times in view of the situation. – H S

March 20, 2001
Hi Henry:

I was looking through some past email from you, and the earliest letter I can find from you is dated April 13th. I think that was in response to something I wrote on April 12th, so I guess it's safe to say that we will know each other a year by April 12th. Wow, did that time fly, or what? I remember that you said you wished you met me two years from then. Well, one of those years has almost passed. What's amazing is that we have grown closer and closer to each other, and the loving has grown deeper and deeper. The sex keeps getting better, and now we're making excellent souffles together, like two old chefs in a great French restaurant. What will we be doing next?

In all this time, I don't think you ever even once, got angry at me. Or if you did, you hid it well. I admit that at times, I have found your wife exasperating, but outside of that, which is expected to some degree, I have had a wonderful relationship with you. You have helped me to discover things about myself that I never appreciated, and I think I have helped you to reach out for the passion inside of your heart to fulfill your dreams and utilize your creative talents. I hope so. I know I got you thinking about your book again. No matter what happens between us, I want you to know that I will always treasure what we've shared together this past year. It is one of the best years of my life, and I hope it is just one of many many more.

I know that you do not openly talk about how you feel. You are great to read what's going on inside of me, but you guard your own feelings well. So well, that you frustrate me. Henry, I am at a crossroad in my life. Part of me wants to stay where I can be close to you, so we can see each other often, and another part of me, is not sure if that is what you want. I may move away, to Westchester, or even South Jersey. If I do that, we will see each other very little, if at all. I am not the type of woman who is happy seeing the man I love once or twice a month. On the other hand, I can stay in North Jersey, but part of me needs you to ask me to stay. If you don't, I will assume that it doesn't make a difference to you, no matter what I think I see in your eyes. One night I said to you, I need to hear the words. And you said, but can't you hear it in my fingers, in my lips, and in my eyes? Yes, I do, but that makes me assume too much. I am afraid to live on assumptions. – H S

March 20, 2001
Hi Ya Hot Stuff:

As far as not saying anything when you talk of moving, and you having me as a consideration as far as where you move to, well, no matter where you move, we will still be able to see each other, if we still want to. Also, I mean this. Only your future should be a factor in where you move, not your porximity to me. Your future is what is important. Although I would like to be part of that future, you shouldn't plan around anyone else. You have done that all of your life. Besides, it doesn't matter where you live or where I live, if we want to see each other, we will.

You mentioned that I don't seem to get angry. Well, that's true. When I was younger, I had a violent temper that was difficult to keep in check as I also had a short fuse. But, as I got older, I found that slowly I became emotionally flat. I don't have real high highs, or real low lows. I get upset or sad much easier than I get happy or angry. It is easier for me to cry than laugh or get mad. I will do almost anything to avoid a confrontation these days as I simply can't deal with them. So, there you have it. I'm slowly going nuts, I guess, or it is most probably seasonal depression disorder. Sunshine always makes me feel better. I felt great in Orlando, but I think that may have something to do with the company I was keeping. See you later...Henry

March 20, 2001
Henry:

By now you should realize that I feel that I am considering my future when I say that living relatively close to you is an important factor in my decision as to where I want to live. If I move to South Jersey, you'll never see me, except on an occasional weekend. Is that enough for you? I've kind of gotten used to our "soup" nights, and I need more than an occasional weekend. Maybe you don't. You say the strangest things. Sometimes you make me think that if you never saw me again, it wouldn't matter to you. It's like you're saying, "come if you want to, and if you don't want to, so what – I'll just invite Elizabeth or Wilma over instead. What difference does it make?" Is that how it is with you, Henry?

Henry, I want you in my future, and if that means planning some things around you, well, what's the big deal? If I get to see you more, isn't it worth it? I think it is. Maybe seeing you a couple of times a week, or whenever you give me time, is more important to me than exactly where I live. We love each other. At least I think you love me. (I'm starting to have some doubts.) Maybe your definition of "love" is different than mine. How can you be so evasive? And, when we're together, we both have real high highs. I know that you do too, and it's not just me. So, don't give me that bull that you're an emotional dud. You have more passion and emotion in your little finger than most men have in their whole being. I'm glad I've never seen you angry, but I think I'd like to see it just once, to see how you get when you do get angry, and what it takes to calm you down. Smile.

I want to explore this subject further this evening, so if you don't show up, I'll know why. I've got to make some decisions as to where I want to live and focus in on it. And, I'm sorry if it upsets you, Henry, but you are a factor in that decision making process, whether you like it or not. Of course, you can always tell me to get lost, and then, I'll factor you out, regretfully and sadly. But, until that happens, you're stuck with me kiddo. I hope that doesn't upset you too much, but that's just the way it is with me. I don't love people half way. It's either all or nothing, black or white, never gray. When I give, I give all of me, not just my big toe. But, you already know this. Why don't you stop the bullshit and be truthful with me? You know darned well that if I moved to South Jersey, it would break your heart. Why can't you admit it? - H S

March 20, 2001
Julie:

If you moved to South Jersey, it doesn't mean that we would not see each other just as much as we do now. Where there's a will, there's a way. I would have no problem driving over to see you for "soup" night there. After all, I wait three hours beyond my quitting time now to see you during the week, so I would just spend some of that time driving over to see you.

As far as not caring for you…well, you know very well that you mean a great deal to me. I give you all that I am able to give. I am sorry if you feel short changed. This is what I have been talking about, when I said that I am afraid that I will hurt you. I know you want more, but you have all that I can give now.

There isn't any more. - Henry

March 20, 2001
Henry:

I'll take whatever piece of yourself you are willing to give. I told you "on any terms", and I meant it. And, if I'm destined to be hurt, what difference does it make if I get hurt now or a year from now? At least I would have had another wonderful year with you. Right? I'm already too far gone to turn back, I'm afraid. The sad part is that you are so convinced that you are going to hurt me. Why is that? Is there something about me that you know for sure will never work out, because you absolutely cannot stand it? If so, what? So far, to date, I have experienced so much joy and happiness with you; I find it impossible to believe that you would ever hurt me. Oh sure, I've had some pain, but nothing I didn't expect or couldn't handle. . .certainly not unusual under the circumstances. You are worth it. The good part overwhelms the bad. As long as you are totally honest with me, I'll be OK. The only thing I really could not handle, and would break my heart is being lied to by you, even if you lied just to spare my feelings. I think I could take just about anything but that. And, I can't sleep with a man who is sleeping with other women. That kind of pain you would never give me. The rest of it – Wilma's mystery calls at 7:30 AM and Elizabeth's butterfly houses – they bother me, but not all that much. Even you not telling anyone about me, or never introducing me to your friends doesn't upset me enough to become a "dealbreaker". But, lying would. It's the one thing I could not handle well. I've been too honest with you to expect nothing but honesty back. And, I believe that you are honest with me. I have to believe it. Call me a fool, call me gullible, but I want so much to believe you when you say you care about me and love me.

And, I don't agree with you about South Jersey. I think it would really hurt our relationship. I know that I wouldn't want to have to drive two and a half hours to see you when I come to visit. I'd for sure get into an accident. Maybe I'm being foolish, but these things are on my mind. - HS

March 21, 2001
Good Morning, Henry:

It's going to be a wonderful day today! After seeing you, and talking with you, last night, I feel so much better. I looked into your eyes, and I saw so much love. It's scary. It's beautiful too. Henry, I consider you a member of my family with all the responsibilities that go along with that. I take these responsibilities very seriously. I felt this way for some time, now. I think you know this already, but I wanted to say it, just in case there are any doubts whatsoever in your mind about how I feel about you. Don't be afraid of my love. Instead, derive a certain comfort level that you can only feel when someone truly loves you deeply and unconditionally. That's the gift I give to you. Have a great day, my friend! – HS

March 21, 2001
Hi ya Hot Stuff:

I'm sorry that I didn't email you today, but it has been crazy here. I will call you tomorrow if you will have time to say "hello". Stay dry, drive safely, and take care of yourself. You are valuable to me... Henry

CHAPTER NINETEEN

I think I wanted so much to believe him that I never let the little things that didn't really make sense bother me. I could see no reason for Henry to ever lie to me, because we didn't have a relationship that had a commitment. Our relationship was free of commitments. The only thing I ever asked of him was to let me be the only one he slept with during the period that we slept together, and if he decided he wanted to sleep with someone else, that he tell me and be open about it. But, I should have known that perhaps Henry wasn't being totally truthful to me.

There were little incidences from time to time that should have been a warning to me. There was the time he said he had to work and somehow tried to convince me that it was very normal to bring Margarita glasses to the jobsite. I always thought that a Margarita was more of a woman's drink than a construction worker's drink. This was a jobsite where men were laying asphalt roads, and not partying. Then, there was another time when he baked a pecan pie for the workers on the jobsite. Pecan pie is not exactly quite asphalt jobsite type food. How gullible did he think I was? I had a feeling that it was more than likely, he was seeing someone else, and he didn't have the courage to tell me the truth. But, in those days I wanted so much to believe him that I let whatever he said pass. Now, as I think back about it, I'm sure he may have lied to me about those days. It seemed that he had to work, or had something to do that didn't include me, part of almost every weekend. Now that I can look back on it, I think he was selfish. He wanted to see other women, yet he didn't want me to see other men. That is the only reason I could think of for him to lie to me about it. I guess I'll never know if it was Elizabeth or Wilma or someone else he was seeing, and I know that if he told me the truth I would have accepted it, but would most probably start seeing other men, if for no other reason than as a defensive action. It would have changed the way I felt about him, but the relationship would have been honest, and we would have remained friends. Some part of him did love me. I felt that. But another part of him seemed to need constant female attention. He got phone calls all the time that seemed suspicious. There were times he wouldn't even answer his phone in front of me. I wondered what he was using as excuses with these other women about the times he spent with me. Did he tell them that he had to "work" when he was with me? Also, I felt that he very much wanted to mend the relationship he had with his wife, and there were times I felt that he was just keeping me in the wings in case Wilma never reconciled with him. Wilma broke up with him over the other women in his life. Maybe I could learn something from her.

He kept telling me that his relationship with Elizabeth was purely platonic. I asked to meet her. I mean if she was such a good friend of his, why wouldn't he want me to meet her and develop a friendship with her myself? And, then there were the visits he had with his son. I have three children around the same ages as his son. My kids have their own lives to live. They come and see me, but the frequency of visits he had with his son, and his son's girlfriend, seemed almost abnormal. Also, he claimed that his son didn't want to meet me, so the three of them would have dinner together. It was the perfect excuse to make me believe that he wasn't with another woman on a Saturday night. Between the relationship he had with Elizabeth, and his reluctance to have his son meet me, I felt that there was probably more to what was going on than what he was telling me. And, whenever we discussed this, he would get very flustered and upset. I was just trying to find out where I stood in his life, and he wanted to avoid the subject altogether. I think it made him feel uncomfortable because he knew he was lying to me, and also knew that I didn't really believe the things he told me. I only questioned this strange behavior to a point, and then I let it go. But, deep down inside, it really upset me. We had a relationship that was stagnating, and yet growing, at the same time.

I had the day of Good Friday off from work, and I wanted to get together with Henry on that date since I would be with my family on Easter Sunday and couldn't spend the whole weekend with him. He wanted to see me that night, but insisted that we leave very early the next day so he could get over to Wilma's house in the early morning to help her cook for Easter. We had an argument over it that almost ended our relationship. I couldn't understand why he wouldn't just tell Wilma that he'd be there in the afternoon instead of the morning. Maybe it was a silly thing to fight over, but I was more concerned with the fact that he was being ordered around again, and was willing to give up some time with me just to be at Wilma's beck and call.

March 28, 2001
Hi Henry:

I'm sorry that I put you on the spot last night. I didn't mean to. It just kind of happened. Your "hesitation" with seeing me on Good Friday is what sparked it all. I did a lot of thinking last night, and you are right. Neither one of us is ready for more than what we have already. In fact, we probably are taking too much from each other as it is. You are being the "responsible" one this time. I guess when you have something really good; you want to keep it always, because it's so precious to you. And what I have with you is really good. I get carried away. I'm truly sorry for upsetting you. I promise it will never happen again. I want you to know that I did make a decision to see other men. But, it's more of a defensive move than anything else. I really don't have any desire to see anyone else, but I will push myself because I think you want to see others, and you will be able to do it with a clear conscience if you know I am doing it also. But, I promise you, that if I decide to get sexually involved with anyone else, I will end the sexual involvement with you first, because I will not become involved that way with more than one man at a time. I wouldn't do that to you or to whomever I decide to become involved with. Right now, I'll just be casually dating on the weekends I don't see you, for as long as you tell me that you need the space. I'm not going to sit home and wonder if you're out with someone else. I'll just assume that you are. Henry, just remember, this is what you want. If you ever change your mind, and decide that you need me in your life, tell me, because I really don't want to see other men. But, as the word of my separation circulates, I have been approached, and I know you see Elizabeth and Sophia and still have something more than what's normal going on with Wilma. I'm only human. – H S

March 28, 2001
Good Morning, Julie:

I may be screwed up, but one thing I know, and that is if someone can stir my emotions to the point that tears come to my eyes, then they must matter to me, and evoke true feelings within me to be able to do that so easily. I am so sorry that I upset you - to bring you anything but joy is the very last thing that I want to do. I am not reluctant to see you on Good Friday, and I am sorry if that is the impression I gave you. I hesitated because I was not sure what date Good Friday fell on. After all, it's more than two weeks away. I hope you still would like to visit this Friday. – Henry

March 28, 2001
Henry:

Yes, I definitely want to visit with you this Friday night. And, I hope we get to go to the show on Saturday, and I most likely will occupy myself on Saturday night while you see your son, and spend most of Sunday with you. Maybe we could go to a movie on Sunday or play in the garden. Would you prefer I came up Saturday AM, and you saw your son on Friday night? I'm flexible. In fact, that might be easier for me since I wouldn't have to drive up in the dark.

I'm really looking forward to some serious cuddling with you this weekend, and I absolutely promise to keep all the conversation "light", and, of course, "hot". Smile – HS

March 28, 2001
Hi Hot Stuff:

I'm real glad you're coming up. Saturday night is the only option for me to see John because he has "stuff" to do on Friday night. So, I will have to leave you for a few hours on Saturday night. If you would rather come up on Saturday morning, I could pick you up at the house as early as you would like. I would prefer it if you stayed on Friday night also, but whatever you want is OK with me. I hope the weather is good this weekend. I really don't mind driving you. And Sunday, if you don't mind me crashing around in the garage for a couple of hours, the rest of the day and evening I will have free. I look forward to seeing you soon. - Henry

March 29, 2001
Hi Hot Stuff:

How late can you stay on Sunday? All day, I hope. I am sorry about Saturday night. I know it will put a crimp in the weekend, but I really do need to do this. See you Friday. And I don't have to read your erotic emails to get horny. All I have to do is know you are coming up... Henry

I sent Henry this poem the next day:

I SURRENDER

Your fingers, cruise over my back,
up and down my spine, tracing every vertebrae -
melting every bone I have, as they make love to my body.
Then, you slowly travel around to my breasts,
cupping them in your hands,
while your lips and tongue play with my nipples,
feeling like a butterfly flapping its wings,
making them swell and grow hard at the tips,
and I begin to strain wildly against the building sensations;
my body becomes unbearably awake to every touch and every taste,
and I ache for you deep inside.

Then, your magic fingers play with me,
and tease me, until you have me on the brink,
begging for mercy, and you smile as you watch me erupt violently,
as orgasm upon orgasm rips through my body,
the release so good it brings tears.
Then, with boyish mischief in your eyes, you ask, playfully,
"Give in?"

March 30, 2001
Hi Hot Stuff:

Phew!!! I am so looking forward to seeing you tonight. That poem primed my pump...and by the poem, I see that yours is already primed.

Can't wait to undress you.
Can't wait to run my hands slowly across your naked body and taste you.
Can't wait to feel the fullness of your ample breasts in my hands, beneath my lips.
Can't wait to surround your erect nipples with my tongue, gently sucking, licking.
Can't wait to bring you to passion with my exploring fingers and tongue.
Can't wait to hear your soft moans as you reach full arousal.
Can't wait to feel you shudder as orgasms wrack your body again and again.
Can't wait to feel that wetness.
Can't wait to feel your soft warm lips surround my arousal.
Can't wait to slip into you and release my own passion for you.
Can't wait for six-thirty.
Can't come soon enough...

Henry

March 30, 2001
Hi Henry:

I loved your poem "Can't Wait"...Grinning and grinning some more. It definitely did some additional priming, as if it were needed. Just a few more hours...maybe we should just skip dinner and do what we really want to do first. Grin. See you later.

H S

April 2, 2001
Good Morning Henry:

I went to bed at 8:30 last night, and when I got up and saw how dark it was out there, it took every ounce of effort to get out of bed this morning. Also, I missed your warm body next to me. I have a very busy day ahead of me today, but I wanted to say "hello" to you before I began it. I enjoyed yesterday very much with you, but I think you probably thought I was getting too domesticated. Maybe so, but it was still fun. Don't worry... I'll remember that you don't want to be suffocated. You have a very subtle way of saying "back off". It came in loud and clear. You never even once, mouthed the words "I love you" this weekend. And, you didn't have to make an excuse for not holding my hand in the car. Do you regret ever starting a relationship with me? I'm not doing what you think I'm doing. Please don't misinterpret what I do. Just because I cleaned your oven, ironed your shirts, and made you a great Italian dinner, doesn't mean I want to set up house with you. I haven't figured out what it means yet, but I need my 'space' too. The scary part is that I enjoyed every minute of it, and I can't figure out why. - Caio – H S

April 2, 2001
Hi Hot Stuff:

I had a great weekend with you. The reason I resist you "working" at my house has nothing to do with worrying that you are becoming too domesticated. It has to do with wanting you to come up, be pampered, relax, and not have you spend time doing work as you work hard enough already. The meal was outstanding, and you say that others don't let you cook... their loss. I think it would have been hard to do better with that meal than you did. I have eaten in many very fine Italian restaurants and your sauce and meatballs were as good as I have ever had. And, thank you for the ironing and the oven cleaning. It saved me so much work. I enjoyed your company immensely, and wish that it could have been longer. And, I do love you, Silly – Henry

April 2, 2001

Smiling now. Henry, you can "pamper" me anytime. But, I very much enjoyed working with you and doing a few little things that needed to be done. And the meal, well you know what they say, "The best way to a man's heart is through his stomach." Hopefully that meal made a few inroads. – H S

April 3, 2001
Hi there, Julie:

Good Friday sounds good to me. I would love to go with you to help pick out the frame and mat for your picture. What are you doing that evening, as I don't have to be at Wilma's until Saturday morning? No problem if you have "things to do" because of the holiday. – Henry

April 3, 2001
Hi Henry:

What are you doing at Wilma's on Good Saturday? Easter isn't until Sunday. I don't have anything to do because of the Holiday. I'm not cooking this year, my brother is. I am off work on Good Friday. I'd love to spend Good Friday evening with you, if possible, but I don't want to have to leave "early" Saturday morning – I would prefer to leave Saturday afternoon, actually. If it would be better for you, we can just skip the weekend. – H S

April 3, 2001
Hi Hot Stuff:

I'm working on Friday, but could get out early, around 2:30 or so. On Saturday I will be helping Wilma cook all day for Easter Sunday. There is a lot of cooking and baking to do as there will be 4 to 6 friends (depending on who shows up) plus my dear, sweet, mother-in-law, and John, and a couple of John's friends over. So, if you don't want to stay Friday evening/night, how about a movie, or we could go out and eat Friday evening, or do whatever.

April 4, 2001
Hi Henry:

I did a lot of thinking last night. I probably shouldn't think, because most of the time it gets me in all kinds of trouble. I mostly thought about you and how happy you seem to be, and how your life was beginning to find meaning when Wilma left you alone for a few weeks. But, now I see you living on "her" schedule again. She calls, no dire emergencies, but you run over there like a sick puppy. And, I guess if you have to ask her "permission" for you to come at Noon instead of nine AM on Saturday, you are doing it again. You must actually enjoy obeying her every command, otherwise I can't figure out why you do it. You say you are afraid of hurting her, but you moved out of the house. Didn't that hurt her?

Henry, you are entitled to a life. You certainly paid the price for it. It seems that you may have moved out of the house, but not out of the marriage. It's obviously the way you want it. I don't think we should see each other next weekend, and I'll somehow figure out what color mat and frame to put on the picture myself. It may not look as good without your input, but somehow the picture doesn't mean as much to me anymore. So, I don't really care. The reason is simple. I only wanted you till Noon on Saturday. She had you the rest of the weekend, and you couldn't say "yes" or "no" without having to confer with Wilma. I can't live my life around Wilma's whims. I can understand you having certain obligations where she is concerned. So do I, where Don is concerned, but you have to draw the line somewhere. I wasn't planning on spending all my future holidays with Don. If I stay with you, I'll be spending my holidays alone. I'm not sure I like that picture. And yet, I know that's the way it will be if I allow this relationship to continue the way it has been. Know that I love you, and I will always love you. Know also, that not Wilma, but her dominance over you, cost you "me" and "us". Try to be happy. You deserve happiness. You're one of the good guys. - Julie

April 4, 2001
Hi Julie:

I just read your email. I understand how you feel. I guess that deep down I always knew that this day would come, because you have a need to go on with your life and mine is admittedly still in limbo. You are a very special person for whom I will always have love in my heart and only have good memories of for the rest of my life. Please, please, can we remain friends? I would find it very hard never to hear your voice, or see your face again. I will miss your touch and your smile more than you will ever know. I don't know what else to say. I am very sad today and am leaving early. I need to be alone right now. My door is always open to you. – Henry

April 4, 2001
Oh Henry:

I'm having the very worst day of my life. My problem is that I don't want to stop seeing you. I can't stop seeing you. Not unless 'you' initiate the break up, and if you do it because you no longer love me or want me. You said you'd be home, so I called and left you a message as to why I changed my mind. Let me reiterate. The message basically said that loosing you is just not worth the four or five holidays a year I might have to spend alone. Hell, I'd be more miserable if you weren't in my life. So, we'll celebrate our Christmas on December 26th – that's all. What's one day in the scheme of my life? And, further, I will spend Good Friday night with you, even if it means leaving you at nine AM. What's three hours anyway? Why should I be miserable all night Friday, rather than be happy? That doesn't make any sense to me either. And lastly, you have a problem with Wilma's dominance. Well, you had that problem for the past thirty or so years. I guess it's going to take a long time to unwind that one. But, I've lived with this problem already for a year, and it's been the best year of my life, so why am I making it so important now? I think you'll eventually work out this problem, and why should I be miserable without you until you do? Maybe I can help you work on it somehow. What we have together is worth putting up with Wilma's whims. It really is. I guess this is what they mean by 'unconditional' love.

And I don't want to take time off from our relationship. What is that going to accomplish? I have an IQ of over 190, and I never have to "think" about anything very long to know what I have to do. Neither do you. Please call me ASAP and tell me I'm not crazy. – H S

April 4, 2001
Hi Julie:

I can't call you to tell you that you aren't crazy, because you ARE crazy to hang in. But, that is one of the things I love about you. I don't like "normal" people. I will call Wilma and tell her that I will not make it by nine AM, and I will see her at Noon on Saturday. I elected to stay at work because being home alone means just that – alone. So, all I would do is brood. I thought if I kept busy, I would feel better, or at least it will take my mind off of my life. I am sorry that I bring unhappiness to your life when I want so much to make you smile every day.

Julie, my life is so screwed up, and I have so many demands being made on me by my family that sometimes I don't know which way to turn. I am so strung out right now that I can't even think straight. I don't know when or how my life will eventually work out, because I feel that I am caught in a rushing river of other people that is just carrying me along, and I have little choice, but to go with it because I don't have what it takes to swim against the tide and forge my own way. I know what you are going to say about that, but I really am trying. It's just that for some reason, I don't have what it takes anymore. I am emotionally drained in that regard, and I just can't handle any more stress. I'm wearing down fast. I think that the best thing for me is to seek some help. So, I have contacted a shrink that I have used in the past when Wilma and I were still living together, and she helped me find the courage to move out. I guess I need some more help to get to stage two. I am reluctant to do what I know deep inside that I have to do, because I am so tired of bringing tears to anyone's eyes. That is a real burden on me, and has a deep and damaging effect on me because guilt is eating me up inside. I am so sorry that I have upset you. I hope you still want to get together tomorrow night...Henry

April 4, 2001
Hi Henry:

I'm certainly glad that you didn't go home. And, you're right, I'm probably not normal. You don't have to call Wilma and tell her anything. I will leave Saturday around nine, as you originally wanted me to. We have a very unusual relationship, you and I. It's not like any other relationship I know of or even heard of. It's unique, and we are unique. I don't know if that's good or bad, but that's just the way it is. The only thing I know is that when I am with you, I am happy, and when I am not with you, I miss you. I wish you would get it out of your head that you bring unhappiness into my life. You don't. It's just the reverse. Sure, I have my moments, but I think the biggest problem with me is that I feel insecure about your feelings for me. I see love in your eyes, and feel love when we are together, but you hardly ever tell me, and for someone who is used to the warm "I love you", that only Italians say often, and they say it over and over again, I feel insecure without it. So, in the back of my mind, I keep thinking that maybe you don't love me the way I assume you do. I think perhaps seeing a shrink might be a good idea for both of us. But, Henry, I think you already know what's wrong, and you are afraid of it. The more I think about it, the more I realize that you need time. And you have all the time in the world. I will not mention anything like this again. I will just deal with it as best I can. But, you are going to have a life. That is, if you want one badly enough, and I know you do. No one goes to all the trouble you did, moving out, buying a house, just to be free, unless that is what they really and truly want. – H S

April 4, 2001

Julie, don't feel insecure. Any man would be lucky to have a woman like you to love him. To me (my limey, stuffy upbringing), it is difficult to show my inner feelings, although I am getting better, but that's because I loose my grip more often now. You have the ability to look into my heart through my eyes. You know what's there. You experience the way I treat you. You know what that means. What do you feel when we are in each other's arms? You know where that comes from. You have seen the tears in my eyes when we have talked of the future and the possibility of parting. You know why I cry. No matter what else may happen between us, you know very well what these things mean. I do have deep feelings for you. I do love you. But, and please don't argue this point – I know deep down, that you deserve better than you are getting in me. And, you already know that I am far from Wilma-free. We share so much of our lives, even yet. It isn't that Wilma orders me so much, as I know that if I do the things that she asks of me, it will make her happy, and that's why I give in, and of course, I know that she is also manipulating me. I have made her very sad in her life, and I find it difficult to make her unhappy again. I don't plan on reconciling with Wilma, because I know that it may make her happy, but it wouldn't make me happy.

I like living up here, and now I have you in my life. But, I must admit to you that in the past when thinking about reconciliation, I had to not think of our relationship as part of that decision. I needed to know how I felt about Wilma, and not how I felt about us. I didn't need to think about that. Julie, you are so important to me. We have helped each other through a very difficult period in each of our lives, and that has helped pull us together. I want you in my life. But, you are nuts to take this on, because the process Wilma and I are going through must run its course. Even she says that she doesn't feel we can put it back together, but she also admits that she would like the marriage back. (There were good times too.) Julie, I am afraid that you will think that I am just keeping you around in case I can't work things out with Wilma. Is that the insecurity you feel? And, that is why I haven't tried to stop you when you have decided to go. I only want a happy life for you. I have learned that a relationship lasts as long as there is more joy than sadness. Julie, I care for you, and about you, more than I think you will ever know. I care enough to worry about the negative effect that I have on your life. If you doubt that there is a negative effect, then, why do I make you cry? That isn't a good thing. Sleep well and stop worrying. At least we can enjoy the moment. Sweet dreams. I love you. - Henry

April 5, 2001
Hi Henry:

I love you, too. Your last email inspired a great poem. Well, not great, but definitely beautiful. I think you'll like it. It's attached. You are getting better at showing your feelings. You actually told me twice in this last email that you loved me. I didn't understand some of the things you said, though. How could you think of reconciliation with Wilma and not think of what that would do to "us"? Henry, everything is connected. It was interesting how you put it...you said that Wilma said she would like the marriage back. The "marriage" obviously means more to her than you. She didn't say she wanted 'you' back – just the marriage. Maybe she likes the feeling of being married, and having a husband who can fix things around the house, and be at her beck and call, whenever she wants him. And, yes, sometimes I do feel that you are keeping me around, just in case you don't work things out with Wilma. And it scares me, because although I am happy when I am with you, I fear that one day you will break my heart and move out of my life. You could never reconcile with Wilma unless that happens. And sometimes, I feel guilty, because I am selfishly staying in your life, rather than moving out, and giving you the opportunity to mend your relationship with her. But, I really believe that you will never be happy in your life again, if you do that. When someone has as much joy as you have given me in their life, they worry about suddenly loosing it. Reading your back emails, I see that I have tried so many times to break away from you, but I keep coming back. I think I keep coming back, because I know, or my instincts tell me, in my heart, that you and I should be together – that we need to be together. Crazy, I guess. I'm looking forward to seeing your eyes again tonight. – H S

NEED

At night, lying close to you
like two spoons in a drawer,
I feel the warmth of your chest against my back;
your thighs touching my thighs;
you bury your face in my hair,
and your lips nuzzle the back of my ear -
I am safe, cuddled within the strength of your arm
and I love the feel of the touch of your hand,
as it cups my beast,
and your thumb gently circles over the nipple
sending erotic sensations throughout my body.

I can fall asleep like that,
and in my dreams, I look forward
to the joy I feel,

and the emotions I can't begin to analyze,
when I once again look into your heart,
and see the love you have for me
through your eyes while
the sweet sharp ache of need
begins to thunder in our hearts
in the glow of the sunrise. . .

April 10, 2001
Hi Henry:

How are you today? I was rereading an email you sent me last May where you predicted that we will definitely make love. How did you know? You made three predictions in that letter. You said that we would become life-long friends, we will become emotional supports for each other, and we would become lovers. And, this was before we ever laid eyes on each other! Henry, looking back now after all this time, you were so right about so many things…it's uncanny. Friday will be one year since the first email I have saved. It's kind of an anniversary for us. We will have to do something special. Why don't you pick out one of those "special" movies you were telling me about that you have, for us to watch? And, I'm not talking about the science fiction movies. You know which ones. Pick out the one you like the best. I'm sure you have a favorite. Grinning. Have a great day! – H S

April 10, 2001
Hi Julie:

Wow! A year already. That went so fast. I knew that we would become lovers. It was so obvious, because we had such a connection from the very start. You actually are quite easy to read, as you don't hide any of your emotions or feelings. That is what makes you so attractive, and yet so vulnerable. You remind me of a rose. . .beautiful and delicate. To be enjoyed, and yet, one must be careful not to bruise it, or prick one's self on the thorns - an interesting mix.

I think that sharing one of my sexy movies would be fun. I don't really have a 'favorite' movie, so I'll just grab the one on the top. That is, unless you would like to go through all of them. Or, we could write our own script. We could teach them a thing or two, Hot Stuff. And, you already know that I will do whatever it takes to bring you pleasure, no holds barred. When we are together, we have no inhibitions and anything goes. That is why our lovemaking is always so much fun, because we get to do anything that we want, and we are both trying to bring pleasure to the other, no matter what it takes. And, that's what's missing with most people. They get embarrassed and forget about the passion then the lovemaking becomes mechanical. That won't happen to us. Now, you have me looking forward to Friday night even more. I am writing this and my pants suddenly got real tight, just thinking about it, and thinking about what I intend to do with my tongue Friday night. See you then. Big Lecherous Grin...Henry

April 10, 2001
Hi Henry:

So, I remind you of a rose, huh? When did you ever prick yourself on my thorns? I don't even have thorns. I think I'm more like the jasmine flower – delicate and free, my scent filling the air with beauty. I have no thorns, or anything else to hurt you.

You pick the movie out. I don't have to go through them. Find the oldest one you have. That would be fun to watch. And, you are right – there are no inhibitions between us. It has a lot to do with our attitudes towards sex. If I detected something in you concerning a certain act that you did not want to do, I would not feel comfortable doing it. Tell me something Henry – has your lovemaking always been this uninhibited? With me, it depends on the man I'm with. The few men I have had in my life haven't been all that uninhibited. I have to say that I feel the most free to do whatever I want with you. It has to do with your views of sex, and your attitude about it. I've never enjoyed sex as much as I do with you, and I know that has a lot to do with you, and the way you think about it. I feel very comfortable with our lovemaking. It seems the more I get, the more I want. I'm just greedy, I guess. – H S

April 10, 2001
Hi Hot Stuff:

I will grab a movie or two for you to pick from. And, sex hasn't always been this much fun. You make it fun. – Henry

CHAPTER TWENTY

I was beginning to suspect that Wilma was making a very strong effort to reconcile with Henry. That became very obvious over the next few weeks. She had an operation on her foot. It was minor elective surgery, and she played it to the hilt. Henry broke a date with me to be at the hospital for her when she came out of surgery, and spent most of that weekend with her. Then, the following week, she needed him to chauffeur her to and from work each day. Henry is the type of guy that would always be there when someone in his life needs him. He'd go out of his way for someone he cares about, and she took full advantage of that. I also suspected that she knew that Henry and I had been seeing quite a bit of each other the past few weeks, and I felt that she wanted to somehow show me that she came first in his life. I tried not to let any of it get to me. I knew that if Henry loved me, he'd see me as much as he could, and if he wanted her back, then I'd loose him, but I didn't want him, unless he wanted to truly be with me. It really didn't matter to me as to whether or not I came first or second in his life. I just wanted to be part of it. My biggest fear was that he would fall back into her trap, out of a strong sense of "duty", and not because he was happy there. She already made him feel terribly guilty about the breakup.

I also had a feeling that Henry was seeing someone else as well – possibly Elizabeth. Every time I visited his house, I'd see little evidence of another woman having been there. It was hard enough when he left me to be with his x-wife, but even harder to think that he left me to be with another woman besides what he was doing with Wilma. It was like he craved, or actually needed, to have more than one woman in his life. Or perhaps, he was so afraid of falling in love, that he needed a 'backup' to convince himself that no one woman could mean that much to him. Whatever the reason, she was taking what little free time he had, away from his relationship with me, and if he spent that precious time with her, then how was I to view that relationship in respect to what I had with Henry?

April 26, 2001
Good Morning Henry:

Too bad about Friday night, but I do understand. Why didn't Wilma tell you before now the date of her operation? Somehow, I see you slowly being drawn back, or maybe, better put, being manipulated back. If it's what you want, then it's OK. If not, I hope you recognize it for what it is, and have the sense to draw some boundaries before it's too late. It took you so long to get this far. Take care, my friend, and try to have a good day. – H S

April 26, 2001
Good Morning Julie:

At least we had two weekends in a row, so we can't complain too much. We both have things to do and live very busy lives. Besides, the amount of time we spend together is not as important as the fact that when we are together, it is always good. At least we do have the opportunity to spend some real time together every week or so.

Your comments about being drawn back in are very to the point. I recognize that Wilma has changed her mind and is making overtures to me to reconcile, but I like my life the way it is. I like being up in the woods, and I like the peace of mind that my solitude affords me. Besides, you have become an important part of my life that brings me happiness, and I don't want to loose that either. I will find a way to call you tomorrow during the day. - Henry

April 26, 2001

You are right, Henry. We really shouldn't complain. We did get to see each other two weekends in a row. Gee, it was really nice, too. I enjoy being with you, and I have jumped through hoops at home to make the time. But, things are catching up with me, and I've been burning the candle at both ends lately. I need to regroup, which is what I'm going to do this weekend. My biggest problem is the more I'm with you, the more I want to be with you. I just like your company so much. You also have become an important part of my life, and I find I'm really happy when I'm with you, even when we're just hanging out and not doing anything particular. You give me a shoulder when I need it, and lots of smiles and laughter, but more importantly, the feeling of being loved and cared for, that everybody needs so desperately. I hope I do the same for you.

As far as Wilma is concerned, I feel good that you wanted to see me Friday, even though you are obligated elsewhere. Just knowing that you wanted to have dinner with me is very reassuring. I also understand that you must be there, and I think one of the reasons why I love you so, is this sense of "duty" you have towards everyone in your life. You are a person one can depend on in time of need. I am attracted to that aspect of your personality very much, and wouldn't have you any other way. The reason why I said to set some boundaries is because you don't want Wilma to think there will be a reconciliation if there won't be. That's unfair to both of you. You've got to allow her to find a new life also. And you need the breathing room for your own sanity. - H S

April 27, 2001
Hi Hot Stuff:

I was so glad to get your call last night. Well, Wilma is home safe and sound. All went well. She is sleeping now and I am cooking dinner. My son John is here also and it has been nice to spend time playing catch up with him. I wish I could see him more. I hope your weekend goes well. Enjoy your time with your daughter. Take care, Sweetie. – Henry

April 27, 2001
Hi Henry:

I'm glad that Wilma is Ok and recovering. I know that she will be in a lot of pain for the next few days. It's good that she has you there to help her. I'm still hoping to go out with Maria tomorrow night, but I think I caught some kind of a bug, because I'm feeling pretty much under the weather this evening. Maybe all I need is a good night's sleep. Would you like me to call you over the weekend? – H S

April 28, 2001
Hi ya Hot Stuff:

I am so sorry to hear that you are not feeling well. I wish I was there to rub your feet for you. Of course you can call me. I will be in and out of the house until about five, and then I am going over to cook Wilma dinner. I hope you feel better. It's too bad you feel crummy on such a beautiful day. Take care and have a great weekend. - Henry

April 29, 2001

How are you feeling this morning? Better, I hope. I got a call from Wilma this morning already, and the doctor wants to see her at the hospital at noon. So, that pretty much shoots my day in the ass. I will give you a call on your cell this evening.

Love you – Henry

April 29, 2001
Hi Hot Stuff:

It's six-thirty and I am finally home and very tired. I had to take Wilma back to the hospital today as her foot swelled up very badly and turned purple. The doctor said she had a blocked blood vessel and did some minor repair work to it. But, the process of getting her down there and waiting for the surgery to be over, and then taking her back home, ate up the entire day. I am so tired. Just sitting around the hospital makes you tired. How was your day today? I missed you a lot this weekend. If you get a chance later, maybe you could call so I can get my "Julie Fix" by at least hearing your voice. How are you feeling? Better, I hope.

Have a great evening and I hope to hear from you, if you get the time. If not, I will speak with you tomorrow.

Good Night Sweetie – Henry

The next week or so we spent time on the phone every night, and didn't email. The calls were long and full of conversation.

May 10, 2001
Hi Henry:

I must admit that I am feeling a bit jealous of Wilma. It's not your fault. I think what upsets me most is that you don't seem to be making any kind of effort to "personally" forge a relationship with your sons, separate from the relationship you had with Wilma. And, I guess that indicates to me that you don't really want to be viewed as a "father" separate from part of their "parents". That probably means that you will ultimately reconcile with Wilma. I think that's a logical conclusion. Am I wrong? I have worked hard to forge a relationship with my kids separate from the one that they associate with me and Don. That doesn't take anything away from them. It just better helps them to accept what is happening in my life, while assuring them that I will always love them, no matter what.

I keep wondering if there will ever be anything more between you and me, or is what we have, all we will ever have? I noticed that you never, not even once, said you loved me this weekend. Was that on purpose? Henry, what's really going on? Please answer that. If you don't want me to back off, as you said last night, do you want me to stay in "limbo" with you forever? You have been separated, actually living separately from your wife, for over six months, and yet, you sleep over there, and she sleeps over your place pretty regularly. What am I to think? I'm not upset so much as I feel I need, and deserve, some clarification. – Julie

May 10, 2001
Hi Julie:

I'm sorry that our relationship still is unsettling to you. I know full well that some clarification of our relationship is what you deserve. I don't plan on reconciling with Wilma, and I am just trying to maintain a friendly relationship with her. I do have a personal relationship with my sons, but Wilma and I remain collectively their parents, and they deserve to have us both. They shouldn't miss out because we are separated. In all honesty, I don't have Wilma and my relationship 'sorted out' in my mind yet, myself, so I don't quite know what to tell you. For some reason, I still am hesitant to tell her what our relationship (yours and mine) is. I guess it's because I still want to avoid hurting her feelings. I know that I must cut the cord sooner or later, but I find that very hard to do. I guess old habits die hard. You are a very important part of my life, Julie, and I hope that I can do our relationship justice, eventually. I know that what I have said in this letter is very noncommittal, but at least it is honest. I am sorry, Julie. You deserve better than I give you. And, just because I didn't tell you of my love for you, doesn't imply that it isn't there. If in the future, you feel that you have waited long enough for me to get my act together, believe me, I would understand. But, for now, thank you for being there. Thank you for sharing your valuable friendship with me, and thank you for sharing love with me. I am in debt to you more than you could ever know.

- Henry

May 10, 2001
Henry:

Our relationship is not as "unsettling" as much as "confusing" to me. Believe me; I do understand where you are coming from. I know that you somehow don't feel totally 'right' about us. That is probably because I cannot make any solid commitments myself, yet. It's just that you seem to be doing things that most separated couples don't do. I could never imagine myself and Don spending more than a dinner together, or a day together, if we were going to some kind of family function. I would never spend the night at his place, or want him to spend the night at my place, because it would not be fair to him to give him false hope like that. My kids wouldn't expect it either. I wouldn't want to give them false hope either. By telling Don a little bit about you and how I feel about you, I have prepared him for any surprise – like coming over when you are here, or running into me at a store when I am with you, or someone else telling him about seeing me with you, so something like that would not hurt him shockingly, if he were unprepared. You, on the other hand, are leaving Wilma "open" for just that kind of hurt. You are not doing her any favors by not telling her about us. Instead you are leaving her open for future hurt. And, Henry, there is nothing "noncommittal" about what we are doing with each other. I, for one, could not just walk away from this relationship. I'm in for the long haul. I feel committed to you for a lot for reasons. Where are you coming from with that remark? Henry, I know that you have a great deal of love for me, and I wasn't implying that you didn't. What I miss is the kind of affection you showed me in all those emails you used to send me. They were a kind of "therapy" for me in a lot of ways. It's as if you make it a point not to say the words that I really need to hear. I don't understand why. It's nice to hear those words. Hardly anyone ever tells me that they love me any more. I'm starting to think that I'm imagining that I mean anything to anyone, and that's not very healthy for my emotional well-being. I need to hear it, as everyone does. You are not in debt to me. Don't ever think such a thing. Just try to understand how I feel when you go an entire weekend without saying one single affectionate thing to me, in spite of the fact that we made mad passionate love all weekend.

I am looking forward to spending Memorial Day weekend with you, if we can. At least it's a time to look forward to, and will get me through all the times you are spending with Wilma. I do have a feeling though, that eventually she will drive me away. As much as I love you, I may have to back off to protect myself, but that hasn't happened as yet. I guess I'm a "diehard". – H S

May 16, 2001
Good Morning, Julie:

If I have to work over the Memorial Day weekend, I will be finished no later than Noon on Sunday, which should put me at your house no later than mid-afternoon. We will have all afternoon on Sunday and all of Monday together. As far as sleeping, I will catch a nap in my car Saturday night at the job site. I know that you don't need me to explain myself as to what I am doing when I am not with you, but there is no secret as to what I am doing, so I don't mind telling you. Soup tonight? - Henry

May 16th, 2001
Henry:

Isn't it unusual that they would be putting in a road during the busiest "traffic" weekend of the year? Is this standard procedure? Are you sure you don't have a date with someone else, and prefer to tell me that you are working, so as not to hurt me? Smile. - Julie

May 16th, 2001
Hi Julie:

You're right. Highways aren't usually worked on during a busy holiday weekend, but we are not doing a road. We are doing a new re-fueling area at Lee Valley Airport. It isn't open yet, so the holiday traffic doesn't impact us. Especially as we are supplying it from a plant almost next door to the airport, so our trucks don't have to contend with the holiday weekend traffic.

I have been given a choice as to when to spend a couple of days at the corporate headquarters. I intend to go while you are in Virginia Beach, if you decide to go visit your son. See you later, toots – Henry

May 16, 2001
Hi Henry:

Please plan your corporate trip for whenever is most convenient for you. It's still more "no" than "yes" on the trip to my son's house because of my own load. I like the fact that you are considering our time together when you plan those trips. It makes me feel important in your life. But, I can live around your schedule. Now, with Don moving out of the house, if I don't see you on a weekend, we can make up the time on one or two nights during the week. Henry, if we plan our time around each other's schedules, we will have plenty of time together, so keep me posted, and I will keep you posted. – Julie

CHAPTER TWENTY-ONE

Don finally moved out. I had my first weekend alone. I loved the freedom. Keeping busy is part of handling being alone, and as much as I loved the freedom, I missed having someone there to talk to and share things with. But, I had so much to do that I really didn't have much time to dwell on being alone. I cleaned the whole house that weekend, and began the task of organizing all the boxes and things still left in the basement. It took all my time and helped me not to think about Henry spending yet another weekend with his wife. That, and Don's move, had really stressed me out. The one thing that kept me from falling apart that weekend was knowing that Henry was coming over after his wife and son left to be with me. He'd been spending quite a bit of time with Wilma, and I suspected that they were seriously considering reconciling. He didn't talk about it, but I felt it. There definitely was something going on between them, and my mind, being the way it is, always tries to analyze what it doesn't understand.

Could all the terrible things he told me about her have been lies? Did he say those things just to make me 'think' she was this horrible ogre who hounds him, sneaks around, follows him, doesn't trust him, puts him down, time and time again, who hates making love with him, and stifles him to the point that he felt he had to leave his own house just to survive? Was it all some sort of sick sordid plan to boost his ego? He knew me well enough that if I thought I was in any way breaking up a happy home, I would never have had the kind of intimate relationship I had with him. But, even people who I knew, that knew her, told me that she was fat, loud, and boisterous. Who would want a fishwife like that? And, who would stay married to one? He told me how when they were married, he'd wait on her every night and how she'd compile these lists of chores that he had to do for her. What kind of a marriage was that? And, why would anyone want to go back to that, after finally escaping? Was it all a hoax…some joke he was playing, a scientific experiment, to prove that he still had what it took to turn a woman on? Maybe he had to prove to Wilma that he could get another woman if he wanted to, and I was the guinea pig. Someday they'll sit and read my poems together, and laugh at the fool I've made of myself over him. I don't believe that he would do that, I can't believe it, but I wish I knew how he really felt about me, or where I stood in the scheme of things in his life, or if I even had a standing.

That Sunday night, he came over as planned. It was late – well after nine o'clock. There really wasn't time to do much else except go to bed. Frankly, all I wanted to do was go to bed, not for the sex, but for the cuddling. I needed to be held closely by him that night so badly. I felt so insecure. Somehow I thought his arms around me would be reassurance that he loved me and would not end the relationship. I had a small night light on in my bedroom. He turned it off. I wanted to light a candle, but he insisted that he wanted the room to remain dark. He said it would be fun to make love in the dark. I should have realized then, that something was wrong. He always liked looking into my eyes when we made love, so he could see the love I held for him in my eyes, and could see the pleasure he gave me shine through them.

We never made love in the dark before. I didn't like it. I couldn't see his eyes. Even though he rarely told me he loved me, his eyes always said it. Suddenly, he said the words, and told me he loved me. It came out of the blue, as if he were reading my mind. It was reassuring and totally unexpected. I was surprised he said it. That night he came twice. I knew it was good for him, and he generously gave me multiple orgasms, as he usually did. It was so easy for him to turn me on. It wasn't because he was a good lover, although he was. It was because I was so much in love with him. I always felt warm and secure in his arms, and he knew my body so well. Since the next day was a work day, in the morning, I woke up before him. I had no time to cuddle. Neither of us slept much the night before, and I had to get ready for work. I didn't want to leave him alone, but I had no choice.

I left for work at my usual time – 5:00 AM. He was still sleeping, and I tried to be as quiet as I could be. I called him later on that morning to make sure that he had everything he needed, and there was no embarrassing encounter with my daughter, Alice, who lived downstairs in the basement. Alice knew that I had a guest over, but I knew he felt funny about it, especially since I hadn't had a chance yet to introduce them formally. But, she left before he was up, and he never did run into her. We talked about how great the evening turned out, and about how much we enjoyed sleeping in each other's arms.

That evening when I went to bed, somehow the bed seemed so much lonelier than ever before. So, I called him again. I probably shouldn't have, but when I love someone, I like to tell them, so they know that they are loved and cared for. I needed to hear it too. I invited him over for our usual "soup" night on Thursday. I was pretty sure I would have Friday off, and could sleep an extra few hours. I guess I assumed that he would want to stay the night. When he said he wouldn't be staying over, I was stunned. I felt rejected and unwanted. He said he had 'things" to do. Well, after soup, there really isn't much time left for "things" to do. I knew that wasn't the real reason. Now, my circumstances had changed. Don was no longer living there and I didn't have to make excuses anymore. I suspected that he didn't want to make it a habit of sleeping over. He wouldn't elaborate. I didn't understand why, and I was upset. I was surprised at how harsh his words were. He had never been anything but gentle with me until this conversation. I wasn't prepared for the words that stung so deeply. I told him that I wanted and hoped that our relationship would grow closer, and his response was, that if he wanted a closer relationship with a woman, he would have stayed married to Wilma. I don't understand why he felt the need to hurt me like that. That statement said it all. I knew then that I may be just a toy, a sex buddy...someone who knew how to turn him on really well. He was different. His words were hurtful. Something happened, either with Wilma, or another woman. Or, maybe it was the fact that Don moved out and I was alone and finally free. But, he changed towards me during that phone conversation. It was the first time I ever experienced his coldness, and the first time I sympathized with Wilma.

All of the warmth I usually felt from him was gone. He said he was afraid that we would get "closer" if he came over too often. He didn't want to get any closer. He wanted our relationship to stagnate – to see each other a couple of times a month, at most. That was more than enough "Julie" for him. His words were hurtful. It was a side of him I never saw before, and it surprised me that he would be so cruel to someone who only showed him love, and never hurt him. I knew my original instincts about him were not wrong. Something happened that he was not telling me.

I think about it now, and it really is insane. To think that someone would go to the lengths and trouble he went through, just to have a "sex" buddy. Sex is so easy to get, and if that was all he wanted, why didn't he just say so? I know also, that I boosted his ego to the sky. People will go to great lengths just to feel good about themselves. Maybe that was worth all his efforts. Or maybe it was because he knew that I wouldn't go to bed with someone who I didn't think cared for me. Just last week he was talking about arranging his schedule so that it meshed with mine, and today he stated that he doesn't want to get any closer to me. I don't understand why he was so afraid of our connection. I was nothing like Wilma, or the Wilma he had described in his emails. I guess the worst moment of the conversation was when I asked him if he was breaking it off, and all I heard after that question, was silence. Why couldn't he just say it, instead of answering my question that way?

Surprisingly, I didn't cry. Maybe I was too angry to cry. Well, I suppose I cried a little bit when we hung up. I was more angry at myself than anything else, because I felt that I made a fool of myself. I let Henry into my heart, and he broke it, just like that, with no second thoughts. Oh, I suppose he warned me enough times that he would hurt me. Maybe I should have been already preconditioned for this. His spending all that time with Wilma the previous few weeks, and his wanting the lights off when we made love on Sunday, were hints that his feelings for me had somehow cooled off. But why? I know it wasn't anything that happened Sunday night. It must have had to do with what went on during the weekend with his wife. Why couldn't he just come out and tell me outright? Why did he have to be so mysterious?

I don't know what this experience did for me, or to me, or how it changed me. I know that he came into my life when I needed a friend, and he saw me through the rough times, and then disappeared quickly. It's as if he were an angel, like the TV show, touching my life, then when his job was done, he left. Maybe I made him up in my imagination, and all the things we felt together and the wondrous experiences we had, were conjured up in my head. I mean, if it were really real, someone who felt as he seemed to feel, could never let this thing go, or risk loosing the one chance he had at being happy for the first time in his whole life. Would he? Or, maybe there is no such thing as real happiness – only happy moments in one's life. I'd like to think that we could have made each other so very happy. There was so much we had in common, so much we wanted to do. I knew that I was good for him and he was good for me. Most of the time he made me feel good, which was why I loved having him around. I thought I did the same things for him. I know I did, but I could never compete with someone who had a thirty year history with him and was the mother of his children. I should have realized this from the first day. It's just that he seemed so unhappy with her – I thought he was as unhappy in his marriage, as I was in mine, and just maybe there could be a chance for us.

To ease my feelings, I wrote another poem for him.

TRAVELING THROUGH YOU

Your magic blurs my vision,
and I lost my way traveling through you.
I ran headlong into danger,
fell into your well-built trap,
loved you with pure innocence and gentleness,
the only way I know how to love,
unwilling to see it for what you say it is.
but, you brought me back into reality,
and it hurt when you asked me, "What did I expect?"
as if you didn't know…
I expect more than just the fire of the moment,
that burns too fast –
not more than you can give, but
more than you are willing to give -
fore as you say,
if you wanted more, you would have
stayed with your wife.
Would you have, really?

As you maintain your distance,
I am just an insignificant subject,
in your lofty reign,
standing behind the wife,
who only knows how to use you,
rather than love you.
Why are you so afraid of
this intangible thing between us –
can you not deny it's substance?
Why does it scare you so?

Is not the rise with me, worth the fall?
and, are you so sure there could even be a fall?
You pull me in, then push me away, then pull me back in again –
each time you say goodbye, you fall into blackness
and, I die a little bit.

So many unanswered questions
wander through my mind -

May 23, 2001
Dear Julie:

I tried long ago to warn you off, as I have no desire to hurt you in any way. You, and the friendship we have, mean a great deal to me. But, Julie, we are so alike in so many ways, and yet so different in others. You see, I am broken and just cannot handle a 'normal' relationship. I know that I am selfish, but would you rather that I pretended, and led you on? I honestly don't know if I will ever be capable of giving you what you need. It is my problem, not yours, as you are straight and forthright in what you want out of life, and the problem is, I don't know what I want yet. I am so very lucky to have a woman like you who loves me. I love you and I enjoy being with you, and I truly don't want to loose you, but I can't handle a full time relationship, a "traditional" relationship, at least not in the way that I know you would define it. I can't see me changing any time in the foreseeable future, and others may see our relationship as a dead end. But, what did you expect it to lead to?

I simply cannot do more, or give more than I have to give, because in so many ways, I am lacking emotionally. You are right about one thing, Julie – I am afraid of becoming closer. I am not afraid of you hurting me, but I am afraid of being hurt again, or hurting others again. To hear you cry on the phone last night was like plunging a knife into me. And, I do hold back some of myself, even if I don't always recognize that I am doing it. I guess I am destined to be alone. Frankly, I still need time to feel sorry for myself. I have some healing to do, and some sorting out of my emotions. These are not your problems, but mine. And, I am going to a therapist and have been going for a couple of months. I am so sorry that I made you feel badly. I only have good thoughts and good intentions towards you. But, Julie, deep down inside, I feel that I am not the right guy for you, and that sooner or later, you will see that too. You are far too loving and have far too much love to give to a guy that has a problem getting through each and every day. I am so sorry that you feel that all I did was "bull shit" you. When I wrote those words to you, I meant all of them. But, now you know why Wilma kicked me out. I am not going to turn you away and would miss you terribly if you were not to see me again, but I would never hold that decision against you, as you do need to protect yourself, and I am very self destructive and tend to push people away who get too close to the "real" me. I just don't want you to get caught up in my self-destruction. Julie, feelings cannot be mandated. We either feel a certain way, or not, and we all have little control over that. I enjoy your company, and for me enjoying the time we spend together is enough. So, you see, we do want different things from life. Julie, I am a borderline hermit who has deep rooted psychological problems that you don't recognize. Julie, I am not going to suggest you do anything but follow your instincts and be careful of your heart, as I have no desire to be responsible for breaking it. - Henry

I did not respond to this letter or call him.

CHAPTER TWENTY-TWO

I feel that every time it seemed like we were moving closer, and starting to build something that would last, we took a step back. And, I think that was due to the fact that Henry was afraid to get close. I did understand why, but it was very difficult. I kept telling myself that I must start to date other men, if for no other reason, a defensive measure…to protect my heart. But, the few dates I've had in the months following his last email, didn't stand a chance, because I kept comparing them to Henry, and Henry always won. I wish it were possible to turn love on and off like a faucet, at will. Maybe some people can do that, but I'm too "human" because I cannot do that.

Every time we had an argument, I felt as if I'd lost him. The argument always centered on the same thing. Our relationship was so intense and so close, that he was afraid that I might swallow him up. He couldn't differentiate me from Wilma. He assumed that I had the same reactions as she did, even though he knew, and I proved to him so many times, that I am nothing like her. I don't react as she does. I don't understand why he was holding back the natural course of our relationship. I couldn't understand what he was so afraid of, and he wouldn't tell me. All I wanted to do was help him overcome his demons, so he could love again, and enjoy his life to its fullest. I think he purposely went out with others, not because he really wanted to, but because he needed to feel free of me. We spent time away from each other when we really wanted to be together. This was all his doing. I think that he felt somehow that I threatened his freedom. Many times I stopped myself from calling him, because I felt that if I called him too much, he might get upset with me. He was in love with me and he was fighting that love. He was fighting his own happiness. What went on in his complex mind? I couldn't seem to connect to that part of him. He said I complicated his life. Ya, I guess I did - but not any more than he complicated my life.

I'm human, and I have feelings, very vulnerable feelings. When I love someone, I don't love halfway. I gave myself to him, trusted him with my heart, and I know that I did not do the wrong thing for myself. I doubt if I will ever be able to love like this again. The pain he inflicted, made me put up a shield, and I am never letting anyone get that close to me again. Maybe this is what hell feels like – to live in a prison of loneliness, to stop feeling, to never share the warmth of intimacy, to just exist until I die – to stop loving, rather than to love and laugh with someone who loves me in return. He has stolen my soul and has condemned me to forever suffer as he does, in a lonely sad existence, never to allow myself to feel the warmth of love again, and never to truly share my life with anyone. Should I thank him for teaching me this lesson and changing my life forever? Don cut off my legs, and Henry cut out my heart. There's nothing left. I don't know if I'm strong enough to overcome it. Part of me is, and will go on, but I will never be the same again. I have forever changed.

I stopped communicating with him – no emails, no phone calls, and no meetings. The perpetual smile I had since I met him, left my face. That sad hollow look has returned to my eyes. There was no more "spring" to my step when I walked down a street. There is nothing to look forward to. I want to somehow remain his friend, but how do you stay a friend with someone who you can't trust with your heart? Shouldn't you be able to trust all your 'friends' with your heart? Isn't that what friendship is all about, and he was my best friend for so long.

So much change has taken place in my life this year. Perhaps I needed this relationship to help me through it all. I know it has made me harder somehow – perhaps less vulnerable, less gentle. I think I liked the way I was before I knew Henry better than the way I am now. I didn't think I wanted to get close to anyone again. I felt totally disillusioned about love, relationships, and about myself. That's probably the worst thing he did to me. He made me doubt myself. He made me feel that the depth of love I had for him and I am capable of feeling, would only hurt me. I didn't think I will ever be able to trust a man with my heart again. This brought me great sorrow, because I have so much love to give. I felt sorrow for him too, because the passion he is capable of will never truly satisfy him unless he allows himself to really love again. His wife will drive every woman he loves away, and he will allow her to do it, because he has allowed her to control his happiness for so long that he doesn't know how to live again without her dominance.

I could spend every minute of every day lost in the memories of how we were together. I missed him. I missed his voice, with its Americanized British accent. I keep trying to hear it in my head, but all I hear are snatches of lost conversations. I missed the look in his eyes when we went into deep discussions. I missed the way he gave me his undivided attention as we talked, and made me feel so brilliant. I missed his hands on my body, and the love that seemed to flow right out of those hands into my heart.

I needed time to heal. I needed solitude and quiet. I needed to be alone with myself and somehow put him into a closet in my heart, shut the door, and not open it again until I can do so without feeling pain. I needed to move on.

CHAPTER TWENTY-THREE

SEPTEMBER 11, 2001

Over three months had passed since that last email from Henry. During that time my house finally sold. I wasn't sure where I wanted to live so I rented a small house nearby. I was busy with the move and had little time to think about Henry, but he was always there somehow in the background of my mind.

I had come into the office earlier than usual that day. It looked like it was going to turn out to be a beautiful day. It was warm and the sun was shining. I turned on my computer to check my email...nothing from Henry. Suddenly I heard a loud crash and everyone in the office went to the window to see what happened. I joined the others. We could see smoke and debris falling from the North Tower, but whatever happened was too far above for us to see. More debris fell past our window and everyone was curious as to what had happened. We went into the conference room which had the largest windows. We climbed over the windowsill to look out. I strained my neck to look up and pushed my cheek flat against the glass trying to see what was happening above my line of sight. I could just make out the caldron of black smoke boiling from where the windows of the North Tower should have been. Debris cascaded down from the floors above me toward the street far below. I heard a crash of glass and watched a computer pass my window on its way to the ground. The air outside the window was filled with, and what seemed like, thousands of papers that fluttered and swirled as they too drifted towards the ground.

Just then, I heard the voice of Steve Black, the company's chief financial officer. He shouted out. "The North Tower was hit by an airplane!" He waved his cellphone in the air as he moved from group to group. Everyone was shaken, but we were in the South Tower. I felt strangely calm, as though I was watching a movie. Then minutes later, we felt the impact of the other plane. A powerful shock wave radiated up and down the building. I felt the building sway. Steve was calling the building for guidance as to what we should do and to find out what was happening.

Steve said that he was told that the fire was above the 80th floor and that we were OK. We should stay where we were and wait for the firemen to arrive. I didn't want to stay put and wait for the firemen. I was scared. There was smoke outside and debris was still falling from the building. Steve convinced many of my coworkers that it was safer to stay inside because we could get hit by debris if we went outside. The smell of the smoke seemed stronger. People were huddled together waiting for the firemen. I didn't know then that this was the last time I would ever see these people again.

It didn't make sense. The firemen would have to climb fifty-four floors to get to us. Some of us decided to leave. We moved to the elevator area. People began pressing the down button.

There was a sign on the wall that said, "Don't use the elevators in a fire." I remembered some of the instructions from a fire drill we had about six months ago. I went back to my desk, grabbed my purse, and then I took the bottle of drinking water I had on my desk and totally wet my scarf. I approached the stairwell and looked in. There was smoke, but not too much at that time. I held the wet scarf over my mouth and nose as I entered the stairwell. My secretary, Diane, followed me. She also had wet a cloth and held it over her mouth and nose. Some others followed.

I could see that the smoke coming from the upper floors was getting thicker and a piece of sheetrock came barreling down the middle of the stairwell from above to the floors below. The lighting was dim as we descended the stairs, down fifty-four floors, to the street. I had my wet scarf covering my face so the smoke wouldn't choke me. We could hear water running but didn't know where it was going. Pieces of sheetrock were everywhere. Down I went, step by step, in high heal shoes, holding onto the bannister as I ducked debris falling from above. When we reached the twenty-second floor we came upon a woman sitting on the side of the steps, with people walking around her on their way down. She was crying hysterically. She was also very pregnant. I stopped and told her to come with us. She was frozen. I grabbed her arm, pulled her to an upright position, and shouted at her. Then I started down the steps pulling her with me. She followed. More people were coming down the steps. More debris from above fell down the middle of the stairwell. We walked faster holding onto the bannister, me and Diane, with the pregnant woman between us. My feet felt like they would explode.

Finally, we reached the street. Soot was flying everywhere. Glass crashed down to the street just a few feet in front of me. A piece cut my arm and another piece cut my leg. The cellphone in my pocketbook was ringing. I didn't have time to answer it. I just ran as far away I could get from the building. Diane and the pregnant woman ran with me. I saw an emergency worker and an ambulance. I gave the pregnant woman, who was still crying, over to the EMT worker and she brought her into the ambulance. Diane and I continued to run. When I was about three blocks from the building, I heard a thunderous crash. I turned around and saw one of the towers collapsing to the ground. Fear filled me as I saw the rubble expand. I ran faster away from the buildings. Smoke and soot was everywhere. I kept going. Hundreds of people were running with me. Somehow I lost Diane in the crowd. Finally, when I stopped running, I found myself in China Town. There was blood on my blouse and streaming down my leg. My feet hurt so much. I took off my shoes and ran in my stockinged feet. My entire body was covered in soot. I didn't stop. When I couldn't run anymore, I walked, but kept on going. I tried to find Diane, but could not see her.

The cellphone in my purse rang again. I saw from the caller ID that it was Henry. I tried to answer, but the line went dead. I tried to call him back, but could not get through. I never stopped and walked all the way to 40th street. All I knew was that I wanted to get away from the city and back home to New Jersey. I didn't care about anything else, but the Port Authority Bus Terminal was closed. The doors were locked. I had to get to New Jersey, across the river somehow. I walked towards Penn Train Station on 34th street. I didn't have a ticket. I just went to the train tracks. There was an AMTRAK train in the station. It was crowded, but I knew it was going to stop in New Jersey. I was one of the last people to get into the train before the doors slid closed. It was impossible to move. I stood against the doors as the train headed for New Jersey. In twenty minutes the doors opened and I was in the Newark New Jersey station. I walked swiftly from the train. Security guards were trying to get all the people from New York and put them in quarantine. I did not want to be in quarantine. I just wanted to go home. There were so many people; it was easy to slip past them. I left the station and went onto the street.

People stared at me, covered in soot, no shoes, runs in my stockings, and blood dripping from my arm and leg. I walked about ten blocks to the courthouse, a landmark I recognized, and sat down on the steps as I tried to figure out how I was going to get home. I reached into my purse for my cellphone and I had a signal. I tried to call Henry again. He answered on the first ring.

"Are you OK? Where are you?" he asked. He knew it was me. His voice was filled with concern.

"Henry, I made it out and I'm alive." Tears were streaming down my face as I continued, "I'm in front of the courthouse in Newark, on the steps. I don't know how to get home from here. No buses run from Newark to my town."

"Stay where you are. I will come and get you." His words were like a ray of hope.

As I waited for him, I just sat there and cried. I cried into the scarf I was still holding. Strangers tried to help me, but I just continued to cry.

It took Henry about thirty minutes to arrive. When I saw his car I stood up and waved him down. He parked, got out of the car, and held me in his arms for what seemed like a very long time.

"You should see yourself." He said as he stared into my eyes. He looked at the cut on my arm and took his handkerchief out to wipe the blood. "Come on, let's get you home."

I didn't say much on the way. I told him my new address and he drove in silence. He could see that I wasn't up to talking. He brought me into my apartment. I looked at myself in the mirror. My hair was white from the soot. My cheeks were streaked with tears mixed with soot. Everything I wore was covered in soot.

Henry saw the cut on my leg and brought me into the kitchen to clean it. He pulled out a piece of glass with my tweezers. I was numb to the pain. He cleaned my cuts with peroxide and bandaged them.

Henry waited as I went into the bathroom and took a long hot shower. I emerged drying my hair.

"Julie, I've missed you. How have you been these past few months?"

"Horrible...I missed you too. Henry, I missed you so much."

I asked him to stay and we sat on the couch, hand in hand, watching the news on the television. As the story unfolded I realized how lucky I was. Henry held me close and when he looked into my eyes, I saw the love he felt for me. When we went to bed, he held me all night. In the morning he made me breakfast. He didn't go to work that day. We talked.
"I think I've finally moved on from Wilma." He stated flatly.

"That's good news. She was suffocating you." I responded. "And Elizabeth?"

"She wouldn't leave me alone." He said. "I ended things with her also. It's been two months since I last heard from her." I saw in his eyes that he was telling me the truth.

"Julie, I've missed you so much. I've thought about you every day, wanting to call, but afraid that I would just complicate your life again. I didn't realize how much I would miss you."

"Henry, I've missed you also." I said. "But, I want a relationship that goes somewhere and doesn't just stagnate."

He took me into his arms, looked into my eyes and asked, "I'm ready to commit to you. Will you give me one more chance?"

Tears filled my eyes. "Are you sure?" I asked.

"I'm as sure as one could be. I want you in my life. The last few months without you were agony for me, and when I thought I had lost you there was a hole in my heart. I realized just how much you mean to me. I know that I want to grow old with you. Please forgive all the hurt I put you through."

Tears filled his eyes. We both cried and held each other for a very long time. I'll never forget that day.

That was fourteen years ago, and looking back, I can say that marrying Henry was the best thing I ever did for myself. It took us time to deal with the baggage we each had in our lives, and being apart for those months helped him heal from the breakup of his marriage, and helped me to move on from my marriage. But, the love we have for one another is so true and so beautiful that I know it was worth all the pain. No one will ever love me again that way.

Now, as I reread these five hundred plus pages of memory, I wonder what next is in store for me. Whatever happens in my life, and as I grow old and frail, I know that I can always go back to these pages and read and reread the wonderful story of a love so deep and so beautiful, that it will always fill my heart with comfort and joy.

www.ingramcontent.com/pod-product-compliance
Lightning Source LLC
Chambersburg PA
CBHW071337020726
47502CB00001B/137